D0722051

Other books by the author:

Providence, poetry

The Chilling Simple

Zana Previti

Livingston Press
The University of West Alabama

Hardcover binding by: HF Group
Typesetting and page layout: Sarah Coffey
Proofreading: Tricia Taylor, Erin Watt, Joe Taylor,
Jayla Gellington
Cover photo and layout: Amanda Nolan

first edition
6 5 4 3 3 2 1

The Chilling Simple

Inhabitants of Chilling

Agnes Slough neé Cates: the village midwife, is married to
Dedlock Slough: a farmer, former husband of **Margaret Cates**. Together, he and Agnes look after
Jim Cates: young brother of Agnes, and
Bonnie Slough: infant daughter of Dedlock and Agnes.
Prudence Reed neé Slough: Dedlock Slough's sister, who has three young sons, named
Daniel Reed, Gervery Reed, and **Romer Reed.**
Faith Ducharme (neé Slough): another of Dedlock's sisters, as is
Priscella Slough and
Charity Benner neé Slough, who is married to
Benjamin Benner, a farmer.

Eleanor Pirrip: a young woman, and only surviving member of her family. Stricken by a mysterious disease,
Philip Pirrip: Eleanor's father
Georgiana Pirrip: Eleanor's mother and
Bartholomew, Roger, Tobias, Abraham, and **Andrew Pirrip**: Eleanor's five young brothers, have all recently died. They are survived only by Eleanor and
Octavius Peabody: half-brother of Georgiana Pirrip and
Catherine Peabody: wife of Octavius Peabody.

Reverend Brewer: the minister of the Chilling church. Working for him, as gravediggers and laborers, are
Joe Gallo: older brother of
Fernie Gallo, victim of an accident which caused the amputation of his left leg. Their mother and father, the latter of whom had worked as the Chilling blacksmith, are deceased.

Alexander Salderman: a British medical doctor who now lives in virtual seclusion on a large hilltop, in Satus House, with his sister
Odette Salderman, a poet and
Paul Lagerkvist, a young medical student working under Salderman and
Jules Demmer, another young medical student working under Salderman. Also in Satus House are
Lily, a young woman who serves as a housemaid, kitchenmaid, and

general help, plus her mother
Mug, who is best described as the housekeeper and cook.

Other Families of Chilling

The Osgoods: a farming family, headed by Lucy and Jeremiah Osgood. They are parents to
Abigail Osgood: currently unmarried and pregnant. She has a little brother,
Michael Osgood. Also living in the Osgood house is
Thomas Osgood: Jeremiah's father, Abigail and Michael's grandfather.
John Nurse: an elderly farmer and last of his family, who lives with
The Cottons: a family unique in Chilling for its four daughters, all born deaf.
The Farmers: an independently wealthy family who live near the center of the village in a large house, and who keep mostly to themselves. They socialize with
The Lockes, the family operating a small mill on the far northeast end of Chilling.
The Lungworts, farmers and cousins to
The Hornbeams, who own the village tavern.
The Nelsons, a family which boasts the village mason and schoolteacher.
The Finches, a family of farmers who live on the very outskirts of Chilling.
The Norton family includes **Dependence Norton**, the cooper. They have adopted and care for a distant cousin, a boy called **Christian Tripp**.
The Flaggs, merchants who own the large general store in Chilling.
The Shoemakers, merchants who own a small shop in Chilling.
The Dials, who work on a farm belonging to the
The Hales, a big family living on a very large and prosperous farm.
The Forrests: a family of shoemakers, one of the original families to settle Chilling in 1715.

Other Individuals

Zeena Cates: now deceased, the former Chilling midwife. Also mother to Agnes, Jim Cates, and

Margaret Cates: once married to Dedlock Slough. She mysteriously disappeared soon after their marriage, and is thought to have been the victim of **Captain Murderer**, a legendary New England serial killer.

James Herrin: a tax collector in Wolfborough.

Steven Storey: currently a dog-breeder; former whaleman and sailor out of Gloucester.

Eliza Bettet: a widow who lives near the center of the village. She lives with a companion and housekeeper, **Anne Coldwell**.

Joy Beddington, the last of her family, she lives in a large house in the center of Chilling.

Dr. Necker: the doctor in the closest town, Wolfborough.

Cole and Samuel Travers: brothers who own a small farm, the closest property to Satus House in Chilling.

Peter Downey: a fairly recent arrival to Chilling, and the village blacksmith.

Hester Osborne: an unmarried woman of independent means who lives alone in a large house near the center of the village.

Scout and About: seven year old twins (real names unknown, parentage unknown).

for Ryan

Chapter I.
Chilling

This is the village Chilling.

It's 1791. Thereabouts. Certainly not 1800, not yet. The ground is mud, because it is springtime, and the sky is dark, because it is nighttime. There have been problems in this village, recently. Men and women, merely days or hours dead, have been dug up—pulled, yanked, heaved, hoed—from their soft black soil beds. Their bodies have been dragged, their feet splayed, and the toes traced twin trenches past Smart Hale and Beddine Hale 'Asleep in the Lord,' past James and Cotton Turner 'Eternal Rest,' past the gravediggers' shed and into the pebbly road.

It is a mist-laden, yawning New England springtime. The season is combing its hair, wiping the fog from the mirror and staring into its eyes. The world is beginning again.

Now, this very moment, in Chilling:
A newly-dead body is being carried from the graveyard. The body wears no shoes. The longest toe of the dead foot is not the first "big toe," at all, but the slim elegant mid-toe, the index toe, the toe we would use to point out our bodysnatchers should we ever, through loss of our hands or voice, be relegated to pointing with our toes. Three toes, the littlest ones, have curled into the foot like a claw; their nails are greenish and black at the cuticle. The grime underneath each nail is hard like shale.

Though it is 1791, and though Chilling is a barely-existent coastal village, these dead toes are exactly like all dead toes. They are like the dead toes of emperors and scientists and prophets. They are turning gray. They have lost their agency. They fall together like exhausted soldiers in a trench, leaning and lolling against one another. In their collapse they collide and bear the weight of the others. They cannot feel discomfort. They are neither cold nor wet. Death has made them impervious, stoic, capable beyond measure.

Inside her house, Agnes Slough is awake; her baby is awake. By

5

candlelight, the kitchen is a maze of moving shadows. Agnes walks with her daughter to the window. The house is warm and the baby is warm and sucking at her breast. Agnes hums.

She can see nothing outside her window but darkness: the merest hesitating suggestion that a world exists beyond the glass. The baby burps and sighs. She burrows her nose into her mother's bare chest, and Agnes kisses the top of the baby's head. Agnes blows out the candle so that the house is black. With her free hand, she feels their way back to bed.

Agnes Slough has seen no thin corpse pulled through the road. She has not observed the lost dead toes, limp in the road. She certainly has not been able to identify the two dark shadows who carry the corpse. She was not looking to see these things, and we miss quite a lot when we don't look for what we hope is not there.

But everything, corpse, toes, bodysnatchers, all of these have passed together not more than six feet from her window. The infant has been in the presence of her first death, drunk it in with her midnight breakfast, fallen asleep again in its wake. The wee, sleep-murmuring Bonnie, fists small and at the ready, dreams milky dreams. She blows small wet bubbles through her lips. She speaks in her sleep: "Bubb, bbb, bub." It's 1791, or thereabouts. Babies make the same noises they always have, and will.

Down the road, Hester Osborne's seven cows huddle together against the damp. They put their heads together under a single tree, and discuss the problems of Chilling. They regard each other.

The body moves past the cows. The cows watch it go. The trees, noticing the angle of the cows' necks, crane their branches. The branches bend, breaking their backs and cracking, splitting, pushing to see the faces of those who heft the weight of the body behind them.

Behind in the graveyard are wounds in the ground where bodies ought to lie. Big holes, holes like black bathtubs, long wooden caskets stained and gaping open, everything empty: what should hold legs and arms and hard sure skulls, all empty, the essential thing gone.

It's the same story we've told a thousand times, isn't it? The story of something being taken away, and by whom? The story of who took it, and why, and what happened then? You lost something once, too, didn't you? Something you needed. Something absolutely essential. Something you've been looking for, all this time.

Chapter II.
The Pirrip Farm

Nora, who was alive, was ready to leave her house. There were three tasks to accomplish before she could leave. First, she would clean out the house in which she and her family had lived. She would lug the mattresses, the furniture, and all the clothes outside. Second, she would set fire to it all. She would keep the heap burning until there was only a charred crater left in the mud. Third, and last, she would find where they had buried her mother, and dig her out.

There wasn't much left on the farm, but a few errant chickens pecking at the grass. "Did you see where they took the dogs?" Nora asked them. She was carrying brush to the fire. She had a very fine pile going already.

The chickens didn't answer her. They made out as if they hadn't heard her at all.

"That's fine," she said. She dumped the load of brush and stood back. "This would be easier if the dogs were here."

Nora put her hands to her hipbones, which stuck out like wings. The flames were small, now, licking little nervous tongues at the bottom of the pile.

"Just wait," Nora said to the chickens. "It'll be a raging inferno. Get yourselves ready." She wiped her hands on her dress. She went back into the house.

It was still early morning; the sunshine lay in limp yellow squares on the floor. Inside, it smelled sour from the sweat of many bodies. Nora tore one of her mother's old aprons into strips, and tied one of the strips across her mouth and nose. As she did, a shout of greeting came from the road.

"Nora," her uncle Peabody called, from the road. He had his hands in his pockets. "Eleanor!"

Nora froze. If he came up to the house, and looked into the window, he would see her. A few people had come by in the past week, looking for Eleanor, shouting their offers of help. They were too afraid to come into the house, though, and she never went out to meet them. Nora was willing to wager that her uncle wouldn't come close, either. But, just in case, very slowly, she sank to her knees and then to all fours; she crawled to the wall and crouched below the windowsill.

Frankly, even if he had walked the thirty steps from the road to the window, Nora's uncle Peabody would not have recognized the person in the house as his niece. He had not seen her, up close, for years. Seven years, Nora counted in her head. She had been twelve years old. It had been summertime . . . she remembered that there were strawberries on the table. Peabody was sitting with his sister, Nora's mother, in the Pirrip kitchen when Nora, all legs and knobby elbows and knees, came running wild through the door. She was soaking wet, out of breath, and covered in leeches.

"Fell. Pond," she had panted.

"Calm down," her mother had said, and rolled her eyes. That was the last time Mr. Peabody had seen his niece. She frightened him a little. Little wiry thing, covered in pond mud, leeches on her face. On her neck!

Nora's body *now,* as it was hunched under the windowsill, would have frightened him again. The illness, whatever it had been, had come least aggressively on Nora than it had upon her younger brothers and her parents, but it had come nonetheless, and it had scraped away large parts of her. She had never been big, or plump, but now she was achingly thin. Her joints jutted from her skin like the edges of tables underneath a linen cloth; she could play her rib bones like piano keys. Her face was all angles and narrow lines, now, a skull stretched over with paper. Her skin was ashy. It flaked off in her hands when she scratched. If the house had had a mirror, and had Nora looked into it, she would have doubted that she had survived the illness at all. The fact that she did survive—and that she *alone,* among her parents and brothers, had survived—was the reason Aunt Peabody had pushed Uncle Peabody out the door that morning, and the reason he stood in the road now.

"You'll have to go and get her," Catherine had said. "It won't be contagious anymore. Right?"

Octavius had grimaced.

"She's our niece," said Catherine. "You go and get her."

Still, when Peabody had arrived, he was not confident. Who knows what had made them sick? What if it was still somewhere in the house?

"Nora," her uncle shouted, "There's a bed made ready for you. Your aunt is ready, any time, when you can come." He waited for a response, any movement or sound from inside the house, but none came. Nora, still on all fours, imagined tying on her Aunt Catherine's old dresses. Nora had no more clothes; everything she wore had been long since torn and used as a bandage or a poultice, and everything else she would burn for fear of contagion. She was skinnier than Joy Beddington who they said had been kidnapped by the Indians and who had come back speaking jibberish, and Nora's arms ached at the thought of winding her aunt's enormous apron strings around and around her own waist. Her throat ached at the thought of speaking to them, the Peabodys, every day. She would have to speak to them *every day*. "Can you just sweep the steps, before you go out?"; "Good morning. Did you sleep well?"; "No, no, that's fine, I don't mind." When really she *would* mind. Every step in that strange house would be a careful step, every word a polite word. All of her private strangenesses, the things her family had come to ignore through familiarity, all of these would need to be either carefully hidden or humiliatingly explained. There would be nothing comfortable and nothing private.

And she feared that she had the illness still inside of her, and that she would kill them.

Nora shook her bald head. She hoped he would go away before he smelled the fire. She sniffed the air.

"So, come along to the house, when you're ready," he called out. He wouldn't step onto the grass or come any closer to the house than the center of the narrow road. He shuffled his feet a little and looked up at the sun. It had just cleared the pines on the east bank of the pond, and he needed to be getting back home. His wife would blame him for not bringing Nora with him, but what could he do? He wouldn't risk infection by going into the house. What if he died? Where would Mrs. Peabody be, then? Who would pinch on her little toe, every morning, to wake her up? Who would go the forest and find those mushrooms she liked? Nora would come when she was well enough, and when she was ready. She was an adult, almost nineteen! She could travel the few miles into the village proper on her own. Or, Peabody considered, she was dead, and there wasn't anything to do. He'd come back tomorrow with Agnes Slough and see if Nora was still in the house. He nodded to himself. He turned away from the house and began the brisk walk back to Chilling.

Inside the house, Nora waited a long time to move. When she considered it safe to stand, her uncle had covered half a mile and his thoughts were not on her at all, but only on his breakfast, and if they had much butter left, and if he should tear off the loose toenail on his foot or let it be.

She stood too quickly and her eyes went star-colored; she bent down again and pulled the rag from her nose and mouth. Then she straightened, more slowly, and surveyed the kitchen. The house ought to have been worse than it was, she felt. It should have been clumsily disordered, thick with dirt and dust, chaotic with debris. How could they all have lain so ill, for so long, and the surfaces reflect nothing at all? One wouldn't be able to guess, by the smooth surface of the table, by the quiet chairs hanging in their places on the wall, that anything much had happened here.

The furniture ought to have been broken and knocked about, strewn across the floors in jagged, splintery chunks of wood. The windows ought to have been coated in black scum, brackish mud dredged from the swamped homes of monsters. There ought to have been dry, dead carcasses of rats and mice and roaches, rigid corpses of spiders and creatures with more eyes than legs. There ought to have been the smell of burning and bile, there ought to have been sinewy cobwebs hanging low from the ceiling corners and doorways. There ought to have been rain and sleet slamming against the door planks and roof tiles and windowpanes, there ought to have been, everywhere, the evidence, the terrible signs of what had happened here. There ought to have been a layer of mourning black on every surface, for each one of her five brothers, and for her father, and for her mother.

But no. The table was clean. The boards of the kitchen floor were swept. The boys' stools arranged themselves in a patient half-moon around the hearth. Her father's boots sat just inside the doorway. Roger's toy duck remained where he had left it, in the corner by the water pitcher. The sun was rising and the air smelled like pine. Everything was ordinary. And everything was terrible, because they were gone. She could sense it, though, just underneath the discernible world: the invisible multiplying body of the disease. She thought she could feel it as it wisped around the house, moving slowly lest it be identified, moving with terrible purpose, propelling itself with many arms like long tentacles.

Nora took a broom from the corner and swung it wildly into the corners of the house, breaking up the soft cobwebs that hung there. "Yah, yah," she yelled. It did not help; she dragged Tobias' stool to the corner, stood on it and clapped her hands. Bad spirits could be driven away by loud noises, sometimes.

She opened the front door and let the air come inside. She stared out at the pond, just across the road; by now the sun had risen over the trees on the far bank. It was pale and yellow and brushing away the strips of clouds with slim unhurried fingers.

"Hey," she said to the sun. "Let's get on with it."

It was wide and quiet. The chickens' small walks and pecks were like the ticking of a clock. There weren't even animals, save the chickens, and chickens didn't count. The people from the village had come, must have come, to take them away, to care for the animals when the Pirrips no longer could. What she needed, Nora thought, was a *body*. Something large, and warm, breathing, with smelly animal mammal breath. Nora felt a bolt run through her stomach, of panic, and she looked left and right for the dogs. Where were the dogs? Where were all the animals? Where were her dogs?

Nora picked up a chicken and tucked it under her arm. It weighed nothing and yet lifting it taxed her strength.

"Let's go see what's left," she said to the chicken. It was a brown chicken.

Inside the barn, Nora stood on her toes to look into the stalls.

"No cow," she told the chicken. "My uncle, maybe." The chicken moved a little, pleasantly. "No," Nora went on, "You're right. She could have been stolen. We'll keep an eye out. Check on the pigs?"

The pig sty was empty. The mud was smooth and brown as gingerbread dough.

"Shit," said Nora. It was the first time she had ever said the word aloud and she felt a little thrill of freedom. The chicken looked at her. "No pigs," she confirmed.

There were no dog tracks in the yard, and no doghair in the house, but Nora wasn't ready to accept that the dogs were gone. She carried the brown chicken back to the fire, and scanned the periphery of the farm, watching for a streak of white or brown, a tail up above the tall grasses.

"Cluck, cluck," said the chicken. Nora put her down on the ground.

"Go ahead," she said, "Go play." She felt a tug in her brain, reminding her of something . . . where had the dogs gone? She shook her head. Her fever had lasted a long time. Nothing was clear. She had to get the fire going. That was clear. She didn't know where the infection had lived in the house, so she had to burn everything. The disease needed to die. That was very clear.

Birds were saying *weet weet weet* to one another, but Nora couldn't see them. Nora needed to see a thing in order to talk to it. When she was younger, she would feel guilty if she washed one shirt more thoroughly than another shirt, or picked one knife to peel her apple over another knife. She believed she had injured the shirt's feelings, slighted the knife, and she would be so plagued by the guilt that she would run to the drying line and grab the shirt to rescrub it furiously, or split the apple into halves and slice each half with the slighted knife. It made sense to her that material things felt and thought; they were *there,* after all. They existed. She existed, and she felt. She thought. Things had shape, substance, form, function. They had defined edges and they began and ended in space.

When her family was sick, Nora had focused on what she could see. Blood concerned her. The sheer amount of blood concerned her. Her father had become ill first, and sores came up on his skin. They were nasty, pustuley things, and after they had grown and swollen, they burst. They pulsed on his neck and ran over with pus and blood. The fluids cocktailed with each other, beaded, and hardened into small swirled marbles on his skin. He began to cough, then cough more, and then he was vomiting blood. Nora had bunched rags in her hands and pushed them into his face so hard that she feared he would suffocate.

"I'm not trying to kill you, Dad," she'd said. "But you'll drown in this gunk otherwise."

He coughed up soggy fists of blood and mucus; he shit out bloody loose stool; he pissed blood and stained the sheets. In the early days, when only Philip Pirrip was sick, Georgiana Pirrip held the baby to her chest and the twins against her thighs, and watched Nora nurse her husband from the doorway. Nora's mother had a face like a fire poker.

Then the little boys got sick. There were five of them, one set of six-year-old twins, one set of four-year-old twins, and Bart, the baby, who was still nursing. He couldn't crawl, yet; if Nora left him on his belly in the middle of a room, he wasn't able to move himself. He screamed and screamed in pain. He burned with a fever but shivered in Nora's arms. His skin, too erupted. Nora tore up her church dress for bandages. She tore up her winter underwear and then her summer underwear.

"There's so much blood," she had said to her mother, when the baby began to vomit. "What should we do?"

"I'm doing my best, Nora," her mother had said. Her mother was not sick, yet. Nora was not sick yet.

"Why hasn't the doctor helped? Should we try to put the blood back in them? Make them drink it? Is that crazy? Where is the doctor?"

"The doctor is afraid," her mother had said. "Like everyone else. Where's the water? I asked you to get water, Nora. What are you doing?"

On her tiptoes, like a thief, Nora began to wring the bloody rags out into bowls. Soaked with blood, the clothing no longer looked like clothing. She couldn't tell if something had been used as a wash towel or as a winter coat. Blood darkened and changed the forms of things so that they were all the same. Nora wrung the rags into the bowls and then emptied the bowls into the heavy black pot on the fire. The pot hung there, the blood black and viscous and waiting to be drunk. By the time her mother began to cough and heave, Nora had filled the pot to its capacity. By then her father had been dead a week. The baby had been dead two weeks. Having the blood there, ready, was a comfort to her.

Well, the blood pot was empty now. She had tipped it into the grass and watched the blood sink into the ground. The cows were gone, the pigs were gone, the dogs were gone, her mother's body was gone. The winter was over; the cold was gone. Lots of things were gone. She did not know who had taken them, or if, ignored, things merely disappeared or wandered off. Watching the fire, she felt guilty, as she had as a child, when she chose one knife over another. It was as though the things themselves had faded because she had not remembered them, as though if one ceased to think of a thing for long enough, the thing itself disappeared. Her brothers were all gone. Her father was gone.

The brown chicken pecked at the hem of her dress. She had only one. It was brown, too, and she had been wearing it for a very, very long time. It stunk.

"How's that fire, chicken?" she asked. "Pretty good, I think. Ready for burning. What do you think?"

She raised the dress and looked at her thighs, where she could see the distorted and pitted skin she had been left with. She touched the scars gently.

By the afternoon, everything the Pirrips owned was outside and spread on the new spring grass. Their lives had come to very little, after food and a place to sit and sleep. The fire was high. Big flames kicked smoke up into the trees. Nora pulled the mask she had made over her mouth and nose; she stood with her arms folded and watched it burn for a while, and felt proud. The smoke wafted toward her eyes and she blinked. She swabbed her forehead with the hem of her dress.

She started with the mattresses.

"Oh no," she said. She felt how weak she had grown. Before, something the weight and size of a mattress would have required no effort at all; she would have tucked it under one arm and used the other to carry a sopping ball of wet laundry. She staggered and flung the mattress sideways onto the fire. It was a poor throw, and so the mattress hung limply half on the brush and half hanging off into the mud.

"Damn this to Hell," she said. The chickens were nowhere in sight. The brown chicken had disappeared in her time of need. She dragged a long branch over from the edge of the field and poked at the mattress. It was from her parents' bed. It smoldered and smoked, until, at the culmination of some series of events too small and hot for her to see, it flamed up furiously. The smell overpowered her. Nora staggered back with the weight of the body the mattress had carried, the smell of the months of slow decay, of violent leaching. The smoke rose over the farm like a beacon across an unwelcoming sea.

She took deep breaths of the scent of their deaths. She felt sick and then not sick anymore. She felt stronger, really very energetic. She pulled another mattress and flung it to the top of the pile. She flung her father's boots. She threw Roger's toy duck as hard as she could into the center of the brush, so it would be buried by what collapsed atop it. Bart's crib she pulled apart with her hands and threw each piece into the fire.

The fire burned into the night. Nora tossed her family's life onto it, then stood back to watch every last breath of infection burn away. To be sure of it, she unbuttoned her brown dress and threw that on the blaze, too. She wore only her thin woolen slip. As she began to sweat, the fabric clung to her legs. Nora looked like a tower of precariously placed white bones. The feelings of intolerable heat, the cold wet of the sweat, the stifling air that made inhalation painful and slow, all of this was familiar to her. It was like being sick again. She wondered if she could give herself the fever again by tricking her body into great heat. Her body crept closer and closer to the edge of the fire until the skin on her face was red and taut, pulled against the bridge of her nose, and the cropped hair they had left on her head dripped with sweat. She reached into the fire with her father's pitchfork, stroking the strands of branch and threads of what remained, stirring flame into pockets of fiery explosion, the smoke rolling off the heap in long sinuous waves. The ash met the soft white wet parts of her eyes and she blinked. The black hollows beneath her eyes shone. When she opened her mouth to pant, her tongue was coated in the same dark ash. She put her fingers in her mouth to trace the tongue down as far as she could reach in her own throat, but could not reach far enough. As she vomited bile and held the pitchfork and stroked the wild blowing hair of the fire, the farm was eclipsed by blackness and the house disappeared, and all she saw was the fire, and the bloody mattresses, and the skeletons of all things twisting and blackening and falling away. Nora felt cold and small and angry.

In the morning, Brown Chicken wandered to the brush pile. Nora sat on the ground. The grass and mud had seeped through the bottom of her dress; the backs of her thighs were cold and damp. The shape of the house emerged, a darker gray against a pale gray sky. The chicken pecked at the edge of her nightdress and shook its head. The fire was a circle of coals, a shallow black crater.

"Listen," she said seriously, to the chicken. "I have to go. I know you will be fine. Because you are chickens. You will either be fine, or something will come and eat you. I can't take you with me."

Brown Chicken hopped a little and wandered toward a tuft of higher grass. She nuzzled her beak into it.

"Because," Nora explained. "I have make sure my mother is dead. And then when I know that she's dead, when I see her body, then I'm going to touch it with my own two hands." Nora held up her hands, "And then maybe I'll come back, and maybe we can start this place up again."

Brown Chicken turned around and stared at Nora.

"No promises," said Nora. "I'll see you later." She got up, went into the house and waited until the night. Then she started toward the Chilling graveyard. She had brought her own shovel.

Chapter III.
The Chilling Churchyard

When Nora was born, nearly twenty years earlier, her mother had disappeared. Georgiana had waited a few months, until her body had healed from the birth, and then she had packed a small bag and left the village. She did not come back, and no one went to find her.

As she grew, Philip would explain to Nora that her mother had died. Everyone in Chilling helped him, too; they were a small community, and a viciously private one. Nora was mothered by no one and everyone together.

Then Georgiana had reappeared, just after Nora's eleventh birthday. She had not died at all. Nora was a logical little girl. She had looked around for explanations. No one offered one.

So when Georgiana had disappeared from the house, in the midst of the illness, Nora could not be sure. She and her mother had fallen sick at the same time. No one was there to care for them, and the pain became more and more unbearable until Nora could do nothing, feel nothing, sense nothing aside from her own agony. One morning, she could not hear her mother's coughing. Another day, she went for water and saw that her mother was gone. At the time, she could not care. Now, though, Nora needed to be sure. Georgiana could be dead. Most likely, Georgiana was dead. Someone may have come and carted her body from the house. But Nora knew her mother was capable of abandoning her family when they most needed her. Nora knew that her mother may have healed and crept off, alone, like she had when Nora had come into the world and chased her away. Georgiana had died before, she had come back. Nora would not be fooled a second time. She would not grieve the death of someone who had chosen to leave her, who had chosen to abandon her to this.

There was no moon. Nora could just make out the steeple of the church. She took stock of her body. Her arms felt good, her neck a little sore and tight, and her legs heavy. It had taken her a long time to walk into the village; the farm was on the outskirts of the village, and her body was not strong. Her calves sporadically blasted into spasms, as they had done since her illness had passed, and when this happened she was forced to bend over in the road and massage her legs with her fingertips until the cramping passed.

She turned left. The path was overhung with dark willow trees that dropped nearly to the crown of her head; branches dipped down to her skull and dropped beads of dew into her short hair. The air smelled like lilacs and water. Nora's legs cramped again. She sat down on the dirt path and dug her thumbs into the hard knots in her calves, and then stood again. She waited for the dizziness to subside, and went on.

When she came to the gate, there was a boy in the graveyard. This was both unexpected and unwelcome. Nora paused.

He was a child still, and he wore a wool cap. His head was down and he walked back and forth on the same segment of the graveyard path, stepping each time, it seemed to Nora, on the same five or six stones. The bottoms of his pants had been cuffed so that they would not drag in the churchyard mud, and his sleeves rolled up to his forearms, as well. On the stone path, perhaps ten feet away from him, the boy had placed a lantern, which cast a long, serpentine shadow across the graves. He was thin, the way that children are too thin in the years before they grow into their bodies. His nose was too long, and he had round ears too big for his head.

"Hello," said Nora from the gate.

The boy turned and looked at her. He put his hand to his head and scratched through his cap. He was perhaps eight or nine years old.

"Hello," he said. Nora opened the gate and stepped nearer to him. She was full in the light of the lantern. She put her hand up to shield her eyes.

"I should ring my bell," he said.

"Oh, no. Please don't do that."

"Do you see any ghosts?" he asked her. He looked around him at the gravestones.

"Right now? I don't. Not," Nora said, "unless you are a ghost."

He didn't answer her, but stared at her. Nora brought the palm of her hand to her heart and let it lie there, as if to feel her heartbeat. She remembered that she was wearing only her woolen underwear; she had sewn them herself, last autumn. They were thick enough, but her arms were bare and the pants came only to the calves. Nora was too tired to feel embarrassment and the sickness had stripped her of modesty and dignity. She squinted at the boy through the lantern light. Her heart had begun to beat slow and low, like thunder still far away.

"Are you a ghost?" she said. She meant to make him laugh.

"Are you?" he said. He squinted at her.

"Jice, no," she said. Her legs cramped below her. She did not lean down and rub the knots out. "I didn't die," she said. She smiled.

"Maybe later then," he said, and he turned away to sit on the stones by his lantern.

Nora watched him walk away from her, and, in another time, she would have laughed at him for his rudeness, his simplicity, his disregard for her presence in a graveyard in the middle of the night. But now she saw only his size and his lantern. His arms were wiry but muscled; his legs were long. His hands were large and brown.

"You're Agnes Slough's little brother, yeah?" she said. She stood over him and looked down at his head. Jim was a strange child; he was quiet and deliberate. Agnes took special care of him. Now, he was twisting and untwisting a bit of cloth, trying to decide whether to eat his bit of cheese now, or to save it for later.

"Later," he said.

"What do you mean, later? I know you, Jim. I'm Eleanor. Nora Pirrip. Do you remember me? I helped Agnes set squash, last spring. Do you remember me?"

Jim looked at her. "No," he said.

"Well, I know your sister, Jim. I know she takes very good care of you."

"Yeah," said Jim.

"Jim," Nora said, "There *are* ghosts here. That's why I'm here."

"What ghosts?"

Nora stepped onto the stone path, and she sat down next to him. She slipped her hand down and kneaded her calf muscle.

"You never heard the story?" she asked. "There was an evil minister, here, a long time ago. Years and years ago. He was a bad man. When he thought someone in the village had sinned, or when someone displeased him, he'd take them down to the basement in the church and he'd hammer them into the beams of the church floors, their hands up into the beams like someone you've seen, maybe. He let them hang there, he said, in retribution for their own sins, and they'd hang down below the floor of the church, naked and nailed into the beams and the blood just dripping out of them."

"What is retribution?"

"Payback. If I hit you, you can kick me in retribution."

Jim considered this. "A lot of blood?" he asked.

"Yes. So they died, painful, terrible, slow, and finally after they were dead the minister came and pulled them down, threw them into a shallow grave in this churchyard here, but never buried them right with words or prayers or coffins. Just threw them into a hole and covered them up."

"Not this reverend," said Jim, "Why?"

"No, not Reverend Brewer," said Nora. "This happened a long time ago, like I said, before you or I were here. But those people that he killed, they didn't ever get buried right, Jim, and so their ghosts are still awake at night, rubbing their hands where the nails went in, looking around for that old minister, that they can torment him and finish their Passions."

Nora pointed to the trees that hung over the churchyard. An owl's eyes shone like moons.

"You can see them, there," she said. "Those are their faces. They watch, like you. They watch over the graveyard at night."

"Jice," said Jim, "the whole time and their eyes on us."

"They wait in the tree because there's no place for their hearts to go. They don't know where to go. So the way to send their hearts off is to do what the minister wouldn't do for them. We dig a hole for them," said Nora. "We need to dig them a new grave, to bury them right."

"Are they going to Heaven? Or if we buried them, would they go down to the pit of Hell?"

"We don't know, Jim."

"The diggers could dig them, the gravediggers. Joe and Fernie."

"They could. That's exactly right. But that's why I am here, Jim. You can help me. We should dig them their graves, Jim." She handed him the shovel.

Jim looked at her. "I'll dig," he said, "if we get to see them. The bloody holes. And everything."

Nora nodded at him. "I think we will see everything."

Nora stood above one large gravestone. Alongside, like a path leading away, were dotted five small flat ones. Nora squatted and touched one of the smaller stones. She looked up at Jim and gestured over at the earth in front of the large stone.

"There," she said, and she sat down in the dirt.

Jim stabbed the shovel into the ground.

"I'll be a gravedigger, soon," he said. Nora nodded.

"You're very good at it," she said.

"Fern'll let me practice with him sometimes," he said. "Fernie only has one leg."

Nora recalled two lanky pale men who appeared from time to time in the village; they worked for the doctor up at his house, and sometimes came down to do work for the Reverend. They had probably been the ones to bury her father and brothers. Sitting atop her family, Nora watched the blade of the shovel clench itself into the dirt. Each time the shovel moved in, and out again, she felt better. She felt lighter, less burdened, less bewildered, as if she herself was the one being unearthed by Jim's shovel. She took the fingers of her hand through the low stubble of her hair. They must have cut it off while she was delirious. She could not remember. Perhaps she had done it herself. Small things, tiny leaves and clods of dirt, had collected in her hair since last night's fire, and as she pulled her hand through she collected a wash of sweat and a palmful of dirt and ash. She wiped her hand across the front of her chest.

Jim grunted and stabbed the shovel downward like a bayonet into the chest of a soldier. The ground was moist and giving, but Jim was not strong.

Nora laid a tip of a finger atop one of the small stones. "You know, Jim, those are my brothers," she said.

"They have wee little baby tablets," said Jim. He stopped digging and leaned the shovel against his leg for a moment, and pulled a piece of cake knotted up in a bit of cloth.

"I had five baby brothers," Nora said.

"You can have some," he said. He held out the seedcake.

Nora stood, but instead of accepting it, she took up Jim's lantern and shone it over the inscription on the large stone. Jim pressed a bundle into her free hand until she took it. She put down the lantern, unknotted the seedcake and broke it in two pieces.

"*Also Georgiana*, that's her, my mum," she said. "And my dad's that one." Nora chewed a little, carefully. When she swallowed, her throat felt as though it had been studded with nails. She did not remember the last time she had eaten. It was as though her body had forgotten how. Nora laid the cloth on one of the small stones—Tobias's—and replaced the seedcake inside. She knotted it up. Tobias had stammered. When he was two, Nora had closed his little finger in a door and split it to the bone. He had had a long white scar. Tobias liked to eat dirt when he was a baby.

"My parents are dead too," he said.

"Do you want this back?" Nora asked, holding out the seedcake to Jim. But Jim had gone back to his digging.

"My mum," she said, when he didn't answer. "That's her you're digging toward. She hated me, I think. And by the end, we were alone, the two of us. I knew she'd leave again. She'd never liked me and wouldn't stay if it were just me. And—oh. Oh, my word. The dog. We got sick together, after dad and the baby were dead, after the boys were on their way to dead. After a little while everyone was dead. Dad, the boys. We'd vomit up on the floor and the dogs would come in and eat it. The dogs died. They all died."

Jim paused, planted the shovel, and rolled his shoulders. "Can I have my cake?" he asked Nora.

She handed it to him.

"Isn't it funny," said Nora, "everyone dead and I'm sad for the dogs."

"Sometimes," said Jim, "I like to put the cheese in the seedcake and eat them together."

Nora tried to smile at him. She knew she should have been hungry. But even the small bite of seedcake had made her stomach knot. She felt an uncomfortable sensation, like a buzzing or vibrating, in her shoulders. She sat down in the dirt again.

"I like cheese, too," she said.

Jim shrugged.

For a little while, she sat and kept her hand on Tobias's stone and watched Jim dig. It was very dark. Outside of the circle of lantern light, there was nothing; just her body, Jim's body, and the tombstones of her family.

Nora made a sudden sound, somewhere between a laugh and a moan.

"She'd just had a litter," she said. "One of our dogs. We let Abraham name her . . . We called her Bug. Stupid. I don't know what happened to her pups. She tried to help, would come lick my face and arms. When she died, I was too sick to get her out the house so we'd lie there and be sick, onto our beds and our clothes, and there'd be the dead dog just a-lie in the middle of the place. Stinking and stinking, too. We could smell ourselves rotting off our bones. You stop caring or feeling like you should care. Everything doesn't matter, when you feel like that. We were too sick to die, even. You get sick enough that no one wants you, even the other dead. The puppies would have been beautiful. She had white feet. She was such a beautiful dog."

Jim looked at her.

"Bug," said Nora. "Abraham called her 'Bug.' She had white feet and she'd go swimming in the pond in the summer all by herself. She'd take a big stick and just go off on her own for a swim, holding her head up with this stick too big for her. You're getting tired?"

"A little bit tired of digging," said Jim, "Do you want any more?" He bit a side of his seedcake.

"No. I don't know if I can eat anything," Nora said. In her mind, she added, *Ever*. Maybe that would be the end of her, she thought. Survived all that just to starve to death in a cemetery. They could just roll her in. She used to think, when she was sick, that she would die stuck to her bed and they'd have to pull her out still stuck to it. When her mother turned over, Nora could see the flesh on her back fall off into the bed. It was as if her mother were made of nothing but wet clay, now falling apart on the bank of a river. She just came apart.

Nora leaned over and looked down in the hole Jim had dug. The dirt was grabbing together, clumping to stay up, but little clods tumbled down nonetheless. Stringy roots were worming free and out of the soil, as if all the bodies deep in the churchyard were still growing their hair, as if hair had grown long and wiry and wildly throughout the earth, out of the skulls and kept and kept and kept growing on, so now the long hairs of all those deep bodies was coming through the dirt walls.

"That's really good digging," she said.

"Thank you."

"That's the thing I think when I watch my mother dying, that she's mucked the bed. I don't even feel sad. I watched her in the bed with her great strips of skin and mashy blood and guts coming all out of her, puddles of our own sickup and our beautiful dog, dead, between us."

Jim reached a hand down into the dirt, and grabbed on one of the hairs, to pull at it, but it didn't want to unroot. He pulled at it hard and a great clump of dirt came free and sprayed across his nose. He stopped his pulling.

"Yes," said Nora, as if Jim had asked her a question. She hung her head back and stared upward. There were dull, dim stars, obscured by filmy clouds. "Maybe you don't remember, Jim, because you're just little. But they told me she was dead, when I—"

"Bodies," said Jim, and he knocked the shovel down onto what could only have been a wooden coffin.

Nora stood and as she did, something large and winged flew low across the sky above them. Jim threw the shovel away from him and flung himself down to the ground. Nora turned and watched the flying thing disappear into the black branches of a tree.

"Only an owl," she said to Jim. Jim lay beside Nora's family's grave, in the pile of soil that he had shoveled away.

"I do not want to dig anymore," Jim said to the dirt. He was tired. He had wanted to see bloody murdered ghosts. He tongued some dirt to the back of his mouth and, turning his head so that he could stare at Nora, he chewed the dirt. It was satisfyingly bad-tasting.

Nora moved closer to the side of the grave and lowered her arm into the earth. She felt around. That it was wet struck her first, and second, that it was pebbly, hard, not soft growing earth. But then why would they, she reasoned, bury men and women in earth that could grow a crop, when there was useless dead earth everywhere, and could serve no purpose but to keep dead things dead? She pushed her fist deeper and extended her fingers. They felt the hard top of a wooden casket. She felt for the sides, to measure the dimensions. Her fingers could move from the top of the box to the bottom, could feel the nails hammered on each side, by only moving her hand so slightly. This was her baby brother, then, this was Bartholomew, who was born with Nora for a midwife. They had sent Abraham running for the real midwife, Jim's older sister Agnes Slough, but the labor came on so suddenly that the boy was barely out the front door when Georgina had felt the head of her baby beginning to emerge.

"Now," she had said, and grunted. Nora had been frantic. She had never seen a birth before. Blood came out of nowhere, it seemed, onto the floor, onto everything. But her mother had been calm. Georgiana had squatted on the floor, took Nora's hand, and laid it on top of her belly.

"Push down when I say," she had whispered. There were columns of sweat down her neck. And eventually, she said "Now," and Nora had placed her palm on the top of the enormous taut belly . . . Underneath the skin he was squirming, moving, he was terribly and desperately alive. She pushed. There was a cry, a gasp, and there he was. Her brother was born. Nora's hands had been the first hands to hold his tiny bloody body. She glimpsed something monstrous about life, that to be alive was a terribly difficult and aggressive thing. He was so alive! So beet-red, so slimy, so much in her hands!

And now that very same little body was there, dead and quiet. She pressed the palm of her hand against the wood.

"Where is she?" Nora asked. She and Jim stood beside the open grave, the five small coffins, and the two large ones. They had opened one, Georgiana's coffin. It was empty.

"Hey," said Jim. "How about the ghosts?"

"She's not here," Nora said. She knelt in the dirt and rested her forehead on the ground. The graveyard's dirt tasted salty. Then she smelled the sweet nauseating scent of those bodies decaying underneath her, not as far down as they should be, and she gagged. She tried to vomit, but couldn't. Her throat stung.

"Maybe Captain Murderer took her," said Jim.

"What?" asked Nora. She straightened up and sat on her heels.

"To the house," said Jim. He turned and pointed west, out beyond the edge of the village, up the hill, to the large looming house on the hill. Satus House, where the doctor lived.

"Sometimes he takes the bodies," Jim said. And just as methodically as he had removed it, he began to heap dirt back upon the graves of Nora's family.

Chapter IV.
The Narrative of the Graveyard

Oh, the bones. I am made of bones! You are made of bones. We're the same, underneath. My forebears are your forebears, though it's been told slightly differently. There is a story surrounding two brothers. Twins, perhaps? I cannot tell. One brother has a very nice big cow. The other brother has a very nice big seedy fruit. For reasons I cannot fathom, the cow is judged in some way superior to the fruit, and faced with this dazzling illogic Fruit Brother runs mad and kills Cow Brother. Fruit Brother, to hide away the physical body of his shame and misdeed, digs a hole and deposits within Cow Brother.

Now there is not one thing better or worse than another thing, as we are all only things upon things in other things. But the Brothers did not know this.

That field where Cow Brother rests, well, from thence we all sprung. It caught on very quickly, dying, and more quickly when more of you began to end others' lives for them, to save Nature the trouble and time. The first gravedigger was a man putting his own brother underground, and I don't wonder much at where he got the idea, or why he did it: it is safe, down here, from the terrible uncertainty above. Safe and dark, for the things you want hidden from others, or the things you want to stop seeing yourself, or the things that have changed so much that you can longer abide their sight. I keep them safe for you. When you have buried them, I keep them, and watch them change, and you may think of them however you choose. You can untrouble yourself. I take care.

I have never told a story before. I have never tried. I must take my time. I must be excused if I tell it wrong, or in a form that is bewildering, be it roundabout or labyrinthine or cruciform. All the forms I know are the forms of graves, of men's bones, of the wandering tunnels of insects, of the spinning whirling basics of stuff. Upon these I must model my own story. Ack! I hear you cry. Ack! How can you tell anything!? You are a graveyard! You are dirt and dumb! These are the things you say, impatiently. The living are always impatient.

I am dirt, but not dumb. I am not insentient, not unfeeling. Before I can tell the story of my failure, of the two young men—brothers, like our forebears—and of the young woman with the dog, you must come to trust me with the telling of the story as completely as you trust me with your dead. I will explain what I know, and what I was able to observe, and try to tell you what happened to all of those lost bodies. You must rival the corpse itself, in patience: allow me to care for you, to provide what you need, to shelter you for this short while. Submit entirely to the story and its teller. Do not question or struggle. Do not waste time on doubt. There is enough, in the world above, to doubt.

I am the Chilling graveyard. Where you have hands, and feet, and ears, long swathes of unbroken skin, I am constructed of the singular earth, of bodies whole and decomposing. I am many-bodied and one-bodied. I am heavy. I sink with weight; I touch the water. I am made of you: I am the product of individuals who seek me out or whom I surprise. I am made of others. I am not, as I have heard a man once say, what I am. I am not dead nothing, no, I am alive and squirming with intrusions. (And what are you, small person, what are you, but that, too?)

The first man to be buried here was a poor pale thing called Jeremy Woodhill. I haven't any idea why he died, or when. I took the man, and became this. His body was pale and he had shrunk, I think, in death—at least, his white skin stretched across the smooth lines of his bones. His hair was nearly all gone, and his eyelashes were nearly invisible. He had markings on his body in blue ink. The letters spelling out *Miranda Woodhill my wyfe*, on his chest, and across his belly and arms, a ship at sail, a flowering tree, a couple embracing, a flying bird with a snake in its mouth, a terrible dragon with a flaming tongue in flight.

Years and years and years ago, there were heavy rainstorms, one right after another. The soil began to wash away from me. Without my soil I could not hold my bodies. Arms and heads began to work their way upwards, through and away from me. Woodhill is thrust upwards. I cling. I grab at his bit of skin with the flowering tree, the bit of skin just above his left breast. A tree like that—heavy branches, large canopy—might grow upon my own ground, so that I and my bodied body could be sheltered from the ravages of such rains in the future. I and all of myself would grow this tree; the rains could come on and the flowering tree would protect resolutely, unwaveringly. I did endure the problem. The problem existed merely to protect me from itself; it existed to destroy itself, to save me from itself. That the rain would stop, and soon, and there would be left behind the beginnings of a grand shelter. And so I wait and cling to my bodies with all my might, knowing my energies to be finite; and surely the rains did taper, and surely the rains did stop. The bodies within me settled back downwards, into their spots. The tree now hovers above us all.

There was a time, too, when a woman would come often to have sex on the gravestones with new and different partners. She, with her long black hair let out and jouncing all curls down and off the edge of the large granite tablet for Mister Coole, saying oohs and ahhs! And from the black dirt the spiders crawl up into her black hair and nestle inside. The earth rises to meet her, we rise to meet them. The man atop her, working away, puts his fists into her hair and screams! He jumbles himself out and up and screams, *Mary, Mary, Mary!* By that time, her hair is thick and crawling with large black spiders, happily spinning new homes between her curls which she has let down for him. She springs up, flailing and swatting at herself, he doing the same, and they run from the place as if pursued. She does not come again.

In my youth I was dispersed through glacier.

Before my life I was dispersed through sky and stars.

I cannot understand the dispersal of joyful spiders as something unpleasant.

Years later, closer to our own day but not by much, a tall, middle-aged Chilling man began to come and visit, walk about slowly and wonderingly, and then unhitch his pants and piss on the headstones. The black-hatted reverend scolded him.

But there is no virtue or sin in piss. We are all borne of waste.

I have Jeremy Woodhill, still. And check on him, occasionally. I think, sometimes, on the strange logic of it. Before Jeremy, I was not what I am, Graveyeard, Churchyard, Burying Ground; I was earth. Wide and consciousless, sprawling space into space, infinite with all other land and air and sea and wind and animal. When the tide yawned, I breathed in. When the seasons turned, we all moved together. There was no I, then, no agent by which to narrate.

When he came, my world shrunk and focused. There was, suddenly, purpose. I was apart from the oneness of the natural world, cut off by my sudden preoccupation. He—his body—made me this,

this singular thing with an identity distinct in the universe. It is, then, funny to think on it: that now he is being whittled away by acid and animals, by time, that he is ceasing to maintain space, that he will soon give up the material wholeness of his body entirely . . . and yet I remain. I remain what he made me.

Justly, the created should disappear with the creator. But progression, process, is full of strange logic. Once begun, there is only more and more. There are no longer creators, only methods of transformation. If the circumstances and stuff of your beginning fall away, it matters not a jot. Once you are made, you are made and begun. And you will go on and on, and on, despite what you lose to the earth along the way.

The story will be great dismemberment and dissection of my body. There are more, endless stories, but this is the one I am telling now. My dead, Chilling dead, were dug up, and taken from me; partly, it was my fault. I had not understood Chilling. I had not seen it in the roads, and homes. I knew only the sad and sodden Chilling, the men and women come to bury and mourn their dead. I knew the religious men and their words, I knew the children who ran and flung the mud, I knew the merry and thoughtful Gallo brothers, my grave-diggers. But I did not know the stories of the living Chilling. I did not know what went on outside my gates, the things that led men with shovels to pull me apart and take what was essential to me. To explain why, and to explain how, you must dig up the dead yourselves. But what, after all, is the story-teller but just that: a digger-up of things long forgotten or hidden away? A digger-up of the things we have once valued, but lost? A digger-up of the things you have, once perhaps, even loved, but could not keep? Who better to tell a story, then, than I? Dirt and dumb! Ha! I will press on, and tell it to you whole.

Once begun, we have begun.

Chapter V.
The Sloughs' Home

In the Slough kitchen, Dedlock was shirtless. The hair on his chest and arms was thick, black, and curly; the hair on his head jutted from his skull in pyramidal tufts. Dedlock's newborn daughter, in the crook of his arm, was pearlescent and hairless, like a little pink bean.

"I'm not kidding," said Dedlock. He scratched at his neck. He jounced the baby twice in his arm and opened his mouth wide at her, to see her mimic the gesture. She widened her mouth and out came a small thin wail. He nodded at her. "Are you going to be a-crying?" he asked, "Or are you going to be not crying?" His voice did not indicate a preference.

"What's that?" asked his wife. "Sorry, what, Dedlock? What?" Agnes was squatting, at her brother's feet, unknotting his laces. She put her fingers to the nape of her neck and prodded. She felt as though all the bones of her neck had been rammed against one another.

"The ghost, Ag," Dedlock said, "Remember what I was saying, about the ghost? I wasn't making a laugh."

"No. Not at all." Agnes turned her face back to Jim's large feet, and spat upon the laces. "Why are you so caked in mud, Jim? And what did you do with these knots?" she asked him.

Jim shrugged. He was watching Dedlock and Bonnie. The baby made sounds that sounded like, "Dub ub ub dub," and Dedlock, holding her along the length of his hairy forearm, swung her out and back. He held her in front of his own face.

"Bonnie," he told the baby, "Don't be scared, now. But your papa did see a ghost, right out there in the north field. Yes, yes he did."

"I was a digger tonight," said Jim, staring down at his sister. Agnes spit onto the knot of his left boot.

"So, where? Again? Pardon. Jim, you have to keep still one moment," said Agnes.

"I dug graves for ghosts," said Jim. He was careful. He wanted to boast, enough for them to be impressed, but not enough to be in trouble.

"That's right, ghosts! But don't be scared, now, Bonnie," said Dedlock, swinging the girl back and forth, "As I think it was a mere past person, maybe a native, back to check up on the land. All dressed in

29

white. See if we're doing right by it."

"Is everyone in this house seeing ghosts?" said Agnes. She lifted herself off her heels. Fat padded her thighs and midsection, pregnancy memories, but her face was still thin. Agnes had sharp, high cheekbones, and the hollows beneath her eyes sunk into purple crescents. Her eyes were very large, almost as if they were lidless, and very dark. Her hair, too, was almost black, smooth and glossy as a pond at night, and she parted her hair cleanly in the center of her scalp. The tightness of the bun at the nape of her neck, and the white center part, made her look severe. She had inherited dark skin, an olive complexion that glowed when she stirred the laundry pot, from her mother who claimed that it came from her great-great grandmother, an Italian opera singer. (In reality, the great-great grandmother was a great-great-great grandmother, and she had been a Scottish peasant. She had lived in the highlands until she was sixteen, at which point— due to a disagreement between her father and herself—she had run away from home and found herself, six months later, in Edinburgh.) Agnes had been the only Cates child to inherit such a deep brown cheek; her sister Margaret had been a red-head, like her father, with skin the color of new milk.

"You walking in the dark to the graveyard every night alone might not be a smart thing," she said. "Giving you bad thoughts. Maybe Ben Benner we can get to walk you over. Ah! There!"

Jim kicked the boot off his foot and flung it into the wall. The baby screamed. Her tongue curled up. Dedlock could see the inside of his daughter's mouth, the ridges at the top, ornate and careful as a tiny, pink cathedral ceiling.

"Ooh! You're going to be crying," he said to her, matter-of-factly.

"Other foot," Agnes said to Jim. This knot came free easily. She took off his boot, and brushed his shoulders with her hard, flat palms. Behind her, Dedlock made soft noises at his daughter, and put his lips to her forehead.

"You did a good job, Jim," said Agnes, "At the graveyard. I know the Reverend is very glad you are there. He's mentioned, though, that perhaps you are falling asleep every so often? He was wondering?"

"I don't fall asleep, Ag. That's the whole point is that I don't fall asleep."

"Well, just make sure. Jump up and down when you feel tired. Do you have enough food to keep you full?"

Agnes clumped across the floor in a pair of leather boots. They were far too big for her and she had to lift her knees high, to the height of her hip, to be able to walk in them. (They belonged to Dedlock, she thought, but they were, actually, the boots of John Nurse, who had just the previous day dropped them at the house for Jim while Agnes was out delivering Esther Cotton's baby girl.)

"I don't want Benner to walk me. I hate Benner," said Jim to his sister's back. Her arms were up above her head, putting away Jim's graveyard bell. Their parents had been gone for nearly seven years: his sister had been his keeper since he'd turned two. If love is born of affection, if affection is born of comfort, and comfort of familiarity, then Jim loved his sister. He was at ease with her. He did not yell at her, or feel angry when she was in the room. The baby was quiet again.

"Sun's getting loud," Dedlock said to his wife, "Jim needs to get to sleep and I need to get out."

"Right, Ded . . . All done. That's safe, there." She stomped cheerfully back to Jim.

"I'm going to tell the Bon my story," Dedlock said, "and whose boots are those?"

Agnes turned away from Jim to look at Dedlock. Dedlock looked up from Bonnie's eyes to meet his wife's. She had waited a long time for a baby.

"My slippers are wet and somehow there's baby sick in my boots. I don't know. Wait a little, and you can tell me about your ghost," she said.

"I'll tell you both," he said, and Bonnie made a noise, a glugging sound, which may have been a laugh or an expression of impatience. Dedlock took her to the window and as the sunlight come down across Chilling, he watched her tiny fingers curl and uncurl, her fingernails pink and impossibly formed, impossibly real on a body so small.

"What *is* a ghost?" asked Jim. "What's a ghost made out of?" He had dreams, when he slept during the day. He dreamt that he was in the graveyard, and that he saw the terrible thing, and that he tried to ring the bell. But when he looked down, he saw that he had lost the bell, that it was gone, and he shouted and shouted and shouted.

The bell had become necessary when the bodies had begun to go missing in Chilling. Last spring, John Francis had complained to the pastor that the land had creased and changed above his wife's gravesite. He had raised some commotion. Sadly, as is often the case, the unrest that John Francis worked so hard to create had a negative effect on his own health; he riled his own heart most. He spent his few widower days worrying and wondering himself to death. But John had been in the grave only a day and a night when his worry proved reasonable, after all. The earth was so badly disturbed one morning that Reverend Brewer himself noticed from the road, and, walking out and toeing the ground, he assumed the only thing he could assume: there had been shovels there, and recently. He had shouted for the Gallo brothers, the young men who worked as the village gravediggers, but they were somewhere far off, asleep or working on some other odd job. No one responded to Brewer's shouting, save the Chilling birds and the Chilling dogs, until the afternoon. Just past midday, the two Gallo brothers had trudged into the graveyard, dirty and rubbing their eyes, and Brewer had stood on the church steps as they dug up John Francis' empty coffin. Fernie and Joe Gallo had stood next to it, enjoying, for the moment, Brewer's aghast face, and then Fernie had knocked Joey's shovel with his own, and Joey hit back, and they had lifted their shovels in two hands like heavy swords and played like little boys above the empty grave.

Three weeks later, Ezipeth Jansom's body was removed; this time, the remover had not bothered to pile the dirt back upon the empty casket. Then, in the summer, Clean Parker who had been kicked by a horse went gone, too, and his wife who died a month later out of hopelessness for him was taken, too. The Reverend Brewer had chosen Jim Cates because Jim was no good for anything else; also, Jim liked the macabre and grotesque tones in Bible stories. He would not be afraid. Brewer had given him a bell, and sat him down in the graveyard at night, every night, even when there had been no burials that day, to watch and keep awake, and to ring it like crazy when anyone appeared. "If anyone comes, Jim," Brewer had said, "You tell them that they've taken quite enough. Quite enough! Then send them on their way." Jim liked his bell. He liked the huge, clanging noise it made, and the power of making noise.

"What's a ghost?" Agnes repeated. "Yes. Someone you see, a person, or a body. But it's not real. It's not made of skin."
"Can it bleed, though? Joe Gallo sees ghosts, he says," said Jim.
"Joey Gallo?"
"Yes," said Jim, "He sees ghosts every night, and they do things.

He tells me about them and what they did."

"I hope you don't bother the Gallos when they're working," said Agnes.

"Does he see them in the graveyard?" asked Dedlock. He walked slowly, away from the window and toward Agnes and Jim in the center of the room, swaying Bonnie from side to side, so slightly Agnes could almost miss the rock of her child's small head. "Spooky," said Dedlock.

"No, no," said Jim, "He says he sees ghosts asleep."

"He sees the ghosts sleeping?"

Jim squinted and rubbed his belly with the flat of his hand. He shrugged.

"Does he see them lying in their coffins, with their eyes closed and what?" asked Dedlock.

"No," said Jim. He looked at Agnes, then at Dedlock. Dedlock swayed the baby in his arms and watched the two of them in the center of the room.

"You mean," she said, "that Joey Gallo sees ghosts while he is sleeping. He sees them while he is asleep."

"Maybe," said Jim, "Maybe." He blinked and squinted. His eyes were not as dark as his sister's; they were paler than Agnes's, paler than Bonnie's, and he had, at the center of his eyes, ringed around the pupil, a thin circle of bright green. "Yes," Jim said.

"Jimmer," said Dedlock, "those aren't ghosts."

"They are," said Jim, looking at Bonnie, who had fallen asleep. Her head lolled to the side and rested on Dedlock's naked biceps. "They are what you said. Not real people but he seen them. He says what they look like and how they have clothes on and what the clothes are, and their smells, and the animals they have if they have animals and if they are sad or if they are happy and what they do."

"But," said Agnes, patting Jim's hair into place across his forehead, "he's sleeping, and so we know that what he sees, these folks, they're not ghosts. Those people are something else."

"What else?" said Jim.

"Dreams," said Agnes, "Those are only dreams."

"But what are they made out of? Can they bleed? Can they be hurt? Dedlock saw ghosts," said Jim.

"One ghost," said Dedlock, "I think it was a ghost."

"If he was asleep," said Agnes, "it would be a dream that he saw. But Dedlock says that he was awake when he saw this person."

"But what if you don't know," said Jim, "if you are asleep or awake? If you can't tell?"

"I'm going to be late," Dedlock said to Agnes. "It's about that time and Benner's likely at our gate." Dedlock turned again, and brought his sleeping daughter to the window. He whispered something down into her head and squinted out the glass.

Benjamin Benner was Dedlock's brother-in-law, having married Charity Slough, Dedlock's youngest and smallest sister. The Slough children had been extraordinary for the way in which their physical sizes corresponded to their places in the birth order: Dedlock's older sister, Prudence, was a mammoth woman, biceps like cannonballs, a waist that strained every fabric tied to contain it. Dedlock, the lone son of the Sloughs, was a size approximate to his older sister's, though his face, when shaven, could show evidence of a jawbone. When he worked particularly hard, in the summertime, the thin line of his skull even emerged, near his temples, and Agnes took the cue to feed him more, to heap food on his plate as though it was a trough. The next Slough child had been a girl called Faith, and her build had surprised everyone with its relative slimness. Faith had knobby knees and bony elbows and a potbelly, though she was almost as tall as her younger brother. She had married a Canadian fur-trader named Pour and they had taken themselves off years ago, somewhere cold where all the Slough fat and muscle could have done her some good; they produced thick-skinned child after thick-skinned child and now had probably more than a dozen sons and daughters trudging through the northern snows and swinging axes in northern forests. After Faith came Priscella, who hadn't spoken a word until she turned seven years old, when she had asked for some more gravy. Priscella was tall and thin. Even now, as a grown woman, she sat in her chair and hugged her knees to her chest in some effort to become even smaller. She spoke in whispers and in slightly louder whispers for emphasis. The last, the baby of the family, was Benner's wife. Charity was whippet-thin and short. Her bones, though, were packed with all of Dedlock's muscle, in miniature; as a child, she had run everywhere and would go missing for hours, running northward to the sea and then for miles along the coast, clambering over the outcroppings of rocks and splashing through the shallow pools during low tide. She had been Dedlock's favorite sibling, and he hers. When Benner had asked her to become his wife, she had turned away from him and run

34

the streets of Chilling until she had found her brother—he had been butchering a sheep, and she squatted down next to him.

"I think I'm going to marry Ben Benner," she had told him, and he understood that it was both a question and a declaration, and he grunted, and she ran off again to Benner and that was that. Charity, at the time, had been only sixteen, but she had grown in mind and intelligence as quickly as she ran, her maturity and her size inversely proportional.

"I hate Benner," said Jim, but Agnes was moving him from the center of the room to the staircase.

"You've really got to stay awake, kid," she reminded him. The graveyard had lost three bodies in four weeks.

"Be awake, be awake, James," Reverend Brewer had told Jim. "You must not allow this, anymore. They've gone too far, now. They've been warned. Keep your hand on your bell and your eyes open. Watch. And keep awake, James."

At the window, Dedlock heard his wife murmuring to Jim. He kept his eyes out the window, where Benner was making his way toward the house from the center of Chilling, Dedlock looked in the opposite direction, westward, where the great hulking Satus House stood high on a sea-facing hill.

"He was exhausted," Agnes said. At the window herself, she leaned her head against her husband's massive arm. Instinctively, Dedlock inclined his head toward hers. Their temples kissed. "I think he'll sleep until I take him to the church."

"I've never seen a ghost before," he whispered to her, "until last night." She laughed.

Agnes lay Bonnie down for her nap. Bonnie had a nose like Agnes's older sister Maga, with little nostrils and a pointed end. Bonnie moved her lower lip in and out while she slept. Agnes could smell, through the cracked window, the smell of a bonfire somewhere in the village, and then she sniffed the air, again.

Not a bonfire, she thought, and stood up straight.

Agnes was almost thirty years old. Bonnie was her first child. She could smell better now, she noticed, after being pregnant. She could smell when her husband was in the next room, and she could smell when he was nervous or when he wanted to sleep with her. She could smell when the baby needed to eat. She could smell her own saliva and her sweat. But most of all, she could smell the weather. Now, through the window, she could smell the spring grasses. More subtly, the mud of the river. Further, the fresh salt of the sea.

Agnes sat straight up in the bed.

She took a long breath in through her nose.

It was fire, definitely. Something large had burned, somewhere, and the wind was carrying the scent down to the village and around the Sloughs' house. Something came along inside the smoke to make her uneasy: her instincts told her to take her baby to her chest and to take shelter somewhere, to leave Dedlock and her brother and everyone else, to get out immediately. She moved toward Bonnie, who was still and pink and sleeping; she breathed in one more deep breath.

But the wind had changed, or else she had imagined it, and the scent was gone. She lay down, with her head on the quilt near Bonnie's face. Then she built a wall of blankets around the child, and went to the kitchen, put water on the fire, and started the bread.

The lingering smell of Nora's fire, far off, came in through the kitchen window. Agnes ignored something, a low hum of warning, and went on with her work.

Chapter VI.
Satus House

"We'll never finish this," said Fernie. He stared at the woodpile.

"Okay," said Joe. He lifted his axe.

Fernie worked on the left side. He had wedged his wooden leg into a small divot they had dug out to make him stable. He, the little brother in age and size, held his axe with the left hand on the top; Joe's grasp was the opposite, so that when they swung their axes up it was almost as though they meant to converge their blades on the same spot. Joe was stronger than his brother, though, and the speed with which he recovered from the swing and brought his axe up again outdistanced his brother's and kept the two from working in sync.

After a little less than an hour, the sun began to rise. Joe wiped the sweat from his temples and chin.

"Someone's coming," said Joe, looking off to the east, down the hill. "Huh," he added, and Fernie let his axe fall and looked, too.

"Jules?" asked Fernie, naming one of the cellar men.

Fernie's eyes weren't sharp. He needed to squint to see at all well far away. Joe, whose eyes were good, saw that it wasn't a man, at all, but something almost monstrous. It appeared female. The light from the east illuminated half of her body and face. Her hair was chopped close to her head. She was emaciated and her skin was badly scarred. She was walking toward them.

Joe looked over at his brother. Fernie was cleaning his fingernails with the edge of his axe, waiting for the someone to walk near enough for him to see.

"Fern," said Joe, "I'll finish the wood."

Fernie looked up. He wiped his forehead.

"What?" he asked.

"It'll be too nice a day to miss. Go for your swim," said Joe, and when he had finished speaking he lifted his axe again and began to work.

"You'll never get it done." But Joe said nothing. Fernie shrugged, then laid his axe against his splitting log and walked off, up to Satus House, and from there down the north walk which led directly to the sea. He did not stop to look behind him, lest his brother change his mind and beckon him back.

When his brother was gone, Joe balanced the axe behind him and lowered onto it carefully, using the handle as a seat. He watched the girl—or small woman? he squinted—make her slow way up the hill from the village. She was painfully thin. The shapes of bones poked up from her skin at the shoulders. If it was who he thought it was, she was probably close to collapse. She made her way up the hill hunched over and stopped often to rest: she would put her hands to the small of her back and lift her face up to where the sun was coming on.

"Yo, hey," Joe called out when she was within hearing, and waved. She stopped, and looked at Joe. She nodded, put her hands on her hips, and moved to take the path that would lead her to the woodpile, and to Joe.

"Good morning," he called to her, as she crested the hill and began the flat walk to the woodshed. Joe stood up and held his axe high, up by the blade. He waved it in greeting. He could see the shape of her skeleton and he cringed. He did not know how she had enough strength to climb the hill.

"Hey," she said when she was close enough to him.

"Jice," said Joe. She was wearing some sort of thin woolen underwear, without sleeves, and Joe could see the shape of her body as clearly as if she was wearing nothing at all. The skin that he could see looked thick and pitted with dark marks. She was breathing very heavily. She either had very big eyes, Joe thought, or a very tiny face. She appeared not to see him; she was looking at the pile of unsplit wood. She was standing very close to him, he thought, closer than people usually stood. He could smell smoke on her. Nora put her hand to the top of her head and rubbed her palm against the bristles of her hair.

"You've been sick," said Joe.

Nora didn't look at him. He kept his eyes determinedly on her big, bulgy, glassy ones. She looked like a starving frog, he thought.

Nora nodded at the woodpile. "Lot of work," she said. She walked over to the place where Fernie had been chopping. She took a long breath through her nose, and then she sat on the ground and leaned her forehead against the handle of Fernie's axe.

Joe looked around him and regretted sending Fernie away. His little brother was better at talking to people. She just crouched there, smelling the wood. He squinted again. She looked familiar, but the person he remembered was not like the person he saw before him.

"If you want, then, to go inside? Get some water?" he said. "You're here to see the doctor?"

She stood up. "I'm Nora Pirrip," she said, "and my family is all recently died, and I think my mother's body—I know it sounds strange, but I think someone here took my mother's body."

"Nora?" said Joe. He stood up off his axe. Then he stopped and stared at her again. "You don't recognize me?"

"I think I know you. Do I know you? Oh, oh." Nora remembered her clothing and looked down. "I'm sorry," she said, "I'm very tired."

"It's alright. I'm Joe Gallo. Joey Gallo. My dad was the blacksmith. Years ago, now."

"I've been sick."

"Your family been sick. We know. I'm sorry. The doctor went to see you a while back. Who told you to come here?"

"We used to catch fish, when we were little, I think?"

Joe shook his head. "That wasn't me," he said, "but I'd hide in the forest sometimes and watch you all playing in the stream."

"Little Jim Cates. Agnes Slough's brother. He was in the churchyard, and he sent me up here. I don't know why. He said Captain Murderer lived here."

Joe lifted his axe and put it over his shoulder. "Come on inside," he said, "and meet the doctor."

(By this time, Fernie had reached the sea, and the day was dawning just as clearly and brilliantly sunny as he had thought it would. The wind was cold but gusted weakly, half-heartedly, and the sea was soft and calm. Fernie sat in the sand and pulled off his boot and threw it behind him; he stood and pulled his shirt over his head and yanked off his pants and peeled off his sock. Then, leaning over to his side and letting all his weight balance atop his good leg, he unbuckled the leather strap that held on his other side. He slid it down and off, felt the wind and the fine mist of the ocean against the healed skin underneath his thigh. He made his way—half hopping, half-crawling—into the water and used his arms to propel his torso fully into the shallow waves. The water pierced his skin like a shower of needles, plunging themselves hard into his arms, his legs, his genitals, his face. It was so cold that, for a panicked moment, he could not breathe and in the panic there came on a blissful break, in which his mind emptied of all thought save the immediacy of surviving the cold. He focused his mind completely on the task of moving his limbs, moving one arm and then the other, kicking his leg like a fishtail, moving fast enough to generate heat, enough heat to be warm enough to stay alive to continue moving his limbs, to generate heat, enough heat to warm his limbs enough to keep moving, moving enough to generate heat to keep moving to generate heat to keep moving. Jerkily, then fluidly, then even happily—he was swimming. The water peeled around his skin. It broke away in foamy explosions where he kicked.)

In the kitchen of Satus House, a servant with a body like a slab of granite and manic red hair looked at Joe, then at Nora. "Woodpile?"

"Getting done," he said to her. "Fernie's out there." He went about cobbling together a meal for Nora: brown bread, a cold potato. Some cheese, too, when he asked for it. She cut it from the wheel with a giant knife.

"Can I have this?"

The granite-like woman shrugged and he took a rough blanket from a bench and tucked it under his arm. He balanced all the food on a great wide plate and began his way across the ground floor of Satus; as he approached the entryway, he found the doctor just coming down the stairs, on his way to an early breakfast, and Nora standing at the bottom. Doctor Salderman had a polished wooden stick with a brass handle tucked underneath his right arm. He opened his eyes wide when he saw Nora, and rubbed his cheek with his left hand. Joe gave Nora the blanket and she wrapped it around her shoulders. It hung to her calves.

"Who's this, who's this? Hello? Right. Hello." The doctor came up close to Nora and, because he was tall, had to bend down to look her in the eyes. She felt dwarfed by him, and she was tired, and thirsty, but she looked up into his face.

Salderman had a long face. His skin was eerily ashen, as if he lived underground, or had never eaten a vegetable. His hair was long, graying, and unevenly trimmed; half of it hung nearly to his shoulder, and the other side was hacked away up around his ear. He would absently tuck the long side behind his left ear, where it would immediately slip out and fall forward, and he would tuck it back again and again without seeming to notice the futility of the act. He had vague brown eyes that wandered around a room even while he spoke to someone and a large mouth that seemed too full of yellowed teeth. One of his front teeth was black. His hands and feet were very large, and he walked as though always on the verge of tripping over something. Those who passed him in the hallways of Satus House found themselves putting out an arm, just in case, though they knew that this jerky, tripping walk was the doctor's normal mode of getting himself around. Still, it was alarming, sometimes, to see him approaching the staircase.

"She found us from the churchyard, Doctor," said Joe. "Came up the hill."

"It's a pile of bones here in my hall," said Salderman. He passed his stick to Nora, who leaned onto it.

"I think we have to leave it alone for a bit, Doctor," said Joe. "Go to Wolfeborough instead. The Reverend is getting annoyed, and the villagers are getting upset."

"This isn't a walking stick," Nora said.

"Oh, no. For Mungbean," said Salderman.

Nora looked at Joe.

"One of Steven Storey's dogs," Joe said, and Salderman shook his head at him.

"*The* dog," the doctor said, "*the* dog. The dog who sometimes comes up the hill, around and about. No, no, not a good dog. A very violent type, needs a stick to keep his teeth at bay. Away."

"The doctor's afraid of dogs," explained Joe. He put the plate of food down upon a side table. "Mungbean came up the hill one time. Months ago."

"Oh," said Nora. She looked over at the cold potato.

"I don't like them, very much at all, no, no. No. Mungbean, though, an especially violent dog." The doctor took up Nora's wrist and pinched it between his thumb and forefinger.

"Hey," said Nora, but the doctor was staring at the ceiling, and counting to himself, and seemed not to notice that she had spoken.

"Found us from the *churchyard*," repeated Joe.

"He told me you took my mother." Nora was still staring at the face of the man before her. He was older, but not old; his hair was only gray at the front, where it fell into his face. She looked down at the hand that pinched her wrist.

"When we were all sick," she said, "were you there?"

"Oh, yes," said Salderman. Even when he smiled, the lugubrious sag of his eyelids kept from his face any suggestion of past or potential happiness. "That you remember. Seventy-four, Joe, remember seventy-four. That you remember at all is good."

"My father had only me and my mother. And my brothers, though some women from Chilling came to help for a little while. To nurse, I mean," said Nora. "The midwife was pregnant. She couldn't come and help us."

"When I heard, oh! I am sorry that I did not hear about your family. Not, I mean . . . until after your brothers had died. I had been away, had been away. But as soon as I could come and perhaps help." Salderman released her wrist and straightened up. He replaced the palm of his hand upon his cheek. "As soon as I heard about the disease—very odd disease—I came to see if I could help at all. It was," he said, as if confiding a secret, "very bad in other places."

"No one else in Chilling got sick," said Nora. "Just us."

"Doctor, I—" Joe began to speak, and even took a step forward, but Nora interrupted him.

"What odd disease? What is it called?"

"I don't know, really. We'll find it out yet, though." The doctor shrugged.

"Did you treat my mother? I can't remember. I was sick and I don't always know what happened and what I made up. Once I think I dreamt I was a fencepost."

Salderman lowered his chin to his chest and shook his head slowly. "No, no," he said. "I can't say that I treated your mother, though I was there just at the very end. I stepped in the house and went straight to you—being the younger—and when I came to your mother afterwards I'm afraid there was perhaps moments left to her. Rattled breath. No hope then—I'm sorry. But no. I saw her, briefly, and was there when she passed."

Nora nodded. "You're the one who cut my hair," she said, and she put her hand on her head and rubbed at her scalp.

Salderman tucked a hunk of his own hair behind his ear, pursed his lips and stared at Nora's hair.

"Yesss," he said, and his eyes narrowed. "Terrible, sorry. I'm surprised, in fact, that it had—but it worked, anyway, or something else, by coincidence. My old teacher, he insisted that hair sucks the vital energies."

"But it was you," said Nora.

The doctor replaced his hand on his cheek. "Oh, yes," he said. "I cut it off myself and burnt it in your little kitchen. That's all I could do for you."

Joe sighed.

"So, Nora came here because of Jim in the churchyard," he said. "She was there not so long ago."

Salderman turned to Joe for the first time. "What," he said, "in the middle of night?"

"Yes."

"Never mind that, no. But you," said the doctor, focusing again on Nora, "you should know how unwise that is. Walking around in night. And being in the cold. Dew. Come with me, now, and we'll check you up."

"I'm better," said Nora, "I'm just trying to find some things. Could I sit down?" She felt suddenly as though the world had begun to spin wildly, and she saw a flash of brilliant colors. In the entrance-way, there was a long trunk for storing boots, and Nora went and sat down on it. Salderman and Joe followed and stood in front of her. She was sweating.

"I keep getting these pains in my legs, and dizzy, and my head hurts. I haven't had water. I could take some . . . water."

"Okay," said Joe. He left.

"I went to the graveyard, but someone must have taken her, because I couldn't find her. She left, once before. They said she was dead. Everyone told me she was dead."

"I remember," said Salderman.

"But she wasn't. She left us. I've only known her since I was eleven, or so. That's when she came back. But anyway, now she's dead, and I need to see her body, because I didn't get to see it. I need to touch it. I don't know why you took her, and I don't care. I'm very tired."

"And then? After you see the body?"

"Don't think, either, that you can fool me. I know her body. My mother had a very particular body. She had very particular feet." Nora could feel a little tide of blackness beginning to creep into her brain. She swallowed and shook her head.

"Most people do," said Salderman.

"Why do you want to see a dead body?" asked Joe. He had reentered with a cup; Nora took it and drank.

"Why do people, usually?"

"Most people don't want to see dead bodies."

Nora felt as though she would either burst or collapse. "Just show me. I'll take a good look, I'll touch her foot, and I'll go away. I won't bother you again."

"Again?" said Salderman, "Again, after what? Joe's brought you some food. Good idea, Joe is a thoughtful thinker. Bread? A little bread."

"Just my mother, please. Please, now."

Salderman took a seat on the bench, at the opposite end, so that Nora had to turn her head to look at him. He spread his knees and held his dogstick between them.

"We had dogs," said Nora, "A bitch and puppies. Do you remember if they were still there? When you came to our house, when I was sick? Were the puppies there?"

"Oh, now, don't cry." Salderman put his hand on her forehead. "Ugh. No. Definitely no puppies. I keep a stick with me," the doctor said, "to keep the dogs away."

"There are no dogs here, though. In this house."

The doctor's eyes skitted toward the door. "Well. It's good to have the stick, though."

"Sure."

"I'm just . . . Nora, I'm terribly, terribly sorry. We did have your mother."

"Hey," said Joe.

"It's okay, Joe. Joey. Nora, we did have your mother but I am very sorry, she is gone."

"Gone where?"

"It is not possible to let you see her or touch her or even her foot."

Nora sat very quietly. Sitting was uncomfortable, for her, because all the fat and muscle was gone from her thighs and seat, and her bones scraped the inside of her skin, and the outside of her skin was ground into the hard knotted wood of the trunk.

"She was here, though."

"Yes."

"You dug up her body and brought her here."

"I did the digging," said Joe. "I did that part."

"She was dead," said Nora.

"I recognized her," said Joe. "Your mother was dead."

"Would you like, maybe, something to eat?" said Salderman.

"No," said Nora.

"Would you like my dogstick?"

Nora reached over and took the stick from the doctor.

"I'm tired," she said. "Could I find somewhere to sleep, for a little while? I don't think I can go back to the village, right now. I think I can just sleep a little, and then, maybe. Then I'll go to my uncle's house."

"Okay," said Salderman.

(Fernie climbed out of the water. The sun shone on his skin. He shivered and wrapped his arms around his body. Naked, his flesh erupted in thousands of goosebumps, and his body looked textured, almost scaled, in the sunshine. His body was long, and very lean, hard and slimly muscled. He was too lean to be a very good worker, like Joe, even if he had kept both legs. But even without his left leg, he was strong, in his own way. His was a body built to move quickly through tight places, a man made for delicate and precise movement. On the sand, tanned even in the early spring and naked, he looked born of the water, and it was no wonder, no surprise to the gulls to find him there, freezing, unable to keep away from the sea. They called out to him and landed around him as he pulled on his clothes.)

Chapter VIII.
Satus House

Satus House was built around a serpentine staircase. It was slick, black and narrow. The steps had been made from slabs of Derbyshire marble. Dr. Salderman's little sister, the poet Odette, had come to America first. A few years later, her brother had followed her. Odette, in charge of the house's creation, had the marble imported from England and used in the house's construction before she had even stepped her toes off the boat.

I want the staircase built first thing," she had written to the American builder. The builder squinted and showed the letter to his friend Mike. "Can you read this?" he asked.

"Looks like a bird shat on the page," said Mike.

"I think it's about the staircase," said the builder.

"I don't know about rich people," said Mike. "I don't know about them at all."

The marble had come on a Tuesday, by which time Mike and his boss had deciphered Odette's instructions. They paid men, in pork and various currencies, to carve and fit the marble into the twisting climbing coil tower. Before there were walls, or floors, before there were windows or stone facades, they built the staircase. It rose out of the grassy hill like a child's model of the Tower of Babel. It went in little circles, turning into the air while moving laterally along the horizon, trekking sideways into spaces left and right where boxed-in rooms, one day, would appear one after another in the fashion of soap bubbles, and contain the air. The walls of the rooms would enclose sleeping poets, overworked maids, snooping guests, and insomniac doctors. One room, on the third floor and entered by the first door on the right, would enclose the small body of Eleanor (Nora) Pirrip, two weeks after the last member of her immediate family had succumbed to some unnamed and violently fatal disease.

She had slept and woken and slept again, on and off, head up, head down, so that when she finally woke, *woke* woke, she had no idea how long she had been in the room or if she had, in fact, been asleep the whole time and had been only dreaming the fitful wake-ups. She was wearing a nightgown that did not belong to her, but felt nice on her skin and didn't have a tight collar. She sat up in the bed. Salderman's dogstick was lying at the foot.

"Dogstick," she said. Her throat was dry.

On the staircase, she grasped the doctor's dogstick in her right hand, and leaned upon it and the banister. She felt tired and sore in her stomach muscles and legs. A man passed her on his way upstairs. He was older than Nora, perhaps thirty or thirty-five years old, tall, thin, with sparse wet-looking hair plastered down to his skull and large moles on one side of his face. He held a hot brick wrapped in a towel. He stopped and stared at her.

"Hello," he said. He pronounced it strangely, hey-loh.

"Hey," said Nora. She kept on her way down, and turned when the staircase turned, and he was left staring after her, puzzled. Then he remembered his brick and hurried up the stairs.

She couldn't figure out the time of day. Where were the windows in this house? Nora stepped into a hallway and looked around for an open room, for lines of telltale daylight or candlelight spilling from cracks. But Satus was painted in grays and blues, soft almost-purples, muted colors that could be dawn or twilight or even dark day, misty noon or rainy morning. Nora opened a door at random and slipped herself into a room.

Arranged in long shelves, thousands of books. Rows and rows and rows, from floor to ceiling . . . but everywhere else, too, on the floor, on tables, on armchairs, on the fireplace mantle, on the hearth itself. Volumes were flung open, spines up, pages dog-eared and exposed to the air. There was a path of clear carpet among the books, from the door to the largest table, but Nora did not walk it. She stood just inside the entrance of the room. On the largest table was a parade of empty teacups. They were large, small, white, pink, blue, lavender, gray with orange flowers, some without their saucers, some turned upside down and some with cold dregs of tea still left.

This room was used. Daily and often. She had stumbled upon it in one of its rare moments of quiet solitude, when it gathered its energy to be of service, when it shrugged its shoulders down its back and rolled its neck from side to side and rested.

"Sorry," she whispered to the room. She left, and closed the door carefully, as though closing the bedroom door of a sleeping child.

Before she went down to the next floor, Nora leaned over the banister and looked down at the black and white pattern of the tiles below. They had been arranged in a mosaic. Nora, from the height of the second floor, could only see a portion of it, three rows of black tiles to one side. She leaned forward . . . but it was too large. She thought it could possibly be a tree, the trunk of it beginning at the front door and winding down the floor to the head of the great entrance way, and the portion she could see, stylized branches. The marble was cool on her feet. Beneath her, someone crossed the floor and Nora backed away and into another room.

This room was Odette Salderman's study. When she and her brother had been living in England (in North Nibley, Gloucestershire, where Alexander was the village doctor) Odette Salderman had published a single volume of poetry that sold unexpectedly well. She moved to London, met a man, a sea captain, and fell in love. She agreed to live with him in America. She published another volume of poetry, moved to New England, published a third volume, and then the ship captain met an unfortunate end. She came to Chilling. Later, her brother Alexander decided to join her in Satus House. Odette still wrote, every day, but she was painfully slow. She wrote very short poems, but composed them in endless drafts, endless repetitions, endless varieties until she had come close to the essential emotion which had prompted them.

This room, her room, she had arranged as carefully as one of her poems. She had heavy curtains hung on the windows. The grate in front of the fire had been wrought per her careful specifications and cast odd shadows across the length of the room: bars and loops of black fell like lengths of velvet ribbon against large travelling trunks in various stages of unpack.

Her writing table was not a table at all, but a child's school desk. Next to the desk, grazing the seat with its lace, Odette had hung her wedding dress. Age had turned it a grayish yellow.

But Nora did not see the dress. She had taken note of the trunks. Odette had never fully unpacked. Clothing, scarves, quilts, linens, boxes and bags spilled out from the trunks and onto the floor. Nora wanted to kneel in front of the trunks and fold each thing, and then to pile the folded things on the floor, and pack everything away. She almost did; she would have. She was almost kneeling when Nora saw, above the trunks, a painting.

It was a man on a horse. He was leading many men, on many horses. All of them were charging, it seemed, away from battle. As he rode, the man held a severed head aloft in his left hand. Behind him, behind the throng of horses and men, a city was burning. The severed head:

1. was a man's head
2. had very long hair
3. was, because of its very long hair, grasped by said hair by the horseman
4. had its skin pulled taut and tightly upward, so that the head seemed to smile
5. had strong white teeth
6. had no visible tongue.

Nora brought her face up close to the painting, as close as she could get on her tiptoes. She studied the bottom of the head, where it had been (presumably) severed by the horseman. But Nora could see no blood dripping, no jagged edges of skin hanging down, nothing loose or uneven. Perhaps this man had been already dead, she thought, when his head was taken. The cut was clean and dry. Perhaps it was removed as a trophy, as some sort of proof or token of something. Not a good prize, Nora thought, on account of the rotting. On account of the fact that when the skin rotted away, all the horseman would have left would be a white skull, which could belong to anyone. Proof of nothing, besides the process of decay.

Nora thwacked the open trunks with her dogstick. Why not pack the trunks? Why not unpack them? Why leave a job half-done, and walk away? She was suddenly very warm. She turned and left the room. She left the door open. If her mother's body had been here, in this house, then it was not here in these rooms. Her body hadn't been stuffed into one of these trunks. And it certainly hadn't been fitted with spectacles and propped up in front of those books, in the other room.

If there had been bodies here, they would go where all bodies went. Downward, below, and into the earth.

The cellar was disappointing. Dusty, fairly smokily-lit with lamps, and lined with thousands of round blank faces, the butts of wine bottles that peered from their pegged slots like idiot toddlers. Nora reached down and lifted up the hem of the borrowed nightgown. It was too long for her and the cellar floor was damp; she tied it into a knot below her knees so that even if she could not walk as freely, at least she would not trip on the hem of the gown, and at least the dampness would not come and creep and creep, soak the fabric until it reached her neck, and pull her down.

So there was nothing there, after all. Wine bottles. Damp. Smoky lamps, and, far off, the sound of humming.

No, not humming. Speech, maybe? Groaning? The sounds were simultaneously thick and soft, as if underwater. She took a few steps away from the cellar steps. The wine bottles came closer together, closer into her body: the miraculous contracting hallway of wine. But as she kept walking, the sounds became more and more clear—there was a human voice, without a doubt. There was a man's voice, and it was louder and then it was not so loud, and it was not like talking, there were no stoppings and startings . . . was it, Nora stopped where she was and listened hard, was it singing? And then, there in front of her, was the door.

Chapter VIII.
Jim Cates Retells the Story of Lazarus

Jesus and Lazarus's sister are friends. Lazarus has two sisters, actually. The one who is his friend is called Mary. She washes Jesus's feet with her hair and has anointment. Lazarus gets sick. The sisters want Jesus to come and maybe help Lazarus get better. But the Gospel says that Jesus didn't go, even though they were his friends. He waited and by then Lazarus was dead. So was Lazarus in heaven? Is there a between place, where you are not alive but not dead? Because if he was all-the-way dead, and in Heaven, wasn't he mad at Jesus for bringing him back again, because Heaven is a Paradise? Or was he not all-the-way dead? So when Lazarus died, he just was in that cave, asleep and that was all, so when Jesus brought him back to life, he was glad? Is death only sleeping in a dark place? Is death only waiting for a long time in the dark for someone to bring you back to life?

Everyone says that Heaven is real, and that you go there when you die if you have lived according to the Gospel. And everyone also says that Heaven is perfect. And everyone says, too, that *everything* that Jesus does is good. He says his best friend is Satan and when he won't go see his mom when he is in her town and she wants to see him, or when he knocks over the stalls at the Temple. Sometimes I want to be angry, but I am not allowed. Jesus can do that. He's allowed to get really angry and smash things and yell. Jesus is bigger than us. So when he does that, no one cares about the people he hurts. He's allowed to hurt other people. Because he has a plan and hurting people is part of the plan.

When Jesus goes to see Martha and Mary, he sees Martha first. She says Lazarus is dead. Jesus doesn't care. He says that as long as everyone believes in Him they won't really die. Then Mary comes to see Jesus. She is sad. Also, she is angry. She says to Jesus that if He was there, then Lazarus would not have died. She yells at Jesus. She was on the one who washed Jesus's feet, with her *hair*, and now she was yelling at him. It must have showed Him how much it had mattered to her.

They all go together to the tomb. It smells bad because Lazarus has been dead a while. His body is rotting. Jesus speaks to God. He says that He is doing what he about to do so that people believe that He is the Son of God. He says, Lazarus, Come Out! Lazarus walks out of the tomb.

I don't know if Lazarus is happy or sad about being brought back to life. The story does not talk about that. It does not show us what happened when he saw his sisters, if he said anything or hugged them or if he said anything to Jesus. I think it depends on whether he went to Heaven, or if he was only lying in the tomb, or if, when he got out, he was still rotten and had to live his life rotten inside and smelling. Also if he was mad at Jesus, who was his friend but who had let him die. Why? To make a point? Lazarus died. Jesus let him die even though he could have saved him. Maybe Jesus wanted Lazarus to die. And his sisters, they were angry. He let their brother die. This means that when people die it is part of God's glory and plan for us. But I think that this story is worse than if your mother or father dies. Your mother and father are much older than you and you know they are going to die before you. But your brother or sister is different, because they were raised with you and know all about you. Lazarus was their only brother. Their *only* one.

I think it must have been annoying to be Jesus. There were no other Sons of God, because the whole point is that he is the only one. The Gospels are always saying how no one understood him when he was talking, even his best friends. He always had to explain himself. Jesus was the loneliest person I've ever heard about. He goes off on His own a lot. Also, I think that He knew when He was being bad to people, His friends and His family. I think He knew that He was hurting other people, and He didn't really care. He has no one to talk to, because no one understands what is like to be so angry and lonely all the time.

Chapter IX.
Satus House

A short dark man stood above the prone body of a naked woman. He held a cleaver in his right hand, and he hacked away like a happy butcher at the woman's ankle. He wore an apron; it tied at his waist and the front had been muddied by dark red handstreaks. The man's mouth was open and when Nora could hear, through her awe which had deadened every sense save that of sight, she heard the song he was singing. Loud, very deep, and in another language. When he held a note for a long time, he lifted the cleaver high in the hair and put his other hand upon his heart. It left a bloody print.

She moved away.

Odette Salderman claimed that interaction with the outside world inhibited her writing and rendered her dull and dumb. Her brother's work—however helpful to the civilization it sought to improve—was criminal, and could be completed only under a shroud of distance. She did not know everything about his work. She did not want to. She did not know how he had convinced the people of Chilling to carefully ignore and even allow the activities at Satus. Alexander went down to the village only when it was absolutely necessary, and when the midwife's powers had failed. He was called in only when the bones had broken through the skin, when gangrene had set in, or when the illness was unknown. These cases were very few. Fernie and Joe Gallo ran errands for him, picked up his post and sent out deliveries, and carried messages back and forth from Satus. Salderman's face was seen in the village perhaps once a month; sometimes not for six weeks. He spent nearly all his time underneath the house.

The Satus cellars had been designed and constructed by Dr. Salderman especially for his own (dark? devious? academic? playful? bloody, at any rate) purposes. When he had followed Odette to Chilling fifteen years ago, he spent a month renovating the cellar. He had paid an enormous amount for workmen to come in from Abbotsville. His secret cellar—that is, the cellar below and behind the cellar—was quite large. There were twelve rooms, each the size of a small bedroom: six rooms on each side of a long, wide hallway. When Nora had descended into this second cellar, she had found herself alongside one of the smaller corner rooms at the very end of the hallway. When she turned, the door to this room was open, and she had seen inside the singing man with the cleaver.

Was it a corpse? Yes, it was a corpse on the table. The man had been using the cleaver to remove the ankles. Nora repeated these facts in her head over and over again. He had needed to use a cleaver because the bone was hard and the joint was hard to break. The woman's breasts had been long and thin and slid down over her ribs like dead snakes.

It had not been her mother.

Nora walked away very quietly. She was grateful that she had no shoes, even though the ground was cold. From the next room issued the sound of two voices—men's voices—speaking calmly. She stayed close to the wall, and listened before she bent her head around the open door.

"Yes, exactly, so you must be very careful to . . . ah, see, now they have torn."

"I don't see how to do it. I was holding it as you said."

"Right, simple, simple . . . Yes! Hold that up. Yes. Perfect. Amazing, isn't it?"

"Ooh."

"No, well, you have to be careful around the bone, here. You see how it connects? Put that . . . perfect. Right."

"Well, that is easier . . . Wait? Wait. I was not expecting that."

"Huh."

Nora leaned forward, so that only her eyes and forehead moved past the doorjamb. There were two men, this time, standing again over a naked body. One of them was Salderman, the doctor. The other was the man from the staircase, the man with the moles. This corpse was male. On the corpse's stomach were two small objects with red strings lying across the chest. The body was otherwise untouched, Nora thought . . . but then she followed the gaze of the two men, who were bending over the man's face. There were, there, two gaping wounds where the man's eyes should have been, and the men were probing the sockets with long thin tools. She looked again at the objects on the man's stomach. They were his eyes, of course. She could see that clearly now; she wondered at how she hadn't known immediately. Nora stepped back from the threshold.

The men had not noticed her. They were intent on their work.

Nora had seen bare flesh before, and lots of blood, too. She had wiped pus and excrement from her little brother's legs; she had stirred her pot of blood. Strips of her father's skin had fallen from his body and left long lines of exposed muscle and jellyfish-like insides.

It hadn't frightened her then, and didn't frighten her now. On the contrary, Nora had found that the closer she came to the bodies of her family, the more deeply she understood them—funny personal habits that she had found puzzling about the twins, sporadic ill-moods of her mother's temper. Three of her mother's toes had been broken, badly, years ago; they had curled like a small black claw. Georgiana must have been in agony, every day, whenever she was forced to walk more than a few steps. And Roger! Poor kid. One of his ears was so clogged with wax that it looked like a yellow earthworm was emerging from his head. Nora remembered, before the sickness, always calling his name, calling and calling and wondering why he never answered her.

"Why didn't you answer me, pumpkinhead?" she would ask him.

"What?"

"I've been calling for you. We have to go get Tobias from the Flaggs."

"Can I bring my duck?"

"You can bring your duck. You need to answer when I call you."

"Okay."

Nora had begun to wonder, those late winter days with a houseful of sick people, how much of her own life was mandated by her body. If she had different fingers, would she speak differently? If her ankles didn't get sore at the end of the day, would she snore? Would she dream violent dreams? Would she like raw tomatoes if she were taller? It became a kind of haven for her, in the small interstitial moments between cleaning and caring for her family, constructing a different body for herself in her imagination and watching the changes manifest themselves in her character. She constructed an ideal Nora, one with a perfect body. She strengthened her arms and pulled back her shoulders. She straightened her nose and stopped her lips from cracking in the winter. She elongated her face, widened her hips. She grew three inches taller. She hardened the skin on the bottom of her feet and on the palms of her hands. Then she translated the perfection and lack of weakness to her personality: perfect Nora was perpetually calm, perpetually detached from fear or worry. Ideal Nora did not fear death or abandonment, she did not feel pain or discomfort. Ideal Nora was strong and healthy enough to live long and alone.

Ideal Nora did not flinch when her father vomited blood and bile. Ideal Nora did not turn her head away from a boy who screamed for hours, as though his limbs twisted in invisible vises. Ideal Nora did not get tired; Ideal Nora did not need sleep or food. Ideal Nora did not have moments of desperate anxiety and the physical need to flee and sit curled inside the snowbank that loomed by the barn, to hug her knees to her chest, to ignore the house and all of its inhabitants. Ideal Nora could work all day and all night; Ideal Nora could ease suffering. Ideal Nora could beckon, and those on the path to death would return again. Ideal Nora opened windows so that breeze could refresh her charges, not so to alleviate the terrible stench they emitted.

And—oddly, to her, even surprisingly—Nora found herself becoming this woman, this strange mechanistic Ideal. So long acting like Her had slowly eliminated *her*. One morning, Nora realized as she was tugging up the window sash, she simply couldn't smell it anymore. The shit, the blood, the vomit, the urine, the other thick masses they coughed up and the yellow pus their wounds oozed . . . She had become inured to it all. The soft parts, the vulnerable parts, had either hardened inside of her or been armored over so completely that the chinks were too narrow to allow the passage of something as clumsy as feeling. She pushed the window up, and turned back around to squeeze a sponge, to trickle water down Andrew's throat.

And so it wasn't the sight of the naked woman losing her ankles, or the eyes ripped from their sockets. It wasn't even the casualness of the men standing above the bodies, arguing, singing, butchering. She felt comfortable with bodies whose integral parts had begun to assert their independence.

In her absorption, Nora had forgotten that she still held the long wooden stick, Salderman's dogstick, in her fist. Her palm had begun to sweat and when she flexed the fingers of her hand open, they left watery skeletal marks. There were more doors. She crept past the eyeless body's room and chose another door. She leaned her cheek and ear against the door, and, hearing nothing, went inside. She held the dogstick like a weapon, up in front of her face.

56

Chapter X.
The Slough Home

Prudence Reed, neé Slough, with her biceps like cannonballs, knocked on Agnes's door mid-afternoon. She would have arrived earlier but she had been subject to one of her stomach ailments that had forced her to spend the earliest hours in her outhouse; she, like Dedlock, suffered from various intestinal disagreements. Food rarely passed through her gut without some friction. Early in the morning, Prudence had woken with a rumbling coil of unrest in her stomach, and before she had walked more than ten steps her gut had forced her into a run. She had lifted her skirts well before he had reached the narrow wooden box and ran with them scooped up in her arms. Then, as her brother had done that same morning, on his own farm, she had stayed in the outhouse. Every so often, she stood and swung the door open and walked a bit with her legs wide, to encourage the digestive process. Even when she was sure she was empty, she was not sure she was empty. It had been an uncomfortable morning.

And so Prudence hadn't got on her way until the tide had gone back out. The Slough house was a rickety weatherbeaten animal, inexplicably sturdy in the way of the ancient bony heifers that grazed in the village common. As Prudence knocked on Agnes's door, the cows regarded her, rolling the grass between their molars.

Agnes opened the door in Nurse's boots, which she had tied at the ankles with a length of leather strap. She was wearing her cap. It made her forehead look higher and larger than it was, and when she raised her eyebrows they seemed to rise to the crown of her head.

"Hello," said Prudence. "My boys here?"

"They're with Jim. Helping with the fence," said Agnes.

"Did they tell you how it went in school? I listened to half of Gervey's speech on the Temptation in the desert. It was terrible. I couldn't listen to the little ones." Prudence had three sons: Daniel, Gervey, and Romer.

"Jim did Lazarus."

"Which one? Never mind. The dead one, clearly. Well, as long as they're going to the class and reading every day. Did I tell you? They can't find Nora Pirrip."

"She died?"

"She's gone from the farm. The house is cleaned out, Octavius said, and she's nowhere."

"Does she have family somewhere else?"

"I think Octavius and Catherine are all. They're afraid she may have . . . they're afraid she may have felt desperate."

"They'll drag the pond."

"I don't know what they'll do. But I have more. News. Abbie's laid up."

Agnes stared at her.

Prudence raised her eyebrows and nodded.

Agnes squinted.

Prudence cleared her throat, and shifted a little. Her bottom, from years of fierce shitting, was almost never without sensation. She smiled a little, then stopped. She smoothed her collar.

"Oh, no," said Agnes, her face clearing like a sky, "Abigail *Osgood*?"

Prudence smiled at her. "Yes, yes, yes," she said, and as Agnes stood aside she came into the house.

"I'm sorry," Agnes said. She began pulling out chairs and clearing them off; large hunks of something brown and dry, stalks of something, were lying on every open space in the kitchen. "Sit, sit," she said. She walked out of the room with an armload of stalks and when she came back again her sister-in-law was sitting at the kitchen table like a small child, waiting for supper. "I'm sorry," Agnes said again, "I wasn't expecting you any particular time. But this is good as any."

Prudence folded her hands atop the table and looked around the kitchen appreciatively. "Busy, busy," she said.

"Abbie Osgood has the hips of a seven-year old. You want tea?" Agnes asked. "I can get you some tea."

"That would be lovely. Loveliest. Where's that baby niece?"

Agnes's mother, Zeena, had been the lone midwife in Chilling until her death, at which point Agnes succeeded her. Zeena had not trusted the doctor, who lived three miles inland in an enormous house with a sister no one ever saw. And if Zeena Cates did not trust Salderman, then the village did not trust Salderman. They tolerated him, but he stayed at a distance, spent his money in the village, and paid the property taxes of some of the villagers. Zeena did not know why, didn't ask, and didn't care. She taught her daughter about the herbs that cured constipation and the flowers that eased a headache.

When Zeena died, Agnes moved the glass jars and wooden boxes to her own home; folks started coming to her door in the middle of the night and at mealtimes, frantic and gesticulating. Agnes, then, felt the foreheads of sick children, cleaned and stitched wounds, brewed, mixed, and supplied medicines. She delivered babies, changed the linens, and walked home unless the family offered a horse. She had no helper, as she herself had helped her mother. She did not keep notes of the births she attended, or of what happened in those rooms; she did not instruct anyone in her methods, or seek out new methods, or even refine her own. Agnes wouldn't have claimed to like her work, but it was her work—she considered it as much a part of her person as the fields were extensions of Dedlock. She had never much wanted to be a midwife, but her mother had been one, and now she was one, too.

What she had wanted, as a young woman, was Dedlock. She had loved him maniacally, as only the young can love, even in those early years when he was charming her older sister. She loved him like a madman loves beheading turnip flowers, or hunting whales, or the taste of ash.

Prudence was already married by the time Agnes was born, and Agnes had been born silly about beauty. As a toddler, she had been attracted to shiny things, even if those shiny things were the glintings of knives. And Dedlock glinted. He wasn't a particularly good man, or a wise one, but it was Dedlock Slough's inherent gift, one he did nothing to cultivate or develop, to be instinctively liked. He was tall and muscular, and he smiled without knowing it. In conversation, he looked directly into one's eyes; I am listening, his eyes said. He was a toucher. He shook hands and embraced. He had unruly, dark hair that he was always brushing from his face. Strands, around his forehead, came loose and fell straight into his eyes; when he pushed them back, he would glance upwards and look ashamed.

His face was open, frank, and happy. His eyes never squinted or narrowed, his lips never really fully descended into a frown or grimace. He cocked his head slightly to the side, when he looked at women, and nodded very slightly forward when he looked at men. I am with you, he seemed to say with these postures, I am on your side. It was nearly impossible to meet him, even casually, to brush up against him in a road, or to watch him pull apples illicitly from your orchard, and dislike him. He had flaws, of course. It was part of his gift to accept his own flaws as parts of his whole. He did not punish or hate himself for the things he did poorly, or the traits that upset his mood or irked those around him. He could take even his most disgusting characteristics and present them to the world in a manner wholly engaging, wholly, somehow, intimate. Even at his edges—especially at his edges—Dedlock glinted.

Inside, Agnes had kicked off John Nurse's boots. She and Prudence sat at the kitchen table, blowing on mugs of tea and discussing Prudence's intestinal woes.

"Oh, but it's been like that for years," she said to Agnes, "at least ten, fifteen years, now." She nodded grimly to herself.

"I'm sorry," said Agnes. "But Dedlock's the same. Just the same. I've tried everything with him. Have you been using the mint?"

"Oh, yes. I have it with me," and she tugged a small satchel from her pocket and undid the leather laces on the kitchen table.

"My sister," Agnes said, "my sister had a bad stomach. She was always in bed, in the late afternoons, curled up and moaning. And who had to empty her pot?"

"Agnes," said Prudence.

"Agnes!" said Agnes. She wiggled her bare toes underneath the table.

Prudence shook the dry shriveled peppermint onto the table, and the two of them leaned over the leaves.

"Maga was a beautiful girl," said Prudence.

"She had beautiful hair. Red hair." Agnes rested her elbows on the table.

Prudence stared up at the ceiling and pursed her lips. "Did you never find any piece of her?" she asked, finally.

"No. Is that Bonnie? Did you hear that? No. We told you all. Never any piece of her."

"Agnes, though," said Prudence. "Everyone else he killed, everyone else that Captain Murderer did really kill . . . well, we found bits of them, didn't we?"

"I don't know what you mean," said Agnes. "By *really* killed. There's no such thing as that ridiculous story. Someone took her or she left. The way Chilling tells that story drives me mad."

Margaret Cates was well known in Chilling, enough to be referred to by first name only. Maga, someone would say, and suddenly conversation would stop and eyes would drift, looking questions.

Margaret Cates was the big sister. Margaret Cates was messy. She broke plates like peanut shells. She stepped on the cat's tail. She nodded her head back and forth when she thought her food was yummy. Margaret Cates never learned to read or write. When she was twelve she snuck out of the house and lay in the road looking at a meteor shower. No one knew, because she never told. Margaret Cates was secretive. Margaret Cates had very red hair that smelled like rosemary. Margaret Cates never caught a cold, in all her life. Margaret Cates was never called Margaret. Margaret Cates was called Maggie, or Magpie, or Maga. Of these, her favorite was Maga. Margaret Cates walked toward the sea one day and disappeared.

"Does Abbie want me to come by?" asked Agnes. She was distracted; she expected Bonnie's wail at every moment.

"I wouldn't think," said Prudence. "How's my wee niecey?"

"Should be waking soon now," said Agnes. She watched the basket where Bonnie slept. She squinted over at it. "Naps get longer every day."

"What a good babe."

"Pray she doesn't get the Slough bowels," said Agnes. She gathered up the teacups and carried them off the table. Prudence took up a peppermint leaf and began to chew it. She scooped the others back into her little bag.

"My boys all shit like their father. I tell them every day, how lucky they are, to have a normal inside, working like that."

Agnes turned her back to the table. "I'm ashamed," she said as she crossed the room, "at how beautiful I think this baby is."

"It's almost," said Prudence thoughtfully, "like having the boys makes up for me. So long as they shit okay. Like normal. Then it almost doesn't matter what terribleness is in me at all. I never liked their father much, may he rest, but he had good insides." Prudence laid her palms on her huge expanse of tummy, which gurgled and rumbled loud enough for Agnes and her daughter to hear. From the basket, Bonnie woke and cried.

Dedlock Slough had been in love with Maga. One day, Dedlock had been carrying a new lamb to Mr. Cates and on his way, saw Margaret Cates hanging up the laundry. Her hands had been sticky with sap, from where she did not know, and she was absently wiping them on the clean pillowslips. Wisps of violently red hair flew out from her kerchief. "Marry me, Magpie," he had called out. She waved at him with her sappy hand. Dedlock brought the lamb around the barn. When he returned to the clothesline, she was collecting the pins that had fallen into the grass. Dedlock smelled the pine so strongly that he imagined for a moment that this girl was half-tree, that she had not blood but cool fresh sap in her veins.

It was about two years later, after they had been married three weeks and two days, that Margaret Cates did not come back from her walk to the beach. This was during the time of Captain Murderer. For nearly a month, Agnes and Jim spent every morning walking hand in hand, their heads down, looking for the bloody limbs and pieces of their sister. They never found one. No one did.

"Prudence's boys helped with the fence," Agnes told Dedlock that night, "and Prudence stayed for a while. She brought six knots of yarn she'd spun. I twisted a few knots of it already. A few families wanted herb bottles and she was putting together some to take over tomorrow. It was cold, today. They went out to the dam, to see the dam. It's nice too, for Jim to have the boys to play with . . . Wasn't it cold in the field? Did you wear your hat? It was funny. Prudence brought up Maga, out of nowhere, and where did that come from? Have you been talking about Maga? Why would Prudence suddenly be thinking about her, now? Bonnie took long naps today. She was thinking, you could tell, thinking very hard in those beautiful eyes of hers."

Dedlock nodded. "Storey's bitch had puppies," he told her. "We'll want one or two, I think." He kissed her dryly on the forehead.

"They can't find Nora Pirrip."

"Oh," said Dedlock. "I'm sure they will."

Chapter XI.
The Narrative of the Graveyard

For years and years, the people of Chilling told the story of Captain Murderer. Some of it was true. Most of it was sad. The truer the story, the sadder the telling of it became, until people stopped telling it, and only spoke of it in whispers when they passed by the spot where he had died, or when they found an errant bone in their garden, or they spotted the whalers coming home off the coast. What they would tell themselves would be sometimes the whole story, but more often it was one part of many sequels, this part, or that part. The parts about the woman he loved, or the people he killed, or the reasons he went to sea, or came back. That he was a good man, that he wasn't, that he spoke French, that he limped when it rained, that he was born without a father, that he could sign his name with the pen in his left hand or his right. That he lived in a whaling town, not far down the coast: Port Daniels, said some, and others said it was Winchester Bay, and others disagreed, claimed that Captain Murderer began on the island on Oyehut.

That Captain Murderer was the captain of a whaling boat, and at sea there was a horrible accident which left him and his men shipwrecked on an island.

That he was not the captain, but he wanted to be, and was jealous of the captain.

That there was nothing to eat and little to drink; after they had killed the few native animals, they began to starve.

That there was nothing to eat and little to drink, so they began drinking the blood of sea-turtles, and the captain grew to crave the taste of blood.

That some died, and those who remained ate the dead.

That the Captain ate his first mate, a man named Onliest Buggum.

That they were rescued by another whaler a few days later.

That they were rescued by cannibals who invited the captain to join their tribe.

That it was the Captain of the whaleship who came home to tell the first mate's widow of her loss. He stood on the steps of the house, but she wouldn't open the door to him, knowing just what it was that he had to tell her, that her husband the first mate was dead and that she'd be lone now in the big empty house. He knocked and knocked and she sat in the house and didn't open the door. Another man would have shrugged and gone off.

That the Captain came home to see his wife, who had thought she had been widowed, and who had moved away.

That the Captain kept up the knocking, that the door was painted blue, that he knocked so long that the paint thinned and wore away. He kept the knocking, until his knuckleskin began to peel away and he left bloody knucklemarks on the wood. He knocked and he knocked steady and steady, into the night and past the night into the red color of the morning, past the sun high up in its seat and down again

That finally, in the evening, then she opened up the door and let him in, cooked ham and onions and rolls and butter and dark ale. He never said what it was he had come there to say because there wasn't ever any need, because she had known it when the boat came along and no husband of hers had walked off the gangplank, and she had turned and walked home and listened for the knocking to come at her door.

That no one ever opened the door, and finally men had to come and drag him away.

That it was in the dinner she'd made for him, and maybe something, too, in her face or her mien, maybe it was the way she smelled or the sound of her foot tapping itself against the floor; the way she crossed her arms over her chest and leaned forward to watch him eat; maybe it was her scarred forehead, dark skin, angry eyes, maybe it was the explosion of forsythia in the front yard or the candlelight glinting off the copper pot in the kitchen.

That the captain fell in love with the widow.

That the captain set out in search of his wife.

That he went away on another whaling voyage, but when a storm arose he turned the ship around, scared that such a terrible thing would happen again, his mind not being able to withstand another round of tragedy and guilt such as the one he'd lived through once, and they came back to port after only a year and very little in the hold.

That the captain disappeared wandering the villages of the Atlantic coast.

That in the meantime, the widow had left, taking everything—

money, furniture, silver, face, life, memory—with her.

That the captain searched for her and could not find her.

That the captain searched for his own true wife and could not find her.

That for the sake of her the captain went mad.

That he found her gone and the pain was too much for a mind already broke and plagued by guilt and trouble and love.

That he began to have fits in which he found himself stranded, again, starving and nothing to eat, at the very eyespot of death where he stared down his own death and that to live he must do the terrible thing again.

That in his fits, he killed men and began to eat them raw, stabbing them in the heart and then wrenching off a limb to gnaw. He would come to his senses and horrify himself at what he'd done and run off, leaving the parts of the body all around him, legs or arms or headless torso, whatever he had left uneaten. Farmers would find bloody pieces of the dead in their fields, housewives on their doorsteps, pastors in their churchyards, children on the beach.

That he never did this, it was only in his dreams.

That he did do this, but only once.

That after a month of this murdering and eating, he was found out. They called him "Captain Murderer," and they imprisoned him in the gaol, where he clung to the bars with his fingers and reached out to them who came to stare.

That there he starved and cried and cried and cried and he died starving and mad.

That, as Chilling tells it, is the story of Captain Murderer.

That, later, years later, when the bodies began to go missing from graves, the villages up and down the coast whispered that he had come back, travelling up and down the shore to murder. That he was hungry for flesh again, that Hell could not contain him, that he had climbed and burrowed his way from the fiery pit and dragged our bodies out with him, to eat silently and darkly in the shadows of the town. That was where they went, into the belly of this dark mad tortured man, to feed him.

Or, at least, so I've heard. All rubbish. It was the Gallo boys. Everything happened, and nothing happened, and there is nothing left in certainty now but the stories. The bodies become me and I am indifferent to the manner of their deaths.

Chapter XII.
Satus House

The dissection of a house into rooms allots, in severing space from space, each room a purpose. The larger the house, the more spaces contained, the more purposes invented (not merely a kitchen, a bedroom . . . but a library, a parlor, a dining room, a formal dining room). The farmhouse in which Nora had been raised had few dividing walls. The boys slept together, most nights, and her parents slept together, and Nora slept alone in an alcove. The kitchen was the only real room. The family ate in the kitchen, they cooked in the kitchen, they cleaned knives in the kitchen and mended hoes in the kitchen. They allowed the dogs to sleep there in the winter. The kitchen was everyroom. They created codes to mark when they needed quiet or a pretense of solitude. When Georgiana began to drum her fingers, the boys left her alone and Nora went about her work quietly; when Alexander climbed up on his stool and sat there cross-legged, staring into the fire, even his twin brother let him be. In this way they could build walls where there were none. In Satus, with its bricks and beams, it was easier to be alone. The splitting of space, like the dismemberment of bodies, can occur by careful plan or by simple nature, by accident or design, whether the walls be real or conjured. And, in either case, the result is the same: the setting of something apart, focusing on a small thing free from the myriad others that clamor for attention and distract.

The room that Nora had found in the Satus cellar was set apart for a special purpose. It was the room of refuse. It housed the things that had been used and discarded, the parts and pieces no longer needed by the aproned, cleaver-wielding Satus men. This room was filled with decaying limbs, organs, heads and globby, formless tissue.

There were large black rats in each of the four corners of the room, gnawing on the meat piled there. The rats seemed to have worked out a system amongst themselves, or perhaps each corner housed an incestuous family; in either case, there were no scaly rat feet crossing the room. They kept each to their corners. Their fur looked like oily feathers. Their bodies gleamed. Their teeth chewed at layers of skin and then tore through muscle. As Nora watched, one large rat burrowed inside the ribcage of a man's torso, eating its way through the stomach. The rat disappeared inside the body and moved toward where, if the men had left it, the heart would have been.

"Hello, rats," Nora said out loud, and then clapped her hand over her mouth and flung closed the door behind her. It banged and the latch slid down; the room was immediately dark, as dark as if Nora had closed her eyes and covered them with her palms. She froze, waiting for footsteps to come hurrying toward her and for the door to be thrown wide, again . . . But she waited, and no one came.

"Okay," Nora whispered. She turned. "Okay, rats." She reached out one hand and felt for the door latch; she took a stumbling step closer and felt the rough wood of the door. The sounds of the room were only those of bodies: the rats' teeth crunching through flesh and bone, Nora's own breathing. She moved against the door, listening for the sound of the rats' feet to come toward her but heard, instead, the sounds of men in the cellar hallway. They were the voices of the men with the eyes . . . She couldn't understand them. They were speaking; their voices did not move up or down; they did not grow fainter; they were standing outside the door.

When Nora was a baby, her father had taught her to greet the things that scared her. Hi horse! Hi snake, hi fire, hi pitchfork. Hi thunder, hi ocean. He had watched her, as a small child, hide her face in his leg when she encountered these things; her instinct was to stop up her sight and hold her body back.

"Let's try this," he said to her, one evening. They were talking a walk to the sea; she was riding on his shoulders. "Say, 'Hi, ocean.'"

"Hi, ohsh," said Nora, "Hi, hi."

"So, when you see the ocean, we'll say, 'Hi ocean!' just the way we would say hello to our friends. And we are not scared of our friends."

"Hi, Da."

"Hi, Nora."

"Hi, ohsh."

"Let's wait until we see it."

"Hi Da," said Nora, and she patted the top of her father's head as though encouraging a slow-moving horse, and she bounced up and down on his shoulders. It had been that easy to change her completely. To change her great fears into expectations of pleasure. Philip Pirrip had felt a tremor of significance at this. Whatever fear he allowed to remain in his daughter, that fear she would carry up onto her own shoulders and into her life. What he said to her, she would repeat. What he did, she would remember. What he did not do, she would never know. What he withheld, she would suffer the lack of; what he gave too freely, she would suffer the glut.

Nora did not remember her father teaching her the language, but she did it without thinking. She did not need to understand the origin of her behavior to behave. She did not need to understand herself to be herself.

"Hello, rats," Nora whispered into the room. "Hello, dark."

She pressed against the door and slid to the left, until she felt the cellar wall on her chest. The wall smelled moist and earthy, and it crumbled underneath her fingertips. She turned and leaned up against the wall to face the room. Underneath her toes something was soft and wet. She wished that she had shoes but allowed the wish to move across her mind like a boat across the water; she watched it vanish. She used the dogstick to push the wet mess at her feet to the side. She did not know what it was, but she did not want to be standing atop it; she did not want, either, to slip and be prone on the floor of this room.

It was dark. She could not see well, but she discerned outlines, barely-there lines on the edges of the arms and legs and heaps of dead skin and severed heads. And like a scent she could barely pick up, she could see the movement of the rats. She caught the quick gleam of their coats. They moved quietly and chewed steadily.

The door and walls dampened the sounds of the men talking to one another. They sounded cheerful. Nora leaned against the wall and closed her eyes. If someone entered, the door would swing to hide her behind it. She had only one job: to remain still and quiet. The rats would not bother her, or they would. She could either be afraid, or she could not be afraid. It wouldn't matter, either way. She would wait until they had gone, and then escape.

She kept her eyes closed. The notion visited her that she had been there, before, in that room. She knew how absurd it was. There was no room like this anywhere: a hidden cellar room in Satus House, full of dissected and dismembered bodies. She had not wandered here, ever before . . . yet the sensations she was experiencing were the same, the same, as . . . it was difficult to arrange thoughts into an order. Her mind refused to capture ideas; they wandered across and exited; they floated and disappeared.

She felt comfortable. Tense, yes, but it was a tension she recognized. There was a familiarity here among these dead bodies and among the creatures that fed upon them. Her own body had come close to this. Closer than close: she had waded knee-deep into death. Everyone around her had swum off, past the break. She'd watched them go. Her mind had been settled on death. She had paddled her hands in its water. The deeper she waded, the more her pain had diminished. She was, for some time she could not know the length of, suspended in the space between living and dying . . . and then, without warning or preamble, with no preparation, she had found herself pulled back. It was her body, not her, that had pulled. Her bones, her blood, her organs, it was they who refused to die. But here, in the basement refuse room of Satus House, here is where she was meant to have been. Here, there were her kind, her peers, her family, the dead and pieced-up members of her tribe. She was skeletal, she knew, pale and deathlike. *Find me*, she thought at the men outside the door. *Look at me all you like. I'm as dead as these bodies. Stare me down and slice my belly open. Pull out my eyes. Hack away.*

Nora felt happy and this made her feel afraid.

Perhaps an hour later, she was still there, against the wall. The door swung open and smashed her in the face. Nora yelped and put her hand to her nose. Joe's face peered around the door.

"Jice," said Joe, "What are you doing down here? Of all places."

"I don't know," said Nora.

"You came down to the cellar for some reason," said Joe.

"I was looking for my mum's body," said Nora, "I saw a painting."

"Right," said Joe, "so, this is not the room you'd want to find your mum in, I promise you that."

"I am bleeding, I think," said Nora.

Joe swung the door back from Nora's body, but he didn't close it; there was light enough for the two of them to see each other's faces.

"Yes, you are," said Joe.

"What's that?" asked Nora. She nodded down at a bucket he carried in one hand.

Joe looked surprised, as if he had forgotten what it was he carried. "Oh," he said, "odd bits and parts. Just went through all the rooms."

Nora bent down and looked more closely. The bucket was filled, as Joe had said, with odd bits and parts. She could make out fingers, or perhaps long toes, jagged chunks of bone, tendrils of pink muscle, gelatinous pods of fatty tissue. She saw a nose, intact, hairy on the inside.

"Sometimes they just fling things down or throw them into the corners. I usually clean the place up around now."

"Mother of God," said Nora.

"We should go," said Joe, "and get someone to look at your face."

"Is it bad?" asked Nora. She brought her fingers gingerly to the small indentation above her lips. She looked at her fingertips.

"You might need a thread to pull it back together," said Joe. "I'm sorry. Didn't know you were there."

"You can do it?" said Nora. She looked down and saw that she had bled on the borrowed nightdress. "Oh."

"Sew up your face? No. But anyone else can. They're all doctors, here. Come on."

The rats had hidden. As Joe led her out of the room, Nora looked backward; she wondered if she had imagined them all, gnawing and working in the corners, the way she had imagined ghosts in the air outside her window as a child, when she had lain in her bed petrified at what she couldn't see until both her body and mind exhausted themselves with stillness and fright, and she woke suddenly without any memory of being released, finally, blessedly, into sleep.

Joe and Nora made their way out of the back cellar, and back up again into the main house. Nora was surprised to see that it was night. Candles dotted the dark halls, and there were stars outside the windows. Joe led her into the kitchen. He offered her a wet rag.

"What is this place?" asked Nora. The rag smelled like garlic. She pressed it against her face; Joe could see only her eyes. They had begun to swell. She was still bleeding, and the pressure made her nose ache more painfully. She pressed harder. "What are they doing here?"

Joe was standing by the door. He looked huge inside the kitchen: the way those accustomed to outside work appear more lost and uncomfortable the farther they move from their mud and rocks and their tools. He put a wide flat hand to the back of his neck and rubbed.

"I'd probably better wait," he said to Nora, "and let Salderman explain it."

Nora's eyes looked at him. They were wide, large eyes, too much white showing to be considered pretty. They were, Joe thought, more like the eyes of a cow than of a frog.

"I think you broke my nose," said Nora.

"Does it hurt?"

"Very much. Joe."

70

When he heard her pronounce his name, it was as if she had reached out and touched him. A very thin fiber tightened inside his chest and pulled up to the bottom of his throat.

"It's a school, sort of," he said. The blood was darkening the rag. "Salderman helps doctors, or men who want to be doctors, he helps them know how the body works and what all the different parts do. And he says that the only way to teach someone about the body is to—you saw—you know. Use the body. Cut it up, they do, and look at all the parts and do things to figure out how it all works. But it's all illegal and immoral. It has to be secret."

"You took my mother's body to cut it up?"

Joe watched her eyes, but the rag covered too much of her face. He couldn't tell what she was thinking.

"They do experiments, too. They come up with ideas about different diseases, how to do things with diseases. They're trying to help."

"My mother?"

"I took a woman's body. We did, me and my brother. It was probably your mother. No, it was definitely your mother. Salderman wanted it, particularly, because . . . Well, I don't know. I think because she had been in a sick house so long and hadn't died right away."

Nora took the rag away from her nose and held it out to look at the stain.

"I didn't die at all," she said to the rag, "They should put me on the table."

"I'll find someone to sew your nose," said Joe. He moved forward, intending to take the rag from Nora, but behind him, from the space beyond the open door, there was a loud scuffle, the crash of something heavy—a piece of furniture, a chair overturned maybe, and the riotous sound of men arguing. Joe turned and ran into the hallway, to the back entrance of the house.

"What in hell, Paul?" he said.

"Well, help us then, Joe," said Paul. He grimaced and for a moment it looked as though Paul had four arms: two of them white-shirted and two of them bare and slack . . . But, no, Paul had only two arms, arms that were full of the corpse's shoulders and giant breasts. Just outside the door, swearing and laughing, too, another young man grappled with her legs. The body's belly rose into the air like a whale from the sea; had she lived, her child might have been born yesterday, a week ago, two weeks. She was heavy. Incredibly heavy, as Joe felt when he moved to take a side from Paul. She was massive. Her dress had come up around her thighs. They were thick and from them her veins rose, jagged purple against pale fat. Joe stared.

"Susanna," said Nora.

"She's mine, mine, mine," said Jules. His hair was black and curly, cut close to his head and shining with sweat.

"Shut up, Demmer," said Paul, "She is mine." They wedged her through the doorway. The frame scraped her hips.

"This woman hasn't even been buried," said Joe.

"Purely by chance," said Paul, "We were on the hill and we saw her fall. By the time we were there, she was died."

"I saw her. I saw her and told you. My find, my study. So sorry. You are welcome to observe," said Jules. He smiled at the dead belly, and then he looked up and smiled at Paul. Paul was very tall and when he scowled at Jules he made it clear he was looking a long way down.

The three of them carried the body through the house, and down to the cellar. Quietly, her face split in two, Nora followed.

Susanna Locke was three years older than Nora. Chilling was a beautiful place: it was green in the summer, with streams cutting sparkling paths through meadows and forests. Springs were abundant, but the locations of freshwater had meant that the village had been settled with its families dispersed throughout a large space. Some were very far from the center of the village, and, in the winter, many were kept by the weather from attending church. Susanna had lived on the very furthest outskirts of the village, with her grandmother; her parents had died when she was a toddler. She had no brothers or sisters, and she lived so far from other families that she had no friends. She was a lonely child, the kind that never truly learns to play alone. She was a little stupid, but kind. Visitors or travelers were surprised by the sight of her heart-shaped face waiting hopefully on the front steps of the house, sometimes holding a broom, feigning work as she waited for company. She would speak to anyone who came along and exuded such a sense of welcome, of cheer, that everyone who passed by the house was pulled inside, offered something to eat, offered the sight of Susanna's raggy ugly doll and invited to talk, endlessly, of any topic at all. Susanna liked people. She was not troubled by judgment, or criticism; she was kind, eager, and blessed with the gift of finding all people interesting and companionable. She wanted to be surrounded by everyone, all the time.

Last autumn, Susanna had married Jeffrey Dial, Buggy Dial's only son. Nora and her mother had gone to the wedding with the new baby Bartholomew. After the ceremony, Susanna had cooed and held the child for hours while she should have been eating cake and saying "Hey!" to raunchy compliments. When Susanna herself had become pregnant, very soon after the wedding, she had spent hours at the Pirrip house, helping care for Bartholomew and helping Georgiana with chores while Nora worked with her father. She had been a friend to Nora, a good woman, a woman who laughed too loudly. She tied bits of string around her wrist, collecting them for some unknowable future use. Susanna's pregnancy was the best thing that had ever happened to her; she would finally be two people. It would impossible to be alone. She would never, ever be alone.

The wound was at the back of Susanna's head. Whatever had happened, it had happened to the back side of her skull; her heart-shaped face was serene. The blood was crusted and clotted in her hair.

"That's Susanna Locke. Dial," said Nora, "I know her." The men didn't hear her. She followed them into a room (the first room, the one in which she had seen Jules, the singing man) and stood in the doorway. They laid Susanna's body on the table and began pulling off her clothes; the sounds of running came from the outer cellar and Salderman appeared, like a gust of wind, suddenly, pushing past Nora and standing above the body, too. He was breathing heavily.

"Good work, men, good work," he said, shaking his head. He laid his cheek into the palm of his left hand and contemplated Susanna's body with his head to the side. "Oh," he whispered, "Well done."

The dark Jules and the mole-faced Paul crossed their arms, put their chins in the air, looked at each other and smiled. Joe looked back and saw the thin, bald girl standing in the doorway with her nose split down the middle and leaning on the doctor's dogstick. Nora's eyes and face had begun to swell. She had blood, still, on her neck and nightdress. Of the two women in the room, it was Nora that looked more like a corpse. Susanna's face was pale, but untouched.

"Wait, please," Nora said. She said it normally, in her speaking voice. Joe gestured at her; Paul and Jules and Salderman all turned and looked at her. How she had known, when asked hours later, Nora would not be able to say. There were signs, of course. There must have been signs: visible things like a movement, or a twitch. The color of the skin, the texture of the skin. Perhaps even the position of the limbs? Something in the curl of the fingers or toes? What she would suspect, but what she would not say, was that it was a scent. That there had been a smell that gripped the body. It left fingermarks of odor upon its neck and arms . . .

"You can't," said Nora, "Her baby is alive."

Salderman looked tiredly at Joe, as if to blame him. "Joseph," he said, "lead her out."

"Idiots," said Nora, "there's a baby still alive there." She moved to the table and elbowed past Jules, who lifted his hands with a closed-mouth smile and backed his body to the wall. He crossed his arms and raised his eyebrows at Joe.

"And who is she?" he asked.

Joe opened his mouth to respond but before he could, Nora had taken up a sharp, slim knife from the table and, without hesitating, hauled up Susanna's skirts and ripped the underskirt and bloomers. She pulled everything off and away, so that Susanna's body was naked below the waist. Her pubic hair was dark and grew down onto her thighs. The men were impassive. Nora leaned over the body and drew a line across her friend's belly and watched the skin gape open like the mouth of a predator; Nora plunged her hands inside and reached down, tugged, twisted, and when her hands came out again they were wet and inside of them was an impossibly small child, a baby with a gray face.

"Heavenly day, it's alive," said Paul. He looked at Salderman. The whole act had taken seconds, less time than it took to latch the cellar door and bolt it across.

"Give me your shirt," Nora said to Joe. She twisted and sliced the cord with the same knife she had used on Susanna's belly. Joe pulled his shirt over his head and handed it to her. Nora laid the baby on a corner of the shirt; she bent down and sucked out the scum that clogged the child's mouth and nose. She spat it onto the floor.

"Let me," said Jules. He had come close to the table, and stood just behind her right shoulder. Nora ignored him. She used the long shirttail of Joe's shirt to wipe the blood and mucus from the baby's skin, then, carrying it to a corner of the room so that she could face away from the men, she unbuttoned her borrowed nightgown and held the baby's skin to the skin of her own chest. It did not cry, or open its eyes. It breathed. No one spoke or moved. The baby breathed raggedly. Nora pressed it to her chest.

74

"She was dead," said Jules, to Salderman. "I swear it. I checked. There was no response, to anything. To *anything*. Paul was with me, ask Paul. Paul, say it."

But Paul could not speak. He had his long face in his hands, his elbows on the dissection table.

"I swear it," Jules said again, "I swear it, I swear it."

Salderman and Joe looked at Nora's back. The baby stopped breathing. It was very quiet. Each of Nora's ribs was visible, and her shoulder blades jutted out from her back like the edges of weapons.

"Idiots, idiots," she said, still facing the wall. "It was a baby girl. You've killed it. You killed a *baby*. You are stupid, stupid people."

Chapter XIII.
Satus House

"Here's what I need, want, want, yes, here's what I want."

Salderman stood at the head of the body, moving his arms as though he were giving a sort of wild benediction. Nora stood at the foot; she had one hand on the dogstick and one hand on the edge of the table. The cellar had quieted down since Nora had delivered the baby; Jules had carried the small body off to a separate room. Joe had said something about finding his brother, and he had disappeared.

After the baby had died, Paul had taken Nora upstairs, brought her a basin of cold water and left her. She washed her face and rubbed at the dried blood with her fingertips. She washed Susanna's blood from her hands, and from her chest, where Susanna's child had died. She dabbed at the nightgown but because she had nothing else to wear, she could not wash the blood out, and the fabric stiffened against her skin. She sat dumbly, for a while, neither thinking nor not-thinking, until Paul reappeared with a little box.

"My name is Paul," he said.

"I remember you," she said, and he guided her to sit on the floor, in front of the fire. He himself sat on a stool, just above her, and took a needle and black thread from the box. As he stitched up the broken skin of her face, he leaned in and his eyes were very close to her face. She could feel him breathing on her. She didn't know where to look, because looking into his eyes felt too intimate and she did not know him. She closed her eyes.

"You will have a nasty scar." He pronounced "will" like "wheel."

Nora lifted her fingers gingerly to her face.

"Ah," he said, "Don't."

But she touched them anyway, the small prickles of the stitching, like the whiskers of a cat. Her head hurt very badly and her face had swollen so that she could see but badly, through a gap in her eyelids that narrowed and narrowed.

"You should go drink some water," Paul said. He slid his needle and the thread he used into a little bag.

"Why are you doing this?"

"What do you mean?"

"Why are you cutting up dead people? This is horrible. It's evil."

76

Paul sat back. "Perhaps," he said.

"Don't you believe in God? Don't you know what you are doing? You'll go to Hell."

"I am a Catholic," said Paul. "I believe and fear God. Salderman, I think, does not think of God, or, if he does, he does only in the scientific sense . . . Jules, now, I do not know. I have never asked him."

"Then how can you do this? You took Susanna. From her grave? When did she die? Where?"

"Did you know her?"

"She was my friend. Yes. What happened to her?"

"Jules was on the hill and could see her. She was on the rocks, the big rocks by the ocean. She slipped. She fell. She hit her head. We saw her from a long way off but when we arrived she was not alive."

"My family is dead. You know that? My little baby brothers, and now Susanna, who never hurt anyone, and her baby. And here you are . . . I don't understand any of it."

Paul stood up and slipped his little box into his jacket. "I do not know you," he said, "and I am not a person to give counsels. But if you do believe in God—"

"Of course I do."

"Then you will see the sense of moving past the unfairness of these things. Why terrible things happen to nice people? I can tell you that there is no sense to it. And though it might look evil, and . . . yes, maybe it is evil, to dissect . . . Ah, do not touch your face. It will make it worse."

"I understand."

"Which part do you understand?"

"I should not touch my face."

"That is right. You can live in your body with God. You can live in your body without God. But you cannot live, you know, without your body. Is not that where we ought to begin our understanding, with this we have? How can we try to understand God, when we do not understand how our own shells, these our bodies, function? That is how I think of it. That is where I leave it. You should go down to the cellar. The doctor needs to speak with you."

Nora had walked downstairs, past the kitchen doorway, down to the cellar. She unlatched and opened doors until she found Salderman in the room with Susanna.

"I'm not at all sure, Eleanor, what we'll do now that . . . But you can be a help, that's very clear. No squeamishness at all. So, perhaps, one or two little tasks, until—you know—decide what might, well."

The doctor put his hand to his cheek and looked at Nora, as though he expected an answer.

"What we do, here, Eleanor, it is not something we can make known."

"No," said Nora. She blinked; she could hardly see him, and her face was throbbing. She felt strange and restless, on the verge of weeping. She wanted to be alone in a dark room and she would agree to do anything that would allow her a moment of solitude. There were so many people in this house. Why had she come down to the cellar? Why hadn't she simply walked outside, and down the hill?

"The village, they know a little, and let us do a little, but quietly. We understand each other and help each other. But this . . . they would not understand this. We have here, this, we have this, and there are some, well, obviously you've done some opening of the body already. Bit of a mess. And we'll get started on it in a few hours, very soon. But," he said, watching her, "I thought you might help us. Might want to help your friend, here."

"Why?"

"No, no reason. I am asking you a favor. The favor is to help us with our work."

"I understand that," said Nora. It hurt to speak. Her face hurt badly. She felt very tired, but not sleepy. Her body felt very tired.

"And also to not mention the work we are doing, until we are done here, fixing up your friend. That is what I am asking."

"Then I am taking her down and telling her husband," Nora said. "Everything, I am telling him everything."

"If you do a small amount of work for us, I will help you with that. Jules and Paul will help you carry her, and we will be very forthright."

"What do you want me to do?"

"Very simple things. If you could just clean the body, very clean, we need it, in fact. You can wash the body—lots of soap and water here," Salderman pointed to a bucket and sponge on the floor, alongside a collection of tools and instruments in a pile. "And then if, possibly at all, you could wash the little knives and instruments, there—what a help it would be to us." He had smiled at her one more time, leaned his cheek farther into his palm.

"This is *Susanna*," said Nora. "She's my *neighbor*."

"Oh, no," said the doctor, easily. He turned and walked to the door. "Not anymore!" he said, and he was gone. He closed the door behind him.

Alexander Salderman was not an unfeeling man. He was a kind man, a man genuinely interested in the process of eliminating pain and suffering in the human condition. But he did not become a doctor to pursue that interest. For Salderman, the alleviation of physical pain was incidental, a servant to the understanding of the developing and growing body. As a young boy, he would run home with his hands clasped around a small dead animal. He read voraciously as a teenager, and spent hours poring over the journals of Leonardo da Vinci; he studied the more anatomically correct works of the Renaissance painters and sculptures. He had never married, unable to see past his obsessions to the humanity of another person. He found most people stupid, unthinking, uninterested themselves in the mysteries of their lives and therefore uninteresting to him. He had a friend in his sister. Odette was such a pattern of secrecy and solitude that her friendship was distant enough to be tolerable and even welcomed.

The Saldermans were a family of obsessives. They were folk who could not do anything a little bit, people who could never practice moderation—if one Salderman liked food, he would eat until his gut gave out; if another enjoyed the open air, she would walk for hours until her toes froze out from under her. Saldermans locked themselves in small rooms with the objects of their minds like new lovers keep to their beds, until clutter, hunger, dirt and thirst forced them into the world, reluctant and doubtful of the use of such an outside place.

Alexander fixed his mind on the insides of human bodies; Odette's obsession was verse. In England her writing gained her a modest celebrity. She and her brother had long conversations with each other in which they compared their studies, and found similarities between them. Odette asked questions that her brother found he had not yet contemplated, and was thankful for; Alexander corroborated for Odette her half-finished opinions and ideas. She was not appalled at his interest in the bloodier parts of man; she didn't try to convince him to be anything other than what he was. He did not understand her fascination with language, but he understood fascination, and this was enough.

Besides, they were not tethered together. They spent time together when they wished to, and when they did not they kept to themselves in their own parts of the house. Odette stayed in the upstairs rooms. She had a writing room, and a bedroom, and when she was feeling gregariously she spoke to the servants and Joe Gallo. Doctor Salderman spent the afternoons in his library, the evenings and nights in the cellars, and in the morning hours he slept. He went about his life and routine happily. He was grateful for this small cloistered village that kept its eyes to itself in exchange for a little money and privacy of its own. He was grateful for his two young surgeons who worked tirelessly at the tasks he set them; he was startled at their selflessness. He himself could never work so well for another's goals. But, most of all, he was grateful for the fact of death—that he could open and examine a dead man as he never could, or would, a living one. The dead were so gracious. They offered themselves indifferently, and asked for nothing.

So, when Salderman put the sponge in Nora's hand and asked her to wash her dead neighbor, it was not cruelty or unkindness; he was as self-absorbed as genius often is, and could think of no better balm to an unsettled and grieving mind than the gift of hours alone and uninterrupted with a dead body. The wonder of it, really, was that the balm soothed.

Susanna had been a very tall woman. When she reached out her arms, Nora remembered, the effect had been that of a great bird with massive wings. She had blond hair, fine as an infant's, which was now gnarled with blood and sand. Her legs, like her arms, were long and thick; when Nora looked closely at them, she saw that the skin was crossed by fine lavender veins, like the tendrils of a flowering plant, and by violently red ranges of jagged, engorged veins. On Susanna's knees, white scars piled upon each other like slugs in a garden. Nora prodded them with her fingertips. They felt pulpy and soft. The black wood of the table, and the pale blush color of the legs above it. The slim trails of lilac vein. The sudden red of the enflamed vein. The disciplined white streaks of the scars. Nora felt as though she would weep, but not for sadness. Because Susanna's body was so miraculous, because the body was a miracle.

In the body, and on the body, nothing was smooth, even, or clean. The wound in the belly was enormous. There were knives and tools laid out on a small chair. Nora slipped a knife into her pocket. Then she knelt and hauled the bucket of soapy water up onto the table, and plunged the sponge into it.

"You, you seen my brother?"

Nora looked up. A man had paused in the doorway, and was waiting for an answer. His body was posed so that it seemed he would move in a moment, halfway between stillness and action, ready to keep walking down the dark hallway toward a new room, to ask again for his brother. His eyes were blue and serious. He looked at the body in the center of the walnut table.

"I don't know," Nora said to him.

He had high cheekbones. His face was thin, very pale, with a large and bony nose. He did not look up to see Nora's face. The other Gallo, she thought. He grimaced at the woman's body on the table. He pushed blond hair, straight like marsh grass, away from his forehead and held it back atop his head. Nora watched him, and, seeing his eyes on the body below her, stretched out her fingers on Susanna's thigh. She remembered that her fingers were dirty, and the nails bitten off. Her knuckles, she realized with something close to despair, they were a man's knuckles, large and bulbous. She could feel, in the throb of her face, her ugliness: her swollen black eyes and stitched nose, her skeletal thinness, her baldness. She felt monstrous. Not as though she merely looked monstrous but as though she was monstrous. She felt ashamed, and angry that she felt ashamed of what she couldn't control: her face, her arms, her hands. She flushed. Nora wanted him to see some part of her body, but there was no part of her she wanted him to see. She curled her hands into fists, and pulled them behind her body. The sponge, behind her, dripped water onto the stones.

The man turned his head and left. As he turned, Nora saw what she should have seen first: that he had only one leg. He limped and dragged his false left leg as he walked. From down the hall, he called out something, a thanks or some other acknowledgment. Nora could not hear it completely, though, and she remained there, watching the door. She put her own hand in her own hair; it was so short that she could not clasp her hair between her fingers. She ran her palm down the back of her head, and felt the depressions and angles of her skull. Her skin was warm.

She lay her palms down on the edge of the table. She heard the man's voice again, from somewhere further down the hallway and she could hear the questioning tone: he was asking for his brother, again. And this time, a laugh, then a deeper voice, another laugh. Nora could smell the body, the beginning of fluids starting to trickle down and out, slowly, through the orifices and onto the wood. She was not repulsed. She leaned over the body's face.

"Hello, Susanna," she said. "Hi."

Upstairs, in his untidy library, Dr. Salderman opened the door and admitted Paul and Jules. They all went to the seats in which they always sat; Jules in a corner, Paul by the door, and the doctor at his desk. Jules picked up a book and leafed through it.

"I feel for her," he said. "I do."

Paul nodded.

"I think it may be helpful for us, though," said Salderman. He spoke thoughtfully. "To learn. After what happened with her family, it seems like heaven has put her in our lap. And possibly there are effects which we should observe."

"You don't think it's strange she's here? Of all the places to go, she comes here?"

"No," said Paul, "I think if she hadn't come here she would have left the village. She's not well, that woman."

"Clearly," said Jules.

"I asked Fernie to keep his eye on her, and to try to find out," Salderman said.

"I mean, she is not well. It has made an effect on her mind. Either the hair is not growing back or—this is what I am thinking—she tears at it, or pulls it out. Maybe she does not know what she does."

"She's lucid," said Salderman. "A sharp mind, I would have said. No? Jules?"

Jules nodded. "There was, though," he said, "what she was saying about her mother. Joe said she was asking to see her dead body. That's not right. That may be . . . something, a symptom, the odd desire or logic?"

"She went to dig her up, Doctor. That is not a healthy mind. We should be watching her closely and understanding this."

"Her mother's body is out of the house?"

"No," said Paul. "But it is not in a good way, and we have hidden it. I do not want to let the boys near it. Jules and I will dispose."

Salderman sighed. "Alright," he said. "I've written to my people in London. I think they will be enthused by all we have learned. I think we've done something, here, yes, I think we have done it. And perhaps this is providence, sending us an experiment in survival, the effects of the disease on survivors. We'll keep her here, and make sure to observe, and we'll use what we learn. Yes?"

Jules and Paul nodded.

In the cellar, hours later, Joe stuck his head in.

"Nose?" he asked, "How's it?"

"Good," she said. She smiled down at the body, but this made her face hurt and she grimaced. "I made a mess of her," she said. She nodded at the wound she had opened in Susanna's stomach. "I've just been looking and looking. I've never seen this type of thing, before. A whole body. You can see the layers of the . . . I don't know. I don't know the names for everything. It's a mess. But sort of a miracle. Have you seen this?"

"What are you doing?"

"You look horrified."

"I am a little horrified," said Joe.

Nora had groped inside Susanna's belly until she had found the placenta and pulled it out. It sat, deflated and veiny, on the table beside Susanna's hip.

"What is that?" asked Joe. "Why is it that color?"

"Afterbirth. It's fine."

"What are you going to do with it?"

"When my brothers were born, my mother had the midwife wrap it up, and give it to my father. The father of the baby has to go out and bury it in a secret place. In the shade of a tree."

Joe came closer to the table and looked at it more carefully. "It looks like a dead animal," he said.

"That's why we bury it," said Nora. "A little helping animal in the womb."

"Well, we can't have Jeff Dial bury it."

"Susanna would have tried to have it buried," said Nora. She moved to bring her hand to rub her eyes, but they were covered in blood. She brought them back down to the table. "We should do it . . . because we were there when she was born. I should bury it."

"I brought you this," Joe said. He held a hunk of bread out to her, over the body. It was covered with dark jam.

"My hands," she said to him. They were wet with blood to the forearms.

"Well, that's disgusting. Open your mouth," Joe said, and held the bread to her mouth. Nora leaned forward and took a small bite. She chewed it very slowly.

"I forgot it once, and now again. How do I know you? I am sorry."

"No need," said Joe, "I'm Joe Gallo. My dad used to be the blacksmith."

"The old blacksmith. Gallo the blacksmith. That was a while back. Oh, that's so good," she said, and leaned forward again to eat more. "There was someone here, before," she said, "He looked a bit like you, maybe. But even blonder hair than you, almost white hair. He was tall. Very thin."

"I'm more like my dad," said Joe, "Fernie looks like our mum."

"He is your brother."

"My baby brother Fern," said Joe. "You had brothers."

"Yes. No. I did. I have five baby brothers." Nora felt Joe's eyes on hers. She wouldn't meet them, though. When he fixed on her, she looked down, or away. "There were two sets of twins. The big twins were just six years, and the little twins weren't quite four. The baby was born last September."

"I'm sorry."

"But you know that, Joe. You buried them."

"I'm sorry."

"Yes," said Nora, "I am, as well. There's a rat," she added, and pointed to the corner.

Joe put the bread on the table. Underneath the table was the bucket used usually for holding the long and slippery coils of intestines. It was empty; Joe lifted it up and watched the rat.

"So what's the point," said Joe, "of burying it?" He walked very slowly toward the rat. The rat had found a piece of something and was sniffing.

"It's supposed to protect the baby."

"It's too late."

"I know. It's supposed to protect the life of the mother and the baby."

"I think," Joe went on, but whispering, "that if you want to bury it, there's the orchard."

"What kind of trees?" Nora whispered, too.

"Does it matter? Apple."

"You should do it, because the father needs to do it. And you're more like the father than I am."

Joe moved once, suddenly violent in one movement, and the bucket crashed down over the rat. Then he was still again, as if he had done nothing at all, and sat himself down on the bottom of the overturned bucket.

"Okay."

Nora tried to smile at him, but her nose hurt. She exhaled, heavily, and smiled again. "Ah, Joe," she said, "My face hurts and I miss my little brothers."

"You can borrow mine," said Joe, "on Wednesdays. And Sundays."

Nora lifted the placenta. "Will you help me bury this?"

"Yes," said Joe.

It was a cool spring day. On the west side of Satus House, the Saldermans kept a small orchard. Joe carried the placenta, wrapped in a canvas sheet, and Nora walked behind him and leaned on the dogstick. They buried the placenta between two apple trees. Neither the Gallos or the other servants had been doing the pruning; the branches of the two trees were tangled into each other. Nora sat with her back to a trunk, and Joe dug a shallow grave with a garden spade.

Nora's blood-stiffened nightgown was not heavy, and the wind blew up against her legs and against her neck. The sun shone onto her forehead. The niceness of it all felt obscene to Nora, a joke played on her by a universe that jostled her from strange place to strange place. After the dark and gore of the cellar, it was suddenly a calm and sunny morning. She did not enjoy how much she was enjoying the weather, the spring day, the quiet obliging company of Joe. Her mind stayed downstairs, in low dark cellars with the stench of the dead people. She closed her eyes, felt the warmth on her eyelids, and saw her mother's body, pulled apart and dissected by men who laughed above her face and pulled her eyes from her sockets. Nora felt as though she teetered on the fulcrum of nature, that the wind pushed her one way, and then the other, and she didn't much care about either, or on which side she would eventually settle.

"Nora," Joe said after the placenta was in the ground. "The doctor isn't going to let you leave for a little while."

"I have nowhere to go."

"I mean you can't leave the house. What he's doing there . . . What they're all doing . . . they would get in a lot of trouble. He's going to make you stay because he can't let you give it all away. Even if you want to, he won't let you leave."

Nora shrugged. "I don't want to leave," she said, "but I need some clothes to wear."

That night, Nora slept in a dark close room, more of a closet than a room. She had chosen it herself; Salderman didn't care where she slept, and she felt uncomfortable sleeping in a great big room with a huge bed. Joe had asked around for old clothes, and a fat teenage girl had brought Nora two dresses, an ancient pair of men's pants, three woolen underthings of varying sizes, stockings, and an apron.

"Thank you," Nora said. "I burned all my clothes. This means a great deal."

The fat girl put her hands on her hips. "I don't know they'll fit you," she said.

"I'm Eleanor Pirrip."

"Lily," said Lily. "You can get your own breakfast? It's just me and mum doing everything. The men do nothing."

In the morning, Salderman gave her jobs and tasks to do around the cellars. The import of Joe's words had sunk in as she slept, and Nora thought of ways she could slip out of the house unseen and return to Chilling. When she had told Joe that she had nowhere to go, she had meant it, but it was not true. She had her Uncle and Aunt Peabody. But Nora had barely known them; he was Georgiana's half-brother, and when Georgiana had walked off and disappeared, Uncle Peabody had gone silent and unhelpful to Nora's father. He had greeted them when they ran across one another in the village, but that was all. When she imagined sneaking from Satus, she imagined meeting Octavius at his front door. She shuddered.

"This is a kidney," said Salderman, handing her Susanna's kidney.

The tasks Salderman assigned her were menial. She couldn't do anything to the bodies, or cut them the way she saw the men do; she certainly couldn't draw out the organs and lay them on the table. You haven't been trained properly, Salderman told her. "Or, really," he said, "trained at all." So in the beginning, Nora cleaned the cellar rooms. She scrubbed the floors with sand and soap. She took over the daily collection from Joe, walking from room to room with a bucket full of flesh. She washed bodies of debris and remnants of illness or accident. She sewed skin back together that the doctors had severed. She tidied up after dissection. She shaved heads and genitals. She removed maggots.

She liked the tasks that allowed her to work alone. She would not help one of the young doctors while he dissected, if she could find an excuse. She would not hold organs or instruments or record weights or figures. If someone entered the room she was in, she left; if she heard voices in the hallway, she ducked into an empty room and occupied herself there until the voices faded. It was ideal, for her, to be living and working at Satus. She could not have borne her uncle's house. She could not have borne the realness, the sameness, the everydayness of Chilling. Nora would have been expected to speak pleasantly, to help with chores. She would have been expected to, over time, entrust her family to God and be a member of the world again. This was intolerable to her. The world was intolerable to her. At Satus, no one knew where she was (save those who worked at Satus, and those who worked at Satus were practiced and talented at keeping more valuable secrets than her presence). If she liked, she could walk away from this place too, and no one would come searching or wondering after her. A meaner spirit would feel lonesome, but Nora was grateful for the solitude. It was as if she had disappeared, and been reconstituted in another life. She spent hours alone, in dark rooms with dead people. And this was where she wanted to be.

The Saturday after her arrival, Salderman had put a pair of tweezers in her hand and sent her to the cellar; the night before, Fernie and Joe had dragged a drowned woman ten miles from the Wolfeborough cemetery. She had been in the ground a long time and her body was covered in maggots.

"You pull them off, little bit, all of them, bit by bit," said Salderman. He bent over the woman's body and pulled tiny wriggling bodies out of the skin.

"I understand," said Nora, and put out her hand for the tool. Salderman handed them over and looked at her.

"I'll send someone to help," he said. "This will take a long time."

"Don't," said Nora, "I'll do it."

She worked alone for an hour, her shoulders hunched over the body. She pulled the maggots from inside the skin, where they liked to burrow and chew on the fat, and placed them neatly in rows and piles on the table. Occasionally she stood up straight and stretched her arms above her head. Occasionally she carried a handful of maggots to a bucket in the corner. She left the room once, to make and drink a cup of tea upstairs in the kitchen, and when she returned, the young man with the blond hair—Joe's little brother—had taken her place at the body's side.

"Hello," said Fernie.

"Hello," said Nora.

"Fernie," said Fernie. He held out his hand and Nora shook it.

"Salderman says we're going to pick maggots?"

"I'm nearly done."

"I don't mind," Fernie said. "Joe hates bugs. But I don't mind them." He pushed the hair from his eyes and pulled a pair of tweezers from his pocket. Nora put her palm to her cheek. She felt her face getting hot and the pulse inside her nose. The swelling had gone down in her face, but her stitches still held, and the black and purple bruising underneath her eyes had begun to seep downward to her cheeks. She hunched over the body's feet and worked with her face near the skin, so that Joe's brother could not see her.

"You've met Jules and Paul?" he said, after a long silence.

Nora nodded.

"Joey says you had brothers," said Fernie.

"Yes," said Nora. "Little ones."

Fernie made a face at the maggots. They writhed inside the navel. "Joey says they died," he said. "I'm sorry."

"You buried them," Nora said. "It was while I was sick."

"I'm sorry." He watched for a moment but she did not look up at him. They worked quietly and once Nora swept a pile of maggots into a bucket.

"That's some bad bruising," said Fernie. "On your eyes."

"Your brother broke my nose," said Nora.

"He feels terrible about that," said Fernie. He moved down to where Nora was working, down by the woman's feet.

Nora pulled a thin white maggot from the body's heel. The skin was wet, white, and came away in long soggy strips. Underneath, the maggots wrestled each other for the scrim of fat.

"Nora?" called a voice from the hallway.

Nora and Fernie looked up.

"In here," she said.

"In here," Fernie said, more loudly. He smiled at her.

Jules entered with a cup. He watched them work. He spat into the cup.

"Hey," he said, "If you want, I have a free breath. We can take the thread out of your face."

"Right now?"

"The maggots will not mind," said Jules.

"They might," said Fernie. "Judgmental beasts."

Jules spat into his cup. "Fern," he said.

"You can't spit while you're taking stitches out of my face."

"Why not?"

"I don't want you to. It will make me uncomfortable."

Jules put his hands up. "Fine," he said, and he spat the mess of leaves entirely into his cup. "No more."

Nora sat on the floor and lifted her face upwards. Jules, slowly, hooked his tiny scissors under each knot, pulled, and snipped the stitching free. Fernie leaned up against the dissecting table. Nora looked sideways at him. He wasn't moving or working. His hands were folded in front of him. He was watching her face. She closed her eyes and felt the little tugs as Jules broke the thread free.

"All done," he said.

"Can I try some of your tobacco?"

Jules laughed. "No," he said.

"Why?" asked Fernie.

"Have you ever chewed tobacco?"

"I tried snuff once," said Nora. She was lying.

Jules put his scissors and tweezers away, zipped his little bag, and smiled. "I'll give you a little piece," he said. "Stay here and I'll get a bit from my room."

"Me, too," said Fernie.

"Fine," said Jules.

When he had gone and Nora had come back to the table, Fernie reached out and tried to touch her face.

"No," she said.

"Did it hurt?" He took back his hand.

"No."

Fernie swept a few loose maggots into his palm and came around the table to where she stood. She felt his body next to her body. They did not touch, but she could feel, as though through an extra sense, that the arm closest to her, beneath his shirt, was hard and thin but muscled, and she felt suddenly the urge to lean her whole body into his body. The maggots made sounds like a hushed orchestra. Nora felt warm. He was very close to her.

Fernie swept Nora's pile of maggots into his palm, and he walked off to dump them into the maggot bucket.

"Can I ask you something?" she said. She looked up at him.

"Yes, go on."

"Do you remember if it hurt when they took off your leg? It is a terrible question."

"Why did you ask it?"

"I would like to know."

Fernie used the inside of his wrist to scratch his nose. He sighed and came back to the table. "I was little," he said, "and I don't remember it. I remember afterwards, waking up without my leg, and I remember a little bit before, when the wound got really infected and smelly. But it . . . No, I don't remember."

"What was it like when you woke up without your leg?"

Fernie smiled at her. "Scary," he said.

"Why do you smile while you say it?"

"I'm nervous talking about it."

"Why?"

"Because that means we're . . . talking about it. You are talking about it."

"I'm sorry. I would smile but it hurts my face. Oh," she said, as Jules came back into the room, "Let me just rinse my hands."

Nora dipped her hands into the bowl of cold water that stood in the hall, and when she returned Fernie had begun to chew.

"What do I do?" she asked.

Jules handed her a few leaves. "Wedge it right inside your cheek, by your back teeth."

She pushed the tobacco inside her mouth. The scent made her eyes water.

"Do not swallow anything," said Jules. "Not anything, like the juice or any little bit you bite off. It'll make you sick. Just move it around, careful, so that you chew on it. Gently. Chew lightly."

"Okay," said Fernie. "Yeah."

"That's all. When you've made a bunch of spit, spit it out. That's it. When it starts falling apart, rinse your mouth out. Just don't swallow anything."

They stood there, chewing carefully in the center of the room. Jules watched them and laughed. "Finish the maggots," he said, and left the room.

"Do you like it?" Fernie asked.

"I can't tell yet," Nora said. "Can you bring that bucket? We'll spit into it."

They resettled themselves on their respective sides of the woman's feet. The maggots were as happy and squirming as they had been before. When they were plucked up, they rose, clasped in the tweezers, and coiled themselves up into little rings.

"Let me ask you something," said Fernie.

Nora nodded.

"Where did your mother go, all those years? No one knows. Not even gossip."

"You know about my mother?"

"Everyone does."

"She never said. I didn't ask."

"Why not? I would have."

"I waited for her to want me to know."

"Did your dad know?" he asked. "She must have told him."

"I don't know. I'll never know, now. He never said."

"That's impressive," said Fernie. "If she kept that secret all the time. From him, from the village, from everyone. That's not easy, keeping big secrets like that."

"For her?" Nora put her pincers down. "Hard for her? Hard for us, not knowing." She spat into the bucket, a thick brown stream across the pale squirming maggots.

"Keeping those types of secrets, they're worse on the keeper. Trust me. Jice," he said, looking down into the maggot bucket, "look at those things."

"When I was little," said Nora, "I used to watch my dad turn the compost. I had ideas that bad little snouty animal monsters lived inside, and that they'd bite you if you put your hand in. I thought I never could do that myself, turn compost. But then one day I did it. And it wasn't terrible at all."

"What made you do it?"

"I don't remember now. I was getting too old to be afraid of things. Ten, or eleven maybe."

"I used to be scared of the water," said Fernie.

"When you were little?"

"Terrified. We lived—I don't know if you knew the forge at all, but where the house was, we could walk through the woods and reach the deep part of the brook."

"Yes, I remember that. I remember taking the boys there, when they were small. We could see your old house if the trees were bare.

There was a little deep spot, where it was shallow enough for them to stand, or they could pretend to swim."

"That's it. Joe and I used to go there. I was so scared. There were these little bugs, water spiders, that used to jump and skit across the water, and I thought they were poison."

"I remember. I remember trying to catch them."

"Once, we were playing at the brook with Oliver and his sister, and Oliver got mad at Joe and pushed him in and Joe hit his head on a rock."

"Oliver Shoemaker? I didn't know he had any friends."

"He doesn't."

"How old were you?"

"I don't remember. Very young, very small. I remember seeing Joe come out of the water, his clothes all dripping and then watching as his head started to bleed. Just gets covered in blood. He must have been fine . . . It must have been just a little cut. But I was terrified and I ran off."

"Did you go home?"

"No. No, I was too scared. I was just running. Joey had to run after me and pick me up, and then he wrestled me over his shoulder, and he carried me back to the brook. Oliver and his sister had gone and Joey sat with me and he dunked his head back in the water to clean off the blood."

Nora smiled.

"He gets knocked in the water, hits his head on a rock, starts bleeding all over himself, and then he has to go chase after his little brother in the woods. When he grabbed me, jice, he grabbed me so tight on the arms that I thought my bones were going to break."

Fernie reached and took both of Nora's wrists in one of his hands, and held them tightly together so that when Nora, tried, instinctively, to free herself, she felt the bones of her wrist push against his fingers.

"Like that! I was scared."

"Okay," said Nora. Nora looked down. Fernie's hand was still holding her wrist and she did not know if she should try to pull away, or if that would be unkind. He waited for her to go on, but she didn't.

"Are you feeling better?" he asked.

"Yes," she said.

"It's not a bad place," Fernie said, looking at her. "We like it here. You get used to it."

"I used to have a dog," said Nora.

"Yeah?"

"She'd swim in the pond. She liked the water." Nora's grief came like a wave. She did not want to be so stupid. 'She liked the water' sounded childish but it hurt Nora to say it as much as eulogies for all five brothers. She pulled her wrist free.

Fernie smiled at her. He had a face like an intelligent horse, Nora thought. His jaw protruded a little, and his chin lacked the definition it needed to stand independent from the neck. His eyebrows were pale, too, so that it seemed almost as though he hadn't any at all. It was his eyes that saved his face from fading away entirely. Fernie had two shards of blue sea with which he saw the world. Her chest hurt.

"This has been a good talk," said Fernie. "I can tell my brother we've made friends."

"Are you going?" asked Nora.

"Yes," he said. "Joe and I have to do some work down in the village."

Nora nodded and looked back down at the foot. She took up her pincers, again, and crouched down so that her eyes were level with the table. Fernie watched her work for a moment and then turned to leave.

"Don't tell anyone," she called after him, "don't tell anyone in Chilling that I'm here."

He left the room. The sounds of the maggots, the munching and the eating of skin and fat, were soft and comforting, like the snorts and grunts of working horses.

Chapter XIV.
The Narrative of the Graveyard

I have never gotten used to burials.

The gravediggers come, first, and dig out a big chunk large enough to fit the body and the coffin. Those days, it was shamefully common to dig something shallow. So many bodies, so many bones piling up, one atop the other like so many layers of a cake. With a little help—the little handcart and, perhaps, Jim Slough or Benjamin Benner or a passing boy, they lower the body into the soil, return the earth, and then spend some time cleaning up the edges and raking out the grass.

The effect is . . . disquieting, for me. I am appalled when I am rent apart, when I can feel the undoing of my wholeness while I can do nothing to hold myself together. It is first the removal of the dirt. What they take, always, is a part I feel lost and terrible without; take another bit, I always think, any other bit! Take from that mound in the corner, take from by the road, where the dirt is all wet and pebbly. Whatever they decide to take, from whichever part of me, is the part to which I am most attached at that moment. It is not as though soil can be removed from soil in the way, say, one can remove a stone from soil. Or even in the way one can remove a weed from the soil. No, it is a different operation, and a different sensation altogether. Soil is soil only when whole, en masse, fully together with all those other, non-soil things that give it health and color. The large stones and mere pebbles, the detritus from flowers and tree seeds and even excrement, what the animals leave behind them. What the folks brush off their footpaths and front steps—a happy confusion that makes a happy thick dark soil. So when it is taken away: oh! There is no whole without the whole. To dig out a part of me is not to cripple me somewhat: briefly I cease.

And then . . . it is all returned to me. And more. They entrust the body. They pile the soil back again, and it forms a mound around him, or her, a shield or orb of dirt. Slowly, the earth settles, and the dirt settles, too. After not very long at all, the ground is flat, and level again, and this is perhaps the genius of the soil. It finds its way back.

I know that there are men and women alive who use their lives only for the telling of things: made-up things and true-ish things, that they find ways to represent these things in pictures, or text, or with their bodies in some way. And I wonder if, like me, the longer they muse on a single idea, the idea begins to seem the same as another, or an object so like another object. Where before there were no similarities, simply sitting quietly and letting the mind settle on a thing expands the thing: and yet the thing, in fact, has not changed at all! It makes me suspicious as to the nature of the universe. If, in fact, all things are the same one thing, and our attempts to describe the multitude are mere repetitions of the same. So it is, when I think about the soil.

For years, Joe and Fernie Gallo were my gravediggers. They came to me when they were only boys, and began to dig with wee skinny arms. Joe did the lion's share of the work, but Fernie was more capable than you would think, considering the leg. Still, Joseph Gallo was the big one, the strong one, the one with all his limbs! He was the Helping Brother, the Knowing Brother, the One Who Leads the Way Through the Brambles; the slim pale brother was the Wandering One, the Brother Who Looks Away, the Feeling Brother, the One-Legged Brother.

The brothers themselves, I thought, were like types of earth: Joe, the blond soft beach sand: universally nice and pleasurable, worn to a fine grain by years of endurance. But sand, warm in the sun and good for digging, is not a particularly healthy soil; you cannot build a house on sand, or grow your peppers in it. No, for things of a permanent and sustaining nature, you need a good dark soil. I have always thought that Fernie, with his storm-like eyes and wooden leg and the gloom about him, that Fernie was an example of a dark soil.

Though in many natural things, darkness suggests menace, as if bestowing the sense of foreboding inherent in the darkness of shadows and night, as in blackened rotting fruit that warns against consumption or in glowering ash-colored clouds that gather to warn of storms; and though some populations have descried darkness as the mark of badness and inferiority; even some pale-tribed humans enslaving and murdering darker-tribed ones, claiming dominion on the virtue of colorlessness and lividity; and though, besides all this, darkness has been made significant of melancholy and mourning, for among the women of Chilling a black dress bespoke a death; and though in other man-made symbols, the dark one is sobering: those found petting a black cat on the boat that hit its hull upon Plymouth

Rock would be flogged for their friendship with the Devil, I heard. You sleep, in memory and practice and anticipation of death, at night when it is dark; you wake and act and love when the darkness lifts; yet for all these compounded associations with bitterness, terrible mystery and ungovernable loss and maniacal unknown, there lurks something wonderful in the inside of the dark, something alluring and healthy, and deeply, silently, unfathomably *good*.

But I go on and on.

I mean to say only this: that the darkness of the soil is sign of good health. Like healthy glossy hair of the young that decays to white. The rich black color means that the soil has combined many things within, diverse parts and pieces of the world that help and complement one another. Soil is lots of rock. Little pieces of stone worn down. Soil is lots of space: water and air. When there is enough space, water can move freely, up or down as it is needed; these spaces can be large, or they can be small, and there is not a size, a specific shape or form to space that is *good* or *bad* but all sizes and forms of space are necessary, opened for purpose and function. Form, in soil, truly follows function. A tiny bit of a healthy soil, oh, a tiny bit, is the stuff that stars are made of, organic us-ness, stuff from life that has fallen off and degraded in form. Lichen, mosses, grasses, leaves, the crumbling rotted wood of old trees. The dead hold everything together, binding rock to rock to water in holey crumbs.

And the rest of the soil is alive. Animals! Worms, sure, worms. But also tiny insects, chewing and digesting, and things too small to see, tiny little identities embodying unity of self, clustering energy and changing what it finds, taking dead life and creating from the corpse-piece nutrients for the living world! For there is much health to be found in that which has died, much to find and salvage, the way a single dead tree can heat a man's home for months, the way a decomposing deer will feed a field of chard.

And, though it is dark, good soil will emit a glorious full scent. It is inimical, the smell of rainy mud in autumn, the scent of living dirt. It *is* the scent of life, paradoxically enough, the densely packed mass of the alive nonliving. Of course it was in ancient days that the land of the sentient dead was rumored underground: because only in the soil, deep within the soil, is there such a union of what is alive and what is not alive, only in the soil do the dead and the living cooperate with such grace and symbiosis.

And of all these living wonders the dark soil speaks. I don't wonder, then, at your fascination with it. At a gravestone, it is the penchant of the living bereaved, often, to stare down at the soil as if it held some significance or message. Some, in fact, reach down and caress the muddy grass as though it were the tousled hair of their loved one. But there are some who take the affection to a level that approaches the absurd, the laughable.

I knew a woman who, having lost her child to a bad cough, used to come and kneel before the tiny stone, plunge her hands into the mud (it was a particularly rainy season) and squeeze the mud in her fists so that it ran through her fingers. Then she would open her hands and, whatever mud was left there, she would smear it on her face and chest.

Of course the soil is no more the child than the child's body is the child, I'm afraid; nor, really, can the soil soothe or enrage. No. It is not the land or nature who has taken the child, I wanted to tell her; something else entirely has taken your baby's personhood—I merely have the carry-case, for use again in the growing of new things.

I blamed myself. I had one job. I had *one* job. Keep bodies inside. Keep bodies safe. Assist in decay and regeneration of said bodies.

When bodies began to go missing, Chilling blamed, first, the ghost of Captain Murderer come back from the dead. This was not a surprising idea—at least not to me, as I had both seen and heard Joseph and Fernie Gallo planning to reconstruct Captain Murderer in the village's collective psyche for some time.

The lame one gave the little boy sweets, fruit, bread, and jam. Sometimes Fernie told the boy stories. And whilst Jim listened and ate, Joe dug and dug and dug, his big broad shoulders straining the fabric of his coat. He dug furiously and threw the soil by the great black shovelful over his right shoulder so that it came down behind him like rain. When he reached the hard box, he jumped in beside it and pried it open with tools he kept tied and jangling about his waist, and then, through a marvel of strength and acrobatics, he hefted the body's weight upon his own back and used the foot of the casket as a step, as he pulled himself up and out of the grave. What I always thought extraordinary was the intimacy the larger Gallo seemed to have with the bodies he pulled from me; he did not cry, like the mourners, and he was not solemn, like the religious. But neither was he cruel, unkind. Joe treated my bodies as carefully as I believe he would have treated a living soul . . . though whether this was by instruction or instinct, I do not know.

When he had the body yoked over his shoulders, Joe would call out, mimicking an owl's hoot. Fernie would find an ending to his story, leave the child with one last piece of bread or cake, and hobble off into the dark road. I expect Joe waited, there, with the body, for any help the smaller brother could give. I was not watching, anymore, I was despairing my loss. They would leave. They would open me up and then just leave me open and gaping. The soil strewn about, the holes empty.

And I never, ever got them back. Fernie and Joe distributed the limbs and body parts around the village: bones stacked in front of the jail, three severed heads lolling in the common, a single slim arm carelessly flung into a kitchen garden. Chilling was all agog, all talk; they discussed the strewing of limbs without end; Fernie and Joe insinuated themselves into the gossip after church, reminding folks of the details of the past, bringing up names of old victims, or asking questions they knew the answer to . . . and Chilling would be tricked into telling the story themselves. The village could only conclude what had proven true, once at least, in the past: that Captain Murderer, the eater and dismemberer of men, had come back.

I suppose it was inevitable. A story, though—at least a good one, like that—is like soil in that way. It finds its way back.

Chapter XV.
The Slough Home

Agnes and Dedlock had not been married long. The early years of their marriage had been slow and dark. Both were still mourning Margaret, and the mourning lingered for the lack of a body. Guilt dogged Dedlock and placed its little cloven hooves in every footprint he made in the Chilling mud. For a year, they had been unable to consummate their marriage; Agnes had wept to herself and Dedlock had lain silent and angry beside her. For months, they barely spoke.

But all through that time Agnes was resolute. She had decided to love Dedlock when she was still a child, and her life had been a series of choices intended to create in him if not a similar feeling—love?— then at the very least a profound and unshakable dependence upon her. She believed she would love him forever, in exactly the same way she loved him first. She cast herself in the role of a tragic mythic figure, doomed to love the same man for eternity, to pine for him if he were ever lost. When he could not sleep with her as a man should his wife, she blamed herself.

She stared at herself in every reflective surface she could find; she put her hands to her dress and adjusted it a thousand times in his presence. She was distracted with the lines of her own face, and the softness of her hair. In the morning she woke knowing that she had dreamed of her sister but unable to remember a single detail save Maga's green eyes which, she was sure, had narrowed themselves into cat-like slits.

Agnes didn't talk much in those days. She became angry at her absent sister; she suspected Dedlock of wanting her. She felt shame for her anger; she prayed to be forgiven. She hoped horrifically that her sister was dead. She was afraid that when she spoke, Dedlock found her stupid and trite. She was always tired. The sky was blue, she loved him and was frustrated, the sky was gray, she removed herself from his presence lest she was an annoyance to him. She imagined that Dedlock thought he had made a great mistake in marrying her. So when she was laying apples in the hay, she was laying apples in the hay for him; when she washed Jim's face and hands, she washed them for Dedlock; when she combed her hair smooth and parted it straight down the middle, she meant to be as plain as possible, as humble and as modest as possible. No one would accuse her of thinking she had been a success. No one would accuse her of pride. No one would accuse her of vanity. She was nothing. If she had been something, before Dedlock, then she went about methodically erasing any trace.

Then Agnes had taken it into her head to solve the problem of Dedlock's bowels. She imagined that if she could cure his body, she would, in some way, own a part of it, be a part of his skin. She steeped mandrake tea for him overnight, so that when he drank it cold the next morning he stepped backwards with its strength. She directed him in a course of stomach prodding she had heard of from Esther Cotton, who swore by it. She prayed, of course. She took away all his favorite foods, walnuts and fresh cream, and fed him soft cakes for an entire week. Another week, inspired by Bonnie's pink gums, she mashed all of his food. One week she eliminated all the meat from his diet. The next week she fed him only fish. The week after that, no vegetables at all, but heaping plates of pork and beef and yolky eggs. He ate it all, raising his eyebrows, maybe, at the plate, but never saying a word.

Yet every morning, before dawn, he clutched his fists into his gut and ran to the outhouse. He would stay there, straining and groaning, things loosening and tightening up without pattern or warning, until he was exhausted. By the time he came back inside the house, walking with his legs wide apart to soften the friction within his rectum. Agnes would twist her face and purse her lips into her expression of sympathy. "No better?" she'd ask.

"No better," her husband would say. Dedlock would stay standing in the kitchen, shifting a little from side to side. He didn't say much in the morning. He knew that Agnes was tired of hearing the story of his repulsive problems. The story never changed. The story never reached a resolution, and she knew she could not help him find one. It had been too long. He did not ever get used to it. It did not ever become something less terrible to endure. Every morning his bowels were a torture; he sometimes prayed to God for deliverance mid-shit, wanting to stop but knowing it must come out, that it had to come out, and there was no other way but this way. He felt exhausted and empty, afterwards, scored and scraped out from the inside. Agnes would place a mug of tea into his hands and he would sip at it, staring blankly through the open window. He arranged his life and work around his insides. But he did not speak about his insides. He never spoke about them.

Jim was a blessing in those days. He chattered and hugged and shouted indiscriminately and obliviously. He filled the rooms of the house. He elbowed Margaret's ghost into the corners. Agnes focused on her care for Jim, on her kitchen garden, on the various spontaneous midwife duties that pulled her out of the house at all hours. She planted squash and delivered the stillborn in barns. She planted marigolds and dabbed at oozing wounds. She carried slop to the pigs and carried the manure from behind the outhouse. She made Mrs. Finch more comfortable, as much as she could, before she died from her hemorrhaging. She cured bacon and hung jerky. She reached inside, rotated the head and neck, and pulled. In the afternoon, she read her brother's favorite stories aloud. Jim liked the bits about demons and plagues. He liked the Book of Job, too, and the Gospel According to John, and Revelations. Sometimes, Agnes would go with him down to the tide pools. While he played, she plucked the green-blue lobsters from the water. And then they would walk home, where Agnes would lift a huge blue body from its basket and plunge it alive into boiling water; it would thrash and scrape the sides of the Slough kitchen pot. Agnes laid her iron poker atop the pot, and waited.

A year into their marriage, when Jim was six years old, there was a blizzard. The Sloughs tucked themselves away into the house and watched the snow creep higher and higher until they had to look up to see out of the windows. Agnes read the story of Lot and his wife to Jim. Jim fell asleep, and Agnes went to bed early, and later, Dedlock went upstairs, laid in the bed beside his wife and fell asleep, too.

Just after midnight, Jack Flagg pounded on their door and shouted like murder until he was allowed inside. He and his son had shoveled and fought their way through the snows, and they needed Agnes right then, right now, they needed her an hour ago, because Mrs. Flagg was bleeding and bleeding and the baby wasn't due for another two months, they knew, and it was very bad, and she was in the most terrible pain and they had waited as long as they could but the pain was very bad, and they needed Agnes, now.

The snow had stopped falling. The night was very still and the sky was black and the snow was high and white. Agnes, following the panting Flaggs, had never seen a night like this. It was as though the world was a sphere filled halfway with snow and halfway with liquid nighttime, and she was striding through the middle of it all, her small track of footsteps blurring the line between the two.

The Flagg house was less than a mile away. It took the three of them almost an hour to reach it. Letty Flagg was lying in blood-heavy linens. She was very pale. Agnes went into the room alone. When she came out again, she had a little bundle that Jack Flagg did not look at. She collected her cloak from the fireside and went out alone. She made her way home without making a sound.

"Is Letty alright?" Dedlock asked when Agnes returned.

"She's alive," said Agnes.

"Do you need anything?"

"No. Did Jim wake up?

"For a minute. He fell asleep again."

"The snow was up to my hip, about there."

Agnes unknotted her cloak and Dedlock took it from her shoulders and laid it by the fire.

"Dedlock," said Agnes. She started to cry.

"What?" said Dedlock.

"Why I am making you unhappy? Why do you get to be the one who is made happy or unhappy? Why won't you worry? Why won't you care about how I am?"

Dedlock couldn't understand most of what his wife had said, because of the tears, but he understood enough.

"I don't know," he said. He did not want her to feel this way, but he felt, also, a part of him wholly indifferent. "What do you want me to do?"

"Jack Flagg loves his wife," said Agnes.

Her face, Dedlock, saw, had changed since they were married. Her eyes were deeper, it seemed, or darker, and her eyebrows slashed across her forehead. His wife was unhappy, he realized, and at the same time realized that she was his wife. He had known it before, of course. He had married her, and lived with her. But it wasn't until this moment that he had understood that it was, in fact, a real person who slept by him at night and scrubbed his dirty shirts. He tried to flex the fingers of his right hand, to pat her on the shoulder but could not. He could not even blink. He did not feel cold or warm. He did not know if he breathed or if he held his breath. It was as if he had accidentally killed a man who he had known a long time, a man who he had valued, an older man, a wise, kind man, and now he stood above the body and saw what he had done.

"Do you love me?" asked Agnes.

"Yes," said Dedlock. There was nothing else to say.

"I will need to have a child," said Agnes. "I need to have a baby, Dedlock."

In the house, Jim sat outside his bedroom door. He liked to sit in the hallway outside his room, positioned in such a way that he could both lean against his door and close his eyes if he wanted to be quiet or, by leaning forward, see down the steep staircase to where Agnes walked back and forth from her tasks with Bonnie tied high on her back.

After Bonnie was fed, she became cherubic and cheerful for nearly an hour. Agnes chattered to her. She named and explained the things of the house and of her own person.

"Chair," said Agnes, "we sit in the chair."

"Ash bucket. We put ash in the bucket. Ash from the fire."

"Nose. Nose. Is this your nose? This is Mama's nose. Nose."

Bonnie's eyes would stare straight and focus on whatever her mother pointed at; "Mama," Agnes said, again, and again. She watched Bonnie for signs of comprehension. She swore to herself, sometimes, that her daughter was nodding. Other times, she convinced herself that the baby understood nothing, and that the sounds that came from her small mouth were sounds and furies and nothings.

"Bonnie," said Agnes, "Your name is Bonnie. Bonnie, Bonnie. Are these Bonnie's toes? Are these Bonnie's little toes?"

When he overheard these one-sided conversations, Jim leaned over the banister and strained to listen. "Don't talk to her," Jim shouted. "Talk to me." And Agnes would call up some gentle question about the weather, or his appetite, or the churchyard.

"She's a baby," Jim would howl. "She can't even talk."

He crouched on his hands and knees at the top of the stairs.

"Agga," he called.

"Yes, Jim, we're down here."

"Agg, come upstairs with me," called Jim. When no one answered him, he called it again: "AGNES. Come upstairs because I want to show you something."

Below him, in the house, Jim heard soft scraping sounds and the soft sound of his sister's voice. She was talking to Bonnie. He jumped to his feet and leaned his body half over the staircase banister.

"I need you," he screamed.

"Dinner, soon." His sister's voice was calm, musical, unworried.

"Mama," she said, softly, to Bonnie. She watched her daughter's face for some sign of understanding. Bonnie opened and closed her tiny mouth.

The back door opened. Jim heard Dedlock come inside. He listened to the sounds of his sister and her husband talking lowly. He could hear the creaks and thumps as they walked the floorboards. Jim strained to hear what they were saying. He crawled on all fours to the top of the staircase, where he stayed very still and tried not to breathe or make any noise at all. It was almost time for him to go to the graveyard and watch the stones. When Agnes called, Jim stood up and went downstairs.

"Are you ready?" she asked him.

"No." He was never ready. He washed his face and hands. Dedlock washed his face and hands. They ate. As Agnes was clearing the plates, Jim pulled off one of his boots and threw it at the basket where Bonnie slept.

"You don't throw shoes," said Dedlock.

"When is it going to be gone?" asked Jim.

"What gone, Jim?" said Agnes.

"He means Bonnie," said Dedlock. As if in response, or because she felt the near-miss of the boot, Bonnie gave a little wail.

"We'll go for our walk now," Dedlock said. He lifted her out and held her.

"Let me feed her first. Talk to Jim a minute."

"Go have your dinner," Dedlock said to his daughter, and he began to bounce Bonnie, gently, in the way that made her look up at him in terror and joy. Agnes took her from him and went into the bedroom.

"Where are they going?" asked Jim, watching his sister leave. Dedlock patted his shoulder.

It was a very quick walk. Dedlock and Bonnie took the road toward the sea before turning down a path that would take them back around to the center of the village. Around the massive common ranged the small stone church and the churchyard, the Parkers' house and the Bettets' house, the schoolhouse and the older, smaller schoolhouse that the village used as a town meeting hall and general hangabout, the Farmer house and the long Flagg garden, the length of stone wall behind which ran Coldrock Brook, the large Beddington house where Joy lived alone and (as some said) mad, and the scaffold. That was a remnant of the not so far removed Puritans. There was a large dog sitting, politely, in the center of the scaffold.

"Hey, yo, Storey," called Dedlock. Steven Storey came out of the dusk. He was followed by dogs, too many and too darkly similar to one another so that Dedlock couldn't be sure of their number. Perhaps five. Maybe twenty.

"Ded," said Steven Storey, "Nice night for a walk. Hey, Bonnie."

"How are the dogs?" asked Dedlock.

"Have you seen the puppies?" Storey smiled. "Beautiful ones. If you want one, you come by." He whistled into the dark.

"Maybe," said Dedlock. He looked down at Bonnie. She had fallen asleep.

"Should I whisper? Where you walking to? Not looking for parts?" Storey referred to the habit of Chilling men to walk at night, trying to catch Captain Murderer in the act of scattering his loose limbs and gnawed bones.

"No, no," said Dedlock. "I heard your dogs found some nasty bits, though."

"More than nasty bits. A whole man's leg, but the thing had been sliced all through and pieces of it hacked away. Not eaten, mind, like an animal, but sliced. With his dinner knife, I guess."

"You think he's real, then?"

"Captain Murderer? I do. When I was in Gloucester, even, I remember hearing of him and my granny telling us, then, that possessed souls like that don't ever die properly. They need to hang around, she said, but I forget the reason. Something with Heaven or Hell or permissions, I guess."

"I meant, you think the story is real . . . about his ghost returning and eating people."

"It sounds silly," said Steven Storey. "But I do believe it. I believe in ghosts, certainly. The dogs see them. I know, because they go all strange in the road for no reason, or get rankled near old places where people have been and aren't, anymore."

"I saw a ghost, not long ago."

Storey squinted at him. "Not still thinking of Maga, then? No one knows what happened to her, Ded, so don't go assuming facts."

"It was the realest thing, but not a man. Ghost."

"Where? Not behind the graveyard? The dogs don't like it there."

"No," said Dedlock, "it was across one of our fields. I was just coming in, you know, late at night, and I saw a figure. So I raised my hand, because I thought it was Flagg or one of the Osborne boys . . .

But he didn't raise his hand, so I thought—"

"Ah," said Steven.

"And then, just as if the wind blew him away, he was vanished. All dressed in white, and thin like a wisp. There was nowhere he could have gone, no trees or rocks or anything to hide behind."

"What did he look like?"

"I wasn't close enough to see. You don't think, now," said Dedlock, pausing in the road, "You don't think it could have been him? Captain Murderer?"

"Did you go up and look around?"

"I did. And, I should say, I found . . . Agnes doesn't believe it, the ghost."

"She seems a tough woman, Agnes. She should have been a whaler's wife."

"I'd forgotten you were come from Gloucester," said Dedlock. Storey was the only black man who lived in Chilling or, Dedlock guessed, in this part of the world for many miles. His family had been whalers for generations, and lived on islands and the coast. Dedlock, like everyone, did not know why Storey had come north to this small place, alone, and no one asked. Chilling respected privacy.

"Born and bred. Speaking of, why, if you know, did they call it Chilling? The wind?"

"For the founder. He took a walk up here with his wife and started up a new place. They had just twenty families, then. Only people they knew, only people who wanted to live outside the prying eyes of the towns and the cities and the church. God-fearing people, but not the sort who agreed on what God wanted. A bit of a haven for the outcast."

"And you, you were born here?"

"Our parents came because my father maimed a man who tried to rob him. They had to leave Providence just after they were married. We were all, my sisters and I, born here. Plus many other babies besides that died. My mother lost five, all told. That's why we keep such a watch on Bonnie."

"Ah," said Storey.

"You think you'll stay here? Or go back to Gloucester? Your family's still there?"

"I don't know how long I'll stay. I don't much care. I can't go back to Gloucester. No real home, I guess. I suppose the dogs are my home."

Dedlock did not know what to say to this. "Hold her a minute," he said to Steven, and he handed his daughter to the man. Storey took her gingerly, and held her at arm's distance. Her eyes opened, and she smiled at him.

"Hello," said Storey.

Dedlock twisted his arm and scratched at a spot between his shoulderblades.

"Ahhh," he said. "Thanks." He took Bonnie again in the crook of her arm. She was awake and her eyes were focused on his; he put his thumb in her mouth and she sucked at it without closing her eyes. They walked on together. The dogs ran and circled around the man, invisibly tethered to Storey's hip. They played and nosed at the grass and dirt, but couldn't bear to be away from him for too long. One would invariably wander out too far, pause, circle back, and trot for a while at his side. Whenever this happened, Storey reached down and caressed an ear, or patted the top of a downy head.

One of the dogs nosed at Storey's palm. Storey looked up, and pointed at the Slough window.

"Jim's waiting for you," he said. They walked together slowly. In the road, before the decrepit Slough house, Storey laid a hand on Dedlock's large arm.

"You never finished your story," he said, "telling me about the ghost. What did you find in the field?"

"Ah," whispered Dedlock. He smiled. "Another time." He and the baby went into the house.

Steven Storey and his cloud of roaming dogs went down the road and into the dark.

Chapter XVI.
Satus House

Nora dropped the body of a fat man. Jules had gone out again by himself and had wheelbarrowed the corpse all the way from the Wolfeborough churchyard. The trip up the Satus hill had been extremely difficult—he had lost his footing and feared the wheelbarrow reversing direction and the massive burden squashing him flat—and so when he arrived at the kitchen door he hollered for help. Nora was still awake, aimlessly walking around the house, looking at paintings and finding the teacups that Salderman left in every corner.

She opened the door to Jules and a dead body.

"Where are the Gallos?" he cried out.

"Asleep," said Nora. "Everyone's asleep."

Together, they lifted the man and they made their way to the cellar stairs. Jules was exhausted, his chest heaving up and down with great gasps of breath, his legs shaking and seizing up beneath him.

"Almost there," he said, at the top of the cellar stairs. "Almost."

Nora's arms hugged the body's fat calves and she moved backwards onto the first step. Her arms were so thin they were almost subsumed by the fat on the man's legs, and as she held them more tightly she felt her bones sink into what felt like a heap of jelly; she could not hold him well. She moved backwards, and took a step down, carefully, behind her . . . but the body was so heavy. Down lower on the staircase, she felt her arms begin to tremble with the effort. Her spine bent; she took another step behind her; her left calf muscle, the one that hated her, roiled itself into a massive, rat-sized knot and Nora cried out in pain. She let her hands drop to her leg, where they had just enough time to feel the hard knot before she fell backwards down the stone steps. The body fell with her.

At the bottom, her face in the corpse's soft belly, she heard Jules laughing.

"My own fault for asking for your help," he said. When she didn't answer, he asked, "Are you dead?"

Jules Demmer was dark and stocky and he chewed tobacco. Of all the men she had met the night Susanna had died, she had disliked

Jules the most. She did not like the way he crowed over the body or the way he thrust out his chest. She found him arrogant and loud. He carried around a little earthenware jug and spit into it delicately and silently. Sometimes, when he was very hurried and put-upon by Salderman, he spoke with a stammer.

The morning after Susanna, Jules had come across Nora on a stone bench outside the kitchen door. It was a humid, gray morning. He had stood in the doorway until Nora felt uncomfortable enough to say something; she remarked that it would probably not rain, but that she wished it would. Jules had sat down beside her and said formally that he had shouldered responsibility for the death of the child, and that he was sorry that he had brought it about. He had gone and prayed over it with Paul.

"Why are you telling me?" she had asked him. "Tell Jeffrey Dial."

"I'm telling you because we can't tell most people in Chilling what we're doing. Some of them know, you know. And have for a long time. But it's not common knowledge, and part of the deal is no advertising our work. I'd like to admit it to someone. I'd like to stand up at that little meetinghouse and have the chance to explain it all, to everyone. But Salderman doesn't care and Paul is moralistic about everything and the Gallos wouldn't like for me to talk about it."

Nora nodded. "Jeffrey Dial would kill you, anyway."

Jules stood up. "No chance," he said. "My uncle taught me how to fight when I was a boy," he said. He spat into his jug. "I had a terrible stammer and it made me very shy. I was very embarrassed. My father tried to beat it out of me but it wouldn't go away. The other boys picked on me. My uncle taught me how to hit so that even if I was picked on by the other boys I wouldn't get hurt, and they'd at least respect me for fighting them."

"You don't stammer anymore," said Nora.

"Not usually. But it comes back to remind me."

"Remind you of what?"

Jules laughed. Nora liked him against her will. She knew that the fair thing to do would be to tell a story of her own, in which she found herself humiliated. She could tell him about her mother. She could explain how she had never felt loved as a child and how she wished she could see her mother again, to ask if she ever loved her or, if not, why? But as she opened her mouth to say the words nothing came. Georgiana was dead. Georgiana was dead and Nora felt that speaking about her mother would be, somehow, a betrayal of her.

Jules had come down the stairs and pulled the corpse from her, and together they maneuvered the fat man through the halls and onto one of the dissecting tables. Nora, remembering their earlier conversation, asked Jules how he had learned to fight.

"Oh," he said, "My uncle gave me lessons."

"What kinds of things did he teach you?"

Jules stepped back from the table and stood with his legs apart. "Here," he said, "I'll show you how to hit someone where it'll hurt them." Nora did what he told her, meticulously. When she punched him, he laughed.

"Like being pummeled by a breeze," he said. "You'll practice and be stronger."

The work in the cellar was not easy; the bodies were heavy and the stairs were very steep. At home, Nora had been doing a half-day of farm work. Not so long ago, she reminded herself. She didn't die, she reminded herself. She had memories of manipulating massive stones, with her father. She remembered wrenching them from the field with a great heavy bar, leveraging her body weight against the weight of the rock. Like a miracle, the rock rising up out of the ground and then the two of them shifting it together onto the sled and pulling it across the field. Nora thought that girl, whoever she had been, was very good. But maybe she was making these things up. Her life before sometimes felt like a dream; surely she couldn't ever have been *that* strong. Surely, she couldn't ever have been that *easy*. Nora began to go for long walks. She woke while it was still dark and walked to the sea and back, away from the village. She sought out the rocks and clambered up their highest points. Lily's mother altered the clothing to fit her body, so she was no longer dwarfed in folds of cloth. She helped Joe with splitting and stacking wood, she worked in the garden and lifted buckets of dirt and manure; she offered to stir the laundry and imagined, as she breathed in the steam, that she was inhaling flesh and strength. Nora asked Jules if she could hit him and, when he said yes, she pummeled his kidneys. She slept every night as long as she could. She forced her throat to swallow whatever Lily put on her plate. She ate piles of buttered potatoes and earthy, sliced beets. Her overtaxed stomach ached.

One afternoon, late in the day, she explained to Salderman that she had recently been having aches in her belly. "It's like hollow terrible pain," she said, "And it starts in the pit of my gut but not the vomiting kind. But a pain that comes like a needle, into my head. And then I can't work or walk."

"You're hungry," he said to her. "That's just hunger."

When she began to menstruate again, she felt triumphant over something very large. Blood was welcome in Satus House.

As she ate more and moved more, and as her bones padded themselves with muscle and fat, Nora felt bolder, more gregarious, more communicative. She made conversation with the stern servant, Lily's mother. She ate breakfast with Joe and Fernie every day, and joked with them. Salderman began to assign her more challenging work and, when it was beyond her skill, she asked Jules or Paul for help and learned from them. Nora could not go to church, and she missed going. But she prayed with Paul every evening, and they sometimes read a chapter together and discussed it. In a few weeks, even Salderman was not afraid of her giving them away, and her routine was so settled within Satus that it was as if she had been born there.

Occasionally, though, Nora's attention wandered away from the scalpel and the sponge, ducked under doorways and jumped through open windows. It listened for footsteps and voices. One morning she looked down at the corpse's shoulder and realized that she had done a line of incredibly crooked stitching. All along her own arms and legs, Nora could see traces of the illness that had killed her family and left her bald, with pale pitted scars. She began to think it was strange, that only her family had been victims. Why had no one else been sick, and what was the disease, exactly? If it came back, what could they do to fight it? What if she still carried it, and was spreading it every day, to everyone in the house? She had never asked Salderman, not once. But he must know. She tore out the stitches and started again.

She did not see him that day, or all that afternoon. Paul said the doctor had gone for a walk, but Nora waited outside and did not see him return. Late that night she could not sleep and she came down to sit at the kitchen table and sew; Lily's mother, who the men called Mug, had brought Nora material for summer clothing. She desperately needed some. When Fernie appeared, she almost did not notice. He had come into the kitchen quietly when her back was turned, and he sat down by the fire so that his head was below the level of the table. He took himself apart so that his wooden leg lay in pieces, some around him and some in his lap. He was working at the leather strap and buckle with his knife. Nora silently moved her chair to a place where she could look at him, and where, should he catch her, she could turn back to her work.

She had never asked him his age, but he couldn't have been more than twenty or so. He was lanky and very lean. He had rolled his sleeves past the elbows and his arms, though strong, lacked the bulk and size of his big brother's arms. His hair was very blonde, and in the firelight sometimes looked even as pale as his skin, and straight. He wore it long enough to tie back in a pig's tail at the back of his neck. He was sunburned, though Nora knew the sun had not been hot or high recently.

"Can I help?" she asked him.

"I didn't even see you," he said. He looked up at her with his leg in his lap, and she sat by him and looked at what had gone wrong. He held the broken portion up to the firelight.

"Ah," she said, "I see. What happened?"

"I wrenched it," he said. "When I move too quickly or take a wrong step, this piece gets pulled off the leather and these two pieces," he held up two round pieces of wood, "get pulled apart."

"Did you try to run?"

"Joe and I had to go out," he said. "What are you doing awake?"

"Have you seen Salderman at all today?"

"No, I don't think so. But he's in and out all over this house."

"I want to talk to him."

"About?"

"I was wondering about how my family got sick, and why no one else in Chilling caught what we had. I thought he would know."

"Probably," said Fernie. They worked in silence for a little while.

"Why did you and Joe go out?"

"We were throwing away the bodies. We heard someone and had to hide so we wouldn't be caught."

"You're Captain Murderer," said Nora. "Oh, I wish I could tell the twins. I told them he wasn't real. They did not believe me."

"Which twins?"

Nora smiled. "My little brothers, the big twins. Abe and Andy. They were six."

"Well, we are only the ghost of Captain Murderer," Fernie said. "Not the original one, not the real one. We just took advantage of the story. If you could hold this part for me . . ."

Nora pulled the leather taut and looked at Fernie's face. She had not wanted to look at his eyes again, since they had struck her so deeply the first time and she did not want to be underwhelmed by them now. They were darker than she remembered. The blue of lobsters, and patterned, also, just like the shell of a lobster.

"This is no good," she said.

"What?"

"There should be a way to make a joint, here." Nora hefted the leg in her hands. "If there was a way we could make something like a real knee? We could use the tendons from the bodies, and maybe you could bend it." She reached and picked up the leather. "Where, exactly, does this connect? How do you wear it?"

Fernie blushed and took the leg from her. "It's fine," he said. "It's fine for what it is."

After another week, Nora's strength was returning, but slowly. "I'm weak as a baby," she said to the Gallos. It was a Sunday afternoon. The three of them sat under a bird-filled apple tree in the orchard. Joe was helping Fernie put his leg back on; Fernie took it off at every opportunity.

"You're okay," said Fernie. "Look at all those legs you have."

"I almost collapsed on Paul yesterday," said Nora. "I was just carrying some buckets up the stairs and my legs just went all wibbley." Though she improved every day, she felt her weakness more intensely. Nora was oblivious to her own progress. She had Salderman's dogstick in her lap and she rolled it lightly along the tops of her thighs, back and forth. She didn't need any support to walk, anymore, but she liked to carry the stick with her. The weight of the stick pressing into the muscles of her legs hurt her a little, but a good, releasing kind of hurt.

"Don't spend time with Paul," said Fernie.

"There," said Joe. He tugged the leather straps of the leg tight.

"Norabones," said Fernie.

"Don't call me Norabones."

"You look a lot better than when you came," said Joe.

She did. The gash on her nose had healed, and the swelling was gone; all that was left of the broken place was a pale scar and two soft bruises under her eyes. She had taken on some weight, and the bones in her shoulders were covered with a thin layer of fat. Her ribs had disappeared back inside her chest. Her stomach had stopped suddenly cramping; she could walk from the first to the second floor of the house without pausing. Her fingernails, which had turned blue during her illness, were pink and white again, and she chewed them to keep them short. Her tongue was clean and free of the woolly white scum that had collected there. But one thing had not changed.

Nora put her hand to her head; her hair was as short as the day Salderman had shorn it off with a kitchen knife. Feeling it underneath her hand brought her back to the farm, to waking up alone in the house. She promised herself that she would ask Lily for something to wear on her head. A cap or a wrap that she could wear all day long.

"You should do all the stairs," said Fernie.

"What do you mean?" asked Nora.

Joe was looking off, toward Satus. "I have to go," he said. "No, you walk back with me?"

"Everyone with legs, you all don't appreciate walking up stairs," said Fernie. "You want to get strong, walk up every stair in that house twice a day for a week. Carry heavy things. You'll be strong enough to pull a plow. That's what I would do."

"You can't climb stairs?" said Nora.

"He can," said Joe.

"It takes a lifetime," said Fernie.

"Ah, you swim everyday anyway. Better than stairs. Really, I have to go, back, now." Joe looked at Nora, but she was sitting still in the sunshine, her back up against the trunk of the tree. She was chewing a long blade of dandelion. She had seen Fernie, in the mornings on her walks, swimming in the sea. He was only a small dot in the ocean, from where she watched, but she could see him.

Fernie squinted at his brother. "Where you off to now?"

But Joe turned and strode across the grass. His hair looked even more yellow in the sun. His legs were long and he covered long distances quickly, without even seeming to hurry.

Fernie looked after Joe until he was out of their hearing. "My big brother the Titan. Nora. Do you know where he goes?"

Nora had her eyes closed and her face toward the sun. "Hmm," she said. She wanted Fernie to ask her questions. She wanted her hair to grow.

"What? You know where he goes?"

"I saw him in the hallway near Miss Salderman's study, the other day, the place with the painting of the man with the head. I don't know if he was there. I just saw him in the hallway. What's a Titan?"

"Salderman calls him that."

"Do you swim every day?" Nora opened her eyes and turned to look at him.

"In the mornings," said Fernie. He pulled himself to stand. He adjusted his bad leg under him, and took a step away, back toward the house. Then he turned, again.

"You should come with me, sometime," he said. He looked at Nora hard in the eyes, and then he looked away far into the forest. Then he turned and walked away and disappeared immediately below the crest of the hill.

She was surprised. When she had been sick, her body had been too tired and too overworked—trying to keep her alive—to spare the energy for much emotion. Nora had spent months so empty and dull inside that she thought her soul had left her body early, and would meet up with her in the grave. But since she had come to Satus she had begun to experience flutterings of feeling. Great sucking tides of sadness that came and disappeared again. Lead-like guilt behind her navel. And sometimes a sudden great confusion in which she was overwhelmed with the mysteries of the shape and size of the world, one that could generate wind and rain and on which her brothers could die and be buried in the ground, how silly, how silly. But now, watching Fernie, she felt gladness. It was a wet, clogging disease, sinking into her lungs. She felt happy to be alive. There were apples beginning above her. Nora waited until Fernie had limped far enough to get to the house ahead of her, and then she went back, too, and climbed the Satus staircase until she gasped.

Chapter XVIII.
Satus House

Sometimes, one corpse would serve many masters, as each doctor took from it what they were most interested in. Jules was the lung man. Nora had helped him hold the ribs open, once, and as he clipped the bits which held the lungs to the flesh, she was reminded of trout. The lungs lay inside the body like twin fish laid out on a riverbed, and when Jules held one in his two hands she imagined him as a sort of fisherman, in the truest sense: a man who fished inside men.

Demmer was from Philadelphia. He was shorter than both Joe and Fernie, but he was powerfully built and very athletic. Every day he stripped off his shirt and shoes and did vigorous exercises in the orchard. He ran from tree to tree, as fast as he could, then stopped and rested for a minute and then was off again. He bent and stretched and once a week he loaded Nora and Fernie on a sled and dragged them up the steepest side of the Satus hill. To Nora, he seemed like a very happy man. His cheeks were always red and he smiled more than anyone she had ever known. He had dark curly hair, which he had Mug clip very short. He liked to talk as he worked and dissected, and if he had nothing particular to say to Nora, he would simply narrate what he was doing: now I am tying off this artery; now I think we'll try that new incision; now this lung is in terrible shape, we'll preserve it. He didn't mind when she asked questions and often interrupted her mid-query, to congratulate her for her observation or her curiosity. She learned a lot from Jules Demmer. But sometimes he was simply too happy and healthy for her, and his talkativeness and helpfulness annoyed her. On those days, she worked alone or, if he would allow it, with Paul Lagerkvist.

Paul was too tall for the cellar. He had to duck into every doorway, and stoop over his dissections. He moved very slowly; Nora thought of him as continually trapped underwater, raising his arms and moving his head through great pressure. His eyes were very close together, and his eyebrows were arched like cathedral domes over his eyes. The left side of his face was dotted with four large moles. He gave the impression of having been fashioned from spare parts, hastily flung together and indifferently joined. He arrived at the bodies last, after everything had been picked through. Paul was the brain and spine man. He never invited Nora to work with him or asked for her help, but would occasionally nod if she gestured to join him. Even when she was with him, he worked as if he was alone, and he rarely spoke. When he did, Nora heard a very slight accent, neither British nor French, but she couldn't identify it.

Paul took religion very seriously, which was rare, Salderman mentioned, for men in his profession. Sometimes, Nora wanted very badly to reach out and smack Paul on the back of the head: he exasperated her with his self-importance and the sense of self-sacrifice. He sighed a lot. Paul prayed every night and every morning and was yet certain that there would be no saving him. He was too far gone, had moved against God and his children with too much violence to be ever forgiven. The surety of his eventual damnation made him pity himself and yet, Nora thought, worship himself at least a little. He carried himself as though he were a spiritual martyr for Science. He made the sign of the cross over the corpses, asking God's forgiveness and forgiveness of the soul who had given its house. When Jesus came again, and the dead rose to join Him in Heaven, Paul knew that these people would be handicapped by what he had done to them. They would be hideously disfigured; they would appear as demons. He had taken Paradise from them.

Doctor Salderman, on the other hand, could be persuaded to take interest in anything. When she had arrived, Salderman had been obsessed with malformation, the process of the developing fetus and how, specifically, babies could come out of the womb with awesome disfigurements. He did not see these deviations as horrifying, or even sad . . . Salderman studied with detachment like artistic appreciation, as when a connoisseur of oils finds a painter innovating and advancing the art. Pregnant corpses were rare, and when they came along he granted himself exclusive access to them. Salderman dissected some of the fetuses he took; the others he preserved intact, to track and catalogue the progress of the growing body. He kept his specimen in variously sized jars, in a special room in the cellar. They hung suspended in liquid the color of stardust, some of them with fingers unfurling and others little more than bean-sized. Nora arranged them in order of how much they had grown and of how close they had come. But then his attention was pulled to the veins of the arm and hand, and the jars were forgotten.

Over the course of a few days, Nora would watch a single body slowly stripped to the very bones, as each man took the parts he wanted most. She watched the body undress and divest itself of layer after layer. She stood above the tables and looked, just looked and looked, as if to memorize the long striations of muscle and branching trails of veins. She learned to recognize the bones, and where they belonged. One day, she passed by the long mirror in the Satus entranceway, and stood for a moment looking at her body. She held her arms out wide to each side, and lifted her chin. She knew, Nora realized, what she looked like underneath all of her skin. The thought was not unsettling. If anything, she was comforted by the knowledge that if she was dismantled, she would know enough to put herself together again.

"Where do you go in the mornings, Norabones?" asked Salderman. She had been living at Satus nearly a month.

"For walks," Nora told him, "to get strong again. But I don't want people from the village spying me out, and knowing that I'm here. So I go early."

"Who would mind, in Chilling?" asked Salderman. "Your family is dead."

"I have an uncle and aunt," said Nora. "The Peabodys."

"Ahh. I know them."

"He was my mum's brother. I don't want to live with them. I can learn more here."

"You like the cellar work, then?"

"Sometimes."

"Cleaning up corpses?"

"I don't mind it."

"And this, do you know what this is?"

"Yes," said Nora, after a minute, "Yes. That's the long bit that connects the right side of the heart to that big muscle."

"And this?"

Nora laughed. "That's a *liver*," she said.

"Hmm. Too easy, yes? Yes. Let's find . . . oh. What is *this*?" In his palm, Salderman held out two tiny spheroid bones, the size of small pearls.

Nora took them in her own hand and rolled them between her fingers. They were cool and dry.

"These belong in the feet. Right under the big toe." She handed them back to the doctor. "I don't know the names."

Salderman took the bones and replaced them in his pocket. "Yes," he said, "that sometimes happens. We know it, but not its name. And yet when we do know the name . . . Eh? Names. Do we know a thing better because we know its name? Well. Just by calling it something distinct? Do we know it better, then?"

"I like to know a thing's name."

"Why?"

"I think when it has a name we sort of put it to one side, like saying, Hey, this is A Thing. It is special, not like the other things. And we can look at it apart from other things."

"And would it be a different thing with a different name?"

"I don't know. When the twins were babies, they looked just the same. The big twins. We called one Alexander and one Abraham. But still it was a very long time before I got very good at knowing which was which. Then my mother had another set of twins. And this time we called one Roger, and one Tobias. And that time it was much easier . . . their names were so different, and somehow it was easier to tell the difference between two when we called them by such different names."

"Having a distinct name, then . . . helps us see what is already there."

"I was wondering about my family," Nora said. "I was wondering what we had, what disease we all caught."

"I only came to the house once, sadly. I had been away. I cannot say, I cannot say."

"Isn't half of what you do is teach Paul and Jules the names of things? The names for all the inside bits and the organs and the different arteries, and the bones, and all of that? It seems they are always trying to memorize the names of all the things."

"Yes," Salderman agreed, "that is accurate."

"I think it would helpful for me to know the name of what killed them."

"Why?"

"If a man had come and murdered them, I would want to know his name."

Salderman sighed and tucked the loose hunk of hair behind his ear. "Perhaps, Nora, instead of going for your long walks in the morning, you could help me with a special project. You have a very good memory, you do, and you seem to have taken the insides here and internalized them . . . you know the body, and what it should look like, don't you? Yes. You know the average specimen."

"Just what I've seen here. And my family."

"But most of all, Nora, I am interested in what is not the average specimen. Well? What I want is the things that go off—what is different. Wrong, even. Malformation. And it could be something large, like an extra finger, or it could be small . . . one bone smaller than the rest, growths, fusions. Anything outside the normal scope. A little bit outside, or a lot."

"My mother said that things like that were marks of the Devil."

"Did she? She was wrong."

Nora stood up and crossed the room to wipe her hands on a towel. It was rough and scratched her hands. Salderman did not look up at her.

"You really don't know? You don't know at all?"

"I could guess, Nora. Possibly something like an infection, or dysentery, or a new kind of pox we haven't seen before."

"If you did know, or had an idea, you would tell me?"

Upstairs, they heard something drop and clatter, and Lily howl in irritation.

"Of course. So," he went on, "you can look for things, specific things, not-marks-of-the-Devil, and let me know what you find. And you can use the bodies in the very early morning, when we are all asleep. That way you won't have to ask the other men, and work in peace, and take your time."

"I would be able to cut them?"

"Yes," said Salderman, "I will show you the way to do it precisely. We will do that, we have a lesson, this afternoon. But, now, come with me? I want to let you see a great thing."

Alexander Salderman's grandfather (William, no. 1) had studied medicine in Berlin and Vienna before settling back home in England. His father (William, no. 2) had been a doctor and a very well-known botanist. Both men gained considerable fame in their fields. Both men neglected their wives and children for their passion, and traveled a great deal to acquire specimens for what would become one of the largest private anatomical collections in the country. William 1 and William 2 were collectors of medical anomalies as simple as clubfeet and as wondrous as two wholly grown men who shared a single heart, who attached themselves through their rib bones. William 2 was an expert on poisons derived from plants—poisons that could, in small doses, cure, and, in high doses, kill. Alexander's father had initially found an heir to his work in his eldest son, William (William, no. 3), but William 3 had no interest in science, medicine, or the human body. In order to escape his fate as a flesh-poker and prodder, he left the family when he turned eighteen. No one had heard from him since, but neither Alexander nor Odette worried. William 3 was a genius, like his grandfather and father and sister, and his genius would one day out. The family did wonder, idly, what form his talent would take. Odette had had suspicions that her brother would surface one day in politics. Alexander said that was unlikely. He thought William 3 would be a painter, and for evidence he would gesture to the canvas Odette kept in her writing-room. Genius, surely. And William 3 had been only sixteen when he had done that.

With William 3 gone, William 2 sighed and looked to his youngest son, the gawky and long-limbed Alexander, who tripped over dust. Alex had, it turned out, an instinctive talent for the scalpel and for the close delicate work of anatomy—not only for dissection, but for the preparation of models and preserving liquids. He developed his own alcohol solution in which to preserve specimen, and his own technique of injecting veins and arteries with colored wax. Each morning save Sunday, Alexander walked a half-block to his father's small foul-smelling anatomy school and stayed there for hours; he napped on vacant dissection tables. When his father died, Alex patted his mother's shoulder, but otherwise took little notice. While he studied with doctors in Germany, Odette published her second volume of poetry, moved to America, and their mother died. Alexander came back to England, where he worked, for a short time, with various military representatives, looking for help with diseases ransacking their troops. He found, at home, that the collection of anatomical wonders had passed to him. When he was forced to leave England, he had it shipped, closely packed crate by closely packed crate, to his sister at Satus House.

When he arrived in Chilling, Alexander Salderman found a room on the ground floor of Satus which he could lock and bar. It took weeks to unpack his specimens and inventory them, but nothing had been lost in transit. A mandible, a huge and curiously shaped mandible, had been broken, but Salderman used an adhesive and Odette told him the break was completely undetectable. It took a very long time to arrange the room, to lay out the glass jars, to reassemble skeletal systems, to curate his small museum in the manner in which it would make most sense to him and to his visiting students. He called in a man from the village, Parker, to build new shelves and cabinets. The walls of the room sagged with the incredible variations, the awe-inspiring fickleness of the human body. On tables, they rose up like ghosts under glass.

Nora stood in the center of Salderman's collection. She held the dogstick behind her back. Salderman walked from shelf to table, to shelf to cabinet, checking on things he liked to look at, talking at her.

"Something goes, quickly, slowly, something goes in a different direction. And who knows when? Perhaps before conception, before anything has even begun. Perhaps *in utero*, at any point. But it goes on! It continues to develop, though something has . . . deviated, yes, something has deviated from the plan but still the life goes. We go on, we progress and it continues as best it can. And all of us have these strangenesses in us. You," Salderman nodded toward Nora's hair, "your hair will not grow. And Joe, Joey Gallo, his ears are the size of a child's ears, though he is big and strong. People become comfortable with their disfigurement and learn either to hide it or to accept it. But all, all . . . yes, it is the same. From small ears to what the public would think are grotesque disfigurements. But not really. *Not* grotesque."

"It would be difficult, though," said Nora, "if that were you. Walking through life with that." She pointed the stick toward the head of a toddler, preserved in a large jar.

"Oh," said Salderman, "yes, but how extraordinary. Extraordinary."

"I think it's horrific."

"No. No. Seen along a spectrum, a continuum, all things seem natural. Well, I mean natural, in the sense of nature, of the changes. If we see what came before, how many slow and minute steps, progressions. So that we may live with the same person every day for fifty years and find that person the same as ever . . . yet if we had seen them once in childhood and then again near death, in old age, we would consider them horribly decayed."

"But no one sees people that way. Most people feel like monsters, I think. Don't most people feel like monsters?"

"Monsters are only signposts for us. Something has changed, it says. We notice the monsters because the monsters are crucial to notice."

"I don't have any hair," said Nora, slowly. "I don't understand why it won't grow at all." She put her hand to her head. She had begun wearing a close black cap. It was thin, and light, and came down over her ears, but she could still slip her hand underneath the fabric and feel her head. There were some places on her skull where she could feel the soft plane of her skin. In some places there was a little hair, but only in small patches, so that her head underneath the cap was dappled and spotted with dark, asymmetrical blotches. "Something has changed with that."

Salderman was staring at the toddler's closed eyes. He tucked a loose bit of hair behind his left ear and then laid his cheek into his palm.

"My father," said Salderman, "was a doctor in England, and his father was, as well. Did you know that? My family was very well known. The government sometimes came to us for help with problems."

"No, I didn't know that." Nora moved closer to the toddler's face. The child had been born with one great eye in the center of its face; there was no real nose to speak of, but two slits like gills which Nora assumed functioned—or did not function—as nostrils.

Salderman stood up and looked around the room. Nora thought he looked a little helpless, his hair long and ragged in front of his face and his hands limp at his sides. She rarely saw him without some sort of tool or implement in his hand, or at least without his hands plunged into the insides of some dead thing. Without his work, without working, he reminded her a little of her brother Abraham. Long before the others were called to eat, Abraham would stand in front of the table, his face and hands scrubbed clean, and watch the family quietly as they moved about the kitchen, slicing bread and spooning vegetables.

Salderman held out his hands and opened the palms toward the child's face. "I have no good answers," he said. "For you. Anyone."

"I know that you do not want me to keep asking," said Nora. "But I feel as though I need to know."

Salderman nodded. They left the room together, and went to the cellar.

It was a good spring. Nora woke early, went down to the cellars and worked for hours until Fernie called down to her. She ate her breakfast with the Gallos while Lily stood by the fire and ignored them. Lily's mother, the general workhorse of the house, was never still; she chopped onions and dug the garden and boiled surgical tools and cleaned bedrooms. Joe and Fernie called her Mug, or Mugger when they felt affectionate and joking. Lily called her Mama. Most mornings, if he could, Fernie limped off to the sea, and, if he could, Joe to sleep. He usually worked through the night, and Nora rarely saw him. Nora would walk up and down the Satus stairs for an hour, or two, and then she spent a few hours in Salderman's library, reading about the body and its diseases and its malformations. When she found something that reminded her of her family's symptoms, she marked the page and laid the book aside. Sometimes she wandered into the Collection, and looked. She tapped the glass with her fingertips and saw her reflection in the jars. In the afternoons, Joe and Fernie walked together into the village to dig graves, tend to the churchyard, or run errands for Salderman, and Nora found herself in the cellar, again. She couldn't stay away. She cleaned up, tidied the rooms, helped prepare solutions for preserving specimens, assisted with Jules' or Paul's dissections. Many days, especially as the weather grew warmer, there were no dissections, and she watched Paul complete his meticulously detailed anatomical drawings. In one room was a great firepit and huge pot, where she sometimes boiled the flesh from particular bones that Salderman wanted cleaned. And because nights were the time that Fernie and Joe brought the new bodies, she stayed up late. She ate whatever supper Lily's mum had put in front of her and took a nap in the early evening. A few hours after midnight, Nora was awake and waiting for them at the door with the lantern, craning her neck to watch for their slow progress up the back walk. Joe would push the wheelbarrow with the corpse, and Fernie walked in front of him, around him, keeping eyes out for anyone, any random villager who may be out for a midnight walk.

Because the nights were still cold, and because she found herself not quite healthy enough to insulate herself, Nora watched for the Gallos with her blanket around her shoulders. She leaned her side into the doorframe and if there was a moon, she kept her eyes on it; if there was no moon, the stars were dazzling and she let herself examine the whole of the night sky slowly and searchingly, moving from the east to the west and back to the south. She would be tired, by then, and her eyes would be tired from the sort of strenuous, scrupulous searching they had done in the cellar. The air was fresh, and clean, and cold; and toward her, coming closer every moment, came Fernie. It was the best time, often, of her whole day, those minutes she spent alone watching the darkness. And yet she was conscious of a restlessness, too, even in those quiet moments. She was waiting for something outside—not just the arrival of the Gallo brothers. She felt something coming, something sweeping in with the sea winds.

At the end of April, it rained heavily for a week. Nora came out into the doorway and held her blanket over her head like an awning.

She peered out but she couldn't see anything beyond the wall of water; it roared down like a waterfall. It would be good cover for Joe, as he dug, and he could maybe get more than one body in the wheelbarrow. But the brothers would be wet through when they got back, and cold and miserable. Nora ducked inside and put a pan of water on the fire. When she came to the doorway again, she could just discern the squeak of the wheelbarrow underneath the sound of the rain. She stood a little taller and the blanket slipped back from her forehead; she came out into the rain and walked to meet them.

"Get inside, mad woman," called Fernie. She couldn't see him, or Joe, or the wheelbarrow, but each of the brothers could see her, silhouetted against the yellow light of the open door. She had clasped the blanket tight against the sides of her body and her head was bare and lines of her head moved cleanly into the downward lines of her neck; she held her face up against the rain as though it were light.

"It's torrents," shouted Fernie. "We're wet to the bone."

She walked into Fernie before she could see him, and she could feel, as she pressed against him in the dark, something large—the size of a child, almost—warm and moving, wrapped in a wool blanket in his arms. Their faces were close, for a moment, and Nora looked into Fernie's eyes. Even in the dark and the rain, they were blue enough to pinch her. He clutched one of her arms and pulled his lips to her ear.

"Don't say anything," he whispered, "don't tell Joe. He wants to see you surprised." Then he released her and she took a step back. Behind him, bent over the wheelbarrow and dripping with rainwater, pushing with his long legs against the mud and stones, Joe. He had dug up at least three bodies: Nora could tell from the height of the stack, by how much of Joe's own body was obscured.

"Inside," said Nora, "water's boiling." She pulled her blanket from her shoulders and draped it over Fernie's head, then ran to help Joe. The way to Satus was all upward. Joe was strong, but three bodies were a large load to push alone in the rain and through thick mud, uphill.

"Thanks be," he said, when he saw her. "Take a side." Nora wedged her shoulder under the left side of the wheelbarrow, and Joe moved to take the right side. They pushed to the threshold.

"Leave 'em," said Joe. "I'll cover them for now and send the doctors out to bring 'em the rest of the way." He put his hands to the small of his back and leaned backwards, closed his eyes against the rain and groaned.

"Inside," said Nora. "Get yourself inside." She could barely see, and her face hurt from the rain which fell like knives.

Joe bent down to unlace his boots.

"Forget the boots!" said Nora. "Mud washes away. Go, go." She was soaked through to the skin, already, and her skirt was heavy against her legs. She pushed Joe through the door and turned to latch it.

Inside, Fernie sat with his face to the fire. He still held the bundle of blankets to his chest, away from Nora. He had made tea, and the big teapot sat on the table, in a half-moon of wet where he had slopped the water.

"It's a storm," said Nora. "He shouldn't have sent you out in this. You'll both get sick and die yourselves."

"You can dissect my guts," said Fernie, smiling at her.

"Go, get off upstairs and get dry and dressed. I'll get the bodies down. They can help me downstairs."

Joe had joined his brother at the fire. Between the two of them they streamed water into the floor, where it rolled and spread across the uneven boards to Nora's feet.

"Nora," said Joe, "you remember how you were telling me about the dogs you had at the farm, your family's dogs."?

"Ah," said Nora. "Yes. They were good dogs. Mine—everyone considered her mine—she was a good dog. We'd just lay Toby and Roger, when they were babies, up against her belly and they'd fall straight asleep. She kept them warm as toast. She didn't mind anything. She let them clutch at her ears and tail, all day."

Fernie, on the long bench in front of the fire, huddled closer to the flames as if he felt a draft. Nora looked at Joe but she felt her eyes wanting to go to Fernie, to whatever he had in the blanket.

Joe tramped to the table and poured himself a mug of tea. "Fern," he said.

Fernie lifted himself up, first leaning off to the right and then pulling the false left leg, and then finally balancing to stand. He turned and offered the small bundle to Nora, who reached out her arms and took it as though taking charge of an infant. And, for a moment, she thought it was an infant. The soft warmth underneath the wool was exactly the sensation of one of her sleepy brothers, being carried to bed. She had a vision, halfway between the horrifying and the sublime, that they had found her baby brother Bartholomew and brought him back to her. He wasn't dead, after all. It had all been a mistake, or a terrible error. Her heart moved in her chest. Her life changed and opened to her again.

She lifted the blanket, and the black-and-white face of a herding pup blinked at her. "Hello," she said, instinctively. Joe slurped his tea. Fernie lifted the animal out.

"One of Storey's," said Joe. "She's a workdog, but she's too small."

"Oh," said Nora. She stared at the dog.

"Jim Cates said you wanted a dog, or liked dogs, or something. But we thought—well, Joe thought—even if you hate her," Fernie held the dog's back legs up and peered underneath, "yes, her, if you don't like her, that's fine, Ded Slough would probably take her."

Nora had her hand clamped atop her mouth. She shook her head. This, this—these two men holding a puppy out to her—she was close to an edge, here. This feeling was an animal itself, caught in a trap inside her chest. It gnawed at its own little limb.

"She's going to cry," said Fernie, alarmed. "Take it back," and he shoved the puppy into Joe's arms. Joe put his mug down, carefully, on the table, and cradled the dog in his arms. She liked Joe. She licked his face.

Nora held her arms out and Joe handed the dog to her. The puppy looked up at Nora but could not see through the mask of her own ears, which had fallen forward onto her impossibly small face. Nora lifted them and stroked them back. "Hello," she said again. The paws paddled for footholds on Nora's chest.

Fernie had kept the puppy warm and dry inside the blanket. Nora put her nose into the dog's fur. She smelled like a dog, exactly like a dog, just the way a dog should smell. Nora made a sound and the Gallos couldn't tell if it was laughing or crying, so they stood uncomfortably and waited until she looked up again. And her eyes were wet, but she was smiling, and she did not look sad, or mad at them.

"Thank you so much," she said.

"Fernie," said Joe, "is that Norabones smiling?"

"No," said Fernie, "I don't think it could be. Impossible."

The puppy chewed on Nora's fingers. Her teeth were like tiny needles, sharp and strong.

Later, Fernie had gone upstairs to change and sleep, and Joe, exhausted but dry, held the puppy in his arms by the fire. Paul had come downstairs to help carry the bodies downstairs and, afterwards, in a rare show of sociability, he'd sat by Joe and occasionally reached out and stroked one of the dog's small silken ears. In the cellar, Nora and Jules pulled the three bodies up onto tables. Salderman peeked his head inside the room.

"Would you mind dismembering a few, oh, these old ones?" Salderman asked them. He gestured to two elderly bodies that they had studied for the past week. "Just take the arms and legs, Jules, if you could saw the heads free? We can send out the boys tomorrow night and then we'll be tidy."

Nora wanted to be back upstairs, watching the tiny eyes flutter and the tiny chest rise and fall, and sitting by the fire with Joe and Paul. But she followed Jules to lay the bodies spread-eagled on the floor.

"The boys told me they brought you a dog," the doctor said, from the doorway.

"Yes," she said, "but don't worry. She'll sleep outside when it's warm and I'll talk to Lily and Mug. It won't be trouble."

"Dogs are a danger," said Salderman, "be careful it doesn't bite you on your fingers. No. You need your fingers."

"It's a puppy, doctor," said Jules. He smiled at Nora.

"I'll be careful," said Nora, "don't worry."

"Maulings, Eleanor, happen with no warning at all. At all! Are you going to call it something, a name?"

"Don't call me that. She needs one. I thought about calling it after Joey or Fern, because they gave her to me, but I can't name it after just one."

"No, no. Yes, that wouldn't be fair. And, yes, we have a Joe, and we have a Fernie already. Enough."

"And it's a girl," said Jules. "The dog."

"My mother liked names from the Bible."

"Ruth. Delilah! Eve. Oh, Eve is a nice name, what about Eve, Nora?"

"But I don't know. I haven't really decided. This saw is very dull," said Nora.

Jules knelt by the first body and used a cleaver to begin separating the arm from its shoulder.

"You know," he said to Nora, "I'm from Philadelphia, and the name Philadelphia means *The City of Brotherly Love*."

"Is that true?"

Salderman frowned and nodded.

"You could call her Phila, like Fee-La," Jules pronounced carefully, "when you don't want to call out her whole name."

"I don't mind that," said Nora. "That's actually nice." She squatted down and began to saw at a pelvic joint.

Chapter XVIII.
Chilling

In Chilling, at half past ten o'clock in the morning of the last day of April, three boys stood on Agnes Slough's doorstep. It was a cool morning and the clouds were thin, ribbon-like spirals low in the sky. One boy, the tallest, knocked on the door with his fist; Jim Cates answered, eating. He had sliced a biscuit in half and slid a thick piece of ham inside, then poured honey over the top. His hands were sticky and when he opened the door, he felt the honey on his hand and on the door handle. He would be reprimanded, later, by Agnes, unless he remembered to clean it off.

Daniel, Gervey, and Romer were Prudence's sons. Gervey asked Jim if he wanted to come with them, to play in the forest. Daniel, the oldest, grabbed the biscuit from Jim's hand and took a bite. It was too sweet for him, and so he handed to the young Romer, who ate it quickly and then bent down and wiped his sticky hands on the grass. The four boys half-ran, half-walked across Dedlock's north field, across the road, and into the woods. Gervey, the tallest with the longest limbs, reached up and clutched handfuls of leaves from the trees as the boys passed underneath. He threw them at Romer.

In a small clearing, Daniel tugged a glass jar from his pocket. The jar was small and empty. He placed it in the center of the clearing and the boys scattered in different directions, each one disappearing into the trees. They dug shallow holes in the dirt, overturned heavy fallen branches, lifted rocks, and slid their hands underneath blankets of needles and old, dead leaves. When they found something large and living, anything with many eyes, anything dark and winged, they clasped it in their palms and ran back to the jar, where they dumped the insect inside and covered the jar with a heavy, flat stone. Romer, tiny and with dark, unkempt hair, fell to his knees by a fallen tree trunk and dug for bugs until he had in his hand a massive, repulsive, many-legged creature. He yelped and brought it to the jar. There were already lots of legs and eyes and bodies, inside, and so he lay down on his belly, crossed his arms by the jar, and set his chin on his forearms. Then Daniel came, and assumed the same position, across from Romer. Then Jim came and lay down to watch the jar, and finally Gervey came and arranged his long limbs on the ground. Their heads close enough almost to touch, they watched the jar. This was a game, their favorite game, watching the insects fight, and kill each other inside this small glass jar.

It was cool underneath the trees. The boys lay on the ground and the moisture of the leaves seeped into their clothes and they felt comfortable. None of them spoke, or even looked at one another. Their eyes tracked the movements of the little disasters occurring inside the jar, and did not look through the glass to the absorbed faces beyond.

"They were looking for someone dead in the pond," said Romer.

"It was a girl," said Daniel, "but they didn't find her."

Jim did not answer.

"They looked on the beach, too," said Gervey. "Jeff Dial's wife fell off a cliff and was drowned."

"Look," said Romer.

"Shh," said two of the other boys.

A black and blue iridescent beetle, huge and with massive, metallic wings, had climbed to the top of the small heap of insects. Underneath it was a spider. Romer had found and captured the spider; it had a bulbous brown belly and twitchy legs that poked and paddled furiously.

"The spider is going to win," said Jim. "The spider is going to kill everything."

"Shh."

"Don't tell me to be quiet."

Gervey looked at Daniel and Daniel looked at Gervey.

"Just be quiet," said Daniel. "We want to watch."

Jim pulled himself to his knees and sat back on his heels. "Don't tell me what to do," he said.

"Come on," said Gervey. He resettled his chin on his hands. "Look."

Jim stood up. The boys ignored him and kept watched the jar. The beetle had fallen and was now pressed hard against the glass. It wriggled and trembled.

"Did they find the dead bodies?" asked Jim. The boys did not look up.

"I see lots of real ones," he said. "Lots of real dead bodies."

The boys ignored him. Jim bent down, lifted the jar and in one motion hurled the jar into the trunk of a wide elm tree. The jar shattered and the insects, both the living and the ones that had died already, fell to the ground. The fortunate ones regained the dirt and leaves, and disappeared.

For a moment, everything was still, and the forest was cool, and the boys were in the shade of the trees.

Then Daniel sighed and Gervey dropped his forehead to his hands.

"Let's go," said Daniel. The brothers stood up and brushed their clothes with their hands. They disappeared together into the forest, towards a place they knew which had a huge uprooted and over-turned tree, one of such size and shape that it could play a fort or ship or mountain.

Jim watched them go. He looked up, where the green leaves were held in place by gray, sullen branches, branches that seemed to him like iron rods holding the brilliant blues and green of stained glass in place on windows he had seen . . . He wished he had another glass jar, filled with animals, to throw against a tree, and another and anoth-er. He lay on his back in the clearing and glowered at the branches, squinted at the sky, and waited until he could feel the insects around him, in the ground, emerge and begin to crawl on his skin. And then he picked them off, one by one, softly at first, before crushing them between his fingers.

Chapter XIX.
Satus House

"What are you doing," said Nora. "Where are you going?"

Fernie was sitting at the kitchen table, tapping the table leg with his wooden leg, like a metronome.

"We're going dumping," said Joe. "Get the body parts out of the house."

Lily handed Joe a small square package.

"Bread and onions and ham," she said.

"Thank you, Lily," he said. She turned around and disappeared into the larder.

"Could you possibly take Phila with you?" asked Nora. "Salderman and I are going to do some work in the Collection and it'll take the whole night."

"We can't take a dog scattering," said Fernie. He smiled. "She'll eat everything we try to leave. No one'll believe in Captain Murderer if the evidence is all in your dog's belly."

"No, that's fine," said Joe. "We'll tie her to a rope and it'll be fine."

From the larder came the sound of shattering glass.

"Lily?" called Joe. "Are you all good?"

Mug's daughter Lily was a quiet girl; her eyes were continually fixed upon the floor and she had a habit of sliding sideways through doorways, as though she were trying to escape the notice of the doorframe. Often, too, she stood against the doorframe, neither in the room or out, leaning her back against the wood and clutching the frame with her two hands.

Lily's mother had hair the color of a sunset, but Lily had inherited someone else's coloring. As a child she had stared at herself in mirrors, trying to find her mother. But her hair and eyes were neither blond nor brown nor auburn, but some shade in between, like no one she knew or had seen. Mug was a haggard but fine-boned woman; she had long eyelashes and elegant hands. Lily was very, very large. Her neck was cowled in fat. Her belly was enormous; the inside of her thighs were always red and stinging. She did not like to walk, because walking hurt so badly.

She was fat because she ate in secret. She would have stolen down the stairs in the middle of the night to eat, but Satus was alive with comings and goings in the middle of the night. Her secret time was right around dawn, when most of the doctors had gone to sleep and before anyone else had woken. Her safe place, her eating place, was the larder. It was close and narrow and had a door that she could bar.

Almost every early morning, she filled a basket with bread, with jam, with unfinished cakes and cold meat. She would feel so excited that the ten seconds it took to cross the kitchen floor to the corner of the larder, the five seconds it took to close and lock the door, these seconds felt interminable and her heart beat furiously throughout. Her forehead beaded with anticipatory sweat. But then! Then she sat down with her back against the wall and she ate steadily, efficiently but not fast, tasting, tasting, tasting and swallowing. It was bliss. And though she felt hurried, because people would wake up soon and she needed to finish before she was caught, she didn't forget to enjoy the feel of every mouthful on her tongue and against her teeth.

Lily was happy when she ate. She filled herself until she could barely exhale short little puffs of breath, until her stomach cramped and forced her to double over. The food filled her stomach, pushed down and piled up, and then came up, pushed at the bottom of her throat. Her heart panicked and beat more quickly. Her breath came in short little puffs. It was very difficult to stand up and to walk. Alone, in this short time, she could put away enough food to feed someone as large as Joey Gallo for two days. It was, however, an exhausting routine and she did not like her compulsion to repeat it. She felt very tired, all of the time.

"Lily?" Joe called again.

"Go check," said Fernie, and Joe went into the larder. The wood of the floor was covered with gleams of glass and black globby jelly.

"Cut yourself, Lily?"

Lily shook her head and took a towel from her waistband. Joe squatted and began to pick up the shards.

"Thank you," said Lily.

"Ah, I don't mind."

"I must have hit it by accident."

Joe found a glob of glassless jelly and stuck his pinkie finger into it.

"It's good, anyway," he said.

"Thank you," said Lily.

133

"You made this?"

"Last summer."

"What is it?"

"It's blackberry."

"Well, it's very good."

"I'm really glad you like it. I like it, too, but I really like that you think it's good."

"Next time, you'll have to break something with cherries in it." Joe laughed.

"You like cherries."

"My favorite. I think I got all the big pieces," said Joe, "Do you see any more?"

Lily stood up with difficulty and looked around the larder. Joe piled the glass on a shelf.

"Did you check under the shelves, there?" she asked.

"I did," said Joe. "You want any help with that?"

"It's fine," said Lily, "Thank you." She pulled a rag from her waistband, struggled down to her knees again, and wiped at the mess.

When Joe returned to the kitchen Nora was sitting at the table with Fernie. Not across from him, but beside him. The room was quiet. Fernie was no longer tapping his wooden leg against the wooden leg of the table. Joe looked at them.

"Are you ready to go?" he asked his brother.

"Let's get something to tie the dog," said Fernie, and stood up.

Later, ducking low branches in the forest, Phila was straining and pulling against the rope that tethered her to Joe's hand.

"This dog is strong," said Joe. "You are a strong girl, Phila-deela."

"Was Lily alright?" Fernie asked.

"Lily? Yeah. Yeah, she's fine. Broke a jar."

"Why do you think she's so big?"

"Eats a lot, probably. She's in the kitchen all day."

"No. She can't be hungry all day. Why would you eat that much and get fat if you weren't even hungry?"

"You're always hungry."

"True, but you say to me, Fern you can go eat or go for a swim, and it's beautiful outside, I'd go swim every time."

"Well, maybe you should take Lily for a swim."

Fernie laughed. "No."

"I'm sure she'd like that a lot. Probably no one's taken her swimming. She'd be very grateful."

"You take her swimming."

"Ah, maybe I will."

Phila stopped to squat into some ferns. The brothers stopped, too, and Fernie looked at Joe.

"Right," he said. "So, where do you want to start?"

"I don't know," said Joe. "What do we have?"

"We have a couple foots, and three heads but the skin's been taken off and one doesn't have a top. Really bad shape. Like the top's been sawed off. And then arms, and four legs, and then some things I don't know what they are. They're old. But those are small and we could probably just leave them anywhere."

Phila pulled at the rope again and the Gallos began to walk again.

"Let's start in the Travers' field, the back one. And then maybe we can do some on the path to the beach. Where do you want to put the heads, though? I hate heads."

"Let's put them somewhere on the Woodhills," said Fernie. "No kids."

Phila barked and both brothers froze. Then Joe jerked the rope and moved to kneel by her and cover her mouth with his hand.

"No," he whispered to her, "no barking."

"Should have thought of that before you agreed to bring her," said Fernie.

Phila sat and leaned her head into Joe's hand. She nuzzled her nose into his palm.

"We can cut across that way and get to the back of the Travers'," said Joe. He stood up and they walked toward the lowest stars of Orion.

"Joe," said Fernie, "what do you think of Nora?"

"What do you mean?"

"I mean, Nora? What do you think of Nora?"

"She seems fine. Why?"

"I think she's up to something."

"What do you mean? I don't think Nora has any secrets."

"She's odd looking. I see her watching the doctors and then she looks away when she sees them looking back. And she eavesdrops."

"This dog is a beast."

"She's tiny."

"Why are you asking?"

"Because I'm asking."

"And why are you asking?"

"I think you like her more than you should."

"She's a nice person, Fern. You're making up stories."

"Jules and Paul says when they're alone with her she asks them questions. Like she's trying to find out something. You don't see girls with no hair, and she's too ugly. You can see the purple lines in her arm, like it was just her skin and then her insides, right there. I think it was anyone else, it'd be disgusting, like a skeleton puttied over."

"That's gross," said Joe.

"That's my point," said Fernie.

"You are her friend," said Joe. "I've seen you two get on."

"I know. I like her. She was happy about the dog. You can talk to her, because she is easy to talk to, but there's something not right."

"I don't know," said Joe. "She's had a loss. She almost died with them."

"Yeah," said Fernie, thoughtfully.

Joe sighed. "I like Nora. I know you like her and Jules likes her and even Paul likes her, and Paul doesn't like anyone. Everyone is fine with Nora."

"I know."

"Salderman likes her."

"Yeah," said Fernie, "I'm going to toss this head and this arm over the fence, okay?"

"Okay. No, do both arms."

Fernie braced his wooden leg in the soft earth by the Travers' fence post, and hurled the head into the sky as though there were something he meant to hit. Phila barked, and tried, against Joe's strong arm, to chase.

In the Collection Room, Nora and Salderman worked almost the entire night. A colleague from Germany had sent a crate of new specimen for Salderman to inspect and study. They had unpacked the crate, spread the contents across the floor of the room and then, slowly, stooping, walked among each bundle to catalogue what they'd received. Differently sized eyeballs of various species bobbed in alcohol solutions; large jars, the size of Phila, were necessary for some of the larger samples.

The real beauty, Salderman had told Nora, does not exist absolutely, or objectively. The thing that is beautiful awaits the singular and unique perception that will, that *can*, identify it as such. And so there is a link, a brotherhood between beauty and genius. Genius will perceive beauty where none has ever been claimed. There is in all things a kind of order; as the complexity of this order increases, so fewer and fewer can make sense of it. The work of the mind is to translate this order to the world: to present the world with its own plain and working beauty.

"My dog," Nora had said, "is beautiful."

"Yes yes yes," said Salderman. "You think that probably because your dog loves you. But just in case, you keep the dogstick around you. Beauty can be vicious! Yes. Terrible stuff."

Back at Satus again, Joe and Fernie let Phila off the rope. Joe opened the door to Nora's room so that the dog could go in to sleep on the bed.

"Hey," Nora said. She could feel the puppy's weight on her chest. Two little prodding, kneading paws under her collarbone.

"Hey, you are home safe," said Nora, and she lifted her head from the pillow. Phila smelled like pine sap and dog hair; she licked Nora's face maniacally, as if she were cleaning it of something delicious.

"Hello, Fee, hello, hello," Nora whispered. "Were you good? Were you a good girl?" Phila's face had much more white in it than black; a thick stripe of white ran between her eyes. Nora ran a fingertip down the line. Even the fur on Phila's face was soft, not hard and sharp like the old dogs they'd had on the farm. There was nothing hard about Phila.

Philadelphia settled and lay like a sphinx atop Nora's chest. "You're going to sleep there?" said Nora. It should have been uncomfortable, but it wasn't. The weight on her ribcage and her lungs was a nice weight, comfortable, secure. Like being swaddled.

"They know something, girl. They do. We'll find it. Don't worry! We will. Are you sleepy?"

The dog's eyes slitted and opened, again and again, watching Nora's face. And Nora's eyes, too, closed, and reopened to look again at her dog, and then closed, opened again, again, until finally, exhausted from looking at one another, they fell asleep.

137

Chapter XX.
The Narrative of the Graveyard

Mostly they came on Sunday mornings or Sunday afternoons, before or after filing into the white church and telling the stories they told each other in that place.

From the west side of the village came the younger Sloughs, Agnes and Dedlock, holding the baby in their arms . . . later, in the spring and in the summer, visiting that same child. From the village, too, Mr. and Mrs. Peabody, Octavius and Catherine, Octavius to kneel for ten minutes at the grave of his sister and the nephews he had not known, Catherine to stand behind him imperiously and pray. She prayed so hard! She was a white-knuckle prayer; she scrunched her nose and pursed her lips. A violent prayer, it must have been.

Also from the east came the Thomas Cockermouths, who lost their daughter-in-law, and the Woodhills, a graying brittle old couple and their thin-cheeked dry-lipped offspring. The buff and hearty Hales walked twenty miles on a normal day and their perpetual windburn paraded through the churchyard every Monday morning, as if to mock the end they vigorously sought to avoid. There came, too, Mr. Cole Travers and Mr. Samuel Travers (brothers who were years later found drowned together in the Pirrips' little pond), the Cottons with their four beautiful daughters (all of them stone deaf), the brothers Gallo (who killed their father), the children Nelson (two boys and two girls), the parents of Clean Parker (who brought a brush and scoured Clean's stone but not his wife's . . . poor Providence Parker who died of sorrow). Also, the Benners, the thousands of them it seemed, all with the same thin face and the same squinty inquiring eyes, the Lockes and the Lungworts, and the Lungworts' cousins the Hornbeams. In the summer the Finches came, with their littlest one in bare feet because he couldn't abide by shoes, forever wriggling out of his coat and pants because he couldn't abide by clothes. Porter Downey, alone and walking through the stones though he himself had no family, having arrived one day from Salem alone and without a crust of bread or a bag of clothes, just walked and walked, he did, through the rows with his hands in his pockets. Cordelia and Aurelia Ridley, elderly spinster half-sisters who had buried their husbands on the same day, through a strange coincidence or (as rumor had it) wicked design. Joy Beddington, who was stolen, as a baby, by a tribe of Natives and raised as one of them until some tragedy of which she never spoke killed them all off, and she arrived in Chilling a somber teenager dressed in animal skin. With the people of the town, she didn't speak much, but when she sat in the graveyard on the stone bench while everyone else was in church, she sang in another language.

Alice Moore, whose grandmother Felicity was hanged in Chilling's sole public hanging (and later exonerated and reburied in the churchyard). Alice visited the grave every single day and told her gran the village gossip—and it was from, in fact, Alice's mouth that I learned of the doings of Captain Murderer, and of the stories about the doctor and poet up at Satus House, and that Joseph Gallo the Elder had been a drunk and a brute, and of the Pirrips falling ill with an epidemic that Philip had brought back with him from somewhere, people said.

There was Anne Coldwell, who came with the young Christian Tripp, whom she had taught to read and write and who was devoted to her; he held her hand and they walked through the graveyard together, reading the stones. She was beginning to teach him Latin, at the beginning of that summer. Of course the Reverend Brewer, who used to come out during the morning hours wrapped up against the cold. It could be quite cold, in the dawn, even in the summer months. He recited and practiced his sermons and this is how I learned many stories and heard many tales that Chilling told one another. Eliza Bettet, who was terrible pockmarked from an illness and who dipped her head so that no one could see her face, she came on sunny days to sit in the churchyard. She didn't meet anyone or talk to herself, she only sat. It was the only place, I think, where she could loosen her bonnet and lift her face to the sun without shame, or fear of reaction against her face. There were the child-twins Scout and About, real names unknown because they were only called in one breath, Scoutabout! who came to the graveyard playing always at some new game or another which usually I could never make sense of. They threw a great deal of mud around the place, and one of them—I don't know which—ate a good deal of grass and flowers and made itself sick. Then there was the man who had all those dogs, and gave them out to the villagers. The pups roamed free and stood up on the platforms and wandered into houses. Steven Storey. He would hurry into the churchyard and lock his dogs outside the gate and go for a moment's dogless walk, and they would wait for him lying in the road and sunning themselves, and one always up and whining for him, holding out a stick for him if only he would come out.

There were the Osbornes and the Osgoods, who lived along the east side of the main road and on the west, the Farmers, and the Flaggs.

And of course there was that heavy-footed woman with the dark bonnet, who came at least once every month at dusk, and whose name I must have not known, because she was never addressed by any man or woman, nor did she speak, nor did she pause before any stone in particular.

But she did come, named or not, and so did they all; living people persist on being, whether they are known to others or not. It is different when you are dead; the graveyard knows you most intimately. Life, I suppose, has that to speak for it: you have your privacy. No one may know you, should you choose it. No one knew them, perhaps, not really. But they were the people who came to the churchyard that year.

Chapter XXI.
Satus House

Nora did not like to begin. There was so much work to do, now, that Nora put an end to her pre-dawn walks to the sea. She spent hours in the library, combing through Salderman's books and, when she found them, his old journals. Preferring to be alone, now more fervently, Nora got her work in the cellars done very early. It was difficult to wake up before anyone else. Mornings, even now, were still cold up on the hill and Nora often kicked her quilt from the bed as she dreamed. Her body would wake shivering and tired, and often her neck was sore from craning over bodies. The muscles of her thighs and calves were tight and taut from standing over the corpses. So she would pull her blankets on top of her again, and Philadelphia would cuddle into her side, and Nora would lie spread-eagled under her quilt for a silent moment, taking her last little bit of pleasure in the bed and puppy and warmth and her own delicious inactivity. Then, in one fast movement, she jumped from her bed and touched her toes twice. Philadelphia would whine until Nora lifted her from the bed to the floor. After she'd dressed, Nora carried the puppy down the staircase. In the pre-dawn kitchen, she would stand and shiver, wrapped in a blanket, and watch the stars diminish through the grimy window. She would open the back door, feel the sudden salt wind-rush from the sea, and Phila would race madly outside. Nora found the parcel of scraps Mug had put aside for the dog's breakfast, and left the bowl outside the door. She stirred the fire, boiled water, brewed tea, and carried a steaming cup of it downstairs to the cellar.

Even then Nora did not like to begin. Sometimes she walked from room to room, blowing the heat from the mug, her blanket-cloak trailing behind her like a bridal train. The instruments were cold to touch, and her hands were so warm on the mug. To work she would have to throw off the warmth of the blanket, too, and wrestle herself into the cold boxy smock stained with pus and blood and excrement.

She drank her tea very slowly. Then, by degrees, she would wean herself from her blanket and mug, slipping the cloak down and off her head, where she kept it like a hood, then off her shoulders, and

141

finally leaving the mug on the edge of the table and throwing her blanket off to the side. She pulled on her smock and every single day felt the temptation to take it off again immediately, to run upstairs as quick as she could and dive under the bedding—probably still warm from her body—and sleep, sleep until midmorning, then wake lazily and eat a large breakfast of ham and coffee and toast. But instead, she tied herself into her smock, lit her lantern, and began to work.

And, once begun, she could never recall why it had taken her so long to begin at all! Here was her life! Waiting inside these bodies, which she alone could explore and make sense of, here was everything she could ever hope to learn and understand. Wholly formed alien worlds met her scalpel. She moved from idea to idea: tracing an artery down the arm, peeling layers of muscle away from each other like onionskin, staring for great lengths of time at the connection of a jaw-bone. The comfort of her body, hours ago, warm and comfortable in its bed, warm and nourished by her tea, these comforts were nothing compared to the fascinating discomfort of work. In the cellar she was never sure, never still, never soft, and yet she had never been so happy than when she stood freezing and hunched before a corpse, opening men and women alike, taking apart a great machine. There was an immensity to her task. She became lost inside of it.

Upstairs, mid-morning, Mug was tying on her apron. Lily measured the flour out into piggins.

"Come bring me that seat, my love," Mug said. The girl dragged a chair across the kitchen floor and the sound thudded down below to the cellar where, though deadened by the layers of wood and stone and brick, it startled Salderman. He dropped a glass jar onto the stones. Tiny shimmering fragments struck Nora's ankles gently, like raindrops.

"Stop throwing things," Nora said. She turned and looked at the shards.

"Dropped. I thought it was the dog. Well. I would. Instinctive move, Nora. I'm so sorry. No harm?"

"No."

"Well, then."

"But one day there will be harm, and then you'll have to do this cleaning up and all the nasty jobs yourself." She walked to the table. "What are you looking at?" she asked.

"Ah," said Salderman, "Something very special, very special. Can you see?"

Nora went round so that she stood across the table from the doctor.

"You've opened that man wide," she said, and then, struck by a new idea, she asked: "Were you the one to cut off Fernie's leg, when he was little?"

Salderman looked up at her. "Of course," he said, and then nodded toward the body's opened chest.

"What's special?" asked Nora.

He had removed the skin and folded it back neatly to the body's sides, where two flaps lay neatly like low red wings. The chest was a cavern. Salderman had scraped away the fat, and Jules had carried away the lungs, kidneys, stomach; Nora had just finished piling the intestines into a large bucket. There was little inside but the bones and the heart.

"When you amputated it, it was because you had to, right?"

"Of course."

"Because I think it might be interesting to practice things, sometimes, to experiment. I bet doctors might want to do that."

"Look," said Salderman, "right here." He used his scalpel to point. Connecting the two parallel sets of ribs, the long perpendicular bone looked to Nora like the sheath of a sword. At the bottom, there was a smooth circular hole, exactly as though an insect had bored through the bone.

"The hole?" she asked.

"The hole," agreed Salderman. He reached inside and put the tip of his pinkie finger inside.

"That's not right, is it? That's how he died, then? For the sake of a wee hole?"

"No," said Salderman, "this man was trampled by a horse."

"It looks like when the beetles eat through the leaves. Are there . . . well, that's a scary thought. Are there beetles within us, eating our bones?"

Salderman removed his finger from the body's sternum and tucked a hank of hair behind his ear.

"Beetles . . . no, I do not think we have beetles. But, you know, Nora, really, we do not know. We can think of life in one of two ways, I think. We can think to ourselves that all the world's life is essentially the same, and we can look at the bodies of organisms to ask ourselves, where did we begin to be different?"

"Like this hole. How did this man get this hole, if no other bodies have one just there?"

"Exactly, precisely. Or we can think this, a second way of thinking: that everything living thing is, at the beginning of its life, a radically different and unique new creation, and then, as it grows, it begins to be more and more alike to something else, gradually taking its place in the world as a certain accepted type of thing. So we look to the bodies of the things to see, where have we become similar? Where is the evidence of our inability to fit? Our last traces of aberration?"

Salderman's hair had come loose again and hung in front of his face like a curtain.

"Aberration?" asked Nora.

"Strangeness."

Nora reached inside the body and put her finger to the hole, as Salderman had done. "One," she said, "that we are essentially the same and become different. Two, that we are essentially different and come to be all the same. I have been reading some of your old journals, did you know that?"

"This little hole, this tiny hole . . . it was made before this man was even a tiny baby. He had his hole here before he could talk, or walk. And who knows—oh, who knows, what it meant to him, how it changed his life. And that he never knew it. Something so important, basic. A hole in your bones, and you have no idea, and what it might be causing you daily! So what we become in the womb, Nora, this is who we are! In the womb, work begins early and goes late: something is making you. At which point are you made? At which point?" Salderman shook his head. "Everything is a mystery, Nora, but nothing more than ourselves."

"They say that in church," said Nora, "When I went to church."

"Where's that dog?" asked Salderman. He looked around the room. "Give me the stick."

"Fernie's with her," said Nora. "He's teaching her to swim."

"Still, the stick, yes?"

"Don't hit my dog, Salderman."

"No, no, right. A good dog, if I never see it."

"You know," Nora said, "I remember people talking, years ago, when Eliza Bettet came through an illness. It killed her husband, and her two little girls. Eliza was the only one who became healthy again, and people—well, my aunt, and uncle, and my mothers' friends, they

144

said it was because Eliza had struck a bargain with the Devil. The bargain being that he'd give her a life again. Make her better. And so in return, she'd given her heart and her soul to him and renounced God. They said that about her."

"Do you believe that?" asked Salderman.

Nora was quiet. Salderman walked to the end of the table and wiped his hands with a rag Nora had left there. In the hallway, outside, he could hear the whines of Philadelphia as she went from room to room, looking for Nora. They had come back early; Fernie must have let her down to the cellar.

"I think . . ." she began. She heard Phila, too; she whistled and the dog's footsteps turned loud and running. "I think that no, she was not evil. But I think that we have more to do with illnesses than we think we do, or I thought we did. Did you know," she said, as Phila came into the room, "that you can make someone ill, on purpose? If you know someone who is sick, and you take something of theirs, you might be able to make someone else sick, too?"

"That is true, sometimes, of course."

"I remember lying there sick, when there were things that were so terrible." Nora shook her head. "There were times when some parts of my body hurt so badly. I couldn't breathe sometimes. Every moment lasted so, so long. Somehow you have to bear the sort of pain that is impossible to bear. I couldn't. I couldn't bear it but I couldn't just . . . die. And I know, absolutely, I would have . . . if I could have, I would have given it all to the Devil. I would have made that bargain and I wouldn't even have thought two times about it. I was afraid to die but I also didn't want to be alive and feeling so much pain. I know it is evil. But the pain was so bad that if my brothers had been alive, I'd have traded them. I would have given them to the Devil, just so I could make it stop."

"Ah," said Salderman, "well." He had crept backwards to the wall, and hung there, watching Phila settle peacefully at Nora's feet. He worried the rag between his hands. "Sick people are odd. You were very, very sick. Yes."

"I feel like I did it without knowing," said Nora. She crouched down and began to scratch behind Phila's ears. "I traded something about me for my life. When I woke up that day and I was, not well, but I knew I would be better, that I was alive—and I put my hand up. My hair was gone and I knew for sure that the Devil had taken it, so that I would remember my bargain. That he had taken my hair as a symbol of my soul, and that my soul was his."

"But now you know," said Salderman, "that I was the one who cut your hair, and it was not the Devil. Look, is it safe to move? Is that dog asleep? I certainly didn't take your soul."

"But it hasn't grown back. And I know that it won't. It's been too long. People say that God uses us as instruments of His will," said Nora. "What stops the Devil, then, from using you? Or me?"

Salderman didn't answer. He watched through the mask of his hair.

"Yes," said Nora, "it's safe to move." She bent and kissed Phila's little head.

"THE DOG," shouted Jules' voice from the hall, "IS NOT ALLOWED IN THE CELLAR."

Nora smiled.

Chapter XXII.
Satus House

The first week of May was hot. The sun was hot from the very moment it appeared and there was no wind. The moon rose hot and the stars burned hot. No use, Salderman said, getting any new bodies; the corpses would only spoil and stink. Nevertheless, the house was too settled into its nocturnal rhythm and so the Gallos and Nora still woke and wandered at night. Nora discovered her favorite part of Satus House during this lethargic week in May. She loved the kitchen floor at nighttime. At home, the Pirrips had wooden floorboards in the kitchen, and dirt floor in the barn and in the boys' room. She had never seen such a beautiful floor: perfectly laid bricks, worn just enough to look smooth and even, worn down at their edges so that in the candlelight the bricks looked soft. When the house had gone very quiet, Nora would choose a book from Salderman's library and carry it into the kitchen. If there was any mess left over from dinner, she would help Mug to clean, and then she would bring a taper to the table and read. Sometimes Joe or Fernie would come in. "You should sit in the chair by the fireplace," Joe would say. "It's more comfortable." But Nora liked the table. She liked the broad expanse of the wood, the circle of light from the candle, the strictness with which she held her spine, and she liked to look up and see the smooth, soft bricks.

Those nights she found deeply soothing. Her mind, she realized when she sat down at the table, had been irascible and restless since she had woken up in her old bed on the Pirrip farm. She had been wrangling with an anger that took time to develop and mature. The marrow inside her bones had been replaced with glutinous resentment and stinging, acidic restlessness. Her skin had been flayed and replaced with a shroud of distrust, and it prickled when she was with the living, who she knew, from experience, could at any moment leave, or die.

But alone, at night, with a single candle and the soft brick floor, Nora felt calm. She did not feel lonely. She did not feel sad. The black cap that she kept always tight against her skull sat discarded on the bench beside her. Nora was surprised to find that, left alone in the dark, her trouble began to smooth itself out, to unclench the fist of despair that had begun curling inside her the day her mother left the house and abandoned her. Her finger moved under the lines of dense medical text slowly, but steadily and surely; her entire mind was absorbed by the descriptions and explanations there. But the moment she heard a footstep, the moment she saw a face or heard a voice—be it Salderman or Joe or Fernie or Lily—the fist clenched again and she shoved the black cap again against her head.

The first Friday in May had been so warm and humid that no one had been able to sleep; Nora tried to rest but she soaked her bed in sweat and so instead sat awake in the dark library all day long. At dinner, everyone was exhausted and hot and miserable and made an excuse to leave the table. Fernie was still picking over his food; Nora hadn't eaten anything. "Too hot to eat," she had said. She was barefoot. She reached out a toe and rubbed Phila's belly. Lily and her mother were kneading dough for tomorrow's bread and the room smelled of yeast.

"Have you seen Joe?" asked Salderman.

"He's upstairs, I think," said Fernie. "He didn't come to dinner." He dipped his fingers into his water and flicked drops onto his face.

The dog rolled over on her back and Nora moved from the chair to the floor. She sat next to Phila's face and scratched her neck.

Salderman tucked a piece of hair behind his ear and wandered away down the hallway.

"It's dark enough. Let's go to the ocean," said Fernie. He pushed away his bowl and Nora pulled herself up from the floor. They left the kitchen without speaking. Phila, suddenly awake and excited, bounded and raced ahead of them.

A while later, Joe came in and picked up Fernie's bowl.

"I'm finishing this, Mugger," he said. He stood, eating, and watching the two women shape the dough into oblong shapes.

"Where's Nora?" he asked.

Lily turned to him. Her hands were floury and sticky with brown dough; she hid them behind her back.

"She and your brother went to the sea," she said. She kept her eyes down. Her chin pressed into the fat of her neck and made a cowl of it. "Took the dog."

Joe stood quietly for a moment. Then he replaced the spoon in the bowl. He drained Fernie's water and left the kitchen.

148

At the beach, Philadelphia barked madly at the surf. She waded in and raced out again.

Fernie and Nora sat with their backs against a long flat stone. It was too dark for them to see each other, but they felt the heat from the rock and the heat coming from their own overheated bodies. It was cooler here, on the beach, than it had been at Satus. The breeze from the ocean could even chill. Nora dug her heels into the sand and wriggled her toes.

Ahead of them, flashes of white appeared and played in the dome of darkness. The fleeting white crests of waves burst and disappeared; Philadelphia's white legs and chest danced into the black of the water and retreated again. Nora smiled at her dog's gleeful distrust of the tide.

"You know how I lost the leg, right?" Fernie asked.

"I know that it was wounded, and infected, and Salderman took it off."

"Yes. That's right."

"Is there more?"

"Yes," said Fernie.

They didn't look at each other. Nora felt suddenly uncomfortable against the rock, but she didn't move.

"Your dog is eating seaweed," said Fernie.

"She'll live," said Nora.

"It was an accident. My father's knife slipped. And he didn't mean to, but he sliced through the back of knee and down my leg. I don't remember it very well but I remember feeling sick and holding onto my mother's hand, and that her hand kept slipping out of mine."

They sat there and let the words get swallowed by the waves. There was no moon. There were few stars: it was a cloudy night. A few dim constellations fought through, but it was dark enough for Nora to feel safe and unwatched. She put a hand to her head and felt the bristliness of her hair under her cap. Fernie took her hand and put it back down on the sand.

"Take it off, if it bothers you," he said.

"Did you see it? Did they let you look?" asked Nora.

"I don't remember. I remember seeing my father crying, which scared me. And being put in my parents' bed, and him lying beside me and crying and touching my hair. The bed felt really clean and nice. And I was numb, or something. I felt really heavy. I wasn't in any pain. I felt peaceful and nice. Having my dad there in the bed.

Later it was very bad, my leg, and all. Everything was different after that. My mother never forgave him, or Joe. I was little, but I knew that. But for a minute, you know, it was good. He really loved me."

"Philadelphia," she called. "Too far!"

Phila stopped and watched the three white gulls disappear into the dark. She turned and trotted back up the beach.

"I was the one with the injury. But it was Joe who never forgave my dad. I never blamed him for it."

"But how do you know he didn't do it purposefully?"

"I was there. I saw it was an accident. When the people you love do something bad, but it's an accident, you forgive them."

"Is that true?" asked Nora. "Maybe you forgive them, but it still happened. And you cannot make things unhappen . . . It will always be there."

"But somehow," said Fernie, "it was worse for Joe, and for my dad. They were the ones who took it worst, me losing the leg. He drank, after. Our dad. He beat our mother and he hit Joe, too. One night he hit Ma with an iron poker and she went down and died."

"Oh," said Nora. She turned and looked out to the sea. She had lived in Chilling her whole life. And no one had told her that the blacksmith had killed his wife. "Did you see it happen?" she asked.

"No," said Fernie, "Joe was there, and he had taken me about the head and he covered my eyes with his arm and my ears, too. He was smothering me so that I wouldn't see or hear anything."

"But Joe saw."

"Joe's like . . . he worries about everyone else. He wants everyone happy and comfortable. He wants everything healthy and strong and laughing. He doesn't talk about it with me, and I'm the only one he talks to and he never really talks to me, anyway."

"Do you talk to him?"

"I do sometimes. But I know that he doesn't like it when I say anything about my leg. If I'm feeling . . . it used to make me embarrassed. The way I walked. I couldn't run or play the way I could before. I was just a little kid. But saying anything like that to Joe made him feel worse and so I stopped saying anything."

Nora nodded. "My mother used to get angry at me," she said, "if I ever said anything like that. She screamed at me, once, when I cried. I forget why. Something silly, likely. But I remember crying and going to her. It was a mistake, because she was so angry. She was so angry with me."

Phila approached the two of them, carrying a limp bouquet of seaweed in her mouth.

"You got tired out, then," said Fernie to the dog. He reached out and scratched behind her white ears; Phila lay down at their feet and lowered her chin on her front paws.

Nora reached out and took Fernie's hand. He placed his thumb in the center of her palm and held his fingers on the back of her hand.

"I understand her more now," said Nora. "It made me a hard person, I think."

"What did?"

"The world changes on you, and you aren't ready for it," said Nora. "Like your leg. You have to change after that."

"Do you swim?" Fernie asked.

"I never learned," said Nora, shaking her head. "When I was very little, I was scared of the water."

"Joe's scared of bugs." He closed her hand inside both of his and they sat for a little while, looking out at the sea. Nora could feel every tiny move of his body, so much so that she thought she could feel his heart pump in his chest and his tongue slide to the top of his mouth when he swallowed. She could not feel her own body for her focus on his. But Fernie was calm, and waited. The smell of the seaweed. The dog's soft breath. Fernie rubbed Nora's thin hand between his palms and smelt the salt air.

"Why are you staying at Satus?" he asked.

Nora didn't answer. She tried to relax her spine against the stone behind her. There was more of her, now. She had matter between her bones and the stone. Fat, muscle, food, thought, work, love, all that which cushioned the hard parts of her against the hard parts of the world. Far out to the north, Nora could see the glint of the Water-town lighthouse. It was so far away that it looked like a star. She could not unclench her muscles.

"I'll go back down to the village soon."

"They think you're dead, you know. They dragged the pond. They think you burned up your things and drowned yourself."

"They'll be glad to see me, then."

"You can't blame people for bad things. Bad things happen."

"They do."

"He forged it, you know. Joey. That was part of it," said Fernie.

"He forged what?"

"Joe. He worked with our father. He was supposed to become a blacksmith, too. The fire poker, the one that my dad hit my mother with, that was one that he had made."

"I see," said Nora. "Poor Joe."

"But no one, Nora," Fernie said, "blames Joe. Why would they? He only made it. He didn't know."

Nora's hand, trapped between Fernie's palms, was warm. Ahead of them, in the dark, the tide began to change.

In Chilling gardens, the lettuces blossomed. The air went warm and muggy in the afternoons; thunderstorms swept through the village once a week and felled great branches which boys split apart. Inside Satus House, Nora pulled skin from muscle, pulled maggots feasting on fat, scraped her knife against wet bone, plunged her arm to the elbow into a mushy gut and removed a handful of liver, of spleen, of bulbous tumor; she lay down on the basement stone floor to soothe her aching strained back, and in the evening she washed her hands outside in the garden. She would find someone, Jules or Paul or Salderman himself, and talk to them, gently, asking questions and listening. She collected journals and books and kept them in her room. She read books about ancient techniques to guard against disease, she read books about modern ideas and experiments.

She listened for days and days, and did what she had to do. She imagined encountering her mother, in the Chilling road, and telling her she had found it out, what had killed them all. Georgiana was proud of Nora, and happy. Occasionally Nora faltered. She understood that no matter what she learned here—what had killed them, how they had caught it, or why—she might not be able to tell anyone, or to prove it to anyone. Or she might be all wrong, about everything, and her mother would be disappointed and cruel to her, again. She was forced to shake off these fantasies bodily, like a wet dog drying itself, lest they drown her and immobilize her there, her hands plunged into the trough, the warm day darkening around her, the stars appearing around her like the pricks of needles, her face angular and blank.

Chapter XXIII.
The Sloughs' Home

In the afternoon, Agnes took Bonnie to visit Dedlock in the field where he and Tim Locke's sons were sorting stock. Dedlock wiped his face and met them at the fence. Agnes handed him the baby.

"Jice, it's hot," said Agnes.

"We've had a man by," said Dedlock, taking Bonnie. "Hello, my beautifulest one."

"Who's that?" asked Agnes.

"One of the Wolfeborough tax men," said Dedlock, "He came to see Flagg, too. They're asking more on the land next year and they want to start taking money on our animals, now. Won't say how much, but more."

"Well, the whole state? Or just in Chilling?"

Dedlock probed Bonnie's gums with his finger. "Yes," he said, "good teeth-growing, Bonna," he said. "Very good of you."

"Is this what you were upset about the other day?" said Agnes. "I came looking for you but I couldn't find where you'd gone." Dedlock handed Bonnie back to Agnes and leaned over the fence to kiss them both. He leaned his forehead against Agnes's and let it rest there for a moment.

"I don't know," he said, finally pulling away. "Flagg hasn't heard anything from his cousin in Abbotsville so he's going to tell us when he knows. They'll have to ask Salderman up there for more help."

"Okay." Agnes bounced the baby on her hip. "Anything in the field?"

"Not ours. The Travers kids said they had arms in their upper field."

"My hand to my heart, Dedlock, if we ever get anything in our land, I want to know. You'll tell me. Right the minute you know."

"I would tell you. But nothing, yet."

"She's going to nap," said Agnes, "and I'm going to set the strawberries. Prudence sent us six pounds of pork. And I'll be at the Osgoods', probably, later on."

"The Osgoods," said Dedlock.

"Abbie's having a baby. I told you."

"We're having a meeting day after next, Agnes. You don't need to worry about it. We'll figure it out, if we can."

"It's not a silly ghost," said Agnes. "You all need to recognize it. It's some man and he's doing this."

Dedlock nodded. He kissed his wife's cheek, over the fence. "These are *cows*," he said to Bonnie.

"Cows," repeated Agnes. "Your daddy is taking care of the *cows*."

"Bye," said Dedlock, and Agnes smiled, but she was tightlipped. She and Bonnie made their way across the grass, back to the house.

The fact that Abigail Osgood was pregnant and unmarried was less a cause for concern than the fact that she refused to name the man. Without the name, the families would not be able to sit down together, slice some cheese, lift it to their noses and smell it before smiling at the cheesemaker—Abigail's mother, Lucy—and finally, chewing and swallowing, set a time and place for the wedding. More pregnant brides were made every day.

"She's being unreasonably stubborn," Prudence said to Agnes. "We've all tried to pry the name out of her. The Reverend had a brainstorm and told her that the baby'd be born without hands unless it had a named father. Abbie laughed at him. He took away the other limbs, too, but she knows it's bosh."

"She's not an idiot," Agnes had replied. She was struggling to cut Jim's hair. He was wriggling furiously. "I'll cut your ear off."

Prudence squatted before Jim and smiled at him. Her massive hands grasped his forearms. "You want to keep your ears, child?" she said. She shook him, playfully. "Do you?" Jim laughed.

"Would there be a lot of blood?" he asked.

"Oh, yes."

"Would I die?"

"Maybe."

"Really?"

"I think you would survive," said Prudence.

"What do you want me to do?" Agnes asked Prudence. She squinted at the back of Jim's head.

"Hmm?"

"About Abbie."

"You don't care one way or another, unlike us. Just go and see her for a little check, maybe. She's been sick and maybe you could go on that, just prod her belly a bit. And while you got her there, just slip in a little inquiry or two. And if in between all those distractions, a wee name slips right out between her lips, well—then we can go ahead and set it all up for before the babe comes."

"I can ask her," Jim said. "Maybe she'll tell me because I'm a kid and she won't think I'll say anything."

Agnes sighed and slipped the scissors into her apron pocket. She brushed the back of her brother's neck with her hand, and kissed him on the top of the head. "Go off," she said to him, and he bolted from the straight-backed chair as though it were on fire.

"Will you go?" asked Prudence. She lifted herself to her feet. Agnes put her hands on her hips and looked out the window. Jim was running toward the blueberry bushes. He swung his arms wildly when he ran.

"Yes, yes, yes."

The Osgood house was close and dark because Lucy Osgood felt headachey when there was too much light. She hung heavy, dark-colored curtains and kept them drawn against the daylight.

"I'm afraid of the part where he comes," said Abigail, staring down at her stomach. It was large now; her pregnancy had been a stealthy one and she hadn't herself known until she looked down one day and a small elbow seemed to be pushing out of her left side.

"It's a thing we all do," said Agnes. "I've done it, your mum and sisters have, too. Every single person alive has a mum who's done it."

"But you think I'm too small," said Abigail. She had deeply red hair, not orange but red hair, straight and thick as hay. She wore it in two braids, like a young girl. The pregnancy had sprayed a rash of red pimples on her white chin and forehead.

"Your hips are very slim."

"And so it'll hurt more."

"More doesn't mean anything. More than what, anyway?" Agnes looked at the girl. She was remarkably small, even for someone in her eighth month. "What you have, down there, is like a wee cave. And the exit of the cave isn't big enough for the baby, so the walls of the cave try to suck in, make the way a bit bigger. Your body will do it slowly to try and make it as easy as possible. But there's a limit. You aren't big at all. Sometimes the walls can't go quite big enough, and the babe gets himself stuck on the way."

"And what do you do then?"

"Well, sometimes I reach in and pull him out."

"With your hands?"

"If I can," said Agnes.

"What about if you can't?"

"Sometimes they get stuck the wrong way round," explained Agnes, "and there's not much we can do."

"The baby dies, then."

"Sometimes."

"If he dies inside of me, and you can't get him out, what happens?"

Agnes looked at her.

Abigail nodded and folded her hands atop her belly. "Oh," she said. She leaned her head back onto the headboard of the bed. The picture of her white face and red hair against the oak headboard would have been pretty, save for the expression of fear. Agnes reached over and lightly rubbed her belly.

"Look at him go," said Agnes. "Restless little one lives under there."

"Ah, he's pretty still most of the time. But when he does move . . . wild," said Abigail. She played with the end of her braid; she had the childish habit, when she was worried, of sucking on her hair.

"You'll be fine," said Agnes, "but I think we'd all like to see you married before he comes. Or she."

"I'm so sure it's a boy." Abigail smiled at Agnes. "Certain of it."

"Something wrong, Abbie? Married, is he? Or someone in some way wrong?"

"I don't want to talk about that."

Agnes sighed and stood up. "I don't care much either way," she said. "You'll do what you do. I'll be here when he decides to come, anyway. Maybe another four weeks. More or less."

"I know. He really is coming, isn't he?"

"Of course." Agnes turned and walked across the room. Abbie struggled to pull her dress down over the belly.

"It's so strange. That he's coming, really. As though for a long time I've been watching something walk across a field, coming closer and closer to me, but I could never really understand it . . . that one day, they'd be here. You watch them coming, and you get so caught up in the watching, you begin to think that's all there is. That somehow once they get to you, that'll be the end. No more."

Agnes had her back to the girl; she was washing her hands in the basin.

"I'm not afraid of the pain," Abigail went on. "That's not what

I meant about him coming. I'm scared of the part when he comes. There's no going back in time, I mean. No undoing it. He's coming."

"It's not helpful in any way to be afraid," said Agnes.

"Is it strange," said Abigail, "that sometimes I feel like he's coming to kill me?"

"Who is the father, Abbie?"

Abigail laughed and shook her head at Agnes. "It's not anyone who I can marry," she said.

Agnes sighed, dried her hands, and left the room.

"Watch the nails," said Jim when Agnes arrived home. Dedlock had dropped a pocketful of straight nails and they lay scattered around the entrance of the house. Some had been kicked, by Jim and Prudence, into the kitchen as they had tramped in and out, but most lay like a welcome mat upon the threshold. Hearing her step, Jim had run from the kitchen to meet her.

"Bonnie's sick," he reported, hugging around her middle.

"She's fine," called Prudence. "Jim just wants her to be sick. She sneezed a bit, that's all it was."

Agnes squeezed her brother, took his hand, and led him into the kitchen. Bonnie was awake; she was swaddled and still in her basket, but her eyes were active and alert. Agnes looked her over.

"Perfect baby," she said.

"Sick," said Jim, "pretty sick. I think maybe she has delirium."

"Did she give you the name?"

Agnes tugged off her bonnet, scratched her neck, and shook her head. "No. Something nasty gave me a bite," she said.

"Dedlock's in a state," said Prudence. "Came running in while you were with Abbie, and dropped a thousand things. He said for you to come out and find him as soon as you were back."

Agnes unswaddled Bonnie and lifted her over her shoulder.

"Maybe he found out about the taxes, then," she said. "He sounded worried?"

"He looked worried," said Prudence. "He didn't say anything about taxes, but maybe. The Flaggs could have heard something. I'm off home . . . I'll ask around. All right here?"

Chapter XXIV.
Wolfeborough

In Wolfeborough, at half past ten o'clock in the evening of the last day of May, three men stood on James Herrin's doorstep. It was a cool night with a three-quarter moon. One pounded on the door with his fist. The tax collector answered in his nightdress. The three men pulled James from his home and into the road. James yelled out in protest. They thrust a canvas sack over this head, and half-dragged, half-carried him half a mile into the woods. James screamed for help, but it was as if all of Wolfeborough had fallen into a deep and dreamless sleep. The neighbors' windows were dark.

In the forest, the men pulled the sack from James' head. A dust-cloud of flour rose around his face. Two of the men took hold of his arms and the remaining man stabbed James in the stomach, twice. He fell to his knees, and then sat backward onto his heels. He put the palms of his hands to his belly and looked down at them. The moonlight shone on his palms. The men turned away and returned to town.

It was a cool and pleasant night. The path from Satus to Wolfeborough cut north, through a portion of the forest in which the sound of the river was everywhere, as though when the nighttime came the river took over and became the sky. Over time, the Gallos' feet had flattened a path through the trees. And so tonight the brothers walked the path they had made until they had come out of the forest and the moon had reached its height. Piled at the edge of the forest were four massive stones in the rough shape of a seated man, not arranged by humans but accidentally deposited there, in that resting posture, by some great flood or glacier or stone storm from heaven. For Joe's sharp eyes, there was enough light to see the earthworms in the dirt, and enough light to see, lying at the base of the great Stone Man, the body of the dying tax collector. Fernie's bad eyes could make out a long trail of dark-colored grass that led from the western branch of the forest.

"Joe," asked Fern.

"Help, please," said the man. He looked confused. His brows were knit together. His hands moved like the wings of netted birds.

He repeated himself. "Help, please," he said. Joe crouched by his side.

"He's going to die," said Joe. "There's nothing we can do to help him." He stood up again.

Fernie and Joe stood together and looked down at the man.

Joe stared at the man and the man stared back at Joe.

"I think someone knifed him."

"Please," said the man, "help me." His eyes were dull and moved inward, as though the irises were circling the drain of the pupil. Joe looked away and took a step backward. He picked up the handles of the wheelbarrow.

"We could put him the wheelbarrow," said Fernie, "drop him in Wolfeborough. By a doctor's house. Who's the man in Wolfeborough? Neck? Necker?"

Joe didn't answer. Fernie, with his false leg, couldn't kneel easily, but he struggled his way down to the ground. He put a hand on the man's forehead and looked at Joe.

"He's white as a ghost," said Fernie.

"He's probably bled everything out," said Joe. "He's going to die in a moment."

It was warm and pleasant night. The air was soft and smelled of new grass. The rush of the river was inside the forest. Joe did not put down the handles of the wheelbarrow.

"What's wrong with you?" Fernie asked his brother. "What's wrong with you?"

Joe leaned forward, into the wheelbarrow. He walked away from Fernie and the tax collector, towards Wolfeborough.

"Pain," said the man. "Please help me." His face shone and slim white strings, like worms, hung from his mouth onto his chin. He moved his hands.

When Fernie turned to find his brother, Joe was gone.

Fernie leaned forward, on the dying man's shoulder, and stood.

"Please," said the man.

Fernie pulled a stone, about the size of a melon, from the base of the Stone Man. He began too gently. He closed his eyes and went again, harder. He could hold the stone in his palm but sometimes it slipped from his hand, and when he paused to pick it up from the ground, he could hear the man breathing and aside from the breathing it was very quiet. The sound of the river disappeared but somehow Fernie could hear the sounds of frogs on the bank, calling to one another with low gulpy vowels. His shoulders began to ache, and the air alternated between the song of frogs and the crunch of the bones: the cheekbones, and the nose, and, at the end, the hard dull split of the skull. And then it was all the sound of the forest and there was no breathing: the breathing was gone, and Fernie was holding his and finally he let it out and felt his heart in his chest. He sat down in the grass. He leaned back, against the legs of the Stone Man. And the frogs were gone but he could hear the river again, moving over the rocks.

When Joe came back, the tax collector's face was so mottled, thick with blood and mash that Joe could not see his nose or his mouth or his eyes. His face was like a winter squash that had been left to rot.

Joe took the dark stone from Fernie's hand and hurled it into the forest. He heard the stone say *thump* when it landed on the forest floor, and then the whistle of leaves as an animal fled. Joe took a step closer to his brother and felt something small and hard roll under his foot; he squatted down and picked up three of the man's teeth. They were not good teeth. They were black and rough. They would have had to come out soon, anyway.

"Hey," he said. "Let's go."

Fernie stood up and used the bottom of his shirt to rub his face. Joe picked up the handles of the wheelbarrow and they began their way back to Chilling. They were quiet for a long time, and the only sound was the even creak of the wheelbarrow's hard wheel.

"Joey," said Fernie, when they could see the Satus hill, "I only hit him with my left hand. I think I was afraid to hurt him. Then I realized I was hurting him more because I wasn't hitting him hard enough. And I knew that I wanted to kill him. But I was afraid to hurt him."

"Yeah," said Joe, "I know."

"I know, though, that after a while the stone was in my right hand. Then I used two hands."

"I know, Fern," said Joe.

"It's fair, now. It feels more fair now."

"I know," said Joe. They started climbing the hill toward Satus.

In the garden, Nora stood with her arms folded, watching her puppy have diarrhea. Philadelphia was growing and she had long legs and huge ears; her body was not yet big enough to match her limbs. Nora heard Fernie's uneven step before she saw him.

160

"Phila has diarrhea," she said, without turning around.

"What did you feed her?" asked Fernie.

"The likelihood that she ate someone's pancreas," said Nora, "is high."

"You have to tie her up, no?"

"She's been at it for a long time."

Fernie came up behind Nora and rested his chin on her shoulder. It was the closest they had even been. Nora was surprised, but allowed it, and leaned her head toward his. Their skulls rested against one another and they watched Phila struggle beside some ferns.

"Something happen out there?" asked Nora. "Joe all right?" She pulled back a little and adjusted the cap on her head.

"It's late," said Fernie. From the window of the kitchen, Lily could see them standing together. She waited for Joe to come up the hill and see them, but before he did, Fernie had appeared inside the kitchen.

"Lily," he said. "Up late tonight."

"I've just woken up," said Lily. "It's morning." She watched out the window. Joe was coming. Nora turned to greet him.

Upstairs, it was as if the man in the woods had never happened. Fernie washed his face and hands. He was more tired than he could remember feeling before. He unhooked and removed his false leg and got into bed. He left his boot on his right foot. He was too tired to pick apart the laces. The effort needed seemed gargantuan. Joe would pull it off when he came in. The sounds of Nora's feet on the floorboards beneath him, his brother's feet, the doors closing and latching and the muffled whimpers of Phila slid together and piled upon one another in his dreams.

Nora and Joe carried the corpse inside and down the cellar. Joe was going to leave Nora with the body, a thin elderly man, but she stopped him.

"Where are you going?" asked Nora.

"Upstairs," said Joe. He opened his palms and looked at his blisters. One had burst, and his hand was wet with the fluid.

"Have some tea with me," said Nora. "The dog's sick and I want to stay until she's better." They went up to the kitchen together. Lily had retreated to a corner, where she sat with something small in her hands.

Phila was still outside. Nora poured from the water jug and hefted the pan onto the fire.

"We had a hard time of it tonight," Joe said to Nora.

"Fernie was off," she said. She measured tea into the mugs. "Someone see you?"

"No, no," said Joe. He came up next to her and put his nose into the tea jar.

"Get your dirty face out of there," said Nora.

"I like the way it smells," he said. He held the jar in his two hands and looked at her over its open top. "Has Fern told you about our father?" he asked.

"Yes," said Nora, "he told about the accident with the knife." She glanced at Lily.

"Right," said Joe. He bent his head into the tea jar again. "Is that all?"

"He said something about your mum, yeah. The firepoker. You want to drink any or just smell it?" said Nora.

Lily made a sound—a cough or snort—and they both looked toward her. But she was intent on some sort of scrubbing or rubbing upon the small object in her lap. Her fat little cheeks were flushed and hung down like curtains around her face.

Joe moved closer to Nora. He put his hand on her shoulder and pushed her, just a little, until her ear was just under his mouth. Nora's body tensed.

"It's not a position for a boy to be in," he whispered. "Feeling like you have to protect your mother and your brother, and not being able to."

"You were just a little kid," said Nora. She spoke loud enough for Lily to hear. She pulled away a bit, but gently. "You weren't in charge. You didn't have to protect her."

"Not that little."

Nora shook her head. "People expect too much from children," she said. "They can't help it."

Joe looked in Lily's direction. Her fingers moved violently. "It's more," he whispered, "about our father." He spoke so low that Nora had to stop breathing to hear him.

"It seems like there's enough already, to me."

"We killed him, Nora. Fern and I."

Nora turned her head and looked at him. Her mouth opened just enough for Joe to see a line of dark between the white of her teeth. The water began to boil and spit streams of tiny bubbles to the edges

162

of the pan.

Joe's fingers tightened onto her shoulder. He lowered his head nearly to the height of hers. Nora felt, suddenly, her smallness, and she did not like it.

"I'm telling you so you know," he whispered. "It was my idea. He killed our mum. We watched him do it. So I made Fernie help me."

She looked at the tea jar. It was brown and glazed and shiny. Joe could hold it in one hand. "How?" she said.

"It was wintertime. He was drunk. We fed him drink. And then we put the fire out in the forge. We stripped him naked, shackled him to the anvil, and then we left him there to freeze."

Nora took the tea jar from Joe's hands. It was wet with fluid from his blisters; she rubbed at the spot with her apron. She replaced the lid on its top and put it back into its place on the low shelf.

"I meant," she whispered, "*how*. How did you make Fernie help you?"

Joe straightened and looked down at her. His brows knitted. She looked straight ahead. The water was boiling violently and silently, huge gasping burps of air releasing up and breaking onto the surface. Steam rose like smoke.

"I told him to," said Joe.

Nora used both hands to lift the pan from the fire, and poured the water into the mugs.

"Careful," said Joe.

"So he froze, then. Your father froze to death."

"Fernie waited outside. And when he heard our dad holler he tried to go in and get him out. But I stopped him."

"Fernie tried to go in."

"I sent him away and waited there alone. It was freezing. I waited and my face was so cold I could not move my lips. In the morning I went in and dressed him, unclasped him, so no one would know. The next week, pieces of my face fell off. Like little gray feathers."

"Joey Gallo," said Nora.

"I thought God was punishing me by taking my face."

Nora looked at Lily. Their eyes would have met, but Nora looked away at the last moment. She smiled and turned again to Joe. "Are you having tea?" she asked.

Joe coughed. "I'm going to sleep," he said, in his normal voice.

"What?" Lily said.

Joe muttered something, looked at the ceiling, and left. Nora turned to face the door; she brought her hands to her hair and clutched there.

"Did you hear that, any of it, Lily?" asked Nora. She didn't turn to look at her. She wanted Lily to say, Yes. She needed Lily to say Yes. She needed Lily to take half of the knowledge from her. She needed Lily to rise and come over to where Nora was standing, to come and take Nora into her giant soft arms and her huge gentle body, to hold her and say that she had heard it too, that she knew it all, too, and that Nora was not alone, they would stand here and know what they knew, that they would know all of this together.

In the corner, Lily's hands stilled. She looked up. Her eyes, when they met Nora's they were black and empty.

"You have any sisters, growing up?" she asked.

"No," said Nora.

"I guessed that might be."

"Tea if you want it," said Nora. She turned again, and nodded at the mugs.

Outside, Phila whined and scratched at the door.

The painting in Odette's study—the one of the man astride a horse and holding a severed head—was dangerously askew. It hung on the wall opposite the fireplace and was bathed in arrhythmic beats of orange light. William Salderman, Alexander and Odette's older missing brother, had painted it over the course of a rainy March.

"Nasty," their mother had said. She had a habit of pouting at things that displeased her, puckering her lips and slumping her shoulders.

"I like it," Odette had said. She had been eight years old at the time. She never slumped.

"It's yours," said William. And then he had left the house to do something mysterious, as he was a mystery entire to his little sister. She suspected that he was a dangerous criminal sometimes. Although he didn't look like one. He looked like a tailor. Or a man who collected seashells.

Young Odette had taken the painting and kept it in her room. She hadn't wanted it hung on the wall, but kept it propped up beside her bed so that when she lay, awake, on her side, she could gaze at the head-toting man and his horse. It kept her brain abuzz, explaining to itself the man depicted therein. Some nights, the horseman was a bloodthirsty general, intent on killing the innocent men and women who plowed peacefully upon land he wanted for his own greedy ends. Some nights, he was a tired and desperate mercenary, driven to horrible acts of murder by a tragic childhood. Other times, in other moods, the head was the head of a man he had loved—a brother or a cousin—and who he had seen fall in battle. He was bringing the head home, to bury. Once it was the head of his lover; once it was his own father's head; once, it was the head of a beggar man he had killed by accident, an act which would bring about his repentance and newly monastic life.

The horse and the rider were, of course, the central figures. The man's massive thighs squeezed the horse's sides and strained the fabric of his trousers, a greenish, brownish heavy-looking material. Perhaps in response to the rider's squeezing, the horse's mouth was open, his teeth showing and even the pale rose of the gums above. The horse's eyes rolled back up into the skull. The mane, black and unbraided, flew up in all directions as if caught in a whirlwind. There was no unity in the two figures; they did not disappear into one another the way a horse and rider sometimes can. They were two distinct, many-limbed animals, each one desperately trying to keep their bodies under their own control as the other distracted and wrestled for dominance.

In Odette's study, immediately underneath the horse's raised front hoof, sat Joe Gallo, perched upon a great latched trunk. For months, Joe came to Odette when he could, when he had an hour between digging graves in Chilling and robbing graves in Wolfeborough and generally doing what Salderman told him to do. He needed to sleep and eat and do work around Satus, he needed to be long enough in Chilling to keep people from asking questions about his work for the doctor. He needed to see Nora, and talk to her. But when he had done all these things, he climbed the stairs to Odette's study, sat on a trunk, leaned his back and head against the wall. Odette stood, facing the fireplace, and let the firelight illuminate the pages of Pope's translation. Joe listened to her calm, low voice read stories about ancient warriors, gods, goddesses, losses and anger, all inside Homer's Iliad.

"*Now*," she read, "*Ajax braced his dazzling armour on;*
Sheathed in bright steel the giant-warrior shone:
He moves to combat with majestic pace;
So stalks in arms the grisly god of Thrace,
When Jove to punish faithless men prepares,
And gives whole nations to the waste of wars,

Thus march'd the chief, tremendous as a god;
Grimly he smiled; earth trembled as he strode:
His massy javelin quivering in his hand,
He stood, the bulwark of the Grecian band.
Through every Argive heart new transport ran;
All Troy stood trembling at the mighty man:
Even Hector paused; and with new doubt oppress'd,
Felt his great heart suspended in his breast:
'Twas vain to seek retreat, and vain to fear;
Himself had challenged, and the foe drew near."

"Ah," said Joe, "stop just there."

Odette placed her bookmark and closed the volume. The firewood was very dry, mossy and gnarled; the flames hissed and snapped out pockets of air and clods of old life. Odette nearly always had a fire in this room.

"If you learned to read," said Odette softly, "you could take this book back with you, and read in your room, or in the garden, or anyplace you like."

Joe closed his eyes and savored this a moment. He pictured himself someplace high up, removed from the sight of Satus or the rooftops of Chilling. Sitting on a stone wall, somewhere, maybe, keeping a bunch of goats company and reading the stories himself. He could watch the battles play out within his own head, stop and ruminate wherever he might, speed past the images he hated.

"It's too late for me, Miss Salderman," he said. "If you don't learn to read when a wee thing it's not likely to change."

"Mug is learning. Lily is learning. Mugger is much older than you."

"I can read enough. I can write my name on papers."

"The whole name? Joseph Gallo?"

"I can write J – O, Joe."

"Did you understand this last bit?"

"Ajax is dressed for battle, and is on his way. Hector is scared."

"Yes," said Odette, "it's comforting to know that truly great men—with, as Homer tells us, great hearts—that even they doubt and falter in their strengths."

Joe stretched his arms over his head again and yawned.

"I'm exhausted," he said, "I'll say goodnight. Or good morning. Thank you for reading. I feel better now."

Odette smiled and replaced the book on a low shelf by the fireplace. "Were you feeling poorly?" she asked.

"Fernie and I . . . we had a bad night. It was a bad night."

"I imagine there are few good nights robbing graves for secret awful nasty dissections, Joe. My brother asks a lot of you. He needs and trusts you so much."

"No, we don't mind. We don't, really. It was Fern. I don't like to see Fern upset."

"Why was Fernie upset?"

Joe stood up. His body cast a shadow on the painting behind him, so that the severed head was almost completely obscured.

"Why did Salderman come out here? Seems like he'd be better off in London, or someplace."

"He had disappointed some of his friends," said Odette. "It is a long and tedious story. But what happened? Are you reluctant to say?"

"We came across a man who had been hurt. Badly. He was still alive, but it was very bad. Fernie wanted me to put the man out of his misery."

"Did you kill him?" asked Odette.

"I didn't want to. I left."

"Did Fernie leave with you?"

"No," said Joe.

"I see," said Odette.

"There are so many bodies," said Joe. "Everywhere we look, we find bodies. Dead ones. Alive ones. Mostly dead ones. It's fine, when they're one or the other. Dead. Alive. Dead. Alive."

"The world is unkind," said Odette. Her eyes flicked to Joe's face and back down again.

"I don't like the part when it's between. Not properly alive, not properly dead. What is that? Did the Greeks have a word for that, like everything else? When you are surely on your way to death, you can look over and see it right there, but you are not dead yet?"

Odette shook her head. "I don't know a word for it."

"It would be helpful if there were a word for it," Joe said, and rubbed his face with his huge palm. "It sounds so nice, when you read it. The stuff he writes about. It's all gleaming armor and fighting for glory."

"And the fear," Odette said. "Always fear."

"Well," said Joe. "I like the part where he can feel his heart suspended in his chest. That's just how it feels."

He said goodnight and went down the black stairs to the cellar, but Nora had gone to sleep. He went to his room. Fernie was still dressed, asleep atop his blankets. Before Joe fell into his own bed, he unlaced and pulled off his little brother's boot.

Chapter XXV.
Satus House

Paul had Nora practice on a series of hands, each severed below the wrist. He filled the needle with blue wax and passed it to her. Nora worried the point of the needle into the flaccid gray artery that dangled from the wrist, and injected the wax. At first, she had been too careful. She had not filled them quickly enough, and the veins had been only halfway filled, so that they appeared to stop abruptly when they reached the knuckles. By the third set of hands she had learned to gauge the pressure correctly, but then filled them too quickly, and the vein walls burst.

"Patient. Steady," Paul said, peering over her shoulder.

"I'll get it," she said. She threw every failure into the corner, where hands mounted like a pile of huge fleshy spiders. And in the evening, when Paul had gone upstairs to eat dinner, she injected one slim, bony hand perfectly. The veins branched away across the top of the hand, filled just enough so that Nora could see them clearly and yet not so much that their fragile walls split open. Perfect. She could see all the paths the blood could go, perfectly. She held up the hand to the lantern light and turned it over. She brushed her fingers over the swollen blue routes.

Her mother's hand had been a map of darkly branching roads. The veins stood up and out: large, purple, pronounced, so much so that the young Nora wanted to reach out and press down on them. One afternoon, after a very early morning in which she had been called to help Zeena Cates with a birth in the village, Georgiana had fallen asleep in the sun. Seeing her, Nora put down the basket of washing she had been carrying. With her index finger, she reached out and pressed down on one huge, purple vein in her mother's hand. It was soft and giving, like the casing of a new sausage. She looked to her own hands but they were smooth and clean, tanned and even. As a child her hands had not become what they would become after her illness: the thin fingers of her mother, the large knob-like knuckles of her father, the dark purple of her mother's veins, the freckled sunspots of her father's leather-like skin. Now, nearly nineteen, she was a perfect combination of the two, she thought: the ugliest parts of each, the least attractive of nature's decisions pieced together.

Nora's mother had bad feet, too. After all the boys had died, when Georgiana fell sick, Nora had drawn back the blankets and seen her mother's feet. The left foot was the one with the broken toes. The three center toes curled in toward the sole like the talon of carrion. Nora hadn't ever asked her mother—she had been too sick, by then, to speak much or to carry on a conversation with any coherence—but she had wondered. Where she had been, what she had done. If someone else had broken those toes with the heel of a boot or walking stick, or if Georgiana had stumbled and fallen, if it had happened outside near stones or inside a building. If anyone at all had sat her mother down on a chair and lifted the heel of her foot into the palm of their hand to carefully, gingerly, examine the damage done.

It was impossible to work in the cellars without looking at each body as though it could be that of her mother. Of course she knew that too much time had passed; Joe and Fernie would have scattered the remaining parts of Georgiana around the forest and dunes. They may have tossed her bones into the sea. They may have left her skull in a garden, or along the road to Wolfeborough. But she couldn't stop looking. Nora's eyes went straight to the hands, to the veins, to the feet, to the toes. She was repulsed by her own hunger for it, the sight of that ugliness. Her mother's uglinesses were what she wanted most to see in the world.

Increasingly, she began looking at herself. Her own ugliness distracted her. She studied it in mirrors with the detachment of a scientist. Her baldness was terrible, but that at least could be covered and hidden. Her eye sockets were dark and sunken, no matter how many hours she slept. Her lips were full but dry, cracked, pale; they faded into her flesh. Her skin was badly scarred and pitted. She understood that she had become an ugly woman. But she couldn't help looking at herself. She could see her father, there. Her mother was in the mirror. Her brothers. Their eyebrows, their freckles. It was as if she were the family entire, as if she carried them around because they had given up their own bodies. Her ugliness motivated her. It made her feel serious and work-sturdy, like a piece of farm equipment. Or like the clumsy metal saw Nora used to open skulls: inelegant, unpretty, unadorned, stained, useful, necessary. She looked in the giant Satus mirror many times each day. Made for work, she would repeat to herself, I am made for work, not decoration. But in the end she attended her own reflection with the sober feeling of loss she would bring with her to a funeral. Something had been killed by functionality.

In the cellar, Paul cleaned up her injected hands and Nora went to find her dog. She found her, playing with Fernie, in the garden. She stood beside the tomato stakes and watched them until Fernie noticed her, and pulled the dog, by the stick she clenched in her teeth, to her side.

"What do you dream?" Nora asked Fernie. "Do you have the same dream, or different dreams?"

Fernie dropped his end of the stick and Phila stumbled backward.

"I don't know," he said, "different ones, I guess."

"Do you remember any?"

Fernie sat down next to the dog and rubbed behind her ears. Phila tried to climb into his lap, as they had allowed her to do when she was a much smaller puppy. She licked his chin.

"I remember one from—I don't remember when it was, the other day. But a few days ago, and I remember it because I woke up in the middle of the night, because I said to myself in the dream, You should wake up, Fern, this dream isn't very pleasant, and it's just a dream, so go ahead and wake up. And then I did."

"What was the dream?"

"I can't remember it totally, but I was underwater. And I think I was trying to do something, like untie something? And I was running out of air, but it was really important that I get it untied. No. Maybe it wasn't something tied, maybe it was I was trying to lift something, or carry it? No. I can't remember."

"But you don't have the same dream over and over, then."

"No, I don't think so. If I do, I don't remember. Why?"

Nora had been having dreams, lately, in which various voices called for her help. Urgently, desperately, now, now. In the dream, she was always doing something, but she would drop whatever was in her hands. She would feel flustered and rush to help. And in attempting to complete the task, she would find that the work would evaporate in her hands; she couldn't make any progress, or even make a beginning. The work simply disappeared when she set herself to it.

Then the dream jumped. Somehow, suddenly, the work was completed; there was a gap of time, and Nora would look down to see the task done. Happy, and proud, she turned around to see the person's face. She expected gratefulness, or approval . . . but when she turned around, she found the person facing her with an expression of horror and fear. She was the thing—the monster, the obstacle—from which they needed help to escape. They hadn't wanted her at all; they wanted protection from her.

"No reason," she said to Fernie. He looked so nice, sitting with her dog. They looked content together.

"Talk to Joe, if you want to know about dreams," said Fernie. "Ask him to tell you about his dreams."

Her mother's belly had been crossed by a giant dark scar. Nora had seen it only once, when she had walked into the room when Georgiana was taking a bath. There were six inches of hot water in the metal tub, and the steam had softened the grip of Georgiana's braids. Wisps of hair clung to her temples. Her eyes were closed. There was no furrow between her eyebrows. Nora had taken the opportunity to walk, slowly and very quietly, as close as she dared; she peered over the rim of the tub and saw her mother's body. The dark pubic hair struck her as monstrous. The frank nakedness of it was obscene. A few long errant hairs had grown onto Georgiana's belly and curled around the scar. It was wide and stark, a line dividing upper Georgiana from lower Georgiana. Nora's face burned. She felt scared. And then the fear dissolved, and she was torn between anger at her mother (for displaying herself, however inadvertently) and shame that she had seen the display. But underneath that, underneath the flush of emotion, Nora was quietly mesmerized by what she saw. The immensity of her mother's resting body. Without looking away, she backed out of the room as quietly as she had come.

In her early teenage years, that image of her naked mother's belly would flash across her mind, and Nora would think of her mother as a woman made of two different bodies. The scar, the marker where the two had been sewn together. When her mother had come back, Nora was eleven, and her mother had taken over the farm as though she had never left it. She worked hard from early morning to late in the night. She carried and bore the boys, the first set of twins and then the second two years later. Georgiana tied apron-strings and bootlaces. She visited families in the village, went to church. But she was never happy. Nora could tell. There was a disdain in the way she sat at the table, a disdain in the way she stirred the laundry and knelt in the garden. She never spoke to Nora of any topic besides the concrete: chores, work, dress. She was militant on the topic of dress. Nothing could be wrong looking, nothing could be messy or out of place. Georgiana would retie the strings of Nora's apron roughly, almost violently, so that the lines lay straight, in parallel lines. She would knock her daughter across the head before staring pointedly at the fallen hem, or at the torn sleeve.

Sometimes, in the late afternoons, Georgiana would become angry. Always the rage was precipitated by some trivial loss or a moment of forgetfulness. Nora had misplaced her good stockings. Nora had forgotten to bring the pork to the Peabodys. Nora had dropped the freshly laundered babies' clothes into the mud. Nora had made a mistake. Her mother's face would distort with rage. Nora would run, crying, to her father, who would lay aside his shovel or his scythe, and hug her to his chest.

"When you were born," Nora's father had told her one afternoon, "your mother had a very hard time. You would not come out right, though she had pushed and pushed, and was crying for a whole day and a whole night. She was pale with no blood. It gushed from her. And still you would not come out. We were sure you would die, and even sure that your mother, too, would die. And I went to Zeena Cates and said, please, do something. And she said that she could try something: she could cut your mother in two, down the center of her belly, and pull you out that way. Georgiana would likely die, she said, but we could save you. And Georgiana said, yes. Do it. But I said no, because I was not willing to lose her. So we went to get the doctor from Wolfeborough, who shook his head and said nothing to be done but wait until death, to call the Reverend and pray. When your mother could speak, she asked us to cut her open and save you. And finally we did.

"For days afterward, your mother lay as though already dead. She was white and cold as ice. She breathed only very little, so that I could put my hand above her mouth and feel nothing. You were healthy! I held you, and you screamed. We fed you by another woman, for a little while, waiting for your mother to pass."

Nora couldn't look up to meet her father's eyes.

"Your mother survived many things, Nora. She was willing to die for you. She may have a temper, she may be unkind. She may hurt you. I know."

"I don't understand why you don't do anything. Why do you let her do that?"

"I know you don't understand, sweet daughter." He leaned down and kissed her on the top of her head, where her hair was parted cleanly down the center. "You are too young to understand what life can sometimes do to someone."

"I'll never be like her," said Nora.

He had smiled at her. "If you were, I would be proud."

Nora had started to cry. It made no sense at all.

"You have to understand," said her father, lighting his pipe, "she never wanted to be here. Here, the farm, Chilling. She should have had much bigger things. Your mother is a different and wonderful kind of person. She's here just for you, Nora. Only because she loves you."

The debt was too large. In those days, Nora often wished Georgiana had never returned. In church she prayed that God would make her mother go away again.

That evening, Nora took Philadelphia to the woodpile to wait for Joe. He had spent the day in Chilling, working at the church. Nora threw a stick down the hill and Phila bounded away to retrieve it, over and over. When the dog saw Joe at the bottom of the hill, she brought her stick to him and they came up together. Phila pressed her body into Joe's legs as they walked.

"How is Chilling?"

"I saw your uncle," said Joe.

Nora snorted. Phila looked at her, then dropped the stick at Joe's feet and backed away.

"He's nice," said Joe. "He's really not a bad person. He said he's having trouble with his feet and wants Salderman to come look at them."

"I have something to ask you," said Nora.

Joe took a step closer to her. He put his hands on her shoulders and pushed her a bit, so that she sat on the cutting log. She sat and smiled up at him, and he stood above her. She could smell the church on him. It was a gray-colored, solitary kind of scent. It wasn't unpleasant, but it was a sobering smell. It didn't match him, Joe, with his giant hale body and smile, golden hair, red hands.

"Sit right there, Nora, and talk to me," he said. He kept his hands on her shoulders.

"You have dreams," she said, looking up at him. "Fern says."

"Yes. Everyone has dreams."

174

"I was asking Fernie if he had dreams. He doesn't remember, but he said you remembered your dreams."

"Ah," he said. Joe took his hands from Nora's shoulders and sat down next to the cutting log, so that she was above him and had to turn and bow her head to see him.

"My dreams are about these stories," he said, "these stories that Miss Salderman tells me. They're from an old book about a war, and a bunch of different men. They all fight in the war, or they're kings or gods or like that."

"So you dream about the stories?"

"No," said Joe. "So maybe Odette—Miss Salderman—maybe she'll tell me the story about how one man gets hurt in battle. Maybe he dies, even. Then I'll go to sleep and I'll have this dream, not about the battle, or the injury, but I'll see the man—I recognize him right away—and he's doing something. Not fighting, or in the war. Like watching his meat cook on the fire, and poking it every once in a while to see if it's done. And the whole dream will just be that, before he goes to war. Just him, cooking some food and not wanting it to burn.

"And other times . . . there's a prince named Hector, and he's a great warrior. And I have dreams about him all the time. I dream about him sitting and holding his baby and making faces at him, to make the baby laugh. Or, I dreamed this the other night, I dreamed that one of his servants or slaves was walking and caught her clothes on the edge of a table, and Hector saw and helped her untangle her robe and then he called for his brother. His brother is named Paris. And then he and his brother moved the table out of the way. So that no one else would get snagged."

"What do you think it means?"

"What?"

"Why do you think you're dreaming these things? What does it mean?"

"I never thought about it. I take them like you take it, sometimes, when you're just sitting and watching people. Just to watch them."

"Yes, no, I see that. But the dream had to come from somewhere, right? And there's only one place it could come from, which is your own mind. And everything the body produces has a function. The stomach makes the acid to digest your food. And scar tissue to protect your wounds. Saliva, blood, bile. All of it has some reason to be there."

175

"I don't know. Maybe just to entertain you while you're asleep."

"No," said Nora. "But entertainment isn't good enough, I think. What do you think the reason might be? The brothers, and the table?"

Joe smiled. "What do you think?"

"I don't know. Do you think the brothers in the dream could be you and Fernie?"

Joe frowned.

"No," she persisted. "Listen. Could it be that your body knows something about you and your brother and it's trying to tell you?"

"If my body knows it, why would need to teach me it? I already know."

Nora stood up. Her face was flushed.

"No," she said. "No, no. Just like you don't know it when your stomach makes the acid. Your body has this whole other consciousness. It's not you. It's separate from you, but it knows you better than you do. It knows how to heal you, how to make you better." She flung the stick for Phila, and the dog took off racing down the hill. Joe and Nora stood watching her. The sun was still quite high, but the hour had darkened the light from yellow to orange.

"In the dream," Joe said, "it was nice, because Hector and Paris were moving the table, and it was nice because they cared about that servant who got caught on it, and it was nice because they both did it." Phila trotted up and dropped the stick at Nora's feet. She sat and waited, but Nora was looking at Joe.

"So maybe," she said, "your body is saying you and Fernie need to move a table."

"What table?"

Nora shrugged. "I don't know," she said. "Probably you know. Your body knows. Something that's in the way, maybe not in your way, but in the way for someone."

Joe reached down and threw the stick for Phila.

"So, what's your dream, then?" he asked.

"Mine?"

"You must have dreams."

"I want to figure out how it is working. It doesn't matter if we're talking about your dream or my dream, so long as we figure out how the dream wants to work."

Joe laughed. "It's not a dead body, No," he said. "Your dream and my dream aren't the same, like livers and bones and stuff. They don't do the same things for different people."

Phila, far down the hill, had come across something with an interesting smell. She abandoned her stick to the long grass, and began pawing and sniffing.

"I wouldn't mind," Joe said, more quietly, "if you wanted to talk about what you were dreaming. I would like that."

"My dog is rolling in a dead bird, I think," Nora said. She smiled at Joe, and walked away.

Joe watched her for a minute, checked the sky, and went inside to wash and eat.

The dreams kept coming. They came every night, actually, and intensified, so that she woke unable to place herself in the Satus world or the dream world. She stayed up very late in the cellar, working on preparations and boiling bones, stringing together skeletal structures, reading books that Jules or Paul marked for her. Salderman had kept journals of his work from ten, fifteen, twenty years ago, and she made her way through them all. She stayed awake as long as she could. The longer she stayed, the stronger her work became, the more adept she became with the scalpel and the names of bodily things. She felt heavy with knowing, and heavy with something else she couldn't name. Her body ached when she woke up and by the time she finally lay down to sleep, every muscle felt as though it had been scored with currycombs. Most nights she felt asleep atop the quilt, fully dressed. During the daytime Nora was seeing her little brothers, the twins, out of the corner of her eyes; she whirled around in empty dissection rooms to find naught but a rat.

The lack of sleep affected her appetite. She stopped eating again, as she had when she had first become sick on the farm. She couldn't stomach food. Nothing tasted right; nothing was nourishing; everything was horrible, and she was frustrated by the sight of food. She snapped at Lily and ignored the men.

"She's in mourning," said Odette, when Joe complained to her. "Her family has passed."

"Months ago," said Joe. "They died months ago."

"We'll be at the end of *The Iliad* soon. We'll have to begin *The Odyssey*."

"There's another one? With all the same people?"

"Some of the same people."

"No one trusts anyone in this house, Miss Salderman. I don't know what it is. But I don't think Nora is just sad, about her family and everything. It's been a long time. It's something else."

"Grief does not have anything to do with time," said Odette. "One has no respect for the other."

"I was thinking we could go down to the village, tell her uncle, have him come and get her."

"He probably knows she's here, you know. Or suspects it."

"Then why hasn't he come and got her?"

Odette pulled away the curtain and looked through her window. She had one of the rooms that looked out to the sea. "Chilling is a strange place. We all have a little silent agreement. It's filled with people who have learned to keep their secrets and let others keep theirs. Nora's family respects that; they've respected the privacy of others, so that they could maintain theirs."

"You mean when her mother left?"

"Yes, like that. Your father, Nora's mother, all these things. A million others."

"But Nora's mother wasn't killed."

"Did you know, Joe, that her mother lived for a short while in Gloucester?"

Joe shook his head.

"She did. She lived with . . . Georgiana had an attachment. She was especially close to another woman here in the village, and they left to live a life with one another. They were very poor, and had to do some very sad things to earn a living. The other woman, as a result of these . . . actions . . . became pregnant."

"She left Chilling to go live in Gloucester?"

"Yes. With her friend. She stayed with Philip until Nora was born, and then they left together. I think that man, the man who gave you Philadelphia, might have helped them. I don't know."

Two boats appeared on the horizon, one large and one very small. Together they inched northward.

"Why did she come back?"

"I tell you this, Joe, because I think—I think—you are a kind young man and, if you think Nora should know this, then you must pass it along. My husband came in and out of Gloucester, and I have friends there, still. They helped her friend after Georgiana had returned to Chilling."

"Why did she come back?"

Odette shrugged. "It should be obvious. Nora."

Joe shook his head. "No. Nora says they didn't get along."

"She came back because she loved Nora, and she couldn't live any longer without her child. She missed her so badly it was making her sick. So she came back. I don't know what she told her husband."

"How do you know this?"

Odette turned away from the window. "Georgiana's friend. Lover, really. I know her quite well. She was heartbroken. I don't know that I have done the right thing in telling you, Joe. There is some uncertainty here, as to the right path."

"You wouldn't tell her yourself?"

"I have work to do. She wouldn't stop bothering me, I fear. Pass it along, if you think she needs to know. Say it's gossip, or rumor. She can confirm it all with her uncle, if she likes."

"How's your poem going?"

Odette wandered over to the child's desk and read what she had written. "I would let you read it," she said, "but you can't. You really must learn how to read, and soon. You're getting too old to be ignorant."

Joe stood up and turned to go. "I don't know that I will tell her, Miss Salderman. I don't know that I'd like to be the one who tells her. She should have learned it from her family."

"Yes," said Odette, "she should have."

Chapter XXVI.
Chilling Meeting House, June 3, 1791

There are three issues to discuss tonight, yes I know Jeremiah Osgood is not here yet, thank you, but we're going on and he can join us when he can join us. First to discuss, first, what there is to be done about the scourge of bones and remains, the Captain Murderer stories that have been going around, and the Reverend Brewer is here of course to advise us. Yes?

There was? In the Flaggs' garden? Was it the vegetable garden or the herb garden? And then more recently the Travers' back field. A head. A head and two arms, yes thanks. So . . . where, what . . . Right, then if we are able to conclude there, we then we must see about the new taxing that we haven't been officially informed of but which we all have been hearing rumors, particularly from our trading friends in Wolfeborough, and then, when Jeremiah makes it in, we'll discuss the town's response to his daughter's condition and what ought be done. Mrs. Slough is here, too, and can speak to the girl's condition in—

Well, no, of course I don't expect that. So perhaps we'll not hear from Mrs. Slough, then, just enough to say all is well with, yes? Thank you, then. Can we first . . . Oliver, have you counted heads? Ah. Then, alright, before the real talks, first, though, to address the concerns brought individually. Mr. Norton's pigs have gotten out twice. Which we've seen is the fence problem . . . Oh? Yes, we knew that fence would be a bad fence, and still, we do need to remedy this. And so . . . Mr. Norton?

Yes, that sounds wise. If families would donate their sons' labor on Thursday noon, they should be able to get the new fence up by evening. Can we see which families can send their boys along?

Perfect, then . . . Oliver, can you write down those names? Thank you, Mrs. Cantwell, I know how busy Simon is. We must get those pigs sorted. Alright, then . . . excuse me. What we are . . . Oh, thank you, yes, Reverend. The children of Rose and Zachary Lungwort have not been seen at church the past two Sundays, first because they were visiting their aunt and uncle and last week because they had a throat complaint. They have been treated by Mrs. Slough and will be in church this time tomorrow. Mrs. Lungwort is staying with her mother who we hear is failing and we will pray for her, certainly . . . Yes?

No, I think a stomach complaint. The boys are being cared for by Daniel's sister, and we can all, I think, lend a hand by sending over whatever we can. What? Oliver? Oh, yes.

Right, those boys are at that stage. Eating quite a bit! Let's try to get through this next bit quickly, less chatter? Oliver? Ah. Joy Beddington asks for assistance in setting her squash in the next week, preferably in the morning, early, before it gets hot. Can we see—oh, thank you. Yes, and . . . Oliver, you have all this? Thank you, ladies. What's that, Jeffrey?

I think this has been discussed, Jeffrey, a few times now. It's a terrible tragedy. But she did insist on walking those cliffs, and—

No, we hadn't heard of that at all. I doubt that very much. It was a very slippery day, very wet and slippery and—

Well, do you want to get up and say it for yourself, then?

Her? No. We did drag it. Nothing there. The places she could have gone . . . Well, Octavius Peabody has been many times and she is certainly not there. Hasn't been coming and going, if that's what you were going to suggest. No word from Wolfeborough or . . . no, no. The Hales have paid for it, almost, and we'd agreed . . . Right.

We have to begin to consider that possibility. Yes, for both. But I admit I think it's unlikely, don't you? But we have agreed, as a community, not to bother—

Alright, alright. We have to respect our word. But maybe we can do about it quietly . . . Busy Tanner comes to mind, I know, and Charles, if you bump into anyone . . . ?

We will consider again. If it has, then we'll—

No, that's a firm no, there.

Right, then, last bit, a happy one: Steven Storey's litter still has three puppies for purchase, if anyone needs a good herding dog. All healthy and good-sized, two bitches and one boy left. Border collies, Mr. Forrest. Good dogs, too, my son took one and it's fine, I'll attest. Thank you, Mr. Storey. To the real business, then: can we hear from Mr. Travers, first.

Thank you. Mr. Flagg, can you speak on what you've found, recently?

Thank you, Jack. I think we all know where this is going. But lastly, perhaps, Reverend, you could just briefly . . . yes, exactly, the churchyard.

Thank you, Reverend. I agree, I agree. We have patience, we have been patient and understanding, but this is too far. Certainly the Captain Murderer story is very strong, among this village. And we must take into account, too, the amount of gore that Storey and his dogs have come across on their wood walks, and the bits the children have seen on the beaches. We cannot be taken advantage of, like this. Almost impossible, as Jack has mentioned, for a single human man to generate the sheer amount of—well, what?

Well, no, no I don't think we do know. We're not going to keep jumping to conclusions.
But I think for now, we can say to those who do not . . .

Right, to those villagers who haven't . . . Yes, yes, Sam. Yes. That Captain Murderer, back from Hell, is to blame for the digging up of our consecrated ground . . . What else is to be done? We depend on it.

Well, yes, Miss Ridley, that's just the question. We're all aware of that. Taxes are rising.

No, Miss Ridley, you're right.

Yes, Miss Ridley. Perhaps I spoke too strongly, there. Well, that . . . No, you're quite right. Are there any other, thoughts, or anyone . . . Yes?

Oliver, can you go and see what the little Cotton girls want?

I don't know. The . . . one with the protruding ears. Frances. And the other one. Go see what . . . Thank you. No, no, Samuel, I think that's quite wise. No sense in making a plan until we know what, exactly we're dealing with. I think the original idea is a good one . . . Hey?

Well, of course. If there's no movement after a week, I'd say. I think a week should be well long enough. What say we, then?

We must be very very delicate, now. Don't go rushing about and . . . exactly. If you do see something, bring it back here and we'll discuss it as a community. We can perhaps bargain for more, if that's happening. And the large issue is decided: we will post a clandestine watch through the night for one week. By next week, this will be found out; it is our most important task; we must sacrifice our sleep and work to its success and resolution. Men, please stay a moment longer and we will sign up for the times and days we will stand watch.

Ah, well, thank you Oliver. You missed the important bit, though, I'd say. We've decided and moving on, now. The Osgoods and their—

Absolutely not!

That is ridiculous.

Because we have chosen to live in Chilling precisely because it is not Salem! Nor is it Lynn or Providence, nor those other places where the folk turn on each other and create havoc. Boston, Gloucester, even Wolfeborough. We came here—or, rather, our fathers and grandfathers—to found a village. A village, in the truest sense, because we've lost faith with the constant attack and defend of those places we've come from. There is no fear, here, no!

Clearly, clearly, we do need to be reminded of this, Thomas! Thomas, your father was one of the first men from the Bay to build his home here. You can say—

Exactly. Exactly that. He would have been whipped. Or he would have been killed, executed for what? For hypocritical leaders, puffing their chests. We won't stoop, not while we live in this solitary place. We will not judge as they judge. Abigail will be protected, there needn't be discussion on that. And we as a village together will protect her. What we need to decide, simply, is what color the cover will be, when the time comes to explain the child to the commonwealth, or to strangers. What can we do? Miss Moore?

You've spoken with the Osgoods?

Yes, I see the sense of that. We will, of course, need to convince Abigail. The child can, for all purposes, be raised as her sibling. After the weaning is done, of course. In this way the girl may remain unmarried and the child can remain in the family. There is no—

Well, of course, that is always the preferred option, but Mrs. Osgood tells us that Abbie is unlikely to reveal the name. They've gone to some lengths and she has resisted them quite successfully. They are open to new ideas, ways to convince the child to name the man. Or, in a like fashion, to convince this man to come forward of his own accord.

Next week, I think, as Mrs. Slough told us earlier, Abigail is far enough along to . . .

Thank you, yes. So we see a decision will have to be made somewhat quickly. As far as I know, the doctor has never even laid eyes on Abbie, or her mother, for months. It shouldn't be difficult to put Lucy in a bed and say it's her child. If need be. Older women have done it. He certainly doesn't need to know.

Exactly! Well, let's make it this, then . . . if Abigail still refuses by next week to name the father, we'll vote and move and act on this. As a village. Are we . . . Oliver, what's the time? We'll stop, then, here? And I shall invite the tax collector Herrin from Wolfeborough to come and speak to us, so we might know more on this other matter. Yes?

Oh. I hadn't heard. Is this true? How awful. Just awful.

Well. Right. Let us pray that no more of these dark times come to us. Reverend, will you lead us?

Amen. Well, then, let's all go home. Men, we'll start watching tonight. Oliver will stay up, and . . . ah, Jack, too, thank you. We'll see what it is, anyway. By this time, next week. We'll know whatever there is to know. It's time this chapter ended, for Chilling. There have been too many bloody things.

Chapter XXVII.
The Chilling Churchyard/The Pirrip Farm

Nora's sleep broke so often with dreams that she had begun to see crystalline arbors spiraling around the bones she cleaned. She fought sleep so that she would not dream. When she did sleep, the dream woke her. Her mind loosened and pried itself apart, so that sensations could not attach themselves to ideas, and ideas could not attach themselves to things or words. Finally, after nearly ten days of this, Salderman gave her something to drink and Nora slept for two days, waking once to urinate and splash water on her face. She did not dream. It was a dark, heavy, unnatural sleep.

"Like sleeping underwater," she told Jules Demmer. "Or like sleeping underneath the earth."

"So, like being dead," he said. He spat into his cup. Nora, also chewing, as she did when they worked together, leaned over Jules's arm and spat as well.

"I think I need to go to see my parents," Nora told him. "I'd like to go visit their graves and my brothers'. Do you think Salderman would let me? I could go at night."

Jules shrugged. "You're staying here now on your own choice. He knows you, now. He trusts you. But take one of the Gallos with you, in case. Oh . . . Nora. No, no. You have to cut the skin much farther down. Much farther down than you think, because you'll need all that extra later on."

"Here?"

"More like," Jules took a knife and made a small nick on the body's calf. "Here."

He was teaching her how to amputate a limb.

Late on Saturday night, so late it was nearly Sunday, Fernie and Nora walked to the churchyard. It was warm, a muggy June night, and Fernie's hair dripped sweat down his neck. Nora had tied a length of cotton around her forehead, in place of her usual black cap. It kept the sweat from running into her eyes. They stood in front of the Pirrips' graves. Nora knelt down and brushed her brothers' tablet clean of dirt. She plucked off the overgrowth.

"I have not been to church in a long time," she said. She could remember, staring at his grave, the soft baby skin of Abraham. When he was just born, she would nuzzle her nose into his belly, and he would open his tiny gumless mouth and smile at her. He knew by smell or instinct that she was his sister. Then, remembering Abraham, she remembered her father, and his expression on the day of the twins' birth when she ran outside to tell him that he had not one, but two sons! Two healthy boys! And he had opened his eyes wide and opened his mouth and stood dumb for at least a whole minute, and then lifted his fists to the sky as though he had won a great battle. He looked so serious! So seriously triumphant. In her memory, her family had begun to freeze: single images sunk inside compotes of feeling.

"I expected Jim Cates to be here," said Fernie. "I wonder where he's at tonight." He leaned up against the iron gate, the barrier between the church and the village, and watched the road. He was unlike his brother: he never looked at Nora unless she was looking at him. Joe stared at Nora perpetually; if they shared a space, Joe angled his head to meet her eyes. It was as if he were trying to read a sentence written on her face. But Nora did not like to be looked at. If she looked away from him, Fernie looked away from her. He knew that she did not feel proud of her face or her body. When Nora caught glances of herself in the windows of Satus, she was struck always by the hard, stern knitting of her eyebrows, the downward tilt of her chin, the stern focus that seemed to plague her even when she was not dissecting, not studying, not working.

Joe was, in his heart, a happy man. He liked to see his brother swimming in the ocean. Joe liked to watch Nora when she played with Philadelphia. When she laughed, her eyes were enclosed in folds and lines like streaks left in a pond by some flitting, fast moving fish. She was nothing, in stillness; she would make a poor statue. But when she moved, when in action, whether walking across a room or dissecting the fragile arteries of a child's arm, she was beautiful. She never saw herself except frozen in a mirror. In this way, Joe thought, she was like his brother, who never saw himself as whole or right. They were similar people.

For years, Fernie had ducked his head and hidden. He was ashamed, in the beginning, of his missing leg. He, too, had felt hideous and wrong and terrible, a twisted monstrosity of a person. He recognized the feeling in Nora and respected it. He respected her and her need for privacy; even when they stood close together, if she did not look at him he knew it was because she herself did not want to be seen.

"Do you want to see our farm?" she asked Fernie. She walked off, away from the graveyard and into the road without waiting for his answer. If he wanted to come along, he would; she was ready to see the place again and needed to see it immediately, before the desire passed. But she walked slowly so that he could keep up with her if he liked.

Fernie again and again brought his sleeve to his face and pressed it to his temples. Before they left the edge of the town proper, they paused and Fernie turned back toward the center of the village. He whistled softly, and Phila, silent as a ghost, flew into the road; one minute, she was hidden by the shadows of saltboxes and high maple trees, the next, illuminated by the yellow moon and running toward them, frantic not to be left behind.

"We'll pass our old forge," said Fernie.

"It's on the way," said Nora.

The Gallos' old house and Mr. Gallo's forge were not contained in one building. Halfway between the Pirrips' farm and the village common, the old Gallo house sat occupied by Mrs. Gallo's widower brother. Matthew Anney had come to Chilling after his sister and her husband had died. He was there, ostensibly, to take over care for the boys, but he was a cold, reclusive man who wanted little to do with them; Joe and Fernie wanted nothing to do with him. They ignored each other, and the forge—a separate small building four hundred feet from the house—went cold and ignored. The village's new blacksmith built his own forge, nearer the common and his own family, and so Joseph Gallo's ghost, if it walked where its body died, was left alone.

"Joe told you," said Fernie.

"Yes," said Nora.

Phila walked in front of them, running madly for a few seconds then pausing, turning back, and waiting for the two of them to reach her with their slow walk. Then she would tear off, again, down the road. Her white tail bobbed in front of them like a torch.

"What do you think?" asked Fernie, "Do you hate us?"

"No," she said. "I understand that he was bad to you. He killed your mother. Killers deserve to die."

"We killed him," said Fernie, "which is not . . . it is not easy, even when you do it yourself, it's not easy to understand how big a thing it is. What you've done."

"People die. We're very fragile, really. You should see some of the bits inside us. It's a miracle we last as long as we do."

"I've sometimes thought I was going to die in the ocean. When the water gets very rough and takes me off. I've thought it a few times. That I was going to die."

"Yes."

"I think that's why I swim," said Fernie.

"Look," she said, "look at how pretty."

In front of them, the pond across from the Pirrip farm was stretched like a sleeping cat, moving with gentle wakes like soft exhalations, glimmering with the same calm moonlight that made Philadelphia's white fur shimmer and the sweat on Nora's temples glisten.

"Let's swim," said Fernie, but Nora smiled and shook her head.

"I don't like the water," she said.

"But I do," he said, and he sat down on the bank of the pond to unfasten the clasps of his leg. Phila was already immersed to the belly, waiting for one of them to throw a stick for her to the center of the pond. Her eyes flicked impatiently from one to the other and back again. She shifted her weight.

Fernie shifted and lifted himself up; he held out his hand for Nora.

"You go," she said. "You can swim."

Philadelphia pranced restlessly in the water.

"Not what I meant," said Fernie.

Phila ducked her head into the water and splashed the water with her nose.

"What did you mean?" Nora asked.

"I mean, come swim with me," he said. He put his hand on her waist.

Phila barked, once, shortly, and Nora bent to pick up a long slim branch. She tossed it as far as she could, toward the center of the pond, and her dog launched herself into the black water, swimming furiously after it.

Afterward, on their walk back to the village, they passed the dark Gallo house and Fernie pointed to a place in the blackness beyond where the forge stood.

"Right there," he said.

"Do you want to go and look in?"

"No," Fernie said. But he stopped walking and stood in the center of the road. "You know, I didn't think he would actually *die*. My father.

I thought we would do it, play a sort of a trick, and I knew, I suppose, that he *could* die. That it was a possibility. But he was my *father*. The man was immense. Like Joe. He was so big, and he was always working or being strong and holding his hammer, and his tools."

"You were too little to know."

"I didn't actually ever think that he could *die*. Even after, when he was dead. Even then, I thought, *No, not really*. He was my father," Fernie said, and shook his head. "Fathers don't die."

"What happened?"

"You know."

"I know what Joe told me. I know what he thinks happened."

"I don't know. I was twelve, and Joe was the only person I really knew. Whatever Joe said, or did . . . I wanted to do, too."

"Do you remember the night?"

"Yes. But I remember silly parts of the night, not the important parts. I don't remember everything that Joe says we did, stripping him naked and everything in the forge. Joe says it was very cold."

"What do you remember?"

"Ridiculous bits. My dad, drunk. He was singing a song. I remember him singing it, in the forge, and he grabbed my hands and we were dancing around in a circle and he was singing, *Hammer boys round, Old Clem! Old Clem! With a thump and a sound, Old Clem!* Sometimes I forget where I'm remembering it from, and I hum it or start singing it and Joe gets angry. But I don't think of it as a sad time, or a bad memory. Really."

"You don't remember Joe sending you away?"

"I don't remember," said Fernie. He shook his head. "I remember the song, and singing the song with my dad."

"I don't believe it," said Nora, "How you could forget so much?"

"It was a long time ago," said Fernie.

"Not that long ago," she said.

Fernie stood still in the road. Nora stopped, too.

Then Phila barked, somewhere ahead of them in the dark, and they followed her home to Satus.

Oliver Shoemaker followed them with his eyes until they disappeared, and then went to straight to the Peabody house, and he hammered on the door until Mr. Peabody, his eyes wet and glutted with sleep, opened the door.

Chapter XXVIII.
The Gallo Forge

In England, winters had been mild. There was rain and snow, but the season had been shorter and the weather less merciless. By March, in the Kent marshes, it smelled like spring. But our pasts rarely equip us for our futures. When faced with the winters of the American New England, a number of God-fearing farmers dropped dead.

So many died, in fact, that farmers began to understand that the winters here were not a season long, at all, but two seasons. At the beginning of February, when, at home, they would expect the weather to warm, the freeze to thaw, the snow to melt and the ice to disappear . . . instead, here, the wind only blew colder. What had been the end, in England, was here only the halfway point. They developed patience. They worked twice as hard in the warmer months. They did these things not because they were virtuous, but because they were necessary for survival. The length of the winter made them pale, diligent, obdurate. They chopped twice as much wood for their fires; their stacks stretched twice as far. They cut twice as much hay for the horses and cows; their barns sagged with the stuff. *Candlemas Day, half your hay,* went the saying. Less than half the store of hay or firewood left at the beginning of February was very, very troubling. When there was an empty minute, they picked up an axe.

But the winter, in its scorn for fragile human skin, could still be a happy season. Over time, the weather was anticipated. Storms were planned for. Expected. Preparation replaced fear, and after a few decades, New Englanders could ignore the discomfort of winter, and focus with redoubled energy on what yet remained good about their new home. The winter meant a cessation of the back-breaking labor of the warmer months. When the snow packed their doors shut, and when the ice frosted their windowpanes, they tended their small fires and closed their shoulders in thin blankets, clasped their children to their thin chests. They told stories and sang songs and slept gluttonously. When the storms abated, they lugged long curved sleds from their workshops, held their children again tight against their bodies, and flew down steep New England hills screaming in delight. It was objectively, coldly, beautiful: a pristine frozen expanse. They recognized the beauty even as they knew it could kill them. Children held icicles to the woodstove and melted the ice into the shapes of animals; they breathed on windowpanes and drew birds and the faces of their playmates. "This is you," they said to their brothers and sisters, pointing to a series of curving fingerstrokes.

But the finest days were the days after the blizzard had come and gone, and after the winds had died down. The boys had gone out with their shovels and dug paths around the farms, and thin footpaths cut like spiderwebs across the village. Outside the air smelled of chimney smoke, the oaky scent of three dozen fires burning. And though the wind was like death, the sky was blue and the sun was there, frozen in place, lending a hint of heat to anyone who could stand long enough and still enough to feel it.

One winter, the night before Candlemas Day, a young man got up from his bed and nudged his brother, who slept in the same bed. The younger brother was a heavy sleeper and so the elder had to shake him by the shoulders. The younger brother didn't speak, but sat up with his eyes still half-closed, and swung his single leg off the side of the bed. The elder brother placed the blanket around the shoulders of the younger, and they went together to put on their boots.

The ground outside was smooth and white. It was too cold for snow. Thick white ice gleamed and reflected the moon in a long, razor-like strip. The brothers walked to their father's forge. The closer they came, they could feel its heat, as though invisible warm bodies crowded around the building and brushed up against them in the dark.

They went inside. Later, much later, they both came out and spoke to each other quietly.

The elder brother went inside the forge again, and the younger brother stood outside. Time passed, and the younger brother pushed his face against the cold glass of the window. It was edged with soot; he had to squint and crane to see anything. He watched, for a few minutes, and in those few minutes he did not move at all, just his eyes darting, following the figures inside.

Then one of them must have made a move that startled him. He stepped away from the window. His eyes were wide and his mouth had fallen open. He went to the door of the forge and pounded on it; immediately, his brother opened the door and pulled him inside by the arm.

For a long time, there was no sound, and then the younger brother flung open the door and lost his balance on the threshold. He cut his chin on the edge of the icy snow; he put his hands on the ice and pulled himself up. He went away, fast, but not running, because he was unable to run. He went along awkwardly, rushing and then pausing, looking back, rushing away again and then slowing, once shaking his head and standing motionless on the ice. He had lost his blanket in his flight. He went home but did not return to bed. He lay down on the floor, and slept there until his brother returned with a red face and ice hanging from his eyelashes, and together they got into the bed.

The next day an old woman came and made them lunch, and told them everything was fine, and that they shouldn't worry.

Chapter XXIX.
Satus House

The corpses had all gone from Satus. The weather was too warm for dissections, and the last limbs and bits finally gave out, and there were no more. The house was very calm and quiet. The men shut themselves all day in the library with their books and their samples suspended in alcohol. In the evenings, sometimes, Salderman wrote papers on the malformed specimen in his collection and records of the delicate preparations they had made over the course of the winter. Fernie spent a few afternoons in Chilling, and he disappeared the mornings and nights. Joe was not well enough to wonder about his little brother's absences; he had cut himself badly on a bone saw, and he was busy sleeping off the infection. Lily and her mother cooked and cleaned and worked in the kitchen garden, Odette read and wrote, and Philadelphia snapped her jaws at flies. She chased snakes in the garden and barked at them until they wriggled themselves back into the stone walls.

Joe's head pounded and felt as though it had been filled with lead and dirt. Two lines of fire ran from his ears to the center of his brain. He lay atop his quilt, his head turned to the door, to press his aching head against the pillow. When Fernie came in, Joe's eyes were there to meet him.

"It's incredibly hot out," Fernie told him. "My shirt's like I jumped in a trough." He opened a drawer and rifled through the clothes.

"Who's helping you dig?" asked Joe.

Fernie had pulled his wet shirt over his head and stood with his bare torso in the center of the room. "Nobody's died! No gravedigging today, or yesterday, or tomorrow. I hope. The Reverend just had me doing some gruntwork."

"You visit Downey?"

Fernie threw his sweaty shirt into the corner of the room and pulled a chair up alongside Joe's bed. "Yes, he's good. And Paul says hello and drink lots of water."

"I hate water," said Joe. His face was very pale.

"I'll tell him you say so."

"What? Tell Nora come visit."

"She said she doesn't like being around sick people."

Joe gave a little breathy snort. His ears throbbed and he closed his eyes. "My head hurts," he said.

"If you die," Fernie said cheerfully, "she'll very happily cut you into little bits. Not today. It's too hot. You know Thomas Osgood said this was the hottest day he could remember ever having been, in this village? The hottest, and he's almost eighty."

"No one remembers the weather."

"Of course they do. Farmers."

"But you don't *remember* it," said Joe. "The way you remember what someone said. Or something you did."

Joe was speaking very softly, and his mouth was half in his pillow. Fernie had to lean in to understand.

"Weather," said Joe. "But they don't remember it."

"You're sicker than I thought. Salderman says you'll be better by the end of the week."

"Kids," said Joe. "Stupid kids."

"You're raving," said Fernie.

"It does," said Joe.

"It does what?"

"The weather, Fern, I'm saying it, the weather knows it all. Inside feeling."

Fernie stretched his arms over his head and stretched his neck. "Ah, you think there's a man in the sky saying, *Ah, Joey Gallo's sad, I see. I'll cloud up the night for him and make it rain.*"

"Natives," said Joe. He tried to lift his head off the pillow, but he winced and laid it down again.

"What?"

"They have dances and calls for weather. I don't know. I heard of it. They'll call on up to the sky and ask for weather. Promise things."

"You want some water?" Fernie went to the pitcher and peered inside, but it was dry as old bone.

"It's the same thing," said Joe. "Asking for the rain and when it rains."

"I'm sorry, Joe," said Fernie. His face, usually so pale and serious, was hot and flushed red. "Jice, it's hot."

"If there hadn't been rain in weeks or months. And maybe nothing was growing . . . you wouldn't feel good at all. Like storming. The weather makes you feel and the feel makes the weather."

"So if you're so sick and miserable," asked Fernie, "why's it such a perfect day outside?" His nails were dirty, and he pulled the knife from his belt to clean them. He leaned against the wall and slid the blade underneath his thumbnail.

"It's not perfect. It's hot, too hot. I'm saying the weather knows. People don't. You can't know another person."

"Does your head hurt a lot? Is it better at all?"

"I'm a good explainer. I explained everything to you when you were just a baby."

"You've got a fever and you're crazy," said Fernie, "The world is like what it's like, and certain things happen and certain things don't, and there isn't any explanation." He looked at Joe, in the bed, squirming with pain. Fernie had never seen his brother in this way. Joe was so big. Fernie had spent his life looking up at him.

"You look bad," Fernie said, more quietly. "You want me to get you anything?"

"No," said Joe. Fernie took up his new shirt and pulled it on. He wanted to leave, but he felt that there was something else left to say. He didn't know if it was him or Joe, who had to say it. Or what it was. He cleaned the fingernails on his left hand, carefully and slowly. Joe said something, but it was too low to hear. "What?" Fernie asked.

"Remember," asked Joe, "when we went to get the puppy from Storey?"

Fernie smiled. "Yeah," he said.

"That was a good day," said Joe.

"She was such a little thing," said Fernie. He wiped the edge of the knife on Joe's quilt. "And she's enormous now."

"It was so good," said Joe. He closed his eyes again. "And remember, how much it rained."

Fernie curled his left hand into a claw and examined his nails.

"I think there was a reason for it," said Joe. "There's an explanation." He burrowed his head into the pillow and gestured with one hand that Fernie should leave.

"Goodnight," said Fernie. "You're crazy with sick. I'll come bring Phila to visit you later. She'll lick the fever off your face. And water. Paul says lots of water. He wants to come pray on you."

"No," said Joe, but Fernie was already out the door.

A few hours later, Nora came up the stairs with a pitcher of water. She was looking almost as thin as she had looked when she first came to Satus in the spring; her bones protruded from her collarbone and face. Her eyes were underhung with black circles. Her hair, which still refused to grow any longer than the half-inch that had remained after her illness, was covered with the close black cap, and underneath it, her face looked very pale despite the sunshine outside. Her skin was slick with sweat.

The trip to Joe's room had exhausted her so completely that she had to kneel in the center of his room and lower her head to the floor so that she did not faint. Joe was asleep. She stayed there a while and then quietly rose again and took the chair by his bed.

"Hey," she said.

Joe's eyes opened and, as his head was turned, saw first the pitcher and cup on the floor.

"Hey No," he said, without looking at her.

"You need to drink some water," she said.

"It's way over there," he replied and Nora looked over at the pitcher.

"Yeah," she said.

"I wish you were here, Nora."

Nora looked at him. Joe watched the pitcher.

"But you're not here," he said.

Nora put her hands in her lap and leaned forward. Philadelphia padded into the room. She held, in her mouth, a leatherbound book. She settled at Nora's feet and began to chew steadily at the corner.

"Oh," Nora said, "bad dog." She leaned down and tugged at the book, but Phila pulled, too, and she had to wrestle her fingers inside the dog's mouth. Phila thought it was a game and growled.

"Okay," said Joe. Nora let go and Phila took the book a few feet away, settled down again.

"It's a compendium on ocular diseases."

"Eyes," said Joe. The glass and pitcher sat, white and serenely, in the center of the floor. "You know who has very bad eyes?" said Joe. He coughed.

"Who?"

"My little brother."

"His eyes are bad?"

"He can't see far away. He can just see a little distance close by him."

"Yes," said Nora.

"You know about my little brother's eyes."

"Yes," said Nora.

"Nearly a doctor yourself."

"No," said Nora. "I'd like to be."

"That's what I call you. No. For Nora. What do you think?"

"I'm not thinking anything."

"Do you think my little brother's eyes are bad?"

"No."

"You think they're good?"

"Yes."

"You think he knows?"

"Knows what?"

"Knows, *knows.*" Joe turned over onto his back. "Help me sit up," he said. "I'll drink some water."

Nora stood up and put her hands on his back and took his arm in her hand. They maneuvered together until Joe had risen halfway from the bed and could lean back against the wood of the stead.

Chapter XXX.
The Sloughs

There were not many times when Bonnie's body separated from her mother's. She was knotted there, most of the day, on Agnes's back or cradled in a sling by her chest. When she slept, she slept in a small crib close enough so that if Agnes rolled over, Bonnie felt a breeze across her face. Occasionally, Agnes handed the baby to another person: Dedlock, or Prudence, or Charity Benner. If Agnes was out midwifing, Bonnie came along and slept or played or watched her mother minister. Bonnie was never left alone. She was never more than a handswipe away from catching her mother's skin. She liked it that way. Agnes liked it that way.

Deep in the nighttime, in the earliest hours, the twins Scout and About began to scream in their beds; when their parents flew to investigate, they found About with a fork protruding from her little side. Her eyes were wide and frightened but she was not the one making noise: Scout stood against the wall, her arms straight at her sides, screaming over and over again: *Accident, accident, accident!* Then About collapsed. Her father pulled the fork from the wound, and the blood began to gush. Their mother, a muscled woman with a face like an intelligent pig, ran for Agnes Slough, pulled her from her bed, and the two of them went off to treat the child.

Agnes, of course, had assumed that Dedlock was in the bed beside her. Dedlock was not in the bed beside her. He had risen an hour earlier, worried and unable to sleep. He had pulled on his boots and jacket and gone outside to walk in his field and smoke and worry. The body in the bed beside Agnes was Jim's. He had taken advantage of Dedlock's quiet absence to crawl in beside his sister, and sleep there happily until her husband returned and kicked him out.

So it was that Bonnie slept in the house alone, save for Jim.

It was dark in the room, but there was moonlight through the window. In the corner, there was a chair. One of Dedlock's shirts lay on the chair. There was a tear in the shirt, by the shoulder. The moon shone on the shirt.

The baby breathed very quietly, only the smallest movement of her tiny chest, the occasional pursing of her lips and, once or twice, a sound from her like a question in another language. Jim stood up and swung his legs out of the bed. He walked to the side of Bonnie's crib. He reached down, very gently as his sister had taught him, and stroked the baby's soft downy hair.

He went downstairs, chose a sweet bun put aside for his own breakfast, and brought it up. He broke off a small piece and held it down near the baby's nose, but Bonnie was too deeply asleep and did not respond.

Jim sighed and put the bread in his own mouth and chewed and swallowed it.

Jim stepped back from the crib and kicked it once, hard. Pain shot through the bones of his biggest toe and through the thousand tiny bones of his foot. The crib rocked and fell over and the baby's little body struck against the floorboards. Bonnie began to wail and scream. She used her arms to pull herself up, but could not and fell down again onto her stomach. Jim kicked the crib again and this time wooden slats of the crib side came down onto Bonnie's body. The baby stopped crying. Jim picked up the crib and stood it upright again; then he lifted the baby—gently, like his sister had told him—and replaced her in her bed. She began to scream. Jim frowned. He held his hand against the baby's little face but she screamed and screamed. He went to Agnes and Dedlock's bed and took up one of their down pillows and held it against the baby's face. When he took it away the baby was not whimpering or moving at all, and her impossibly small eyelids, with their impossibly small lashes, were closed.

Jim took the pillow from the crib and replaced it on the bed. Then he lay in the bed, all alone, all by himself, curled into the position from which he had woken Bonnie. He fidgeted and fidgeted. He stood up. He made his sister's bed and smoothed the quilt. He returned to his own room. He lay down in his bed, atop the blankets, and put his forehead on his cool pillow. He could not close his eyes.

The moon made its slow orbit. The light moved through the glass of the window and slid down the length of the white sleeve, then down the bare rods of the chair legs, and finally, swept like a wave onto the floor. The moonlight was window shaped, molded into long stretching panes of yellow. The night deepened and the light moved slowly until it touched, with a corner of its pane-light, the leg of Bonnie's crib.

Gently, it pushed, and the crib rocked.

But Bonnie was no longer alive, and the sound of her breathing had gone. There was only the creeping sound of the moon on the floor, and the creak of the wooden crib.

The moon retreated behind a cloud, and the room was dark, and the shirt and the crib waited for Dedlock to return.

Chapter XXXI.
The Narrative of the Graveyard

The small bodies return to the earth much more willingly than those bones that have been hardening and hardening over long years. There is no word for what I want to explain. I want to explain how there was purpose when I began and how the world opened like the mouth of a god and how, since then, the world has shrunk to the disintegration of bodies and the darkness of process, how every day is the same as the one before and the one after. Those that die and are buried mean nothing to me and I watch with businesslike attention as parents and children collapse with grief. My purpose has not changed. But it has become rote. There is no beauty to vocation. There is no magic or celestial aroma to the work of turning bodies into soil. There is no grandeur. There is only slow, plodding process.

The girl with the dog came, quite a lot, in the summertime. Only, though, at night. Occasionally, she came with one of the Gallo brothers. They watched her as if they expected her to turn on them. Always, she came with her dog. It was black and white and trotted around and sniffed and ran and circled around the stones, trying to herd the graves. The girl visited the site of her family: she had five dead brothers. All of them, small little things, small bodies that disappeared immediately. The girl talked to each one, one at a time. She told them stories about her life and things she had seen and done. She told the littlest one, long gone inside me, stories about her dog and going swimming in the sea, how the dog barked at the waves and was afraid of them at the same time. She told stories about dropping a bowl of dry beans on the floor and watching them bounce and roll away everywhere, how she ripped her sleeve and was caught on a door until someone came and let her free, about how she started singing in the cellar and some people caught her out and laughed at her poor voice. She told them stories to make them laugh. They were paralyzed at the age they had left her. She never said a melancholy sentence, when they could hear her. She never used a melancholy voice and when it began to break, when she could feel her voice begin to waver, she stood up and went to the dog, and the dog reminded her to be glad, and she could begin again.

She came so often that I began to grow accustomed to her. She only came at night. I recognized her step on the path and so I knew the moment she would join us and I waited to hear her voice and the stories of her house, Satus. Though they have ways of telling me what I need to know, the bones never speak. I am a quiet place. When she spoke, we all listened; I listened. When she spoke to her brothers, she was speaking to me because I am them, and more, but this many-bodied life does not make my time less lonely. She, separated from them, felt their absence. I, joined with them, could not feel comforted.

Solitude has not freed me from loss, but it will not allow mourning. I have learned many voices but I fear I have lost my own. I do not understand the marks upon the stones, or the symbols in the windows. I do not understand what these things mean to those that create them. To me they mean nothing.

I will say that she loved the dog. She would sit and speak to her brothers for a long time, in the night, and the longer she spoke, the more her face drained of color and movement. There is an expression on the faces of men that speaks to me; it tells me that they will come, soon, and return to the earth. Or send someone there. And after hours speaking to the soil, the girl had this look. And then the dog would come, and lay its head in her lap. This small thing, the love and closeness of the animal, this small thing would change her entirely. And she returned to herself, and left me.

Chapter XXXII.
The Slough Home/The Chilling Graveyard

A house grieving is a man walking under a yoke. The road is endless, and the yoke unbearably heavy. But still, plod, plod, plod, blank-faced, the man walks as he has done every other day, one foot, the other, the other, over and over again.

Dedlock's sisters had all come, their daughters had come too, and Missus Woodhill came, and Cordelia Ridley and Anne Coldwell. The Osbornes sent food and the Hales sent food, and the Cotton girls were tending Agnes's garden and Daniel and Gervey had come to keep Jim company. Agnes sat in a chair with her hands folded on her lap. She watched them all as she might watch the waves at the ocean: not uninterested, but dispassionate, unconcerned. She could think of nothing to do. There was nothing to be done without Bonnie. How much work the child had been! Feeding and cleaning and working! Agnes had barely time to bathe her face during the day. And now all of that work and occupation had gone. She could not think of a single task that was worth doing. So she sat in a chair in the kitchen. Sometimes, when one of the women put something into her hands, she nodded. It was difficult to see. Her vision was cloudy. She tried once to smile but it felt as though a bone was cracking. So she did not smile. She did not move. Moving her body stirred and unsettled the emotions inside of her, and when they were riled, they rose up into her gut and shoulders and throat. But when Agnes was very still, and stayed still, they settled at the bottom of her body and slept there. Occasionally Dedlock would walk past. She remembered that she had once thought that she had loved Dedlock. She almost laughed. As if that was love. As if anything, other than her child, could ever be loved.

In the evening, when the women left and Jim had gone to sleep at Prudence's house, Agnes could not bring herself to climb the staircase. She slept in the chair. She liked going to sleep. She sat by the window and closed her eyes as soon as the sun showed any sign of sinking. She dreamed exclusively of Bonnie. In the dreams, nothing happened; only her little baby was alive. Bonnie was alive and laughing in her arms, or alive and breathing in the crib, or watching the birds outside the window, or kicking and squealing in her bath. "Nose," Agnes would say to Bonnie. "Is this Bonnie's little nose?" In her dreams, she could touch Bonnie's nose.

Waking was a nightmare and the day was a long attempt to cope with the fact of waking.

She could not look at the children of Dedlock's sisters without imagining them dead. She did not share this with Prudence or Charity, of course. She spoke very little. When she heard Priscella Slough whispering about preparing Bonnie's body for burial, she stood up and said a few sentences. She would do that, she said, and no one would need to help her. But if they would not mind collecting what she needed, that would be very kind.

Agnes soaped and scrubbed the little body, kissed her belly and her forehead, and wrapped her in white linen. The Slough sisters walked with her to the church. Agnes handed her baby to the minister. She sat in the church a long time until she heard shouting outside, in the graveyard and she walked outside. The gravediggers, the Gallo brothers, were kneeling on the path, pulling the weeds that grew up between the stones and throwing them, dirtclods and all, at each other's heads. The lame one was laughing and Joe, the large one, was smiling but he was not laughing; if Fernie's missile caught Joe on the head, Joe would let out an annoyed shout, fire back, and kneel again to his weeding. Agnes watched them and then she stepped onto the path herself. Her shadow fell onto Joe's curved broad back.

"Good morning, Missus Slough," said Joe. He jumped to his feet. He wiped his forehead.

"It is hot today," said Agnes.

"Yes, pretty hot," said Joe. He looked at Fernie. Fernie, still on the ground, shrugged. He turned towards the weeds.

"I've just prepared my daughter's body, Joe. And the minister says you'll be burying her. You and your brother will bury her. Later today, he said."

"Yes. I'm very sorry, Missus Slough."

"It is very hot. It is very important, to me, that my daughter be buried very deep."

"We bury everyone at least man's length, Missus Slough. You don't have to worry."

"I do. And so for my baby—for my baby, Joe—you have to bury

her deeper. I don't want anyone taking her. I don't want the robbers coming and taking her. I don't want her hot. I don't want her to . . ." Agnes paused and closed her mouth. She stared at Joe. "I want her cool and so far deep that no one even if they dug all day would find her."

Joe shook his head. "No bodies taken any time recently, Missus Slough. I would not worry about that. Captain Murderer must have gone off and left us."

Fernie looked at Joe.

Agnes turned around and looked at the graveyard. It was a broad and sunny day; the gravestones were warm and dry. The grass around each plot was green.

"Deep," she said. "Deeper than anyone else."

"I'll do my best."

"And stones," said Agnes. Her stomach heaved and she put her hand to her mouth. She knew she needed to return home. She needed to be in her chair where she could still smell her baby on the blanket and where she could be alone to strangle down her grief. "You put stones on top. No one takes her out of the ground."

Fernie stood up awkwardly and walked Agnes down the path to the gate. Down the road, the pregnant Abbie Osgood came out of her front door and stood a moment on the step. She lifted her face to the sun and smiled. Her red hair was loose from her braids, and it reflected the sunlight like a mirror. Her belly was enormous. Agnes froze and watched the girl stretch her neck and put her hands to the small of her back.

"Are you all right?" Fernie asked.

"Yes," said Agnes. She did not take her eyes from Abbie's body. s face, Fernie thought, was like a mask. Not like a real person, at all, just the sort of lines and colors made to impersonate a human.

"Should I walk with you home?" asked Fernie. But Agnes did not answer, only strode away from him, and Fernie returned to his brother. Dedlock Slough, now, was standing over the grave, rubbing his beard with one hand.

"Oh," Fernie said, "I didn't know you were here. Missus Slough just went." He pointed to the gate.

Dedlock turned to face Fernie. "Whose grave is this?"

Fernie looked at Joe. Joe shook his head.

"Ours," said Fernie. "Joe's, at least. He's the one making it."

"No," said Dedlock, "I mean, who will lie in this grave when you have dug it out."

Fernie gazed down at his brother in the dirt. He gave a short laugh. "The dead don't lie," he said, and moved off to sit on a small edge of moss. "They're truthful, most of the time."

"Stop it, Fern," said Joe. He paused in his work and leaned onto the shovel. "Hello, Mr. Slough."

"Joe," said Dedlock, "Whose grave? What man?"

Fernie shrugged and lay back with his arms under his head.

"No man, sir," said Joe.

"Oh. A woman, then," said Dedlock. He dropped to his knees by the hole, and leaned in close to Joe.

"No . . . not a woman, Mr. Slough," said Joe. He took up his shovel again, and then laid it against the wall of dirt. He looked at Dedlock's face. Dedlock's eyes, which had always been the reliable part of him, the eyes that always focused and probed, they wandered now. His eyes were vague, off center, dumb.

"Did you know they'll probably take our farm?"

"What's that?"

"For taxes. Because they raised the taxes and our farm is more acres than . . . not good soil, but still a lot of acres. If we can't make the payment. They'll take the animals."

"I'm sorry. That is terrible."

"You don't spend much time in the village," said Dedlock. "It's not a surprise that you had not heard."

"We have a lot to keep us busy up at Satus."

"Satus! Tell Salderman to come to a meeting sometime! Satus! I'm keeping you from your work," said Dedlock, sitting down. His legs hung down into the grave. "Please, please. Dig. Dig away. A big grave, it seems like."

"Not so big," said Joe. He took up his shovel again. Fernie, the sun on his face, closed his eyes. "This is a small one," said Joe. But Dedlock did not hear him, or did not mark that he had heard. He watched Joe shovel dirt.

"How long have you been digging graves for us, Joe Gallo?" he asked.

Joe did not stop working. "Since our mother died, Mr. Slough."

"Ah. Of course. Your mother did have an accident. We were sorry she died. And your father, too, I remember, close behind her. Gone to God."

"An accident," said Fernie.

"Stop it, Fern," said Joe.

"How long ago, now, was that, Joe Gallo?" Dedlock swung his legs. His heels struck the dirt and dislodged great hunks of it into Joe's blond hair.

"It was eight years ago, Mr. Slough," said Joe. He brushed the dirt from hair and kept digging.

"Eight years," said Dedlock.

"And when did you marry Missus Slough?" asked Fernie.

"We had a baby," said Dedlock.

"I'm very sorry," said Joe. "We both are."

Fernie sat up and shielded his eyes from the sun. "That's true, Mister Dedlock. We're very sorry for the baby."

"What name will go on the stone?"

"Her name, sir."

"No, I meant will it be the name we called her by? Or the name we christened her?"

"How do you mean?"

"In my wife's family, everyone goes by another name than what they are. Her sister was Margaret, called Maga. Jim is not a Jim at all, but he hates his real name so much that we call him by his second name, his father's name. He was christened Doleful James Cates. Dolje, we used to call him, but he did not like it. Agnes is fully Agnes-Rose, and Bonnie . . . Bonnie was named Annabelle."

Joe looked at Fernie. "What do you think, Fern?"

"I think they'll put on the stone what you want, Mister Slough, as you loved her best."

"Agnes was here. Agnes-Rose. My wife. I saw her speaking to you," said Dedlock.

"About how deep the grave."

"How deep will it go?"

Joe stopped and leaned against his shovel. "I'm digging her a man-size grave, plus a bit," he said. "So a little more deep I'll dig now."

"Does it matter, really?"

Fernie answered. "Not a whit, Mister Dedlock. The body, it'll go to pieces no matter if it's a hundred lengths down."

"The body," said Dedlock.

"That's true, sir," said Joe. "But I think Missus Slough was thinking about the grave robbers."

"How long? How long will it take to . . . the body?" Dedlock looked at Fernie.

"What?"

"What is going to happen to her little body?" asked Dedlock. "Will she still be my little Bonnie, when I come back and . . . her little hands, and her little eyelashes."

"Most men are already rotten, Mr. Slough," said Fernie, "long before we get hold of them."

"Stop it, Fern."

"How long before she's gone, entirely? Just nothing at all?"

"I don't know, exactly. I heard, eight year or nine years," said Fernie, "Around there when there's nothing left but bone."

Dedlock looked at Joe, still leaning against his shovel and blinking up into the sunshine. "Why have you stopped?" asked Dedlock. "Keep digging! Keep digging Joe! Dig it deep!"

"I've struck a stone. Fern, pass me the bar."

Dedlock stood and walked along the edge of the grave.

"Joe Gallo," he said, "you do such good work. What do I do? I grow a bit of food, a bit of flower. And it all withers away within the year. Cows . . . they take my cows. And that's not only me. Porter Downey, you think, well, his work will last. Metal. Or Nelson. A mason's work will last! But think, really . . . how long can things stand? A hundred years, a thousand years, before the stones wear away and tumble down? Worse for John. The carpenter's got rain and rot coming into the wood. And if you build a boat, it'll sink one day. All work. All this effort, all this work we do. All for what?"

Joe heaved his weight against the stone and it came free of the soil, leaving a black velvety hole alive with the bodies of insects. He yelped and threw himself backward, against the wall of the grave. The stone thumped down again.

"Got it," said Fernie, and he lowered himself into the hole.

"But you, the Gallo. The gravedigger. What you build is forever, isn't it?"

"What," said Joe. He hadn't been listening. Carefully, he heaved again and held the stone up. Fernie crawled underneath and plucked the crawlies from the hole. He held them in his hand and threw them up onto the grass, where Joe couldn't see them.

"How comforting," said Dedlock, "to know that what you made there, you made to last forever."

"I suppose."

"It's a very good feeling. To look on something you made, and say to yourself, this will outlive me. It's a very good feeling."

Joe looked at Fernie. Fernie looked away. He bent to pick up a worm.

"But you have never said, Joe Gallo. Who is this grave for?"

Joe looked up at Dedlock. He squinted at him. "No sir," he said. "I never said. But you know, don't you?"

"Hello, little worm," Fernie said to an inch of flesh in his hand.

"Ah," said Dedlock. "Worms. This is it, then? This is where . . . this is where the," Dedlock closed his eyes. "My little daughter. My daughter? This is where she'll go?"

"Yes," said Fernie.

"Here," said Dedlock, "with the worms."

Fernie smiled and held the earthworm up to Dedlock. "It is okay. It's good to have playfellows," he said, "I was never lonely as a child because I had my brother Joe. We played together and talked and kept each other busy. Fought sometimes."

"Playfellows," said Dedlock.

"Ignore my brother, Mister Slough. Go on, let me do this digging. I'm sure your wife will want you. Come back when I have finished. It'll be soon. Tell your wife that I have taken care of what she told me, and I will do it. Tell her how black you see the soil, how deep it is. Very, very deep, tell her that."

"It is a deep grave," said Dedlock. He looked around him help-lessly. "What have I done?" he asked. "Did I do this? Did I do this? Why punish the baby? What sense is that?"

"Go on home, sir," said Joe. Dedlock turned and wandered away, the seat of his pants wet and dark with the soil.

At home, Dedlock did not work. The men from the village came and worked shifts on the farm, to allow him time to grieve and, they thought, to be with Agnes. But Dedlock and Agnes did not see one another. She could not look at him. His face was too much the face of their daughter. The shapes of her, the smell of her, the skin of her, all of this was inside of him and she could not bear the weight of memo-ry in Dedlock's body. Agnes sat in the kitchen, or slept, and Dedlock's body was electrified. He could not sit for more than a moment; he ate standing up. He couldn't sleep. He paced the house and looked out windows, repaired table legs, folded and refolded blankets at the foot of their bed. He had taken the crib out to the barn and sometimes at night he went to see it. His stomach and gut were worse than ever. No one had been able to say how the baby had died, only that children did die, sometimes, even healthy ones, with no warning. Dedlock wanted very much to *see* Bonnie. He was distracted by his desire to see her. There were no paintings, no likenesses of his child, and now that she was dead there was nothing like her left in the world. Nor would there ever be, he thought, because she is dead now and no one will ever be able see her again. He would live the rest of his life and never see her again. Her face, her body, *gone, vanished, disappeared.* There was no way for Dedlock to understand how this could be true. The truth of this was too large, too unwieldy, and his mind could not lift it.

Chapter XXXIII.
Satus House

Lily came into the kitchen with a bowl of cherries. She came in butt first, opening the door by jutting her body into the wood. When she swung into the room the three men who had been speaking all fell silent at once. Salderman stood up and put his palm on the side of his face. Jules Demmer spat into his cup.

"So, so," said Salderman, loudly.

"Right," said Joe.

Jules stood and smiled at Lily.

"So you'll get the compost turned and take a look at the stone wall," said Salderman. "That'll be a full day for you, unless the Reverend needs you. All good. All right, for me."

Lily looked at Joe, who looked at the floor. She stared at the floor until all three of the men edged past her. There was not much space between her great bulk and the kitchen wall, and Joe could not help his arm from brushing against hers as he went past. Lily felt him jerk and shudder.

"Sorry," she said. Her eyes stung and her face flamed. She froze where she stood and waited for them to be gone. Then she sat down at the table with the cherries but did nothing. She folded her hands in her lap. Satus House was a different house now, she knew, than it had been when she and her mother had first come into it.

When she was small, Lily had lived in Gloucester with her mother and her aunt. They lived in two small rooms close to the docks, and it smelled like fish. Her mother and aunt had fought a lot, until finally her aunt left and did not come back. She had not then understood what her mother had been doing those nights and days in the side room, or why, later, she and her mother had been forced to leave Gloucester.

But then, when they had come to live at Satus, her mother seemed happy for the first time. Genuinely happy, not the feigned, smiling and nodding genre of happiness she had tried to project all through Lily's earliest childhood. Suddenly, there was enough food, every day. The beds were soft, the fires burned all through the night, and, soon, Lily would have a baby brother or sister. She did not know, when they arrived at the great isolated house, what was happening in the cellars. She did not know what the noises were, at night.

At first, Lily had been lonely in Satus, and she had asked if she could walk down to the village that lay at the bottom of the hill.

"To meet some friends to play with," she explained to her mother, who sat at the end of her little bed.

Lily's mother smoothed the blanket and then reached over and fiddled with Lily's limp braid. "Aren't you tired?" she asked.

"No," said Lily.

"Miss Salderman and her brother did us a very big favor, Lily. We are very lucky to work here. And one of the rules about working here is that we have to keep some very important secrets for the doctor."

"I can keep a secret," said Lily. "I won't tell anyone."

"Beauty," said Lily's mother. "Beautiful girl, I know you can. I know absolutely you can keep a secret. You have kept too many, already. But this isn't like Mama's secret, this isn't the same kind of thing. We can talk about it later, when you are a little older. But for now I would like for us to try to be happy in this house."

"There is no one to play with," said Lily.

"Your little brother or sister will be here soon," said Lily's mother. "And I'll need you to help me. And then the baby will grow up very quickly and you two can play together."

"Can I feel?"

Lily's mother moved to lie beside her daughter in the bed, and took Lily's small hand and rested it on her enormous belly.

"It's not doing anything."

"No, the baby is sleeping now."

Lily turned her head and laid her ear on her mother's stomach. She did not know how to convey to her mother how badly she needed to know other children. She tried again and again, but each time her mother only smiled and shook her head.

Her mother had given birth when Lily was ten, but the child was stillborn. Lily had wanted and prayed for a sister, but in the days afterward she was sure she would have loved a brother just as much, and she felt guilty for the prayers. She grew up. She divided her time between working in the kitchen, talking to her mother, and playing alone. She spent too much time alone.

But despite the loneliness, Lily grew up with a sense of security in her position. She came to understand what her mother had been and done in Gloucester. She did not blame her mother. If anything, she was grateful: her mother had traded something of herself to be able to care for Lily, to be able to feed her and provide a roof and home. They were very close to one another. They loved and felt loved in return. Lily came, too, to understand what was happening underneath the house. She never said it out loud, and neither did her mother, but they both knew. Lily felt as though she were part of something very great and very intimate, and she went on feeling this way until Joe and Fernie Gallo came to the house and changed everything. Lily fell in love with Joe. She knew that he did not love her. She knew it was never even a possibility and she was not bitter. Having a home and food and safety was enough. Anything else would have been greedy.

When Nora wandered into the kitchen, Lily still sat unmoving at the table. She had closed her eyes.

"What's happened?" asked Nora. Lily opened her eyes just a sliver, enough to see Nora's whisper of a body. The bones below her neck jutted, sharp as elbows. She was an assembly of empty space. It was a body in terrible pain, Lily thought. As if she still suffered from that nasty dread disease.

"Is something wrong?" Nora asked again. She sat down at the table across from Lily and grimaced at the bowl of cherries. She picked one up by its stem. "I love cherries," she said. "I used to. They were my favorite thing to eat in the summer time and I'd eat them all. I never shared with anyone. Then, oh, what shits I'd have. But I loved them."

Lily couldn't help herself. She pushed the bowl toward Nora. "Eat some," Lily said. "Please."

Nora made a face and pulled back. "Really," she said, "I almost want to be sick, here looking at them."

"Are you ill?"

"Not that ill. Off, maybe. Not ill. What're these bound for?" Nora replaced her single cherry in the bowl.

"I was going to make a pie. Or jam tarts. Maybe tarts."

"Joe'll be happy. He loves cherries. I just passed them in the hall. He was with Jules and Salderman, coming away from here. Were they here?"

Lily took a towel from her apron and spread it on the table. She took a cherry and pitted it by digging her thumbnail into its wet red flesh, popping the pit onto the towel. "They were just here," she said. She went on pitting. The pit of each cherry was worried free in less than a second.

"They smell so . . . well, they smell like cherries. But strong, aren't

214

they?"

"The cherries? They don't smell at all."

"Do you know what they were talking about?"

"No," said Lily.

"I could smell them in the entrance way. The back way."

"That's where I carried them in."

"I could smell them when I came inside. And I saw Joe and Jules and Salderman, and they didn't look at me, and then Joe looked like he was going to say something and he didn't. So I wonder if, you know, there's something they're doing and they don't want me to know. Oh, jice, I've left Phila out and she's probably digging."

Nora stood up and paused. She put one hand to her forehead and another onto the table to steady herself. Lily would have stood up more quickly to help—she tried—but her body was large and it was a process of inching and wedging and pushing. It took a moment before she could lift herself and move over to Nora.

"You're ill," she said. "You look very ill. Let me get my mother."

Nora shook her head. "Stood up too quickly," she said. "I'll tell Joe about the tarts."

"It's not about you," said Lily. She sat down again and began pitting again. She pitted the cherries quickly and efficiently, sliding her sharp nail into the fruit with the precision of a surgeon.

"What?"

"They shut right up when they saw me, is what I know. So they don't want you to know. But they don't want me to know what it is either. So it's not you, Nora. They don't want us both to know."

Nora stared at Lily. "That's right," she said. "That does sound right. Do they do that a lot?"

"What?"

"Make secret plans and have conversations we can't hear."

"Sometimes, yes." Lily shrugged. "It's a strange house. Leave it alone, that's what we do. We're happier not knowing."

"I'm going to get my dog now, Lily. Then I'll come back and help with the cherries, if you want. The tarts, or whatever you're making."

"No need. I'll be done sooner without your help. But . . . I can watch Philadelphia. If you want."

"Do they do anything else?"

"Who?"

"So they have more secrets than just the corpses? Is that the only secret or are there other ones?"

"There are other ones."

Nora nodded and left.

Behind Satus, in sight of the sea, a portion of the stone wall had tumbled and needed repair. Some of the larger stones had rolled some way off, as the ground sloped downward on the north side, and as Joe loaded them onto the sled Fernie waited with the ropes to pull them up the hill.

"I feel strange about tonight," said Joe.

"Careful, your toe."

"It'd be different if we'd been doing it more, but just the one, alone. And a baby, that makes it different."

"Are your ears all better?"

"They're better."

"Because if you can't hear good, you know. Trouble with that."

"I can hear okay," said Joe. "What does he need it for, anyway?"

Fernie shrugged. "If you don't want to do it," he said, "Jules or Paul'll come. I can do it without you."

"Fern," said Joe. He pushed a large round rock onto the sled and then sat back in the grass.

Fernie looked up. His lashes, like his eyebrows, were almost colorless, so that when he was alarmed he never looked alarmed; his eyes only opened slightly wider, revealed slightly more blue, but the pale expanse of his face remained unfurrowed and unworried. His face had always been a serious face. But until recently, it seemed to Joe, it had been serious and careless. Now—and Joe couldn't say when it had changed—his little brother's face had become the face of a man. Fernie had outstripped him, somewhere along the way. Despite his limp, his fear, his size, Fernie had made his way silently past his big brother, and was striding toward something.

"What, Joe?"

"Do you know why Salderman had to leave England and come here?"

Fernie stared at his brother. For a moment he let his mouth hang open; then he closed it, pursed his lips, and nodded. Joe nodded back. He felt as though he was going to vomit.

"Okay," said Joe. "That's good."

"Did he tell you?" asked Fernie.

"Does she know?" Joe tried to swallow. His throat closed and he panicked, and for a moment he could not breathe. He spit on the ground and again feared he would vomit.

Fernie shifted and adjusted his leg so that it stood more securely underneath him. He dropped the ropes of the sled and walked to the top of the hill and climbed up on the tumbled portion of the wall. Up by the house, there was a hazy figure that he thought was Nora, and a small thing next to her that was probably Phila. He rubbed his eyes. "Joe," said Fernie, "I don't know. Sometimes I think she does. Salderman asked me to find out. I've been trying but she's too strange. I don't know."

"How did you know? When did you know?" Joe concentrated on breathing. He breathed in and then he breathed out and this helped him feel less sick.

"Salderman. Last year. He needed my help."

Joe watched his brother's back. "You think Jules or Paul told her?"

"I don't know," said Fernie. "It's possible. I've seen her talking to them, but I don't know."

"Odette said he'll go back to England, soon. Because it went so well."

"I don't know about that," said Fernie. "But if Nora knows what he did . . . and how he did it . . . she'll do something before he leaves. She's not right."

"Yeah," said Joe, "How did he do it?" He did not know how long he was going to be able to keep standing. His stomach had dropped out of his body entirely; he was going on now purely by force of will. He felt himself perspiring with the effort.

Fernie sighed. "A few weeks before they got sick, he asked me to bring them a few jars of jam. He said we had extra, and they would go to waste. He said to bring to their farm, only, because they were so far away from the village. They'd be the best ones."

"Go on."

"I asked what he meant, and he said the jam might make them a little sick, but that it was a harmless little experiment and they'd be fine."

"Go on."

"When the father started to get bad, he left and went to Boston. I don't know why." Fernie climbed off the rocks and came back to the sled. Joe could not stand any longer. He sat down on the ground and put his hands on his knees. Fernie piled all the loose stones in small pyramids. When Joe was able, he stood up, and together they hoisted the ropes over their shoulders and pulled.

Chapter XXXIV.
The Narrative of the Graveyard.

One of my favorite stories is the story of Lazarus, a man who dies and is buried and is brought up to live again. The minister has told it; he recites his sermons sometimes in the night air, with a cigar. He stops and speaks then walks and smokes. Stop: speak, walk. Smoke. Stop again, speak, walk, smoke. Stop: woman sees that her brother is very sick. She loves this brother. Her brother is her family, a man whom she has played with when they were children, quarreled with, the man who knows her more honestly than most men because he can love her without the temptation of sex; he has seen her since she was a little girl, and she has seen him. How rare this love is, between brother and sister, a bond we forget because passion, pain, love, because all this interferes.

Speak: Come, please, come heal my brother. Come, please. Come save my brother. Come heal my brother; stop and turn with me and walk to my home where he is and come and heal my brother to save him the brother walk and stop and come with me heal save brother walk stop heal come come heal save brother.

Walk. The minister told the story of Lazarus in the summer. It was rare that the Gallos took anyone in the summer. It was quiet and warm at night and humming with starry insects. The minister could walk here unmolested and the sweat dried on his neck with the breeze. He would pause before a grave and address it, waving his hands so that the bright tip of his cigar drew great meaningless letters in the black air.

Smoke. But he the healer would not come. He sat and smoked, lay resting against a rock in the dry desert air watching the colors of sunrise once, and then again. She was frantic at his feet. She tugged at his clothes, held his face in her hands and screamed into it as she would have yelled to a dying child down a well, she pulled him away from his seat. But the healer would not come.

Stop, he said, stop.

And finally she gave up. She walked days back to her home, where her brother was dead. She sat in the corner as they anointed him. She sat in the corner as they wrapped him in a burial shroud. She was dull and dumb. She felt like the inside of a stone, before the mason finds a shape. When they forced her to move, she knelt and pressed her forehead against the ground. So she stayed and the dust settled on her for four days until the healer came with his men and he pushed her a little with his toe, which was dirty. She looked up and spat in his face.

"I am sorry," he said. "I never had a brother, myself."

And it had been so, yes. He had grown up alone. He had played alone, and walked alone. He had eaten his meals alone, and gone to bed alone. When he was a child playing with stones in the mud, he made sounds indicating speed and force, whoosh, rawr, but these sounds were for no one, because he was alone. His parents loved him, but sat apart from him, sat at the end of the table and watched him eat; they feared him and feared to lose him. Is it to possible to understand "brother" if one has no "brother"? So, to understand, he walked himself to the tomb where he saw the body of Lazarus, and the body was dead.

Oh, it was pleasant! The minister smoked his cigar. He leaned his head back when he exhaled. Telling stories and the fresh night air! Him and I and all I had within me, like children gathering round to hear a tale. We listened. We are the finest listeners. The smoke does not bother our eyes; we cannot blink or see. The smoke does not tickle our throat; we cannot breathe or speak. We have stopped entirely, to hear your story.

The healer stopped a while in the tomb and sat with the body. He unwound the shroud from the man's head and saw that the man looked like very much like the sister. This made the healer feel sad, because the healer was a human who could feel sadness and sorrow and despair.

He said, Lazarus, come back.

And Lazarus did.

Lazarus did!

The minister's cigar, alight in the nighttime, was like a furiously dying star, and when he had told his story he dropped it down into me and the fire went out. A slim arm of smoke stretched upwards.

I think I am in a rare place. It is a happy story, the story of the risen man. It is the story of impossibility! Because no one comes back from here. No one has congress with me and lives to gossip about the softness of the bed. It is a chilling, simple ending, but it is the ending to every story. It is a happy story, always, when you hear of a man who can do what no other men can do. Perhaps it encourages you to inch like a worm outside your own limits. I don't know.

But the story of Lazarus is a tragedy and I feel that I am in the rare way of understanding it. When I accept the body, I assume it is forever, because in every case, it is forever. We meet and marry in a moment; we are bound irrevocably through hell and high water. There is no other choice.

And when someone comes and takes from you what you have joined with, body to body, it is as though they remove your limb, an essential part of yourself which cannot regrow or regenerate. The forgotten sadness is the dark empty hole of Lazarus's tomb. How sweetly they had prepared his body! How fragrant the oils, how lovingly his sisters' hands wrapped the shroud! How they cared, how they cared, for those final concrete acts, for their brother's body . . . and then he was taken, brought back to the living, and he stepped out of that shroud as though they were rags, left the tomb that sheltered him as though it were a mere hold of rock and air, with no thought to void his life would make.

What is a tomb without a body? An empty belly, a barren ship's hold, a fruit scraped clean of pulp.

And so I was, when Joe and Fernie returned in the nighttime to dig up the baby who they had buried in the daylight, when they removed her tiny body, when they took her away.

Chapter XXXV.
Satus House

In the Satus cellar, the men were dervishes of removal, whipping old bones into bags, tossing skulls one after the other to roll like cabbages in huge flat garden baskets. The air in the cellar was dirty with the smell of the decaying dead and the sweating men. They were all of them up and moving, up and leaving. Everything was falling down. Jules shouted, Paul heaved a man up the stairs, and even Mug ran back and forth with armloads of blood-stained sheets and rags and smocks.

Nora had been working for hours, too, dissembling and packing a number of Salderman's most bizarre and didactic specimen, loading them into crates and hammering them shut. She moved slowly, though, slower than everyone else. She was feeling so tired.

"Thanks be," she said, when Jules came into the Collection room. "You need to explain. What's happened? Why is he leaving?"

"I don't know," said Jules. "I only know we need to be out and erased by the morning."

"Has he been called off to a new place? This doesn't make sense. He's leaving so much behind." Nora gestured at the long rows of jars and preserved flesh and bone. "If he would just wait, another day, we could pack it all up."

"I don't know," said Jules. "He came down, happy, and told us to pack it all up, and that we were heading to England. I haven't seen him or Fernie since. Have you seen Fernie?"

"No," said Nora. She put down the hammer and looked at him. "I gave him Philadelphia this afternoon and he said he'd look after her."

"We can't find him."

"Which one?"

"Either."

"Did you ask Joe?"

"Joe's upstairs. With Odette."

"Well, did you ask him? Fernie doesn't hiccup without Joe knowing."

"Joe is . . . not himself."

Nora stood up and ran to the head of the cellar stairs.

"Phila?" she called. She ran to the back door, to the kitchen. Phila

221

was not in the places she should have been. Lily had not seen her. No one had seen her.

"Where's the dog, where's the dog?" she cried, running from door to door in the cellar. Paul caught her arm before she tripped over an ash pail.

"Calm down," said Paul, "she's around here. Likely chewing a piece of someone's leg."

"Or rolling in it," said Jules.

"Or rolling in it," agreed Paul. He smiled crookedly at Nora.

Nora had gone still. She put her hands out to Jules and Paul, as though to hold them at a distance. "She's dead," said Nora quietly. "She's dead."

"Okay," said Jules, "why are you so wild all of a sudden?"

"Your dog is of course fine," said Paul, "Everyone is just busy at the minute, Nora." He whistled for Phila.

"I can feel it," said Nora. "I can feel her gone. I shouldn't have let her out of sight. I should have kept her close to me and not let anyone take her, ever, away from me. It was too risky. I am stupid, stupid. What did I think? What?" She picked up an empty bucket and threw it across the room. It clunked to the floor. Paul and Jules looked at each other and then turned back to their work.

Upstairs, Odette rifled through the pages of a book.

"I've mislaid the Homer," she said. Joe sat on the trunk with his eyes closed.

"I don't care," said Joe.

"Would you mind a little Shakespeare? You probably won't understand a word. But I can try to read it so that you might glean the sense."

Joe didn't answer. Odette glided to the corner of the room and leaned against the wall; she tilted the book so that the firelight fell upon the pages. When she leaned her head to the right she could brush her cheek against the dress that hung there.

"I'll read from a comedy, I think, because I don't think you'd survive a tragedy. We'll find something. There is a play, this one, and in it there is a man who has been shipwrecked. He finds himself lost on an island ruled by a strange and cruel man, and the sailor falls in love with the man's lovely daughter. The cruel man, though, forces the man to work very hard, to do heavy labor."

"Why does he work so hard for a man he hardly knows?"

"For the love of the daughter," said Odette.

222

"Go on, then."

"Well, here he's talking about the work he's been set to do. '*There be some sports are painful*,' he says, '*and their labour*

Delight in them sets off: some kinds of baseness
Are nobly undergone and most poor matters
Point to rich ends. This my mean task
Would be as heavy to me as odious, but
The mistress which I serve quickens what's dead
And makes my labours pleasures: O, she is
Ten times more gentle than her father's crabbed,
And he's composed of harshness. I must remove
Some thousands of these logs and pile them up,
Upon a poor injunction: my sweet mistress
Weeps when she sees me work, and says, such baseness
Had never like executor. I forget:
But these sweet thoughts do even refresh my labours,
Most busy lest, when I do it.'"

Joe shook his head. "I didn't understand a word," he said.

Odette put her finger in the page and came to sit on the trunk with Joe. "You can follow with me," she said, and opened the book on her lap. When she read again, she traced each word with the tip of her finger.

"'There be some sports that are painful, and their labour delight in them sets off.' He says here that there is sometimes work that is hard to do, but it is the very difficulty of the work that makes it worthwhile. Then he says that 'poor matters point to rich ends.' So that perhaps other kind of work—maybe not such fun work—that can be good, too, because it's leading to something very good. And so he can put up with the pain and difficulty now, for a reward later."

"That sounds like church," said Joe.

"I suppose," said Odette, "this writer was Christian. And he had his own ideas. This man, in the play, he goes on to say that his work is, in fact, very hard. But he says that he does not feel upset, because he is doing the work for someone he loves."

"They won't love him if he doesn't do it?"

Odette shook her head. "No, in fact she already loves him. Later, she offers to do the work herself."

"So then why is he doing it?"

"Well, it's a comedy. There are ones that makes even less sense."

"It sounds like misery."

Odette sighed. "Yes. Well. It's a comedy. There is misery. It ends up happy in the end," she said.

"You keep saying that. Comedy. What does that mean?"

Odette began to answer him, but she was interrupted by a knock at the door. Nora leaned her head inside the room.

"Joe," she said.

Joe closed his eyes and leaned his head against the wall.

"Where's Phila? Where's Fernie?"

The night previous, before Salderman had received whatever news he had received and before the doctors knew they would be travelling across the sea, Salderman sent Joe and Fernie on an errand. They had gone out together just after midnight. Jules, knowing their errand, had gone with the wheelbarrow to Wolfeborough and walked with them as far as the bottom of the hill. "If the old man gets a summer body," Jules had said, "I get a summer body. And not a piddling little baby body." The brothers had gone into Chilling and Jules off into the forest. Oliver Shoemaker and Octavius Peabody had been waiting by the steps of the church; they watched Fernie stand at the gate, they watched Joe dig up Bonnie Slough and tuck her small body into his pack. Together they followed the brothers back through the village, and then up the steep hill to Satus.

Joe explained this all to Nora without looking at her. Odette sat, the book in her lap, and watched them.

"Your uncle came into the house. He spoke to Salderman," said Joe. "He said, this is too far, and that babies were never allowed. And Salderman tried to calm him down, and said he would send something down to the Sloughs, to help, and that made Peabody more angry. They fought for a long time."

"My brother is returning to England. He has taken a position working with the British military."

Nora ignored Odette. "I am surprised," said Nora. "My uncle. He should have woken the whole village. They should have come and arrested him. And you. They should have arrested all of us."

"Well," said Joe. "Your uncle didn't seem very surprised. Just angry. But I haven't seen Salderman since this morning, so maybe he went down to the town."

Nora turned to go.

"Wait," said Joe. "I want to bring the baby back. I want to bury her again. But it's in no shape. Paul did . . . Paul got to her." Joe left the room. Odette and Nora stood in their places: Odette by the fireplace and Nora in the doorway.

"I'm Nora Pirrip," said Nora.

"Yes," said Odette. "I've met you through Alex."

"Does he speak about me? Or my family?"

Odette raised her eyebrows. She gave a soft, short laugh. "You have to understand, Nora. His heart is good, but the path to progress is bloody and can seem, even, evil. You should talk with my brother. But I am sure that the arrangement is that you will go to your uncle's house."

Nora opened her mouth but Joe had reappeared; he carried a bundle of dark wet rags. When Nora took it she could feel the child, who had been methodically pieced apart, a jumble of soft flesh and hard bone within.

"Jules and Paul are getting rid of everything," said Nora. "How did they forget this?"

"I hid it in the apple bag," said Joe. Nora looked at his face; as they always were, his eyes were the color of the sea, like Fernie's, and they were fixed on her own. He looked pale; his cheeks, usually flushed and ruddy, were gray. Wisps of blond curls had flattened under his cap and lay on his scalp like hair shorn from a corpse.

"I just need you to put her back together," said Joe, "as best as you can."

"If you're going to bury it again," said Nora, "there's no point in me sewing her up. No one'll see her." But Nora pulled a corner of the rag free and folded it back. She saw what was left of Bonnie Slough. It was the first time she had seen a baby since they buried Bartholomew. Her heart fell beneath her.

"I'm sorry," she said, "it wouldn't take that long. I'll do it now."

"Thank you," said Joe.

Nora tugged her black cap low into her forehead and left the room. She had forgotten to ask about Fernie; she had forgotten the dog.

"Nora," Joe called. He heard her footsteps pause on the staircase. "Fernie's bad leg splintered a bit on the way up the hill. The buckle broke and he slipped. He's trying to fix it, out in the woodshed. He took the dog."

Nora ran down the stairs and into the cellars again. She swung herself into each room until she found Paul, alone, in the corner room. He hadn't cleaned it out, yet. Paul stood with his arms folded. He stared moodily into the partially dissected pit of the stomach.

"Ah," he said, when Nora came to stand next to him. "Jules

brought this one."

"We need to get this body out of here," said Nora.

"Jules has begun the burning," said Paul. He sighed. And in the damp air there was, just perceptible, the woody scent of a bonfire.

Paul leaned forward, so that his head hovered directly over the open stomach.

"You know," he said, "an interesting fact here, we can try it out." He took Nora's hand and stretched out her index finger; he pressed it into the cavity of the man's stomach.

"Taste," he said, and Nora touched the tip of her finger to her tongue.

"Salty," she said. "It's a little salty."

"See those little holes, there. There. The gastric juices—yes, salty, I think so too—they go on with digestion. Even afterward. After death, the stomach is still with the acid. So I used to think that these little holes in the stomach were symptoms of disease. But no. Time at the table. With time and experiment, you begin to see how wrong everything you thought . . . at the beginning . . . in course. Time, ignorance. So now we understand this."

"This burns holes in the stomach, if there's no food to dissolve," said Nora.

"Yes."

"We need to get this body out."

Paul straightened up. His face was long and morose. He had aged, since Nora had been at Satus, more than a young man should have aged.

"Salderman thought it would, in the end, save lives."

Nora stiffened. "I don't know what you are talking about. Dissection? Of course."

"Nora. The books you have taken, the questions you have asked. Years ago, many many years ago, a group of men came to Salderman. They wanted a way to make their enemy very sick."

Nora listened but her face did not change.

"They wanted to end battles before they had begun. If their enemy's soldiers were all sick, they could not travel or fight. There would be a great reduction in death and war."

"He couldn't do it."

"Not well enough. It is easy to make people sick . . . it is another to make sure the right people stay healthy. He needed to sicken some, and make sure his own people stayed alive. He promised to find a way to contain and control the disease, and taken much money, but he could not do what he was asked to do. They were angry with him. He came here."

"No one told me this."

"Of course, we could not."

"We worked very hard to keep it to only one family, and to observe, from a distance. It was highly infectious."

Nora laughed. "I know."

"Of course."

"So what is it?"

"It is not really new. It is a sickness that has been around a long time . . . Originally, he wanted to infect a large amount of people with multiple diseases, at the same time—dysentery, plague, typhoid, others—we could topple a whole army in days. That was what he wanted. But of course that couldn't work. We cannot control the spread of so much disease. Salderman wrote to doctors abroad, and asked about contagions. He imported one body . . . we had been told it was unlike anything we had seen before, violent and terrible and fast. We have been working a long time to find a way to find a cure for it, so that we may keep our own people safe from infection. That, Nora, was you. Salderman cured you of this. Salderman has been called back to London to share what he has found. They are pleased with what we have uncovered."

"But it's not perfect," said Nora. "My family all died. He did not cure them all."

"For now, one out of eight, this is good enough."

"Why? It is a poor result."

"Because he tried something different with each of you. It was your cure that worked."

Jules appeared at the doorway. "Have you seen Salderman?"

Paul shook his head.

"We can't find him. I sent Lily down to Chilling but nobody's seen him there, and he's not in the house."

Paul looked at Nora. She shrugged and looked away. Paul turned and his shirttail flapped behind him. He and Jules strode off. The men bustled in the hallway, talking and climbing the stairs.

Nora stood above the man's body. She held her finger up to her face, to see if the stuff that had torn that ugly black diseased-looking hole in the stomach had had any effect on her skin. But no. Her fingertip was pink and she could make out, even, the ridges of skin that ran in perfect ovoid tracks. She placed Bonnie on the table.

Chapter XXXVI.
Satus House
The Osgoode Home
The Chilling Churchyard

She did the best she could. Bonnie had been dead a few days already; the weight of the child in her hands was almost featherlight. Nora had never worked on a baby before. She had never even worked on a child. She stood above the body in her smock and wondered if the men had kept her from these bodies on purpose, because they feared her feminine instincts would overwhelm her intellectual curiosity or her work ethic. She felt, suddenly, very alone.

The baby was a girl. It was hard to look at her. Nora did not want to feel sentimental; she had dissected and sewn together so many bodies, and she did not want to admit that this was different. There was a part of her that did feel, instinctively, love for this small mangled body. Nora wished the dog was with her. She wanted to leave the house and go out to look for Philadelphia, pick her up though she was now too large to really be carried, and take her upstairs to sleep and sleep until all of this had ended and it was day again.

But she did not. Nora made the stitches small and tight, and she swaddled the baby in a clean blanket. Upstairs, Joe stood by the window and watched the clouds begin to turn from gray to black. She showed the bundle to him and asked if he wanted her to come along, to keep watch while he dug and buried the child again. Jules, passing, overheard.

"Neither of you should go anywhere near the churchyard right now," he warned. "We need to find Salderman and the village is angry at him just now. They know about Bonnie. If they know you did it, Joe, it will be bad for you down there. We'll burn it."

Joe shook his head. He took the baby's body and replaced her in his pack. "Tell Fern not to follow, if he finds out," he said to Nora. "Try not to let him find out."

Paul's dissected corpse was still on the table, though he had sewn portions back up with big loopy careless stitches. If she had had the

228

time, Nora would have unpicked and sliced out the thread and done the whole job over again. She did not like to see sloppy work. But there was no time: the sun would be up in a few hours, or less. She hooked her arms under the corpse's armpits and dragged it off the table and into the hallway; one of the men would come and drag it onto the fire. Then she set to work on the room itself. She threw the bits of flesh and muscle into buckets, kicked the rats and began hard scrubbing on the bloodstains. She was sweating and the sweat poured off her forehead onto the table, where it mixed with the blood and water and soap.

"Where is Joe?" called Fernie down the cellar steps, but Nora couldn't hear him.

"Nora!" he bellowed, "Eleanor!"

She paused, a dark-stained scrub brush clasped in her hand. "Fern?" she called back. Hearing her voice, Phila barked.

"Where is Joe?"

Philadelphia appeared suddenly, crashing through the hallways and coming up on her joyfully. They had been apart a long time and the puppy knew that Nora was her mother: Nora loved her more than anything else on the earth, and the dog could smell this the same way she could smell food cooking, or a skunk coming.

"You are here, Feela-deela," said Nora. "My best girl." She could not help it: suddenly she began to weep like a child, like one of her brothers who had fallen down and hurt his knee. She could not stop, either. She tried. She tried to stop. Nora kissed the dog's nose and Philadelphia tried to climb into Nora's lap.

"Nora! Where's Joe?"

"I can't tell him," she said to the dog.

"Nora!" yelled Fernie, "Answer me!"

"At the churchyard." Nora closed her eyes. She was tired and she had not eaten. Her head swam with color; she felt pressure behind her eyeballs. She clung to Phila's neck. "He's gone back," she shouted, "to rebury the baby."

There was no response from the top of the cellar stairs. She waited, then knelt down and brought her forehead to the dank foul-smelling floor. She understood the idiocy of what she had allowed Joe to do; she understood that she should have stopped him by holding her hand out to him and asking him not to go. She could not muster the energy to care. Everything was named, now. Everything had been put in its place. Why it had come upon them so suddenly and strangely, so violently, only them, and why no one could help.

Philadelphia sat, half in Nora's lap, and whimpered. Nora stroked the dog's soft ears. Phila smelled like the woodshed, fresh and invigorating, and there was still sawdust clinging to her belly. When Nora could stand again, she left her work and climbed upstairs.

In the kitchen, she looked at Lily, who nodded toward the kitchen door. Through the mist, and the storm that was coming up the hill, Nora could just discern Fernie's slim shape making its way awkwardly, lurchingly down the grass. He would fall many times, she thought. His leg was not fixed. He must have wanted Joe to help him, because he could not fix it himself. He was not wearing any hat.

"Fernie," she called out after him, "Joe will be fine. It's Joe, Fern."

The darkness and the mist and the slope of the hill swallowed him up; she could not see him.

"Joe! Fern! It's Joe! Our Joe!" she yelled, as loudly as she could.

"No way he hears you now," said Lily. "It'll be pouring rain in another minute, now."

"I had to let him go," said Nora. "He said as much. Joe did. He wanted to do right by the baby."

Lily looked at her and smiled. Her face was pale save for two feverish spots high up on each cheek like spots of blood. Her hair had been carelessly twisted back into her cap, and a limp, sweat-wet tentacle of her braid lay flat against her neck. She wiped her nose with a pudgy hand and came so that she stood close—very close, very close to Nora; their noses nearly touched. When she breathed, Nora thought, Lily's breath smelled of a windowless room, closed with a corpse inside.

"What have you been doing?" asked Nora. "Are you feeling alright?"

"We've been burning horrors outside in a fire," said Lily. "Nothing is right. No one can find the doctor and there are horrors in the garden."

"I know. I know. I'm sorry, Lily. This is wrong. It may be my fault."

"We haven't seen him for hours and hours," said Lily. "I think there might be something wrong. We've looked everywhere."

Nora whistled, and Phila came like a thousand horses, all eagerness. "Go," she said, flinging her arm in Fernie's direction. "Go on with Fernie."

Phila started, but paused. She looked down the hill, and then back at Nora. She couldn't go. She wouldn't leave. She turned and returned to the house. She wouldn't leave Nora.

The heavy rain, when it came, was less terrifying than the wind. Down the hill, past where Fernie slid and fell and stood again, past the churchyard where Joe was just opening the gate, past the cows who huddled together under the single tree, past the Flaggs' garden in which the water pounded the peppers back into the soil and forced open the leaves of the lettuces, past the huge muddy puddle before Joy Beddington's front door, the wind blew through the village center and shuddered the doors and windows of the Osgood house. Inside, hours ago, Abbie Osgood's belly had begun contracting like a vise, again and again, around her son.

Agnes Slough squatted at the end of the bed; Lucy Osgood poured water into a bowl; Abbie was silent and pale and sweating so much it was as though she had just come inside from the rainstorm.

"It's raining," said Agnes, "Raining very hard."

"Yes, the boys said it was coming down in buckets," said Lucy. "Agnes, what can I get for you?"

"Nothing, nothing. Abbie, sweet, just pull your nightgown up there."

Abbie heaved forward and bunched her nightgown in her fists. She couldn't see Agnes's head behind her own massive belly, but she sat and up and craned her neck.

"What?" she said, "What is happening? Is it going to be quick?"

Agnes took each of Abbie's thighs in her hands, one at a time, and rubbed the muscles until they relaxed, at least a little. The wind howled like an animal; the tree outside Abbie's window threw its branches against the glass and they scraped themselves across the pane.

"It'll be a little while yet," said Agnes. She licked her fingers and wheedled them inside of Abbie. "Just a little while longer, Abbie."

"I don't want to die."

"We don't want that either."

"Can we wait a little longer?" Abbie looked at her mother. "I'm not ready. I need more time. Momma," she said.

Lucy came to Abbie's side and kissed her face. "You'll be patient and very strong."

"You'll need to be patient," said Agnes. "Patience and calm will help."

"Nothing will help," said Abbie. There were tears on her face but her voice was very steady. "I don't want to do this. Please, please don't make me. Please don't let me die. Don't let me die."

"Pray to the Lord," said Lucy.

Inside her body, the muscles of Abigail's uterus suddenly tightened and quivered there, holding on, holding on, and staying tight, tight, tight around that small child inside.

"Momma," gasped Abbie.

"Remember to be calm," said Agnes. "Remember when pain begins, it means only it is soon to end."

Lucy put her palm on her daughter's forehead.

"You are a strong person, Abbie. God is good, Abbie. We will help you. We're going to stay here and help you."

Every breath that Abbie took was drowned or muffled by the shrieking of the wind, the shaking of the house, the beating of the rain. The candles burned slowly and steadily, enough light so that Agnes could see the widening and stretching of Abbie's small body, the smallest and youngest person emerging, and coming into the room.

It was nearly dawn when Agnes came downstairs.

"Hello, Michael," she said to Abbie's small brother. "You have a little nephew," she said.

"Momma said that I was getting a brother," Michael said suspiciously. He stood up and took a step toward the staircase.

"That's right," said Agnes. She put her hand to her forehead and closed her eyes for a moment. Her forehead was warm and she felt a stone in the bottom of her stomach. "Brother."

"Can I see him?" Michael asked.

"Have you seen my cloak, Michael? I had it when I came."

The cloak, though, was not on any of the pegs in the entrance way, and it was not, when Agnes trudged back up the stairs, anywhere in the bedroom or in the hallway. The family was crying and rushing about and so Agnes drifted around the house, looking into room and opening closets. Her legs felt numb, and cold. She wanted her cloak for its warmth and heaviness and did not want to be forced to look for it, walk aimlessly around this house that was not hers. She dreaded walking out the door, into the rain and the cold, and trudging the long way home in the rain, but she could not tolerate another moment in the Osgood house. The storm had not let up; the house was loud with the noise of the water on the roof and the wind on the windows. There was a fire in the kitchen, Agnes knew, because they had been boiling water all night, and she went to stand by it for a moment to warm up before setting out cloakless into the night.

She smelled it before she saw it. Someone, in the rush and confusion of the birth, had thrown her cloak by the fire to dry, and it had been thrown too close. The fire had scorched one side almost completely, and there was a large hole burnt through the center. Seeing it, Agnes's eyes welled with tears and she was deeply annoyed, less with the thoughtlessness of the Osgoods than with her own reaction. She wanted to sit on the floor like a child and cry at the unfairness: here she was, helping as she always helped, and they throw her things into a corner and burn holes through them. She wanted to run upstairs and force them to apologize, to provide her with something new and clean and rainproof, so that she could—at least! at the very least!—walk home dry and warm. But in the end she did none of those things. She listened to the sound of the storm outside and the rushing happy family upstairs. She pulled her cloak around her shoulders and smoothed it and pulled the hood over her head and stepped out the door.

The wind came from the east, from the very direction Agnes need not go: her house was west and so she could walk there quickly, with her face away from the hard horizontal rain that was coming down, now, in buckets and sheets, not in drops or showers at all. The rain was loud, too, the wind in the trees and the water against the roofs and ground, the sound far off of the waves crashing maniacally on the shore, against the rocks and up the steep sides of the cliff walls.

And then Agnes did not turn west, toward home. She turned east. When Agnes turned into the rain she was almost thrown backwards and she needed to hunch herself and stagger forward. It was a decision made without thought, merely the knowledge that she could not go home. Not yet.

Agnes dropped her chin to her chest and pushed, headfirst, through the wind and the rain. The thought occurred to her that if only she was big and powerful, like Prudence, everything would be easier. Prudence, who had biceps like cannonballs and Prudence who had laughed through each of her childbirths, Prudence who would stomp her way through this storm without thinking it any effort at all. Prudence with three strong sons. The road was a river of mud;

Agnes tried to walk on the grass but it had become so soft that she sunk and the water came to her calf.

There were two trees in the churchyard. A low willow in the southeast corner spread out over the fence and onto grass beyond. During the day, the willow would shade almost half of the road. Then, by the entrance to the church, just to the east of the doorway, stood a giant elm tree. The elm folded its arms like a sentry, impassive against the rain. Joe had placed the bundle containing Bonnie's remains at the trunk of this tree while he dug her grave again.

Joe was resting. He was wet to the bone and had been for so long that he didn't mind the rain and, really, he was beginning to enjoy it. He had taken off his shirt and he had wanted to take off his pants, too. They were wet and heavy on his legs when he was digging; the mud clung to them, too, and rubbed against him. But he did not take them off. The rain felt so good on his chest and his arms, and even when the water came into his eyes and he had to stop to wipe them clear, he thought of how the rain was good. It had been a bad day, a bad few days, a bad many days, but that the rain was good. It would be okay, in the end. Salderman would go to England, and all of this would be over.

He put his hands to the small of his back and leaned backward. He turned and looked toward the elm and there, bending over the bundle, reaching a hand to draw it open, was a dark, hunched figure.

"Hey," shouted Joe. "Stop."

"Yes," said a voice from the darkness. The wind and the rain carried and changed the sound, though, and to Joe it did not sound human, like a man or a woman.

"What do you want? Go home."

"Joe Gallo?" The figure stood and straightened. It was a woman, Joe saw, in a long cloak with the hood up against the rain.

"Yes. What is wrong? Why are you here? It's stormy and dark, go on home, now."

"Nothing is wrong." The woman crouched again and reached for the bundle.

"Don't, don't . . . please don't, for your sake."

Agnes drew away the folds of material, untied the ties, reached in, and drew out her Bonnie. She had been sewn roughly back together with dark coarse thread. Agnes brought her face close and then away again, to stare at what had been done to her.

"Who did this?" she asked Joe.

But Joe had thrown his shovel aside, as soon as he had seen her reach out her arm, and he was running and jumping over the tributaries of rainwater and the slick stones; he ducked into the forest, to cut the distance between himself and the hill. But the forest was dark, much darker than the road had been, and even if the rain was lighter here, held off by the dense branches and leaves, the air was colder and Joe was running sightless, barreling and tripping toward the hill. He could hear the rushing of the brook and he steeled himself for the leap he would have to make, over the running water that was probably now high and rising. And as he did he saw a small figure, off-balance, standing in the way, in the middle of the rushing water, unsteady on a rock.

"Stop, stop!"

But Fernie had shouted too late, and Joe knocked into his thin unstable body with all the force and might he carried with him through the forest. Fernie went down heavily into the water, and the back of his head cracked against a slab of granite. When he stood up again, he was wobbly on his feet for a moment, and put both hands up to his face and then down, again, to his sides. He took a step forward. "Joe?" he said. "My head? I hit my head."

Joe linked his arm through his brother's and they sloshed through the brook together, to the other side, and Joe pulled and led Fernie back to Satus. They were both soaked through to their skin, and they stripped naked in their room and pulled blankets over them like capes. Fernie lay down in his bed without taking off his boot. "Fire," he said to Joe, at one point. Joe unbuckled and pulled off Fernie's false leg. "My head hurts," he said to Joe.

"I'll get Jules," Joe said. Joe took the leg downstairs and laid it by the kitchen fire to dry out.

For a while, Joe sat there, alone, and listened to the rain. He felt very tired. He couldn't hear anyone in the house at all. He stirred the fire and piled two more logs on top. Then he remembered Bonnie. He left the house and went down the village again.

There was no one awake. The darkness, the storm, lulled everyone into late sleep. Bonnie's body was still there. Agnes had replaced her in the little bundle, and placed it inside the open grave that Joe had dug, now, twice. He reburied Bonnie as the sun was coming up, darkened and obscured by the rainclouds. The handle of the shovel was wet and kept slipping out of his grasp and as he reshoveled the mud back upon the grave he swore over and over again, just a litany of swearing, the same word again and again and again. The largest blister on his hand burst and stung. When the grave was filled, he went back to Satus, built up the fire in the kitchen, drank a great deal of water, and got into his bed.

Later, when Joe had almost fallen asleep, Fernie started to talk again. "There might be in the pit. Let me in. No, no irons."

"Okay, Fern," Joe had said. "Go to sleep." He was very tired. His body hurt. His head hurt.

Five hours later, when Joe woke, Fernie was dead.

Chapter XXXVII.
Narrative of the Graveyard

It is a strange relationship, you and me. You do not like me. You do not seek me out on a sunny day, for an afternoon of ease and quiet happiness. If it has been a long time since you stepped foot here, you do not miss me. You not sit and think of me, quietly, sadly, feel my absence in your life. You come when you must, when obligation or decency compels you to come, or by chance, chasing after a loose animal or laughing child.

I don't mind. I am never too fond of visitors, anyway. Or maybe I have simply grown used to the lack of them.

A little unfair, I think sometimes. That I must, through necessity, understand loneliness because you inflict it upon me. Unfair that my existence depends on you. Unfair that I spend my days waiting for you to arrive. Unfair that you avoid me. You hold your breath when you walk by, you hurry past; some of you are afraid. I do not totally understand why, though. I have thought about it and I have some ideas: maybe the immensity scares you. I am large, I contain multitudes, and you are merely one. That, I suppose, yes, is frightening. But when I see you, there is a portion of my heart made glad because I recognize you as part of myself. I wish that you could see yourself in me, too.

Or perhaps it is just that: the fact that you do see yourself in me, that fact that frightens you and keeps you away. That feeling, that sensitivity at the nape of your neck, the feeling of being watched? Kinship with those within me. Perhaps you know very well that you are being watched, every second, that I am feeling you breathe and counting the spaces in between the pumpings of your heart, measuring how long it will be. I am aware of you; I watch you, and perhaps, maybe . . . yes, I think you do know it.

But do not be frightened. There is no reason. It is always difficult, of course, to be seen exactly as you are. And that is how I see you, exactly as you are. You cannot charm me, or woo me, you cannot deceive me or ply me with gifts or lies or compliments. Alive, as you are, you have nothing that I want. Alive, you have hurt people. You have meant to hurt them: I saw you do it. Alive, you have hurt most deeply those who have loved you most profoundly; I have seen you do it. You have not been honest. I know you; I see you exactly as you are.

I am waiting for you. I do not care what you have done with your time, or what you have not done. I do not care if you are kind or cruel. I do not care if you are a genius or an artist the likes of which the world has never seen nor will ever see again. You are compost, like everything else. If you have told lies, I do not care. Your lies are not your flesh. They do not last. They do not matter as matter only can. I do not care, either, if your flesh is ugly or deformed, or terribly butchered, injured beyond repair, riddled with cancer, swollen with pus. I do not care if you are the beauty of the county, if your skin is dusky perfection or your eyes like gems. It is all the same. For me and for what I am, you are perfect as you are, or however you will change. There is no way that you can be imperfect. This is not sentiment. It is plain, undecorated fact. We are all made of bones.

I see you, exactly as you are, blood and bone and brain, frantically alive. You think—oh, you think it in error!—that to be seen is to be judged. I do not judge you. I do not judge you for what you have done. I do not judge you for what you feel or think or seem to be. I accept you. I wait to accept you; you are wholly, entirely accepted.

The price of this acceptance is everything: your very life and the lives of all you know and love. Those who wander inside my gates of their own accord (the loose animal, the laughing child) have not reckoned with the price. They have no fear of me, no fear of death, no fear of what dreams may come. But neither do they need that fear. They have been accepted already by the primary source of their universe, their own fleshy hearts. They have not learned the comedy of life, that every moment they are alive they are less alive, that everything, one day, will end for them and something new will begin. When they stumble across this information, accidentally, as it were, as you brush against a spider's web in the dark, it is in that very moment that they cease to accept themselves exactly as they are and begin to measure and weigh. They think: if living is temporary, then surely there must be better ways to live, and better ways to be than those to which nature has inclined us!

You all forget, so quickly, and so irrevocably, that you are perfect, made for the perpetuation of the earth and for no other purpose than for the good of the soil. You are here to serve the earth, and there is no possibility that you can fail at this task. You have everything you need; you will be called to do your work, in time, and you will do it.

Chapter XXXVIII.
The Slough Home

Abbie Osgood's baby was enormous. Even Prudence, with her half-ton of sons, was impressed that Abbie had birthed him without managing to die afterward.

"She must have rearranged her insides, that little thing," said Prudence.

"It's a beautiful child," said Agnes.

"They're all beautiful," said Prudence. "But not all of them are that size. It'll have her red hair, I can tell it. What's that? Is that a scorch?"

"The Osgoods left it by the fire," said Agnes.

"Give it here," said Prudence. "I'll mend it for you."

"Thank you, Prudence." Agnes left the room and came back with a scrap of heavy material and her sewing box.

"How dare they leave such a nice piece by the fire! You should have left their baby by the fire! See how they like their nice things that gets holes burned through them!"

"Prudence."

"I'll bet they didn't even see you home."

"No," said Agnes.

"In the rain! With a holey cloak!"

"It was very rainy," said Agnes, "very wet, and windy. I went to the churchyard, on the way home."

Prudence stopped sewing and looked up at Agnes. She lifted one eyebrow and pouted her lower lip.

"To pray for Bonnie?"

"I saw her," said Agnes. "I saw her."

"It's good to go and visit, at the beginning, Agnes. That's fine. You should go and see her as much as you like, if you can. We'll help you out here, and we'll make sure Dedlock has help. Should you just peep out and see how Jim is getting? He's been out a bit long."

"Jim stays out of the house now. We never see him."

"Growing up," Prudence said.

"Prudence, why are doing this? Why do you come to the house? You have your own family. Your own boys, work, everything. I don't see what you come for, unless to watch all this misery."

"Don't be stupid. You are my sister, Agnes," Prudence said. "That is mere fact. I don't know what you mean by watching the misery. I'm here to watch the misery and make sure you don't get left alone. Sew your cloak up. Take your bread to the oven on Wednesdays."

"I haven't been kind to any of you who have come to help."

Prudence squinted at the needle and smoothed the cloak across her knee. "This is done," she said. "Not pretty, but it'll keep the rain out."

Agnes hadn't told. She doubted herself, in the daytime. When she woke up, the morning after, the sun high and bright, Jim shouting with his friends in the road, Dedlock's smell on the sheets, she regarded the whole thing as a dream. And it had been like a dream, she told herself. It was so dark and the rain seemed to come from all directions, and the wind sometimes could have blown her off her feet. She dreamed of Bonnie every night. But until now the dreams had been good dreams. Bonnie had been healthy and laughing, grabbing at fingers, sleeping and moving her lips. She had loved those dreams, while she dreamed them. When she woke, though, the pain was worse for having been soothed. Now, after this nightmare—her baby torn apart, as though by dogs, and sewn together by some dark and clumsy hand, the body deflated and wretchedly dead—the morning awake was a good morning. She could breathe, she felt. Her chest felt light. She was glad to see Prudence, she was glad of the company and the voice in the house.

Jim, sweaty and panting, ran into the room. "We found this," he said, and held out a raggedly pulled white flower, the buds tiny and clustered, the roots still earthy, to his sister.

"It *looks* like it," said Agnes, "But what I need is a different plant. Remember, yarrow has smaller leaves. This is helpful. I can keep it. But we still need the yarrow. Say hello to your aunt."

"Hello."

"Are my boys helping?" Prudence asked, but she did not look up.

"Yeah."

"Ah," said Agnes, "that's all fine, Jim." She stroked his hair back from his forehead.

"I'll go again and look again," said Jim.

"No," said Agnes, "You'll go out with me and we'll find some together. I need to take a walk outside, Jim."

She pulled Jim to her side and hugged him there. Jim turned and wrapped his arms around. He buried his face in her stomach. Prudence smiled and Agnes smiled back at her.

"Come on," Agnes said to Jim. "Let's go out."

"What's this called? What we found."

"That's spikenard. It is good for a cough, so we will keep it and dry it. But it has other names. Our mother used to call it Brother's Blessing. And Prudence, her family calls it oglethorne."

"That's confusing," said Jim. "Things should just have one name."

Prudence coughed into her sleeve and stood up. Earlier, she and Agnes had made the dough for the week, and the shaped loaves had risen. She cleaned a knife to mark them for the oven. "The problem with names," she said, "is that they are too easy to change. Look at me, Jim. Prudie, they called me, as a baby. Then Dedlock was born and he couldn't say my name right, so he said Oodi, which was close, and then everyone got to call me Oodi, and Prudie disappeared. Then I married John and out went the Slough. I used to be Oodi Slough."

"That's a funny name," said Jim.

"A funny name, but I liked it. But when I was married, Prudence came back, because my husband said a grown woman couldn't be called Oodi or Prue or Prudie. I was used to those names, and being called Prudence was strange now. I had been so long away from it. I had a whole new life—new house, new home, new bed to sleep in, a man who slept in it! And no one said my name, anymore. They called me Missus Reed. Prudence Reed was a new person and I didn't know her very well. Then I had the boys and they called me Mama and I turn around now, when someone says Mama. John started calling me Mother, too. I hear that more than I hear Prudence. And no one says Oodi. We should have a name for our whole life, shouldn't we? A lilac is a lilac its whole life, when the bush is flowering and when it is not flowering. And when the whole thing is dug up we can even say, That's where the lilac used to be. When my husband died his name didn't die: I am still called by his name. And I'm the one alive! A name should be something stronger, more like a rock and less wooden. You shouldn't be able to cut down name, kill it, burn it to ash. If it must go, let it be worn away over great swaths of time, by dogged determination of the sea and wind and the elements of God. If it must be changed, let it only be carved into a new shape. But never gone. Never taken away and destroyed. What are we, if we are not our names?"

"Flesh and blood," said Agnes. "Faces. Wombs. Without it, no name."

"Ah, that's the midwife speaking, isn't it?"

"The body will say the truth," said Agnes, "in a way no name will ever say anything. They say you can see a baby's father in his face, the way he has his father's eyes." She paused.

"What's that?" Prudence looked up.

"Or his mother's nose or the shape of his grandmother's chin. And so without saying a word, not even knowing the fact himself, the baby has a body which betrays the truth of things, how things are, have been, what has happened in the past."

Prudence motioned Jim over to her side. "Help me make these marks, Jim."

"What do I do?"

"Just hold the knife right here. Perfect. And we are going to make your sister's marks on these loaves. One, two, three swipes, just like that. And then we'll do my marks on those."

Agnes watched the two of them slice her initial, A, into her bread. Jim was careful, very slow. After each mark, he turned his head to watch Prudence's quick swipes and back again at his own.

"Our gran used to say," said Agnes, "that when you lay with the Devil, the Devil marked you on the body. And this mark would remain forever and it would mean the thing you had done. Because it is something impossible to hide: you cannot ever be separated from your body, can you? It's you, after all. You can cover it up, maybe. You can hide it. But you can't ever change it or discard your body, not really."

"Agnes," said Prudence. She pointed her knife at Agnes's nose. "You know that we came to Chilling just to spite all that. We've left behind all that way of talking."

"We came to Chilling because it was a place that kept secrets," said Agnes.

The next morning, Dedlock came downstairs to find Agnes awake in her chair.

"My stomach," said Dedlock, "my stomach is very bad today."

"Jice, Dedlock," cried Agnes, "why is it so bad? Every day? Every day we have been married, you have been like this. Nothing helps. It never gets any better. What is it? Why is it so bad?"

"It wasn't always," said Dedlock.

"It has always been," said Agnes, "as I have known you, it has always been."

"I was here before you knew me," said Dedlock.

"Help me, I know it, Dedlock. I know it. I know very well you have a life away from me."

Dedlock turned and looked at his wife, but her back was to him. "Agnes?" he said. She did not turn around. He walked to the staircase but did not climb the stairs. He turned and came back to Agnes's chair. "Octavius Peabody told me what they were doing. Up the hill. Do you want to know what they were doing there?"

"We knew the council'd made some deal. It was better not to know then and I don't want to know now. He's paid half the town's debts. Paid ours."

"They had Nora Pirrip. She was living there. And we dragged the pond, everything."

"Where did you put the little knife? We had it yesterday, and you put it somewhere."

"She's been up there, at Satus, this whole time. Not a mile off."

"Then she didn't drown herself. Good. The Hales still get the house?"

"Do you want to know what they were doing? Up at Satus House?"

"I need you to take the knives to Downey. They are all dull."

"I sharpened everything on Thursday."

"They're dull. Downey will do it right."

"I want to tell you about what they were doing."

"Dedlock, I don't want to know."

"Oh," said Dedlock. "That's a bad feeling. My stomach is bad."

"I am sorry," said Agnes. "I know you don't believe me, but I am sorry. I don't want to know. I don't care."

Chapter XXXIX.
Satus House

They did not find him.

Salderman had left behind everything: his clothing, his books, his favorite medical specimens, his medical bag. Letters. All of his papers and documents. He had taken nothing with him, it seemed, but the clothes on his back. And in the rainy weather . . . no cloak or cover at all. No hat. Simply gone, someone said, like Maga Cates all those years ago.

They waited a week. For a letter, for a message, for his footstep in the hall. Finally, Jules and Paul gave up. They packed and left for Boston. They needed jobs, now.

In the days following Fernie's death, Lily waited for Nora and Joe to pull against each other. She expected them to engage in a competition of grief, a tug-o-war for the claim of deeper mourning. But just when she expected them to yank and pull, to turn on each other and drag the other down, they silently put down their ends of the rope, and walked in opposite directions.

Lily and her mother cooked, still, but began to make less and less food. There were four fewer mouths to feed. Nora wafted around the house like a ghost. They saw her maybe once or twice; she ate almost nothing at all. She spent her days in the Collection, packing and boxing and preparing every misshapen skull, every suspended fetus for the long trip across the sea. In the evenings, she went upstairs to the library and read dull passages about circulation and wound infection and cataracts. She replaced all the books and journals she had taken. She cleaned the room, too, removing the teacups and the plates hardened with food, organizing the texts on the shelves.

"I'm almost done," she said to Odette Salderman. "I'll go away, when everything is packed, and sent. And when the library is back in order."

"That's fine," Odette had said.

"What are you reading?"

Nora had felt Joe enter the library. Philadelphia, who had been sleeping beneath the desk with her head on Nora's foot, lifted her head and resettled it again. Nora kept her eyes on the page so that Joe would think she had not noticed him and go away again. She turned the page. It was a heavy, hard bound book with sharp edges. Joe came closer and stood by her elbow.

"What is that you are reading?"

"This man dissected an elephant," she said.

"Pictures?"

"Yes." Nora handed the book to him. Joe stood over her chair and paged through.

"This is amazing," he said. "I've never known an elephant was as big as this."

"Are you leaving?"

Joe closed the book but kept it in his hand.

"Heavy," he said.

"I wondered what you are going to do."

"I spoke to the blacksmith," said Joe. "Downey. He's agreed to let me work with him, and I can live behind the forge. I'll go there after I finish up here for Miss Salderman."

"Downey. That's good," Nora said.

"What are you going to do?"

"You know. I'll go to my uncle."

"Yes, I knew. I don't know why I asked." There was no second chair at the desk, so Joe swung himself up onto the desk and sat facing Nora. He put the book in his lap. "I won't see you every day, anymore," he said.

"No."

"You could come, sometimes. You could come to the forge and we could go to the sea, sometimes." Joe reached out his hand and he touched the top of her head. She had stopped wearing her black cap. He ran his palm over the short, uneven bristles of her hair. Nora jerked her head away.

"Stop," she said.

"What?"

"He died coming after *you*," Nora said. "As if it wasn't enough what you did, what you made him do nearly killed him with guilt. He was devoted to you. He would do anything for you. That's what killed him. You're what killed him. He was going after *you*."

Joe lifted the book and hit her hard against the side of her face.

Immediately Phila leapt awake and tensed herself in front of Joe; like a shot Nora's hand went to the dog's neck and held her back. Phila's eyes were furious and she growled so lowly and softly that Joe could barely hear her. The growl vibrated in the room and he could almost feel the pages of the book tremble. He thought about what would happen if Nora let go. If he would have to kill the dog. But Nora held Phila's neck. The wound gaped in her cheek like the mouth of an animal.

"I'm so sorry," he said to her. He looked down at his hand as if it had acted independently of him. "Nora, I am so very sorry. I didn't mean to do that."

With her free hand, Nora reached down and dabbed the end of her apron at the blood. She clenched Phila by the scruff at her neck and dragged her to the door of the library. "It's okay," she whispered, and then shoved the dog into the hall and closed the door. "I very much deserve it." Joe looked at the books on the desk. He reached down and turned a page. The printing was tiny. He looked for J's, but there were not very many. He put his finger on one and tried to smear the ink but it did not smear.

Nora stepped very close to Joe, so that he could feel her breath. She reached and took his hand from the book. She held it inside her own hand for a moment. Then she guided it behind her back, and positioned it low, just below her waist. He could feel the hard and irregular knobs of her spine. Behind the door, Phila whined.

"When you do kill me," Nora said, "you should aim right here. It won't do much to hit me in the face."

Joe pulled his hand and with it came Nora's body. Her face was underneath his and he felt her breath on his chest. She felt very small. She felt very much like nothing. He pressed his palm against the small flat of her back and when she wouldn't be pulled any closer, he stepped toward her. He could feel her face get hot. He leaned in and bent down to her height. With the tip of his nose, he traced a line from the corner of her eye down to her lips. Then, without making any sound, he began to cry. He tried to stop, before she felt the tears on her skin, but he found that he could not. Nora put her arms around him and pulled his face down, against the heavy fabric of her dress. He knelt and pressed his face against her body and circled her waist with his arms. She rested her chin on the top of his head. "I know," she whispered to him, "I know, I know, I know." They stayed like that for a long time. When Joe stood, and stepped back to see her face, it was striped in blood.

Nora moved through her tasks so efficiently that she was done before she was ready to leave the house. She planned to speak with Odette, but she had been relying on Joe to open the door for her, to chaperone their talk, act as an ambassador. She hadn't understood Joe's relationship with Odette, but she did not care. Now, though, after what had happened in the library and the way in which they had parted, she gave up hope of Joe's intercession on her behalf.

"How well do you know Odette?" Nora asked, in the kitchen.

"We know her grand," said Lily. "We're only women in the house now, right, Mama?"

The woman they called Mug laughed and looked up. "What dooya need? Odette'll help. Where's that pretty girl? Hey, Feel! Feels-beela!"

Mug bent to kiss the dog on her head. Philadelphia sat and looked up at her patiently and expectantly. Lily and her mother had been very kind about Philadelphia. They let her sit in the kitchen, after she'd grown out of her mad puppy weeks, and Lily had taken the time to teach her to obey when asked to sit and heel and stay. In fact, Phila had spent more time with Lily and her mother than anyone besides Nora and Fernie, and she preferred to be in the kitchen when she was evicted from the cellar.

"We could keep the dog if you want," said Lily. "Mama and I don't mind."

"Oh," Mug's face lit up but she was careful to sound calm, "we could, just, look affer her. If you cannut take her with you." She looked at her daughter and smiled. "We'd make her a part of our family."

"The littlest cook," said Lily. She looked at her mother and they both laughed.

Nora felt sick, as though she might vomit. She coughed and put her hand to her head. "No," she said, "I need her with me."

"Of course," said Mug. Her face fell and she turned back to the soup. "They huvvent found the doctor yit?"

"They sent out searchers to the forest," said Nora. "They couldn't find him."

"Someone dun away witthum," she said.

"Mum," said Lily, "no one would do that."

"No?" said Mug. "Oh, no?"

"I have to go speak with Odette. Do you think she'll mind? I don't know her well at all."

247

"Ah, Lil, lovely Lil . . . Go up with Nora, make her feel all well?"

Lily struggled up from the bench and Nora followed her up to Odette's study.

The room was stifling. It was midday but the room was dark as midnight; Lily didn't seem to notice and she and Odette spoke brightly about two people Nora did not know.

"She just wanted a talk," said Lily. "We thought I'd say hello. Mama's making the soup and we'll have some pie with it."

"Perfect," said Odette. "You'll come up?"

Lily nodded and left, and Odette gestured for Nora to sit. She put herself on a trunk.

"That's exactly where Joe sits," said Odette.

"Who's Heck?"

"What?"

"The man you were speaking of to Lily. Just now."

"Ah. Hector. No, he is a character. In a story that we are reading, all of us together. We are learning to read."

"You are?"

"Lily and her mother are learning to read. They have been working very hard."

"I had no idea," said Nora.

"No."

"I am sorry about your brother. That they can't find him."

"Which brother?" said Odette. "I have two."

"I'm sorry. I didn't know that."

Odette smiled and looked down at the page in her lap.

"The other one disappeared too. Runs in the family. Where have they gone? To Egypt. To study with the masters. To draw apart the man he hath killed," she said.

"I'm sure they'll find him," said Nora. "Wherever he has gone."

"He left something," Odette said. "When our mother died, she left Alexander a little clock. A little gold clock. He kept it by his bed. Never lost it, never traveled without it, never mislaid it." Her eyes flicked to meet Nora's and then down again. "He said it kept the time of his life."

"I didn't know about that," said Nora, "did he take it?"

"As I told you, he left it behind," said Odette. She stood up and the paper on her lap fluttered to the floor. She trod on it as she crossed the room to Nora. "It is very strange that my brother would leave that behind."

Nora made a sound, between a cough and a sob. She felt, again, as thought she might vomit. She did not want to vomit in this room. The air was extremely close. Dense, almost. Stifling. Dark. She closed her eyes and cleared her throat.

"Why haven't you let your hair grow out?" asked Odette. She put out a hand and ruffled the short crop of hair on Nora's head. "It would be very nice hair, if you let it be alone."

"It won't grow," said Nora. "It's been like this for months. I don't . . . I don't know. I don't cut it. I don't know."

"Ah," said Odette, "I see." She caressed the brief snips of Nora's hair between her fingertips, so that the firelight glinted off the ends. "My brother is a very good medical man, a very excellent surgeon. But he is not intelligent in the way William was intelligent, or, really, even in the way of our mother. They, Eleanor, they had a wonderful ability to see a whole body. Not like you or Alexander, who can perfectly see a bone alone or a tongue severed from the throat, a system of veins and whither they went."

Nora ducked her head from Odette's hand. "Stop, please," she said. She walked to the fireplace and then back again. "I'm going to have to go to my uncle's. There's nothing left."

Odette smiled. She returned to her place before the fireplace, and stooped to take up her draft again.

"My mother and my brother William," she went on, "had among their brains a certain way of seeing all places in a man and the roads that connected them, the lakes that separated them, the skies that clouded over them. By which I mean they would have been terrible surgeons. But they were very nice people. Alex and I are terrible people but we are good at our work. Attention to detail is destructive to the heart."

"He was your brother. You must have loved him."

"He said you were a very good student and help."

"I was. I am."

"Well, then," said Odette. She nodded. "I am writing." She turned her back on Nora and bent her head to study the paper in her hand.

Nora wasn't ready to leave the room. She stood up from the trunk and took a step toward the fireplace. The room, the whole house, was very quiet; for the first time since she had entered Satus, there was no hum of scalpel-wielding men working below her feet. Fernie was gone, and now, too, she feared she had lost Joe . . . She wanted, suddenly, her dog. She wanted her dog immediately. She felt frantic; she had no idea where she was, if she was in the house or in the garden or on the hill, and she did not know how long it would be until she found her, until she could kneel down and bury her face in Phila's neck and rub at her belly.

"Get out," said Odette.

In the kitchen, Lily and her mother were standing in front of the window, watching something outside. Mug had her arm around her daughter. Lily's head was on her mother's shoulder and she had one hand was resting lightly on the top of Philadelphia's head. The kitchen floor, Nora's beautiful brick floor, spread out under their feet, looking as soft as a blanket.

Nora snapped her fingers and she and Phila went to the door. Lily and her mother followed.

"Weell miss you soo varry much," Mug said to the dog. Philadelphia licked the women's faces and hands. Lily was crying.

Before she left, Nora went out to the orchard and dug out what remained of Susanna Dial's child. She wrapped it up carefully.

Chapter XL.
Chilling

Nora and Philadelphia spent the morning walking from Satus, down the grassy hill-path, the way she had first come. It was a cold morning; the dew made the bottom of her dress wet, so she tied the hem into a knot by her knees. Phila rolled in the grass and paddled her paws in the air. At the bottom of the hill, Nora turned and tried to remember the day she had first come, the morning she had found her mother's grave empty and come struggling up the way to find Joe Gallo waiting for her. But the memory would not appear. She couldn't picture the day, or feel what the weather had been doing, or where Joe had been standing. She did not feel sad about this, but she was not happy. Nora turned around again and began the walk toward Chilling.

She took her time. Phila, impatient, darted into the forest and the brush, disappearing until Nora gave a whistle or a shout, and then the dog would come bounding from nowhere, covered in leaves and dirt. Left alone on the road, Nora stood bone-still, often, to watch a bird on its branch, or bathing itself in a puddle. She moved so slowly and stopped so many times that when they reached the outskirts of the village, the day was warm and sunny; the bees were out, and the breeze kept the sun from its own strength. The world smelled like flowers and grass. When she stepped out into the road that led to the common, Nora kept her head down. Phila kept close to her, now. Along the path, scores of snails lay scattered. Some had been trampled by horses or heavy feet, and lay crushed and oozing. The others made squeamish, slow progress, and she was careful to step around them. She had to pause, once or twice, and study the little thing in her path, to discern whether it was a small stone or a moving snail. The walk took a long time.

"Should we visit our family?" she asked Phila, when they could see the church and graveyard. "We could visit our family and we could visit Fernie. Fernie lives there, now, too."

Across the common, someone whistled. Philadelphia pricked up her ears and looked up at Nora with a question.

"We live down here, now," she said. "You can go."

She was gone like a comet. Her little white tail streaked across the green and straight into the arms of Steven Storey. Nora watched Storey kneel down and scratch Philadelphia's ears and neck, and then, when the dog lay down and rolled, rub her belly. Nora made her way to them slowly.

"Ah, she's yours," said Steven Storey. "We'd wondered where you'd got to, Eleanor Pirrip. Thought perhaps you'd done yourself a wrong and thrown yourself in that wee pond."

"Not a wee pond," said Nora. "It's quite a large pond."

"That is, that is," said Steven Storey. "How's the dog been working? Good dog?"

"She's the best dog. Thank you. But we haven't had her working. This one's never done hard work in her life."

Storey looked up. "Oh, Miss Pirrip, I'm not pleased to hear it. These dogs, they're put on earth to work. This one, to herd, but all of them to work. You can't take it away from them. They'll become low. Have nightmares and twitch in their dreams, howl it out."

"Do dogs have dreams?" she asked him.

"Everyone does," he answered. "Dogs have them, you have them, so I have them."

"I used to have the same dream every night," said Nora. "But then that one stopped and I don't dream it anymore. It's hard to fall asleep. It is strange that you said they thought I had drowned, because when I was sick, after my brothers had died, I used to dream that I was drowning. In my dream I was at the bottom of the pond, my family's pond. I was at the bottom in the center of the pond, but I wasn't drowning. I was just lying there at the bottom, looking up. And I could see men in little boats on the surface. They had long poles and they were reaching them down into the pond, to poke around, because they were looking for my body. I was lying very still and then when they came too close I would roll out of the way so that the pole wouldn't get me. But then I rolled the wrong way and into a pole, and the pole got me right in the chest. But instead of coming off, the pole stayed there, right on my chest, and then the other poles came and they poked me and stayed there, so that there were poles on my chest and my legs and my stomach and my shoulder, and then I realized they were trying to keep me down."

"You are a strange one, aren't you, Eleanor?" said Steven Storey.

"I only just remembered that dream."

"That is too intimate a thing to tell a stranger," said Steven. "Care-

ful now. Chilling keeps secrets but you have to keep them private!"
He laughed.

Nora shrugged. "I am sorry to have bothered you."

"No bother. But you cannot go around the village and speak to everyone like this. They'll think—"

"I won't," interrupted Nora, but she was already walking away from him, and Steven felt inexplicably guilty, inexplicably ashamed. She made him feel shame when he had done nothing wrong . . . in fact, he reasoned, he had been trying to help, to steer her toward an easier transition back into the village. And so why had she looked at him like that, dismissed him so utterly? He was in the right! He had been in the right and she had made him feel like an idiot. Steven's face was flushed and he shook his head in irritation. Ah, he thought. She takes after that mother of hers. Georgiana had been just the same way. Mean, just mean. Both of them.

"Is Jeff Dial still here?" she asked over her shoulder.

"Same place," Storey replied. "Lost his wife, poor man."

Philadelphia was still crouched by Storey's side. She had trapped a spider between her paws: her ears were high and her tail was up. Nora whistled. Phila snapped and gulped down the spider, and trotted after her.

When she finally arrived at the Peabody's house, it was nearly twilight, and Mrs. Peabody was out front, lighting the doorlamp.

"Nora?" she said, softly.

Nora stood in the road and looked at her aunt.

"Where have you been?" Mrs. Peabody asked.

"There were so many snails," said Nora. Then she walked past her aunt, into the house, and upstairs to a bedroom. She stripped herself naked and pulled the quilt over her body. Philadelphia climbed up on the bed and slept beside her. Nora could not fall asleep until the dog began to snore.

In the morning, Jeffrey Dial found that a corner of his garden had been dug up.

Chapter XLI.
The Narrative of the Graveyard

Oh, the bones. It all comes home to the bones.

Abruptly, the men stopped. They stopped digging and stealing my bodies; I was left in peace, and I was left whole. All, again, was well.

The brother buried his brother. I have him now, and he is pulling himself apart to become the little seedlings and tiny bugs and mulch. There is little left of anyone, now, but there are bodies I recall even now in this late hour. I wonder at this species of specificity. What pattern dictates the memory held in the stones and dirt? Who does the earth remember and who does the earth forget?

Those alive remember the bodies they have loved. The village of Chilling came, again and again, to kneel and speak to the bones. They come, still. They remember the bodies they have hated, the bodies to which they were cruel. They remember, most of all, the bodies that were cruel to them. They remember, too, the bodies that owned many things or much money; they remember the bodies that owned superlative brains or motor skills. They take papers and chalks and mimic the gravestones of these bones. It all comes home to the bones.

But the earth remembers other bodies. You have your memory, the living memory of love and emotion and awe. And I have another memory; I am here to help and complete you, to remember what you cannot know, what you forget too quickly.

There was, in the beginning, Cow Brother and Fruit Brother. The land has not forgotten them! And even the men alive have not forgotten them! But there is more, more to the story and more to the reason. They were terrible, in their own way. They did things that evoke terror in the living . . . and I do not only mean the way that Fruit Brother killed Cow Brother. No! Cow Brother, Cow Brother, he accepted his privilege at the expense of his own Brother, though it was not earned nor deserved. He took up the weapons of his privilege as sure as his Brother took up his weapon of murder, and they both struck with the weapons they chose. We do not only remember the dead body, composting away in a far away bed, but we remember the terror.

There were no witnesses to the first murder, save the land itself. I watch; I must watch and accept. I change as I am changed. The beginning is always chaos: there is no pattern extant to follow, no sure path to trod, nothing to do that we know can be right, good, appropriate.

The earth remembers beginnings. Cow Brother. But the earth remembers, too, when it has been turned upon, when it has been attacked: the earth remembers when it has been terrorized. I do not comment; there is not a right, not a wrong here. Fernie Gallo, the younger Gallo, he was a terror unto the land. He tore into the earth and took what belonged here, to us. He took our bodies and ripped the land apart. I accept all.

And so I remember Fernie Gallo, and I watch as his body comes apart and becomes the earth, again. He is the earth, like all others (like you, soon) and yet there is inside the earth the memory of his distinctness, his presence as a living thing, the wonder of his life.

If you do what is right, will you not be accepted? This was the question your god asked to the Fruit Brother. Why choose this god? Why choose this way? You have created a thing that does not accept you unless you are what it demands.

You are already accepted, I try to say to you. You feel the way the earth bends underneath your feet? The way it crumbles between your fingers? I accept you. There is no right and wrong, in the earth. I remember you. I accept you. Brutalize the earth, envelope it with joy and love, spit upon the trees, bend down and kiss the sand: nothing matters. You are accepted. This is how you will end. This is how you will end. This is your beginning, your end.

And so do not seek acceptance, as we have accepted you before you were made.

Chapter XLII.
The Peabody House

Nora was not happy at her uncle's house. She terrorized her aunt by alternately not speaking, speaking only in monosyllables, and speaking under her breath, to herself. Nora left rooms when Catherine Peabody entered them. Catherine attempted conversation at meals. She tried local gossip, details about clothing and food, observations about the weather and tides and phases of the moon. Catherine interrogated the visitors from Wolfeborough and brought home information of a wider, sometimes even national, stage. Catherine told stories, gossiped, reflected, chattered. Nora never said thank you. Nora never said anything.

Nora killed a chicken for dinner and, instead of cooking it, dissected it.

"She's gone mad," said Catherine to Octavius. "She dissected a chicken on the table."

"Can we still eat it?" asked Octavius.

"I guess," said Catherine.

Nora hated them. She hated them while she knew that they were kind to her. They were genuinely concerned for her health. Catherine made elaborate meals and consulted the midwife on restorative teas and herbs. Every night, pure maternal worry woke Catherine at least once, and she padded to Nora's room. Nora feigned sleep as her aunt adjusted the blankets. Octavius was concerned for her soul. He read aloud from sermons at night and woke her in time for church. Nora understood that they were intelligent people, that they were competent people, and that they were good people. She believed that they loved her.

She still hated them. She despised the way they spoke of money, of everyday affairs, of dinner and chores. She hated the way they looked at her . . . as if she were something to be pitied and helped. She hated the way they looked at her emaciated frame and her bald head and saw only the body presented there, the way they feared her body and feared for her appearance.

But most of all, she hated the muzzle. Her aunt and uncle would not mention Satus House, and they would not ask her about Salderman. They never alluded to her time there, or the work she had done. The work which she had loved so much, and which had given her life purpose, which had contained her life within its small and regular movements. Every day she woke up and felt filled with talk. Her mind was pregnant with the circulation of blood through the neck to the brain, with the black knots of tumors entangled in lungs, with the beautiful myriad bones of the foot. Nora wanted to share what she had learned and all that she had done. She wanted to carefully lay out what questions had yet to be answered, and to discuss ways and means to answer those questions. She wanted to think out loud through the moral problem of dissecting human bodies. She needed to tell people who Jules and Paul and Salderman really were. She wanted to talk about death, and all of those who had died. And though Nora's uncle and aunt were capable of these discussions, they refused her the privilege. They pretended she had only just risen from her sickbed. They pretended she had been nowhere and seen nothing and done nothing.

Nora could only find one way out: she would have to go away, either down to Boston or even abroad in Europe. Not Chilling. She could not stay in Chilling. She suspected the town of complicity . . . in something, in part of something. Chilling was filled with secrets and agreements to keep secrets and she would not feel safe ever again. She would go. She did not care where . . . she would go anywhere. She could go on learning and become an anatomist. Or a military nurse, those were always needed. Maybe she would just make things to help, so that she could be alone. She could find a way to make a prosthetic leg with a knee joint that functioned properly, one that allowed running and maybe even jumping, and did not chafe, and did not hurt.

Chilling was a small place. Every house had many windows. When she left the Peabody house, someone always caught Nora up, took her arm, chattered, and gently led her away from the road she wanted. And in this way, frustratingly, June passed away and July took its place.

One morning Nora woke to the sounds of her aunt's screams. She wrapped herself in her blanket and when she had run downstairs she found Phila cornering a snake in the pantry. The snake was mostly brown, large, and it coiled itself up and occasionally leapt up towards Phila's face. It knew that it was in a tough place. It was, diligently, making every effort it had in its little arsenal to get itself out. Philadelphia was very calm and very alert. She arranged her body and widened her stance and perked her ears. She moved carefully and mirrored the movements of the snake.

Nora held the blanket closed with one hand and with the other clasped the snake at the neck. Catherine flung open a window and, with one swift toss, the snake was gone. It wriggled and disappeared into the stones around Catherine's herb garden. Phila looked at Nora in stunned disbelief.

"Sorry," said Nora. The dog galloped off and in a moment they could see her through the open window, sniffing at the stones.

"Thank you, Nora," said Catherine. She had her hand on her heart.

"It was only a garter snake."

"I'm glad she didn't eat it. Would she have eaten it?"

"I've never seen her eat a snake," said Nora. "But she'll do what she wants. Oh, what is that? What is that smell?"

"We used to have a pet garter snake, when I was a little girl. Well. No, we didn't really. But I thought we did. I used to see one in the garden and think it was the same one every time. I named him Gumus the snake and my parents never disenchanted me of the idea it was the same one every time. That snake lived twenty years!"

"I'm going to take the dog to the sea," said Nora. "This place smells of something . . . I don't know what it is. But it's making me sick. What is that?"

"Nora," said Catherine. "I know you do not like living here."

"You've been hospitable to me. I am grateful."

"I was speaking, yesterday, to Dedlock Slough. He and his wife, you know this, they lost their baby daughter not very long ago. You know this?"

Nora nodded. Catherine walked into the kitchen, still talking, and Nora followed her. She put her hand over her nose and mouth.

"They've had a difficult time. Agnes suffers. She had been a little better these last few weeks, but we cannot go on, all of us, chipping in for her forever. She is still not able to do every thing she needs to do, around the house and the farm. They have Agnes's little brother, too, but he's not a smart boy and he's not helpful. He spends most of his time avoiding work. Playing in the forest."

"Agnes Slough, is she still midwifing?"

"She is, but it's a strain. This is what Dedlock and I were talking about. I think it could be best for everyone if you went to live at the Sloughs for a little while. You can help Agnes with the work and assist the midwifery. Octavius mentioned . . . Octavius said that the idea of working as a midwife might hold some attraction for you."

"I'll do what you want. Let me go upstairs and get dressed," said Nora.

"You know," Catherine called as Nora was staring up the stairs, "your uncle has not—will not—tell anyone. He won't say a word about anything."

"I'm not ashamed," said Nora.

Catherine came to the foot of the stairs. "It's not about shame, Nora. He loves you, you know. He wants you to be safe. He only wants you to be safe."

"I'm going to take Phila to the sea," said Nora. She went up the stairs with the blanket trailed behind her. "Jice, can we get rid of that smell?"

When Octavius came home for lunch, Catherine was waiting for him.

"What beautiful tomatoes," said Octavius. "I've sweat through this shirt."

Catherine kissed her husband on the throat. She was a tiny woman, growing shorter as she aged, and even standing on her tiptoes she could only reach his Adam's apple. Octavius liked to feel her eyelashes on his skin, and he bent his head and kissed the crown of her head.

"Joey Gallo's back blacksmithing again," he said. "Downey's taken him in. Did you set the beet?"

"And the turnips."

"What's in your mind?"

"Could we tell her, do you think?"

"About her mum?"

"About Georgiana, about Maga, about everything. It might make her feel more tethered. I am worried she'll go on making mistakes. If she knows why Georgiana came back, if she can understand that . . . I think she'll be better. She'll understand."

Octavius sat and scratched his neck. Then he shook his head. "She was clear, Cath. She was clear from the day she returned."

"Octavius, Nora is pregnant. I am sure. She is just like Georgiana was. Smells and everything. Just the same way."

Chapter XLIII.
The Forge

He did not like to begin. Joe's first week of blacksmithing was terrible. His hands had lost the muscles and the instinctive, spasmodic turning of the tongs. By noon, his back and legs throbbed with pain. It took him ten blows to achieve a shape he used to be able to hammer in two.

Porter Downey worked alongside him. Downey was infinitely faster and better. Joe was too exhausted, though, even to feel frustrated; his whole day was sweat and hurrying and pain and concentration. At night he fell onto his thin mattress and was immediately asleep. He didn't dream. He didn't even move. If he fell asleep on top of his right arm, then his right arm would stay there the full night, waiting painfully for morning. He slept like a dead body. And then, roused by nothing, he would sit up suddenly and stretch his shoulders in the dark. Then he stoked the fires and took up his hammer again. Every morning was terrible. He hated beginning, all over again.

It was not only the pain and the incompetence. It was as though he had become a new person, and not a better one. Joe had always been the strong one. The skilled one, the one everyone trusted with the delicate or difficult task. He had been, too, always with Fernie. He had never been without his brother. Never. Without him, it was as if Joe had lost half his own body, half his own mind, the ballast of his soul. It was as though the admirable, strong Joe had died along with Fernie. Or maybe, Joe sometimes thought, that strength had never really existed in him at all; it had been only Fernie's idea of him, and one he loved so much that he had adopted. In any case, no one admired Joe anymore, or relied on him. No one was left to love him or be his family. Joe had done terrible things, and he knew he was being punished for them now.

And then, without his noticing, Joe's body remembered how to be a blacksmith. Old muscles, long unused, awoke and took over from the fumbling clumsy ones. His spine shifted and resettled itself into its old shape. His arm swung in its old rhythm; the tongs danced back and forth, high, flat, down, up, on the anvil. His brain counted the heat in the fire and measured the time for each metal. Throughout it all Joe did not think a single thought except, sometimes, that he was thirsty. His mind was blessedly gone.

One evening, Porter left early to wash and attend the village meeting.

"You don't want to come along?" he asked.

Joe shook his head.

"You're welcome to. Part of the village again, now."

Joe smiled and clasped Porter on the shoulder.

"Then who would be left here to finish these? I'll come next time."

Porter nodded, put his cap on his head, and disappeared. The sun was slanting through the southern window. It was dinnertime, or about, and even though he felt hungry he decided to keep working. He wanted to finish and go home for the day. There were only ten more hooks to shape and dunk, and then he could sharpen a few axes and be done.

He felt her before she said anything, but he didn't turn around.

"Hey, Joe."

"Hey there," he said.

"I've come to apologize for what I said."

"There's no need," Joe said. He put the iron in the fire and turned to face her. She was wearing new shoes. He had never seen these shoes before.

"No, there's need. I'm sorry it took me a long time. I've been with my aunt and uncle."

"Yes, I know."

"Where's the dog?"

"She's just outside. Oh my word, she was sad when we left the house. She misses you. She misses Fernie. She didn't eat. She didn't eat for a week and I thought she was going to die, and it was really, really horrible. I couldn't have borne it, you know."

"I miss her, too. She's a good dog."

"She's the best dog," said Nora. Joe thought he heard emotion in her voice, but she coughed and looked at him with dry eyes.

"I'm sorry for saying it was your fault," she said. "He loved you and you loved him and he died because he died, and it wasn't anyone's fault. I was angry with death. I was never angry with you. The wrong people die, the wrong people."

Joe nodded. He picked up his tongs and pulled the iron from the fire. Nora was silent while he hammered a point.

"What are you making?"

"Hooks for the Cottons."

"Can I help?"

"No." He pulled another piece from the fire and hammered again. Nora waited.

"I haven't seen you in a long time, which is strange because Chilling is very small."

"Lots to do," said Joe. "I have a lot to do here."

"I wanted to say I was sorry. I am sorry."

Joe put his work down and pulled off his gloves. "Sit," he said, "Have a visit." He pulled a bench from the wall and wiped it clean with his sleeve. "I'm the one who hit you," he said.

"I don't blame you for it," said Nora. "I would have done the same."

Joe sat on the bench and patted the seat beside him. "You lost brothers, too," he said, when she took the seat. "We're the same."

"No one's the same," said Nora.

"I mean families. Your brothers, my brothers. Your parents are gone and my parents are gone."

"People keep on leaving. When my mother left, I was really too young to understand. And when my father died, and the boys, and my mum, I was too sick to really understand. With Fernie dead . . . Does it ever feel like a joke, to you? As if it couldn't have really happened? What we've done we haven't done? It can't really have happened, I sometimes feel."

Joe went to the door and whistled. Phila came like a whirlwind; Joe squatted, the dog climbed onto his knees and licked the sweat from his face.

"Hello, beauty! Hello, beautiful girl. I missed you."

"She knows something is different," said Nora.

"Of course she does. New home, new people, no Fernie, no me. No stray bones to chew on."

"I mean with me. Something's different with me."

Phila was panting. Joe filled a cup with water and put it outside.

"Be good," he said. Phila drank and lay down in the sunshine. Joe came back inside. "I always felt bad, about that. That we didn't have your mother's body by the time you came to look for it. I think that would have helped, for you to see it."

"When I was a little girl, I used to think that if I had her back in my life, then everything would be good. If we had her back, if my father and I had her back, then I would be whole. The family would be whole. Everything complete and good."

262

"That's how Fern and I felt about our dad, when he was drinking. We used to say to each other that life would be right and fine if he could just stop."

"When she came back, though . . . It wasn't. It wasn't complete. Or good. I couldn't separate her, the flesh and blood of the woman, from the idea of the mother who had left me behind. When I looked at her I only saw the woman who never wanted me. I couldn't look at her without feeling so . . . I felt so unwanted, when she came back. I felt more unwanted when she came back than when she was gone."

The forge was very hot, and she wiped her face with the edge of her sleeve. Joe had half an eye on Phila.

"It's so often like that, isn't it. You think something will make it better, and, of course, it doesn't."

Joe was still standing in the doorway. "She never talked to you? She never explained where she went, or why?" He raised his arms over his head and grabbed onto the top of the doorframe. His armpits were very dark and sweaty. Nora could smell him. She pretended to rest her chin in her hand while she tried to cover her nose.

"No one ever explained it," she said. "I am still trying to find it, that reason. I used to think, when I was sick, after she died, that if I could see her body, to make sure . . . I think I thought that she had abandoned me again. And if she hadn't—if she had really died—then maybe I could find an explanation somewhere, written on her body. Just seeing her body, Joe. That would have told me something. I'm still missing something."

Nora paused and looked up at Joe. He was the very picture of health, she thought. Standing like a giant in the doorway, the sunshine behind him, his great blacksmith's arms.

"Do you ever think of Job?" asked Joe.

"Job? From the Bible?"

"I've been going to talk to Brewer. Brewer and I have become good friends, now. We've been talking about the *Book of Job*. I think, well, he lost his whole family and everything he owned. And he had boils and illnesses."

"Why do you think of all that?"

He chanced to look at her face. She did not look well. Her skin was blotchy and broken into a rash on her forehead. Underneath her eyes, purple pooled in half-moons. As though she had been beaten.

Joe shrugged. "I think because sometimes I look, like you do, for an explanation. Why this happened, why that happened. And in the end it doesn't mean anything. Or the explanation wouldn't be any good. Job didn't suffer for any reason. Just the whim of Satan. The whim of God. His family that died, they were good people. And Job was a good person. The servants, the pigs, the cows, all suffered and died. The pigs and cows certainly hadn't done anything wrong. But they all died."

"I'd never thought of that," she said. "But how apt. And I alone escaped, you know. And I was like him, too, with the boils and the sores. All stricken but not dead."

"You're like Job?" said Joe.

"When I was got better and saw that everyone had died, gone, well, then I thought, that's all! There is nothing left to take away. I had to burn everything we had, to kill off the infection. I had to burn Roger's duck."

"You killed a duck?"

"His favorite toy. In Salderman's cellar, I used to strip the bones. I'd peel away the skin and slice through the layers of muscle, and of fat, and underneath, you'd find the bone—I'd pull it out and scrape it absolutely clean. Boil and dry it. So in the end that is how I felt. A bone without tissue, everything pulled off for some other purpose, and me left over, sitting there dull and white and useless."

"The doctors used the bones, I thought."

Nora rolled her eyes and laughed. She was suddenly arrogant, too proud of her small amount of learning and narrow scope of skill. If she was cruel, Joe thought, she was cruel now—in making him feel inept and stupid and as though no matter what caliber of thought escaped him, she would find it—and him—imbecilic. It was in the short, hard laugh, her exasperated looking away from him as she listened to him. It was her scorn that shot from her breast like needles. She was truly ugly, then. When she wielded her mind like a weapon, and struck with it. She had never been this way, before, Joe thought. Or she had, and he had not seen it.

"We did use them," she said. "We strung them together and hung the skeleton on a stand. Some of them. But that's not the point. That's not what . . . the thing is that I thought that was the end. I keep thinking, Joe, that this is the end. My mother comes back, it must end. They die, she dies, now it is the end. And then I find . . . I don't know the word. I find Salderman. I find out why they died, and how they died. What I did to find these things . . . That should have been the end."

Nora paused again. She stood and walked to the doorway. "It is never the end, though." She put her hands to Joe's face, a palm on each cheek. He did not flinch. "I can see your skull clear as your face," she said to him. "I know everything underneath there."

Joe put his hands around her wrists, and she pulled them away.

"I'm angry now," said Nora. "I have become only that. I am angry in my sleep."

"I don't think there's a reason. That's what I'm saying. There's no point in getting angry about it all. It's whim. The whim of the Lord. Or of the Devil."

"No," said Nora. "There are reasons. Things make sense, things need to have a sense, a direction, a rule. Why show me what we love and take it away?" Her voice was very cold. She did not sound like herself.

"Are you talking about Fernie?" he asked.

She waved her hand. "Of course I am talking about Fernie," she said. "And my father. My mother watched her husband and all five of her baby boys die, right in front of her. Susanna Dial. Everything."

Joe pushed past Nora and returned to the fire. Nora turned and watched him; Phila, too, came inside and sat, watching. Joe pulled on his gloves and took up his tongs, pulled a piece from the fire and hammered so loudly that Nora clapped her hands over her ears. Phila yelped and ran. What Joe knew, what he wanted to shout at her, was that it was the messenger who alone had survived, who returned to say it. It was not Job at all. And that she was arrogant, and sad, and he was sorry for her.

When the hammering stopped, Nora began to untie the kerchief on her head. "My hair still hasn't grown any. My aunt thinks I'm possessed by a demon."

"Nora, do you ever think of anyone? Anyone else? Do you only think of yourself?" asked Joe. He kept his eyes on the fire and the hook he was heating.

"Maybe I am a demon," Nora said, but her last words were lost. Joe had pulled out the piece and begun to hammer. She waited until he paused. He put his glove to his forehead.

"Joe," she said, "I think I'm having a baby."

In the corner of the forge, just inside the doorway, Joe kept a white pitcher filled with water and over it he had draped a white bit of cloth to keep out the ash and smoke. He stood and went over to it, pulled the cloth back, and drank from it. The water tasted of metal, no matter how he tried to cover it.

"Taste this," he said. Nora came over to where he was standing and drank from the pitcher.

"It tastes of salt," she said. "It smells terrible, though."

"It tastes of metal," he said.

Nora sipped from the pitcher again and held the water in her mouth for a little while before swallowing.

"No," she said finally. "I think probably you are tasting your own lips and your own mouth. That's you."

"When?" he asked.

Nora shook her head. "Agnes Slough guessed maybe four months, or so. It's only a guess."

"You can marry me," said Joe. He went back to his place by the fire, and Nora reseated herself on the bench. He thrust his work into the fire and they watched it gradually change from black to orange to red very red. Joe pulled it and started to hammer. With each strike the metal grew more dark.

"I love you, anyway," he said, when the piece had gone cold.

"Joe," she said. "That's not true at all. It'd be too much for you, on top of everything else. You can ask me the question you really want to ask. I'll tell you."

"I don't want to know what you did," said Joe. "I want to marry you. So marry me. End. Stop."

"You don't like me very much, Joe."

"Not right now."

"There is no need to ever explain myself, with you. You know most of the reasons for things, either because I've told you myself, or through Fern. Of course," she said when Joe opened his mouth as to interrupt, "I know you two spoke about me, sometimes. You were brothers. And because you know me in those different ways— through me, through Fern, through your own eyes—I bet you know things about me that I can't even see myself."

"I do," said Joe. For the second time since she had entered the forge, Joe looked up and met Nora's eyes. No, her eyes were not as bad as he thought. They were looking at him, after all. He smiled at her.

Nora smiled back. "No," she said.

"Look," said Joe, "it's done. It's enough. You're selfish. I've done some terrible things, too. You know what they are. But at least we know what we are, and we know what the other one is. You need a dad for that baby. We'll have a family. We'll be okay."

"But that won't work," Nora said. She was still smiling, and looking at his face. "Not the way I feel about the world. Even now. God. I hear the ocean. My skull—can I explain this? My skull feels tight. I need to get away from here . . . I remember the smell of that cellar, and those bodies. I will always have that smell with me." Nora closed her eyes. "I would have died with them, you know, if someone had asked my opinion. After Abraham died, I wanted to go too. But my body decided for me, otherwise, and I got up and walked out of the house."

She was quiet for a little while. Outside the forge, some village boys had found Phila and were throwing sticks for her to fetch, and they were laughing and talking. Joe pulled a new piece from the fire and drove the hanging hole into the top.

"My father used to tell me that love was from God," Nora said. "He said that the Lord showed him my mother. And that like all gifts from the Lord, love was a thing to work for and tend to everyday, like a garden or a new baby. But I don't think I love anything, now. I have nothing much to work at. My work feels done."

"No?" said Joe. "I don't know."

"Did you know that Chilling had made a deal? That the whole town would ignore him and his work, if he'd just keep to himself and pay money for the privilege. They would trade their dead for privacy and money."

"He was a good man," said Joe. "I know you cannot believe that. But he made poor choices. We knew they were poor choices. I wish we hadn't done the things we did."

"Do you know why I liked it so much, being at Satus?"

"Yes, I think so."

"Why?"

"I think you honestly liked the work Salderman is doing. I think you enjoyed the work."

"It's very difficult. It took me a long time to do something well enough for Jules or Paul. But I felt like I was doing something. Not avenging them, not that, but moving toward something that would give us all some peace. I know you hated your father, Joe, but I loved my father. I loved my father and every day I wake up and my father is dead. I am still trying to figure this out, that he will never not be dead. I had brothers. Little baby brothers who played with wooden ducks and peed on my skirt. They were my brothers. And now they are dead. Nothing will ever occur that will unmake their death. My mother left me—twice! and I never even knew her. Sometimes I feel like I never even met her. Whenever I was in that house and not working at something, I wanted to rip my eyes out of my head."

"I know, Nora. We all know. You're sad. We're all sad. People die. Do you think I don't know about this? Our family, they're dead too. Half the village dies, it seems like, every winter. Accidents happen. People die. Children die. Babies. Mothers and fathers die. You are not special, Nora. This doesn't make you special. It only makes you less able to handle what we've all been handling for a long time."

"You killed your own father," said Nora. "You murdered him."

"What does that have to do with my brother?"

"I am trying to explain. Fernie was my favorite thing in the house, except for the dog," said Nora. "I liked him very much and I liked to be with him. But the world is dangerous place and we are not built to survive. If I have learned anything, I have learned that our bodies are always right there, right on the cusp of death. They're vulnerable. There have so many ways to fail, so many different fragilities that it is a miracle that you and I have survived long enough to speak these sentences to one another. The world conspires to kill us, Joe. We would be best to be unloved and to live away and apart from all others, because they will leave us, and we will leave them."

"I don't know why you're telling me this, No. I don't want to hear it."

"Don't," said Nora. "Don't call me No. I'm sorry. Yes. I'm . . . not telling what matters. I'm being selfish. Yes, Joe. You are my friend. But I couldn't ever marry you, because I think I would come to hate you. I would hate you. You would remind me of everything. You are Satus. You are the cellar, and your brother, and Jules and Paul. You are Salderman and all the books in the library. You, just looking at me, that would be a sort of violence. I know. I would be cruel to you because I would not like to be reminded of what I had to do at Satus."

"You don't know, Nora, what will happen. You are saying this because you are grieving, and the past year has been difficult and strange. Mourning happens, No. You'll mourn. I will, too. And all of these emotions will settle into something more . . . manageable. It seems this way now. It will not always be this way. You might see my eyes as a comfort, Nora. I find comfort in you. And for the same reason. You can remind me of my brother."

Nora laughed a little. "This would be the end of you, a marriage to me. You, kind as you are, heartsick of anger and violence, you would accept me, when I turned horrible. You have always accepted me just as I happened to be. You would put up with—even defend— every horror I could show you. Can you see? Can you see this? What your life would be if we married? You would be giving up your life to live with a devil. And I . . . do you know the worst part of being a devil, Joe?"

"You are not a devil," said Joe, quietly. He was looking away from her.

"It's that every moment you are awake, you know that you are a devil. You know it. And cannot do anything to change."

"What will you do?"

"I'm to go and live with the Sloughs," said Nora. "They need someone to help. I can help Agnes. There's nothing to do here."

"The baby," said Joe. "And the baby?"

"Oh, Joe," said Nora, "I am not going to have the baby."

For a moment her words rang inside Joe's head. It took him the full ringing moment to understand what he had heard.

"Wait," he said, "Nora?"

"Shut up. Why is it so quiet?" Nora walked outside and scanned the road and grass. She whistled and waited. "Joe?" she said, "Where is my Phila? Where is the dog?"

Chapter XLIV.
The Chilling Churchyard

What Jim Slough had done was very simple, and he had done it very quickly. Philadelphia had followed him happily, and he threw the stick for her again and again as he walked, so that by the time they reached the churchyard she was friendly and eager. He had taken the rope from the gravediggers' shed, then wrestled the dog down to the ground and tied her front legs together. Phila, to this moment, had only ever been touched by hands communicating love, affection or, occasionally, when she had been very bad, half-amused frustration. These were new and different hands. She was frightened and, as Jim was tying her back legs, she urinated and the urine was very pungent and it soaked his shirt sleeve.

"Disgusting," Jim said. "You're a bad dog. You're disgusting and I'm going to kill you." He pulled his stained shirt off over his head and threw it onto the ground by Phila's face. Philadelphia was frantic, now. She struggled and craned her neck and whimpered.

Jim looked around and saw a pile of smooth gray stones. They had been arranged at the base of Smart Hale and Beddine Hale's single tombstone, a little offering built up again and again by their grandchildren every Monday. Jim walked over to it, chose the largest stone, and returned to kneel by Philadelphia's skull. He took the stone in his right hand. He raised his arm and the dog, sensing her death, became very still. She froze and then, suddenly twisting against the rope, she lunged up and sunk her teeth into Jim's left wrist, and he yelped in pain and anger. And then he looked down at the animal and he smiled at her, and raised his arm again. When he brought the stone down, it crushed the piece of her skull round her right eye, where the bone curved around in an ovoid and protruded at the circumference. Phila's head began to bleed. She was able to smell the blood. The blood seeped into her eye. She cried and Jim brought the stone up again.

Then Jim felt something very cold on the soft flesh on the inside of the elbow of his raised arm. A hand grabbed his wrist, and the stone dropped onto the ground.

"Hey," he said, and twisted around. "This dog bit me. It's bad!"

"Hey," said Nora. She spoke very softly. "Calm down. Look up."

Jim looked up. Nora held the point of very slim blade to the inside of his elbow. His skin there was very white, almost translucent. He could see his little blue veins pumping, and the tiny edge of a silver blade.

"Do you know what it is that I am holding?"

He shook his head. "A little knife," he said.

Nora nodded. "It is a little knife," she said.

"Let me go."

"I am sentimental," said Nora. She sighed. "I like to have things. I like to have small, physical things to remind me of the things. This is not a knife. You are a stupid little boy. This is a special tool. A very good friend of mine used this tool to slice the skin from dead bodies. It is very sharp. I have kept it sharp, because he was my friend, and he liked it very sharp. He is gone, now. It has a very fine point. See?"

Nora pressed down. A thin ribbon of blood snaked down the length of Jim's white arm, toward his bony shoulder.

"Yes," he said.

"I bet you didn't even feel that."

"No."

"Here is what I am going to do," said Nora. "My friend would always explain to me what he was going to do before he did it, so that I could follow along. He also chewed tobacco. Have you ever chewed tobacco, Jim?"

"No," whispered Jim.

"I have. But, in any case, here is what I am going to do. It won't take very long at all. I am going to make one quick slice, a straight slice right up your arm." She tugged on Jim's wrist, the one she held pinched in her hand. "I will cut just to here, to where you feel me holding you. After I do that, you will begin to feel a little dizzy and very light and very strange. You will faint. When you faint I will do the exact same thing to your other arm. My dog has helped me a little. She's a very good dog. Then I will sit here, right beside you, and wait for you to bleed to death. It will not take very long."

"Please," said Jim. "Please, you don't understand."

"I do understand. Very well," said Nora.

"I do, please. I won't touch her. I won't hurt her ever again. I won't. Please. I promise. Please." Jim had begun to cry and the tears streaked through the dirt on his face. His nose began to run and mucus dripped onto his lips. Nora smiled down at him.

"Oh, Jim, you'll only torture another animal. The world is painful

271

enough. We are all better without you."

He was sobbing now, and though he continued to speak, Nora did not understand him.

"You're a bad person," explained Nora. "You don't deserve your life. I am angry, just standing here looking at you, still alive. You shouldn't. You shouldn't. My dog is a very good dog, Jim. And look what you've done. You've taught her how to be afraid and to know that she will die. Pain. She knows that now. She will never un-know it."

Jim sobbed. Nora wasn't smiling anymore. She brought her face a little further down, so that Jim could feel her breath in his ear.

"If you touch my dog—any dog, any animal, even a bug, even a spider—ever, with the intent to make them hurt or suffer or die, I will come and murder you. I will murder you, Jim, you stupid little boy, with gladness and joy. It will make me happy, Jim. Do you understand? Do you understand that your life will depend on how you treat other living things? Do you understand the price? Do you understand me, little stupid boy?"

"Yes," said Jim.

"Look at me."

He looked up into her face. "I understand," he said.

"Do you understand that I am ready, and willing, and happy to kill you? That I have worked very hard, with Captain Murderer, who was a better person than you, and he taught me how to cut out men's hearts? And that I will cut out yours? If you ever hurt another living thing, boy, I will slice open your chest, and I will break your ribs, one by one, and I will cut out your heart."

Jim nodded. "I believe you," he said.

"Go home," she said. "Go to the house where you and I both live, and tell your sister how you came to your dogbite. Tell her exactly what you did."

Chapter XLV.
Narrative of the Graveyard

The worst part of everything is not being understood. Careful! I don't say misunderstood. I wouldn't mind being misunderstood. That would mean that someone had understood something and then took the liberty of missing it. But no, not for me. You try communicating legibly when your brain is sediment and your soul is water. It's very difficult.

You, for example. I wonder if you are. Are you there? Someone to whom these communications go? There is the strong possibility that all my talk of cow brothers and darkness and the cataloguing of the village has gone nowhere at all. My fear is that it has all been a little silly. Cow brothers. I hear it, now. I apologize, phantom You. Did I really make you listen to the names of everyone who came to mourn their dead? I did. I really did. I thought it might be important. I thought it might be interesting. My intentions were good. I suppose, positioned against a measuring stick, the big notched stick of life and death, interesting does not reach very high. I should keep on with the real work. My work is spread here before me, and I go with it. Compost and the water cycle. There's no choice. It'll be done.

No. Sorry, no. I retract that apology, phantom You. This other thing I do, the not strictly necessary work, the telling about it . . . the endless attempt to communicate, to fashion a story out of the shapes I recognize: I consider this work to be just as good! Just as important! Just as endlessly complicated! Certainly, just as unseen. I can turn a man into a tree but no one will ever see it. And I can tell you a thousand twisted tales of dirt and death but without your language and your brand of voice, they'll never be heard.

It's frustrating. I spend all my time folding and refolding, trying to fashion a message to you. I would like to say something worth listening to. Nothing seems worth listening to. I am never asleep, and so I go on composing and writing and singing or drawing, whatever the word for it is. It is an endless barrage, endless attempts on the part of the low and simple earth to say something in a language you will first, hear, and second, understand.

Sometimes, you do hear. I send out my emissaries and, though you cannot see them as they march up and down the street, maybe one of you will catch a whiff and smell him as he goes by, or one will possibly brush up against him in the night, jump back and be afraid. But that it the best I can hope for, I think. But understanding? Never. Don't blame yourself. I haven't found yet a translating phrasebook.

I wish there was a dictionary. I wish there was a way for me to pass my language through a portal and out it would come, sounding just like yours. To translate me, though, to move me from the ground and into text, it hasn't happened. I know. I know. I've failed at that.

There might be a reason I've found it so impossible. A story, stolen from the mouth of the good Reverend Brewer: the story of a tower built by men to reach Heaven. "Impossible!" said Reverend Brewer. He said this was impossible, to build a tower tall enough to reach Heaven. "Why?" asked the child he was counseling. (The child had, I believe, an inclination to pride.) "Because it is wrong," said the Reverend. "It is a sin to think you can reach so high."

The impossible, then, is what is wrong. The wrongness is nicely cordoned off, outside our reach. We cannot grasp it. Impossible. (I retell this story only to console myself. The impossible decays into the possible as quickly you yourself decay to rot and mud. But it is comforting to think that what is behemoth and difficult is impossible. We wriggle free the hook, escape the prison of long and maddening labor. And of course it is even worse when we catch someone else in the attempt. They have locked themselves in the cell we secretly covet. How dare they think themselves up to the task!? Kill 'em! Hang them so that everyone can see them swing. Fine. More mulch for me.)

I think, in the end, I have tried to say too much. A stranger in a strange land should learn one word. One word at a time, the most important word first. What must be conveyed at the expense of all else. And the minute he arrives, he must utter this word, in perfect accent, so that, whatever deficiencies there else might be, this single, crucial thing is conveyed.

Here it is.

You are scared to die. I know. It is frightening, after you have been alive so long, and done such a good job at keeping yourself breathing. Perhaps, too, there have been obstacles in your way. Perhaps when you were young, you were not cared for. Perhaps you became sick. Perhaps you were injured. Perhaps you were left alone in a dangerous place.

And yet you lived. This is enough, you know. This is enough.

But I suspect that you have done even more. I cannot guess what, but I imagine you have done some sort of work. You may have created things, been a maker of things, fixed things, cleaned things. Perhaps you did not like this work. Perhaps this work was difficult, back-breaking labor. Perhaps it was painfully rote, painfully tedious. Perhaps it was thankless. Perhaps it was all for naught. Or, I consider, perhaps this was work you loved deeply—but the others did not find it valuable. Perhaps they did not like your work. Perhaps they mocked it, insulted it, found it pathetic, vague, valueless.

And yet you did your work.

Have you done even more? Have you bound yourself to other living things, and, by being alive yourself and working each day, helped them survive? You may have married, or mated. You may have had children. You may have thrown in your lot with your friends, pledged yourself to them. You may have taken in a body that, without you, would have no other living body on which to rely. Perhaps they did not ever thank you. Perhaps they ignored you. Perhaps they did not think of you highly; perhaps they did not like you. Perhaps they did not love you. Perhaps, when you needed them most, they abandoned you.

And yet you bound your life to the lives of others.

You are scared to die. I see it in your eyes when you sense your death is near, and it is often nearby in a churchyard. You are scared to die. You are scared to die. You are scared to die.

Guile does not exist in me as it does in you. I cannot be but what is real and honest: I can show you what will happen.

Here is what will happen. It is only mechanical. Your heart will stop pumping your blood to your veins and arteries. The blood will simply slow and then draw to a halt, like a train arriving at a station. The conductor will get off, bone-tired, and he will make his way slowly home, where it is warm, and he can sleep a night in his own soft bed. When your blood stops flowing, your skin will become pale. Some have dark skin and you will hardly notice. You may look the same as you did before. Some have very white skin and it will whiten even further; you might look like wax or ivory.

After life's fitful fever, years of talking and walking and worry and care, you will cool down. The furious rushing and whirling within you will slow and stop. Your body will get colder and colder until it matches me. I am warm in some seasons and cold in others. Your body will drop itself down just to where I am. It might take a long time. Don't worry. There is no need to rush. You are coming, I know. I will wait for you. I am here.

Do you understand me? This is me, comforting you. This is me, the great big world, saying you have done enough. You will die and you will have done much with your life. Your life has been worth the wait.

Do you understand? Do you understand?

You will become the earth. You are, even now, the earth.

Chapter XLVI.
Cotton Home

Agnes put her hand to her mouth. The child's injuries were very bad. Even Nora, who had disemboweled men and took saws to skulls, flinched. She exhaled sharply. Frances Cotton was four years old. Her hair was very curly. She had thick corkscrew curls, the lone Cotton daughter with curls. Her mother had to braid it into two long tight tails, one along each side of her head, to save it from knotting and tangling. The braids, wound around the child's head like a crown, would hold for a week.

"What happened?"

Agnes sighed. "No one saw. She found a bottle and kept drinking. And when it took hold of her she must have stumbled into the fire, or fallen. They only found her when they came home."

"But the gashes? These cuts?"

"From the grate. There are spikes at the top."

"There's no saving her, is there? We need a real doctor," said Nora. "This is very bad. We don't have the things she needs."

"Necker is coming, from Wolfeborough, but it will be a long time." Agnes began to unpack her bag. "Here," she said to Nora, "you can sew up those? On her arms? Just enough, maybe not too tight in case Necker wants to open the wound again. I'm going to flush her out with oil."

"Oil?"

"For the spirit she drank. That alone could kill her. Dot Cotton is making salve for the burns and when she brings it we'll get it on as fast as we can."

Nora chipped the soap into water and began to flush the wounds. The skin had broken raggedly, and parts of the girl's flesh hung from the bone like fillets of beef. Nora could see the lines and striations of red muscle and the thin pinpoints of yellow fat that leaked from between each layer.

They worked quietly for a long time.

"She might lose this arm," said Nora.

"Necker will decide," said Agnes. "It might be better that way. At least it won't pain her after that." She looked over and her face spasmed, as if she could feel what the unconscious child could not.

"She might," said Nora suddenly. "Fernie Gallo. They cut off his leg, but he could still feel it. It hurt him, something, and the foot itched."

"What did he do?

"Nothing," said Nora, "there was nothing he could do and so he just felt it. And sat with the feeling. This was harder than anything, I think. Sitting with the feeling and just feeling it. Giving up the idea that you could do anything about it." Nora tugged and the thread broke. The girl's lashes fluttered.

"She's awake," said Agnes. "Hold her down."

"What?" said Nora, but the child had already begun to move. She turned her head and saw the wounds in her arm and chest and began to scream; she jumped up and thrashed, to get the women off of her and Nora tried to hold her at the shoulder but there was no part of the body, no uninjured skin, that she could press on. To hold her, Nora and Agnes only put her in more pain. She screamed and screamed until they could hear people running, and then there were many bodies in the room, and someone put his hand over the little mouth, and they all held her down.

Later, the doctor came and Frances, sedated, slept. She was going to lose the arm, Necker said, but it couldn't be helped. He would stay at the Cottons' overnight and amputate in the morning. Agnes and Nora went back to work, and began to close all the small wounds.

"You are good at this," said Nora. "All of this. Thank you for letting me help."

"I'm glad to have the help. You have been, Nora. A great help. Did Jim apologize? I told him to apologize to you. He told me he was teasing Philadelphia."

"Yes."

"He won't do it again . . . Boys are so rough sometimes. How is her eye?"

"I think she will probably be blind. There was a piece of bone inside. She can see from her left one, though. She's a tough girl."

Agnes nodded. "You have very neat stitches," she said, leaning over Nora's work.

"How did you learn all of this? Did you follow your mother around? I don't remember you at the house with your mother. It was just her, and then it was just you."

"I wasn't supposed to be a midwife. My sister was, and she was the one who went along with our mother. I learned to read and write, and Maga was jealous of me for that. But then Maga went missing. Just . . . gone, one morning. Then when we came to the fact she wasn't coming back ever . . . so I went out with my mother and I'm the midwife now."

"My mother did that."

"Ah, but she came back, didn't she?"

"But do you like it? Do you enjoy the work?"

"That's a silly question, Nora Pirrip. I do the work God's called me to do."

Nora bent over the child's head and drew her needle through the skin.

"I like this. Helping her," Nora said. "I like doing it."

"It's hard work and it gets old after doing it a while. When I was just learning it was . . . different, because everything was new. But it's been a long time now and women have babies the same way they've always had babies and kids fall off roofs and men stab themselves with the same tools they did last year and the year before. Fevers and warts and stomach-aches."

"You could go off somewhere, learn new things. Go to a different town or a city."

Agnes looked at Nora. "I think women have babies the same way in every place," she said.

"Did you deliver Frances Cotton?"

"I don't know." Agnes sat back on her heels and wiped her hands on her apron. She sighed. "I don't know why I say that. Yes, I did. I remember very well."

"You delivered my brothers. Twins. Two sets."

"Oh, I remember them," said Agnes. She shook her head. "Your mother was the strongest woman I ever knew. Like a . . . I don't know. I couldn't believe her at the time."

"Why?"

"She must have been in incredible pain, both of those times. They came a bit early, twins do . . . but she was like a soldier on the field. Just straight on and iron-willed. Patient as the moon, too. She wasn't willing to say a word against her babies or your father, and most women, they do. They get angry. But she was always repeating, *Lucky, lucky, so lucky* and she wasn't going to forget it one moment."

"Who was lucky? She was? The babies? Dad?"

Agnes looked up and frowned. "I don't know. I can't remember exactly just what she said. Just kept saying *lucky.*"

"I think she loved my brothers," said Nora.

"Of course she did. Mothers love their children. I loved mine the second I felt her in my body."

"I'm sorry."

"She died," said Agnes, "and there's the reason for your mother to feel so lucky. When you have the baby, and it's alive, that's a lucky day. And every day it's alive after that, every single day you wake up and that little beautiful mouth is open and breathing, that day is luck and a gift and we don't all receive it."

"You'll have another child, though?"

"That is not in my hands," said Agnes. She finished and tied off the bandage on the girl's chest and smoothed it with the palm of her hand. She was hot to the touch and her face was flushed; her hair was matted with sweat and clung to her neck and forehead. "We'll give her something for the fever," she said.

"You can have mine," said Nora, and she meant her baby.

"No," said Agnes, because she knew what Nora had meant.

"I don't want it," said Nora.

Agnes turned and struck Nora flat across her cheekbone. Her palm stung and she shook it out in front of her and turned back to her work. "Oh, Nora, my love," she started, but the rest of the sentence caught in her throat and stayed caught there.

"Agnes, if there was someone else who could help I wouldn't ask you. You're the midwife. The only one we have. I'm going to the midwife and I'm asking her to help me. She'll help, I think. I know her a little, from mum, and the boys, she wasn't there for Bartholomew because he came early but she was there all the other times. She knows me."

Agnes had gone still. When she did speak, her voice was a cold whisper. A blade of a voice. "Nora."

"Agnes," said Nora, "I know I am not supposed to be a mother. I know it. Whatever is in you—that need, that urge, that love to hold your child and keep that small packet of a body near your chest, to hold his hands up over him as he takes a step, then another . . . I don't have that part, Agnes. When I felt him growing, you know what I thought? Over. Done. My life was no longer a life, but an endless servitude, a chain of exactly similar days in which I sacrifice all my will for the care of someone else. Oh, Agnes, I love him. I do love him. There's no way to avoid it. He presses against my organs and I feel, in the pressure, the heaviness, the great, anchor weight, of my love for him. He is my family, again, when all my family has left me. He is a miracle, my son, a miracle that restores my father and mother and my brothers all—to me again. He is my family."

Agnes put her palms over her face and eyes. She dug the heels of her hands into the eye sockets.

"And I, desperately, terribly, violently, Agnes, I do not want him. I do not want the burden of him because, oh, Agnes, I cannot do it. I cannot see him and be reminded of where he came from, and what I did, and why I did it. I cannot wake up every morning and fear that he is hungry, cold, dead. I can't live thinking about him, his life, the dangers he will be exposed to daily, hourly . . . it is too much. It will drive me mad. It will turn me rotten. It will rot me away. I will descend to an animal that is concerned only with the survival of its young. My life will slip away from me. I will give it all up so that he will live, and live long, and be well fed and healthy. That he not die. Simply that—that he not die."

"What did you do?"

Nora put her hands to her head but didn't answer.

"Nora, what did you do up there in that house? What happened?"

"In Chilling," Nora said, "we keep the secrets. Right?"

Agnes stood up and took the needle and thread from Nora's hands. "Wipe her down once and we'll go," she said.

Nora leaned her head close to Agnes's ear and whispered. "If I am forced to have this child, Agnes, if I cannot stop this, I will die inside my body. I will shrivel up and become a shell of cotton and needles and fear."

When Agnes took her hands away and looked at Nora, her face was a white waxen mask. The pallor made her look more severe than ever, made the blackness of her hair more black and the lines of her face like the edges of knives.

"Nora," she said, "You cannot want it dead. It is a child, Nora."

"It is a boy. I know. And I love him. I can love him without wanting him! It is possible to love a thing and not want the thing, Agnes. I do not want him to be born. He would have a monster for a mother. He will have a soulless thing watching him sleep and eat; he will have no father. He will come into the world with nothing, and I will guard that nothingness with every fiber of every muscle. And I am very strong, Agnes. I do things well when I attempt them. If I guard him, he will not be able to get out. He will live in a prison of my love. He will grow to hate me," Nora paused and reached out for Agnes's hand. "Help me, Agnes. Help me get him out."

"No," Agnes said. "What you want to do, Nora, is monstrous. It is demonic."

"Oh, God," said Nora, "please, please."

They stood together and looked down at the child swollen and blistered and crossed with black stitches. Nora clutched Agnes's hand and Agnes was unable to withdraw.

Nora made her first attempt later that night. She had taken a taper candle from the cupboard downstairs, early in the afternoon. It was white and slim and she did not know if it was going to be long enough. She lay in her bed until the moon rose enough for her to see it through her little window, and then she went downstairs. She was very quiet.

She lit the candle by the low kitchen fire and carried it back upstairs. On her knees, and facing the wall, she prayed until her back ached. Then she extinguished the candle and hiked up her nightdress, rolled onto her back, and pushed the candle up inside her until she felt the sudden sharp wall of pain, and then she pushed harder. She could not scream because they would hear her so she tore her cheek and lips with her teeth and groaned like an animal. Then she pushed harder and something inside of her burst, or broke, and then she went dark and lay unconscious on the floor of her small room.

When she woke, in the morning, the blood had stiffened her nightgown. She could not walk for two days. She was still pregnant.

Chapter XLVII.
Satus House

The black staircase at Satus House gleamed and rose up, first floor, second floor, third and highest floor, wound around like the curve of a woman's waist. Whereas before the staircase has been leapt upon by Joe Gallo, hobbled up and lurched down by Fernie Gallo, trudged by Salderman, and determinedly mounted by Nora, it was now touched only by three sets of feet: Lily and her mother, going up with some tray or task, and Odette, coming down to ask for someone to light a fire, for a cup of tea, for dinner.

The patterned floor tiles at the foot of the staircase remained the same patterned tiles whether they were trod or not, studied or not. The untouched wine in the cellar squatted mutely and dumbly, butts in the air. Through the Satus windows, the sun shone on the sea. The eaves of the house were dark at night, lit up with broad day. The kitchen table stood, brown and sturdy, sometimes covered in spills and spoons and sticky brown dough, but always there, heavy and worn and immovable.

Houses, thought Nora, as she crept inside the house by the kitchen door. She wished she had brought the dog with her, but Philadelphia was still badly injured, and long walks made her whimper in pain. But it was strange to be without her . . . she felt unarmored, and as though she was intruding. Not on Lily or her mother; Nora did not do them the service of considering them. Neither did she feel as though she was intruding on Odette. It was as though she were interrupting the house itself: the stones and bricks and planks.

But this wasn't a new feeling. The Pirrip house, which Nora had loved and felt loved within as a child, became terrible when Georgiana had returned. Nora slipped through rooms on the balls of her feet, she hid in her room, she did her work with her head down because to be noticed, in that house, was to be criticized, and Nora felt herself eroding under the unrelenting judgment. She dreamed of living alone, of sleeping in the woods, of going off to Boston or Providence and living some place where no one knew her name, where her sins and faults could go unnoticed. She no longer dreamed of being loved, or accepted, or nurtured; she only wanted to be ignored. To float in the calm, warm water of anonymity.

When Nora was small, she had fantasized the return of her mother. Because the woman was supposed to be dead, Nora felt free to imagine the sort of woman she most loved: someone large and motherly, warm and soft and perpetually glad, perpetually untroubled and kind and comforting and accepting. Someone to whom she could tell her thoughts and feelings without fear, someone from whom she could learn, a warmth and a refuge from the hardness of her life.

Then Georgiana had come back, in flesh and blood. There was a long period of explanations that explained nothing, of head-shaking, of her father stuttering and her mother sighing, and in the end Nora knew no more than she ever had, save that her mother was not dead, she was alive, and would live in the house with them forever. She would never know what her mother had done all those years, or where she had gone, or who she was with. Nora had believed that one day, someone would tell her. She had truly believed that.

Entering Satus again was like entering her old home with Georgiana inside. It was no longer her home; everyone who had made a refuge for her was gone, dead or changed, and there was nothing that beckoned her inside or promised to shelter her. For the first time in a long time, Nora felt tears in her eyes. She shook them away. In the kitchen, she nodded at Lily, who was turning the spit, and then she went upstairs.

Inside her study, there was no fire and Odette was standing by the window. She was sewing a tear in a white dress by the last bit of sunlight; when Nora came in, she looked up and smiled. Nora, struck by the evenness and the whiteness, complimented her on her teeth.

"Oh," Odette said, "they're not mine."

"I am back," Nora said.

"You are," said the poet. "My brother is gone, but you've known that. I don't think anyone will see him again. The cellars are empty. There is nothing here for you to do, girl."

"I came to speak with you," said Nora. "I need help." She put her hand on her belly. "The midwife won't help me," she said.

Odette hung the white dress on its hook and led Nora to one of the trunks. She closed the lid, latched it, and Nora sat down upon it. Odette took her place before the fire but stood with her back to it, so that though she faced Nora straight on, her face was entirely in shadow.

"Do you know," said Odette, "that my family is from a small village in England, a village called North Nibley."

"No, I didn't," said Nora.

"We are. Alexander and I, and our brother William, we were all raised there. Our father was a surgeon. A very famous one. There are things named after him, I think. Procedures. Tools. Our mother sang. She was a very talented musician and singer, though she largely gave it up when William was born. North Nibley was a nice place to grow up. And it was famous, too, because William Tyndale was born there. Do you know who William Tyndale is, Nora?"

"No," said Nora.

"William Tyndale translated the Bible into English. He was the first to do it. He wanted everyone in England, not just the rich and educated, to be able to hear what the Lord had said, to know the stories the Lord wanted told."

"Yes?"

"The Lord, Nora, loves a good story."

"Okay."

"What they did, Nora, was kill him for it. They tied him to a stake, choked him, impaled him, and then set fire to his body."

"That's terrible, Miss Salderman. For translating? I'm not wholly understanding this."

"For blasphemy. And the people who killed him—this is the important part—the people who killed him really did think he was perverting the word of God. They truly and righteously believed he should die for a great sin. And now, of course, we look back and we see only sound logic in what he did. If God's speaking a language that only fifteen people can understand, then we're putting a lot of trust into their reading of the idiom.

"There is no act that we can judge, Nora, as good or bad—there is nothing in the world that is good, or bad, nothing at all. There's an illogical decision, or a logical one. There things done in haste and things done with great care. But how they are done does not make them good or bad, any more than the weather on the day they are done. The sureness we have, the certainty we have that what we are doing is right or wrong, has absolutely nothing to do with whether it is right or wrong."

"I appreciate this, Miss Salderman. This is very interesting. But I have heard enough about what is good and bad and I've already made my decision. It's not any use."

"I was sure, once, that moral decisions were easy to see. But as you become older, Nora, you find that there are many ways to be kind. Right and wrong . . . these things, we cannot know."

"I just need the library. What I've tried, it hasn't worked."

Odette smiled. She gestured to the dress. "Do you know what I was doing when you came in?"

Nora waited.

"A mouse must have gotten inside this room," said Odette. "There was a little hole, and I was sewing it up. That, there, that's my wedding dress. I made it myself."

"I didn't know you were married," said Nora.

"Oh, I wasn't. I was just thinking to myself, when you came in, if it wasn't time to rip the dress to shreds. To make it into napkins or a tablecloth."

"What did you decide?"

"That I don't need any napkins, or a tablecloth."

"There can't be any harm, I think, in keeping something that won't hurt anyone."

"Who is it? Who is the father?"

"I won't say that," said Nora.

"It must have been one of them. One of the Gallos? Paul or Jules? I pray . . . I pray very hard that it was not my brother. Will you at least tell me that? Was it Alex?"

"I can keep a secret, Miss Salderman."

"Then we have something in common," said Odette.

"Did your husband die?"

"Oh, you know him. Not personally. You were probably too young. But you've heard of him, or what happened to him. They put him in a cage and he starved to death. I heard that birds pecked out his eyes and his nose. But I only heard that. I don't know if it's true."

"You were the woman who jilted Captain Murderer?"

Odette Salderman smiled. "No," she said, very softly. "I did not jilt him. I have never jilted anyone. I wrote some poems about him. Love poems! They were very good. Everyone said so. But it broke him, that last voyage. Like the child's rhyme, you know. He couldn't put himself back together again. In the end, he was not the man I knew."

"I heard that the woman didn't love him and he went mad," said Nora.

"Everyone loves stories," said Odette. "We were made in God's image. God loves good stories but He doesn't care if they're true or not."

"It wasn't your fault," said Nora.

"No," said Odette, "but it was a horrible time. Then one day, there was a storm at sea. On a particular day, in a particular place. Consequences. And everything is changed."

"I'm sorry."

"No need."

"Do think I should have the baby?"

"Personal certainty, Eleanor. The sureness of the chooser on the correctness of any choice does not have any bearing on the outcome."

"I don't want to make the wrong decision. I don't want to be wrong."

"You've told me you've made your decision, that there is no use."

"I know."

"There's no need. It doesn't matter. I think now that I really hardly knew him. Not really. But I loved . . . oh, there was a way of being, he had. My brother showed me, once, how the bones of jaw fit together. I had thought there was only one smooth surface of skull . . . But he showed me how the jawbone fit neatly inside, to open and close. And that is what we were like. Two independent pieces, built to work together, neatly, each with our function and our full range of movement."

"What did he look like?" asked Nora, "And what was his real name?

"You know, I forget his face. It was all so long ago, and very soon after he died I couldn't see his face in my mind."

"I see Fernie's face," said Nora, "I see it all the time. And sometimes when I'm walking on the road I see him, out of the corner of my eye."

"Large, very strong. Sunburned, always, because of all those days in the sun, on the ship, without a hat. He lost a hundred hats to the sea. He was very beautiful, I thought."

"What was his name?"

"I cannot tell you," said Odette. "I keep his name, so that it is only for me."

"We have that in common, then."

Odette smiled.

"I'd like to ask for your permission," said Nora, "to use some of Doctor Salderman's books, the ones he left behind. Just a few of them.

Specific ones. I know which ones."

Odette looked at Nora's stomach. "I won't bother you," she said, "You may use the library as much as you like."

"Thank you," said Nora. "I won't bother *you*."

"I know," said Odette. "That's why I allow it."

When Nora had gone, Odette stood for a little while longer, staring at the painting of the horseman and the severed head. Then she walked to the desk, picked up her pen, and began to write.

Chapter XLVIII.
The Slough Home

The second attempt was a tea.

Nora spent three days in the woods and in the fields of the neighbors, plucking leaves and mushrooms, consulting the book she had borrowed from Satus, stealing surreptitiously from Agnes's herbs, drying and mixing the ingredients, measuring, re-measuring, and then another two days steeping the mixture. When she woke, early in the morning of the sixth day, the liquid was black and thick.

On her tiptoes, like a thief, Nora poured the mixture from the bowl into a mug. The morning was only just the earliest morning; the air still smelled like nighttime. Dedlock was in the outhouse; Agnes and Jim were asleep. Nora took her mug outside and stood on the stone threshold. It was cold. She went back inside and wrapped herself in Agnes's cloak. The tea hung in the mug: it was a heavy, dank liquid and it smelled like the stinging bitter earth. It was black and viscous and waiting to be drunk. Nora watched the sun move like a spider over the clapboards of the neighbors' homes, and drank.

"What's wrong with you?" Agnes asked at midday.

"I'm not sure," said Nora. "Nothing. Nothing."

The pain was excruciating. Nora felt as though someone had inserted a screw with sharpened edges into her belly, and throughout the afternoon it revolved and revolved and sheared off strips from her insides. She bore it for a long time, and she sweat through her tasks but eventually she could not help it; she fell to her knees in the garden and lost consciousness in the dirt. Phila barked until Agnes came.

Nora came to her senses and vomited. She was still pregnant.

That night, Agnes sat on the edge of Nora's bed and sponged her forehead with water and vinegar. Nora had drifted in and out of consciousness since she had collapsed in the garden and now she was sleeping, but badly, and she was feverish, and the dog had been so agitated that they had been forced to tie her up outside for the night.

Dedlock came into the room. He sat, too, on the edge of the bed, on the side opposite his wife.

"Will she recover from this?" he asked.

Agnes looked at Nora. The girl—the woman, she corrected herself—had the face of a dead animal. Her hair had been cut from her head, and poorly. Someone at Satus must have been cutting it, and Nora clearly had gone on cutting it herself, though Agnes had hidden her knives and scissors. It hadn't grown at all since she had arrived. There was no color in her face. The usual blush of the pregnancy, the rose of the chest and arms, was pale as snow on Nora's skin. Agnes remembered her own pregnancy. The delighted growing, the taste of food, the way the scent of her body had deepened and sweetened. Dedlock used to kneel on the bed, at night, and lower his head onto her massive belly. He would listen to the baby making waves inside her little ocean home, turning somersaults and kicking furiously, happily, tapping her mother on the ribs to say hello. Dedlock would lay his great hairy hand on top of the belly, and Agnes would slide it to where the baby's foot was, or her head, or her little elbow. Dedlock would talk and talk and talk. He would tell the baby stories about when he was a little boy, how he and his friends had gone sledding, and lost control of their sled on the ice, gone too fast and narrowly avoided the tree. They had laughed and laughed and felt alive. He told the baby that he loved her already, though they didn't know she would be a girl, or what they would name her. Agnes had asked Dedlock to tell the story of how they met each other, and Dedlock would lean over and kiss his wife on her lips. Then he told the baby the story of how one day, he had come to see Agnes's father, Mister Cates, and when he had come to the house there was a little girl playing inside. He asked the little girl, "Where is your father?" and the little girl had stopped her game, put down her toy, and taken Dedlock by the hand. So boldly, so easily, so without fear or pretense, so much like the trusting and kind woman she would one day become, and led him outside to the garden where her father was staking tomatoes with Zeena Cates. And as Dedlock told the story he kissed his wife's great taut belly and the baby, too big for her little home inside, tried to elbow her way to her father, and the next day, brought into the world by the story of her parents' first meeting, Bonnie had been born. Agnes looked up at Dedlock, sitting across from her, on the other side of this sad, pregnant girl.

"I don't know," she replied.

The third attempt was steam. Nora waited until Agnes and Dedlock and Jim had gone to sleep; she crept downstairs and, with the bellows, roused the fire to a blaze. She hung the soup pot and filled it with water; when it began to simmer, she rubbed dry herbs between her fingertips and sprinkled them into the pot. The kitchen began to smell musky and sap-like, fresh and heavy at the same time. The scent was pleasant but there was too much of it; Nora feared it would wake the Sloughs and so she opened the front door and the windows and let the summer breeze sweep away the perfume. The water came to a boil and bubbled furiously. It was awkward, the next part. Nora knew, as soon as she began, that she would need to be quick, or it would all be for naught. Ideally she would have help; she needed another person who was strong, and who could lift the pot from the fire and place it on the floor. But she was alone, and so she did the job alone. She heaved it up and the water spilled and the water burned the skin from her bare calf and foot, but she didn't make a sound. She paused and was more cautious; in the heaving and the balancing, the water calmed from the boil. But there was nothing to do; she stood up and squatted over the pot so that the perfumed steam drifted up the insides of her thighs, scorching her as it rose, then upwards into her insides, where she burned and the fragile skin spasmed in sudden, rose-colored pain; and then it came inside of her, scalding the tunnels that led to where her child was growing, and it burned, there, too, it burned and burned and burned and Nora bit through her lip and her tongue and she did not cry out until she heard the hurried footfalls of Agnes on the staircase, and the strong arms of Dedlock pulling her off and away from the steam, and she sat splay-legged on the kitchen floor and wept.

The next morning, she was still pregnant.

Chapter XLIX.
The Chilling Meeting House
The Slough Home

At the village meeting, in her seventh month, Nora stood up and explained that she did not want the child to grow up thinking that she was his mother.

"On account of his father and us being unmarried at the time," she said. There was a short silence in the room. The old woman Woodhill coughed.

"Religious reasons?"

"Yes. Morals. All that."

"And will you tell us the name of the child's father?"

Nora would have looked at Joe, but he had not come. He didn't like meetings. Oliver Shoemaker smirked.

"No," sighed Nora. She stared at Oliver and Oliver stopped smirking. She kept staring at him. She wanted to hit him with something heavy. She imagined hitting him with Salderman's old heavy dogstick. It gave her some pleasure. "Still no. Always, no."

A number of men and women stood up and offered suggestions. Dedlock and Agnes Slough, having a relationship with Nora, offered to adopt the child and raise it as their own. Octavius Peabody and his wife offered, as well, but their age was so advanced that the offer was ignored as mostly symbolic. Cordelia Ridley suggested that the village could do again as they had done for Abigail Osgood: obscure the child's parentage and raise the baby as Nora's youngest brother. They would tell him, or her, when the child was old enough, that it too had survived the illness that had claimed the rest of the Pirrips. Nora could be spared the pain of motherhood, at least nominally.

"You would need a helpmate, though, Nora, and it would be best you married."

"Or the Sloughs could raise the baby, and then . . ."

"We will give you the time you need, of course, to decide. You can marry, and raise the child yourself. As your youngest sibling. Or you can abandon it and reap the consequences of that."

Oliver coughed and looked at his list. The village began to discuss again the property tax changes, and how they would fill the coffers now that Salderman's funding had dried up. They argued. Then they moved on to the dispersal of the Hale land.

Afterward, in the road, the Peabodys found her. It was a new moon; Catherine clutched at her husband's arm.

"The choice is fair enough, Nora."

"There's another. I could go away. I could go to Boston, or even further. I could say I was a widow. No one would know."

"You would still have the baby, Nora. You cannot change that, now. It could come any time." Octavius put a hand on Nora's shoulder but Nora shrugged it off.

"It is a fair price, Nora," said her aunt. "Joey Gallo is a good man, and it will be a good marriage. And he wants the child, he wants the marriage. It is better that, than giving the child up to the Sloughs."

"Is it?"

"I know you do not want it. It is not only *your* child, Nora. It is your child, but also Georgiana's grandchild. Philip's grandchild. To give the child up to the Sloughs, the secret becomes massive. It is more difficult, then, you know. The larger the secret, the more difficult it is to keep. You would be nothing to him, your aunt and I, nothing."

"I don't mind it. I want to be nothing."

"But you force all of us to be nothing. All of us! We want this child. We will raise the child as your brother. You need not be a mother."

"I will be, though. I'll be a mother, no matter what we decide or what story we tell."

"I know this is difficult, girl. But you are no longer one person, Nora. This means you are two people, at once, and more. You contain more than your mere self. You cannot think ever again the way you have thought."

"So the choice is not actually mine, is it?"

"It is wholly yours. Ah. I see Dedlock, just coming. Talk it over with them. Agnes is rational and a good woman. Dedlock, too. Talk it over. But your aunt and I hope that we can cradle this baby as our kin. It is a good decision, Nora. Marry Joey Gallo. Have a family."

Dedlock Slough and Nora got along well, though Nora would never have claimed that she trusted him. There was something, to her, too earnest about his smile, too steady in his eyes when they fell on hers. She understood why Agnes had loved him and why she had wanted to marry him. His face was a good face: a nice strong jaw, a nice beard, nice brown eyes and even forehead. Dedlock smiled a lot. He was physically very powerful, and he held himself with a sort of aggression, a sort of hardness in his limbs. Occasionally, when he was talking to her, or talking to Agnes, Dedlock reminded Nora of someone, or of something, and she annoyed herself with her inability to remember who, or what . . .

"The fact that the village is going to keep this secret from him," Nora said to him as they walked home, "I cannot really believe it. That everyone can agree and do it."

"They've done it before," said Dedlock. "Chilling was made on that. Keeping things secret and private. The whole reason the village was founded was that . . . Scoundrels and wasters and people living outside the church, taking some land as a haven. Strange people begun Chilling and they begot what it is now. We're part of it, whether proud or not. It's not as hard as you might think. It becomes very easy, when you decide on your story and keep telling it. It's very easy and you forget the truth, eventually. The lie is all anyone knows and so it is all they can tell."

"Do you know what I want? What story I want told? I want to know where my mother went, and where she was during all those years. When she came back no one said a thing. Not where she was, or why she went, or why she had come back. No one said anything even though someone must have known . . . People don't vanish and reappear."

"Everyone knew your mother very well. She was born here." Dedlock stopped in the road and squatted down to rub Phila's neck. "I knew your father well, too. Philip was an honorable man."

"He loved me."

"But even your father kept secrets. Everyone has their secrets. Mothers and fathers included; you don't stop being a person . . . a scoundrel . . . when you have children. And people keep their secrets because they have good reasons for keeping them. Sometimes other people agree. Chilling agrees to keep secrets because Chilling needs to be of one mind. We want to be safe, here. Protected from the laws of the other places, protected from their judgments. But it has nothing to do with the person . . . It has nothing to do with the person . . . It has nothing to do with you."

"Of course it does."

"It has nothing to do with the person who doesn't know. From whom we keep the secret. Like your baby: it is not because he is a bad or untrustworthy person that we're going to keep the secret of his parents. It is because of you, and the father. It has to do with the person who needs to keep that secret. What's inside their own hearts."

"Can we keep walking? Agnes will be waiting."

Dedlock stood up and they went on. Philadelphia jumped ahead; she liked to snap at the lightning bugs.

"I never felt loved," said Nora. "By my mother. And yet she loved me."

"Some people need to keep secrets. She needed to."

"I don't see how I can be a mother."

"You'll be fine. You don't need to be the same person as your mum. You don't even need to be the same person you were in the past."

"I never want to keep secrets from the child. But I don't know . . . if that is possible."

"I myself, I keep myself far off. I've kept a secret from my own wife for a long time."

"What is it?"

"That's just it, Nora. That's what you are not understanding. Secrets are not told. Secrets remain secret. They remain mysteries. That's the nature of it. I won't tell you and I won't tell Agnes. I won't tell the other men—the men I trust with my life. And it has nothing to do with you. You are all good people: you would be kind. You would forgive me. You don't have choices with secrets. Your mother, likely. She didn't have choice."

"Why?"

"For me . . . because my heart won't let me say. I am ashamed. I cannot say my shame out loud, because to make a thing into words is to make it real and public. Once it is real it can go out and attack. Words cannot be unspoken once spoke, Nora. They turn into other things. Words conjure. Words make. And hearts don't say, so you keep terrors there. They're safe. They cannot get out, hurt other people."

They could see the Slough house. Agnes had kept a lamp in the kitchen window and they could see Phila, who had run ahead, waiting for them by the door.

"If I marry Joe Gallo," Nora asked, "what will it be like?"

"I don't know," said Dedlock. "It is a mystery."

"You are married."

"I don't know. Marriage is a mystery. It is a deeper mystery when you are inside of it. It is hard to see a thing from the inside."

Nora proved to be more competent with deep wounds than Agnes, and so she went out, huge as she was, and sewed up gashes and slices. Coming home, one day, from Janey Farmer's kitchen accident, she took a turn toward the forge.

"Hey there, Nora."

"Hello Porter."

"Who's been hurt? Not a bad one?"

"No, not bad. One of the Farmer girls cut her finger."

"Ah." Porter glanced at Joe, who had not looked up from his work. "Well. I've had the thought to go and get these to the Hornbeams. Have we got them all here, Joe?"

"All of them," said Joe.

"Grand. Back in a wee time. Best to the Sloughs, Nora."

Nora waved and, after Porter had gone, leaned up against the wall. "I've been talking to Dedlock and Agnes," she said. "We are getting along. Prudence Reed made me this dress. It fits me."

Joe looked up. Nora patted her belly.

"You're so big," he said. "I can't believe it. You were such a skeleton. Here, can you sit farther off? That fire will burn you."

"Joe," she said, "I have a question for you, a specific question." She lowered herself into a chair.

"What?"

"I don't want to ask, if it will offend, or if you don't want to make any reply, then don't."

"What?"

"I was wondering why you told me about your father. I wanted to know why it was you wanted me to know about that."

Joe put down his hammer. He pulled a piece from the fire, wiped his forehead, and shook his gloves off onto the floor. He pulled a small bench from beneath a table and dragged it next to Nora. He sat on it and unlaced his boot and pulled off his sock.

"I'll tell you why," he said, "if you take care of my toe."

Nora put her hand to her back and turned toward Joe. "Give it to me," she said. Joe swung his leg so that his immense foot rested on Nora's knee. His big toe skimmed her enormous belly. Inside of her, the baby shifted uncomfortably.

"Oh, Joe. What happened?" said Nora.

"I dropped something on it."

"You feel that? You broke these two. I can set them, if you want. You can keep them broken but they'll look funny and hurt. I can set them."

"I told you because I wanted you to know."

"Why's that?"

"I don't know. Fernie and I were bound together our whole life because of it. We were closer than brothers because of it. And I think I wanted to do that to you, to bind you to us with it."

"I'm sweating. We couldn't do this outside? More light would be nice. I need some sturdy sticks."

"We can't talk outside," said Joe.

"You did," said Nora. "You did bind me to you. Look, I'm here in your forge setting your disgusting toes. For no charge. I care about your feet. But you didn't care that you were telling me something that would mean you were a bad person? You didn't care about that?"

"Look," said Joe, "you dissected bodies. You let Fernie and I talk to you, you made friends with Paul and Jules, you let us all hang about you, you never went to church. You didn't talk about God. You didn't judge Salderman for what he had done. You didn't judge Lily's mom."

"Why would I judge Lily's mother?"

"You didn't seem to mind the things that they all had done. You seemed, instead, to like those things. It gave you energy. You liked working with those bodies. It made you happy."

"But that is different."

"I'm not ashamed of what we did. What I did. I don't feel guilty about it."

"Did you not love your father at all?"

"I did love him. And when I say I'm not ashamed . . . I just don't want to have to talk about it. I am ashamed. I'm not and I am. I am sad about him. Of course, I love him. He was a good person who got ruined by accident and changed into a devil. He wasn't born a devil. But it is hard to be alive and he was soft, and he got hammered and split and shaped like the way the world made him."

"Fernie thought you hated your father."

"I did. I do. He killed our mother. He would have killed me, or he would have killed Fernie."

"But you never said to Fernie that you loved your father and felt sad about him dying?"

"No, I never did."

"I don't know why you'd keep that a secret. That you loved him isn't shameful."

"I lost the right when I left him in that forge, Nora. I never doubted my father loved my mother, even when he killed her. And Fernie always knew that Dad loved him, even after the knife slipped and he lost his leg. But once you've done something like that, something so terrible, you can't show love anymore. You've lost the right. Because no matter what you say or do you can't ever make it up. You've dug too far, you might say, and it's impossible to climb out of the hole. You ruined them. You don't get to love them anymore."

Joe yelped in pain.

"I had to set it," said Nora. "It will be sore a few days, and you should try to not walk on it very much. Can you struggle through with these toes until tonight? You can come by the Sloughs and she'll bandage them right. This is all I can do, for now."

"Thank you."

"We had a meeting," Nora said. "They have all agreed, that we could tell the baby and everyone that I am his sister. And we survived the illness together."

"And then?"

"Dedlock and Agnes would raise him, they said. I like them very much. And they lost their child."

"It's your decision."

"What would you like for me to do?"

"I would like to stop all this and stop the worrying and the decisions and the fretting over what is going to happen. We know what is going to happen. The baby is coming. And you'll want him when he comes, Nora. He's going to look like someone, Nora, and I'll know who it is, even if you never tell us. And all the stories in the world won't change his face. He'll have the truth written in his eyes and his hair and the way he walks and stands. If you have to be his sister, then be his sister. But I want to raise him. I want him as a son. He's a fatherless thing and no one deserves that. He's mine. And I love you, in a strange way, at least a little, and I want to stop all of this and have it over. I want it all done and decided, so that we can go on."

"Give me your boot. I will pad it up as much as I can."

"Will they be straight again, when they are healed?"

"I think they will," said Nora. "But maybe not. I have tied them straight with these sticks—see?—but we'll do better tonight. Set them a bit stronger. And as long as they stay tight, and you do not let them get loose, or walk too much on them, I think they will heal straight again."

"When will the pain stop?"

"I don't know. Sometimes it does not go away and sometimes it goes away very quickly, and sometimes it goes away and then comes back in sudden pangs."

"What are you going to do, Nora?"

"I do not know."

"What happened to Salderman, Nora?"

"I do not know."

On her way back to the Sloughs', Nora saw an elderly couple ahead of her in the road. They were walking very slowly and, even as massive and swollen as she was, she passed them quickly.

"Nora," said the woman. Nora turned.

It was her aunt and uncle. They were old. She had not seen their age, before. She had been too busy seeing her own unhappiness. Her uncle's hair was very thin, very gray, and so sparse that Nora could see the shape of his skull and the delicate staining of his scalp. Her aunt was speckled, like an egg, with age and liver spots. Her hands clutched at themselves like the talons of a dying bird. She stooped; she looked very small.

"Hello," said Nora. She turned and waddled back to them. The baby kicked her ribcage and she gave a little grunt. "Oh," said Catherine, and she put her hands on Nora's belly.

"Here," said Nora, "that's his foot right here." She maneuvered her aunt's hand so that it lay right over the baby's little heel.

"Octavius," said Catherine, "feel this!"

"May I?"

Nora took his hand. "Of course," she said. She stood and looked down on them, crouching by her stomach, their hands on her. Catherine looked up and met her eyes.

"Incredible," said her aunt. "Just incredible. Thank you. We never had one of our own. We're very excited, Nora, for him to come."

Nora left them in the center of the road. They stood and watched her until she was out of sight, and then they started again on their walk to the sea. They liked to watch the waves and see if any ships were passing.

Chapter L.
The Gallo Home

Nora's son was born in the beginning of February, on a cold and snowless Sunday afternoon. He came early, and was a very small baby. Nora sat in a chair by the window, the child sleeping at her breast, and looked out on the spare gray ground, the empty gray sky, the far away shore dismal and motionless. Agnes was sure the child would die before he was a week old. But eventually he did suckle, and he did survive, even if his limbs were thin as straw and his eyes big as moons. Joe asked that the baby be named after Fernie, but Nora didn't want that. They named him instead Philip, after Nora's father.

In their bed, Joe played with the tiny boy. "He's getting stronger," he said to Nora. "Look at that!"

Nora laughed. "Oh, yes, Joe. He's a brute. Look at him. He's the size of a seed."

"Are you a little seed? Are you our little pip?"

"We'll see if he ever sprouts."

"You're not a pip! Don't listen to your mother."

"Sister, Joe." Nora frowned. "I'm his sister. You have to start now."

"We'll have you with a hammer and tongs next week," Joe said to the baby. He watched Nora tie a brown kerchief over her head. She pulled it halfway down her forehead so that if she raised her eyebrows she could feel them graze the fabric. Her hair had begun to grow, slightly. She hadn't mentioned it to Joe but she could feel wisps on the back of her neck, where before there had been none. She felt timidly excited; she was ashamed to be excited by such a thing as hair.

"Put him to bed," said Nora.

Joe lifted the child and handed him to his mother. "You do it," he said. "I want to just go to the back and check the sky."

"It's not going to storm," said Nora. She was working hard to learn Joe. She wanted to be perceptive and observe the fluctuations in his face and body, to determine when he was sad, or angry, or one of the other thousand emotions. But she did not enjoy it. Unlike her work in the Satus cellars, there was no mystery to this task. Joe was honest with her. He said what he felt. He explained what he thought, or knew. He asked when he did not know. Nora listened to him half in wonder, half in disbelief. *She* felt as though every movement of her life was an effort at disguise, and that every shape she made with her eyes or mouth or body masked something too terrible to show.

Since the baby had been born, she had felt the absence of the absence of what she loved. When she looked at Joe's body, and then at the little Philip's tiny one, their whole and healthy beauty made her sad. She realized she had been harboring a ridiculous hope that the child would change her. But he did not. He was the physical manifestation of what had happened to her heart, or to her soul, or to whatever was that strange and dark and tumorous thing that gaped within her body. Observing her husband, listening to him speak and watching him move around their home, she was annoyed by his goodness, and his complete honesty. Nora hated her feelings, her resentments, her desires. She devoted all of her energy to hiding them.

When Joe came back into the room Philip was asleep in his crib at the foot of the bed, and Nora was squatting over the little pot.

"It's very cold tonight," he said. "Does he have enough?"

"He does, but we can take him in the bed with us if you're worried." Nora stood and pulled her nightgown over her head. Joe liked for her to be naked when she was in the bed with him, and she had come to like the feel of his skin on hers as they slept. She and Joe climbed into their bed, each from their opposite side, and took a minute to layer on top of them the four blankets and fold another at their feet. Nora liked the feeling of weight when she slept, and even if she became too warm she would not kick off a blanket. Sleeping by her, Joe sometimes felt as though he was being smothered, or had nightmares in which a woolly monster came to strangle him; each time he awoke, sweating and panicked, but he did not pull off the blankets.

But of course blankets were not the price of the marriage, or they were not, at least, the full price. Nora slept with him, she opened her legs to him and took him in her mouth. She kissed him. She rested her head on his chest. When he was exhausted after working, she would lay his head in her lap and stroke his hair and his forehead; she would lay her hand on his wide back and he would feel such comfort, such love from her body that he could have wept. She smiled when he was happy and listened when he was upset. But Joe knew that Nora didn't love him and Nora knew that Joe knew this.

After he had rolled off of her in the dark, Joe wiped his forehead and leaned against the cool wood of the headboard.

"How can we be so close," he asked her. "How can you be with me like this?"

Nora was lying on her stomach. She was almost asleep, but she reached out and patted Joe on the chest.

"Don't," she said. "There's different ways of having something. This is what we have."

"I would like you to tell me," Joe said. He closed his eyes and waited. "Everything. I think you will feel better. Everything that happened up there—whatever it was that you did, or felt you had to do."

Nora was quiet a moment, then pushed herself up and turned so that she was sitting up beside her husband.

"Joe," she said. She rubbed her eyes. "I am so tired."

"I don't want him to get cold," said Joe. He swung himself out of the bed and took the baby from his crib.

"Does he feel cold?"

"No," said Joe, but he got back into bed with Philip anyway, and pushed his feet under the blankets. "Fernie's first word was *Joe*. My name."

"That sounds right."

"He used to follow me around everywhere. He'd say, 'Hi, Joe,' and then I'd say 'Hi, Fernie,' then again, 'Hi Joe!' and 'Hi Fern,' and 'Hi, Joe,' 'Hi Fernie.' He would have gone on forever. And then my mum used to say whenever I went outside or into another room, he used to just look sad and wander around and say, 'Hi, Joe? Hi, Joe?'"

"Maybe we should have a shorter name for Philip. It'll be easier for him to learn and say."

"We can call him Phila."

"Did we name him after the dog?"

"He could do worse. We could call him Pip," said Joe.

"I wouldn't mind that. How old was Fernie when he started saying your name?"

"I can't remember. Little."

"How old were you when he was born?"

"I was three. Three and a half? And then when we were a little older, when I was around eight or so, Ben Benner used to come around to the forge. I was working with my dad then and I heard a lot of things they were saying, and one of the days they were talking about witches, and what they'd do down in the Bay when someone was a witch."

"You mean when they would burn them at the stake?"

"I was eight years old. I went home for lunch, tied Fernie to a chair in the pantry, and set the ropes on fire with a candle."

Nora laughed. "It's not funny, I know," she said, "but I can laugh because I know he was okay."

"I told him, 'If you die, you're not a witch,' and the great thing was, Fernie was fine with it. Completely unbothered. The ropes smoldered a little but didn't really light up the way I expected them to. I left them smoking and getting all black at Fernie's feet and I went to find mum.

"'Mum,' I said, "the ropes won't catch fire the way I want them,' and so she wiped her fingers on her apron and she followed me to the pantry and then I opened the door, and there was her baby Fernie all tied up and the ropes absolutely smoking and curling up."

With his fingertips, Joe stroked Pip's tiny head. He touched the tip of his nose very gently.

"Did you give Phila those crusts?" Nora asked.

"They were still in her bowl when I went downstairs," said Joe. "She was watching something outside the window."

"I hope she comes upstairs soon," said Nora.

"She won't until the fire dies."

"Do you think she is mad at us? Angry about the baby?"

"No," said Joe, "I think she is confused by him."

"What did your mum do?"

"She screamed. And then she fell to her knees and started smacking the ropes with her bare hands. The whole house smelled like burning. I got very nervous and I got out of that pantry fast, but then later she found me and she looked at me, like, oh, she was angry. I'd never seen her like that. And she couldn't undo the knots I had tied so she sent me in to untie them, but even I couldn't untie them."

"Did you have to cut him out?"

"That's what my dad's thinking was," said Joe. "When he got home I was crying and my mother was yelling, 'Joey tried to kill Fern.' I think about it now, what it must have been like to come home that night. His wife was crying, one of his sons was crying, the other son was bound head to foot to a chair in the pantry, and the house smelled just like the forge. Everything loud and wild. And when I come home, you're so nice and calm, and the baby is here. We have a good home. Peaceful. He's going to be such a happy boy."

"Joe," said Nora. She put his hand on his thigh. "I didn't know this was what you were telling me."

"And so he got the knife and he sawed through some ropes, and then something must have happened, and the knife slipped."

"Did you see?"

"No," said Joe. He shook his head. "Mum and I were in the kitchen. Just Dad and Fernie, in the pantry alone. Because I tied him to a chair too tight."

Joe placed the child between them and then sunk his head into Nora's belly and reached around her with both arms. Nora kept one eye on the baby. She bent over her husband's head, rubbed his back with her hands and put her nose in his yellow hair until he fell asleep. She did not love him. She could admit that. But she loved the feeling of her body giving comfort to his: it was so easy to make him feel happy. It was only her hands, or her lips, and her legs or her belly, and she would give them to him and then he was content. It made her feel peaceful and powerful, to do these things for him. She pulled away, took the baby back to his crib, tucked him in, and went to sleep.

Joe dreamed. In the dream, Fernie had been tied to a chair for hours, and Joe was Fernie. Five years old, and he could hear himself—Joe—crying loudly somewhere in the house. His father was tired and hungry at the end of the day, and when the knife slipped, they both watched it go into the back of Fernie's leg. Fernie was sure that he had seen the knife go into his leg, but he didn't feel any pain. And then Mr. Gallo pulled the knife out again. There, the dream changed, and they were outside; the air was thick and solid. Everything was blue: the trees, the wind, the smell of dung. It was all blue. Then, looking at the blue knife in his hand, Joseph Gallo knew exactly what had happened. He looked up at Fernie with the wild and sure hope that it had not happened, at all: that there was a moment in which you could erase the previous moment. It did not happen, he said to Fernie, and Fernie agreed. No, dad, he said. If, together, they ignored the fact, perhaps the fact would not be. Their bodies were not blue. Everything was thick and blue around them, but they were not.

An eternity later, a second later, the blood and pain came. Joe was trapped in Fernie's body. His leg was on fire; his brain was on fire. He wanted to scream but he did not want anyone to know what his father had done. But the elder Gallo knew. He nodded at his son, who remained silent as long as he could, and finally, with great reluctance and with a great intake of breath, he cried out so piteously that a young Maga Cates and a young Dedlock Slough, young and blue and walking in the road, both dropped the armfuls of blue gourds they had been carrying. Blue, pimply, misshapen, the gourds rolled to the side of the road where a horse had shit, and where the flies were swirling and screaming in joy.

Joe woke and lay in the bed. He did not move. He listened to Nora breathing.

Fernie's wound had turned gangrenous within the week, and he lost the leg soon after. Doctor Salderman, with help from the shoemaker, fashioned him a wooden prosthesis that attached to his small thigh with a leather strap and buckle. Fernie had stopped talking for a month or so. He rarely left his mother's side; he became anxious and restless if she was out of his sight for more than a few moments. He followed her to the outhouse; he slept in his parents' bed, sat at the kitchen table while she cooked or baked or washed. In the weeks it took him to adapt to the wooden leg, Fernie fell a lot. He broke his nose thrice in a month; his eyes were underhung with violent yellow and purple half-moons where the blood had pooled. Joseph Gallo the elder began to take liquor with his breakfast, and then with all meals. Then, throughout the day. When he was sober, he heard the thin guttural screams of his baby as the doctor sawed through his leg and bone; he saw the phantom limb dancing in front of him, the piece of his child he had sacrificed for nothing. He had done this, the sight of his child daily reminded him. Things could not unhappen. Mistakes—no matter how passing, how careless, how silly, how unnecessary—could not be unmade. The injustice of the temporal world was too much for him. He drank as much as he could; as he drank more often and in larger amounts, he became increasingly violent. He began strike his wife at night. This continued for years. The boys spent whole nights cowering. Occasionally, Mrs. Gallo would take them out of the house and they would go to sleep at the Cottons', or at the Woodhills'. Joe got older and began to intervene on his mother's behalf; Mr. Gallo struck Joe. Nothing ever turned better; every night was worse than the one before. One night, just a week after the new year, Joseph Gallo struck his wife in the back with a fire poker and severed her spine.

Then, three weeks later, he himself was dead. He had frozen inside his forge. Benjamin Benner forced the door and found the body, curled in a corner, cold and blue.

Chapter LI.
The Pirrip Farm

The day before the Pirrip farm was legally handed over to Jeremy Hale, Joe and Nora and Phila and Pip packed a lunch and spent the day at the abandoned house. Nora promised Oliver Shoemaker and her uncle, who had arranged everything with the Hales, that they would be out by the evening, and that they would leave no trace behind them.

It was dry, scorching heat, odd for September. Nora spread a quilt on the grass by the pond, close to the edge, where they could easily slip from scratchy New England sun into the cool dark of the water. Occasionally, either Joe or Nora would fall asleep, dozing face up in the sun, and awaken again to the sound of the other's body easing into the water. From a distance, from across the pond, their vastly different bodies would have looked the almost the same, two spots of movement against the landscape. From time to time, too, one of them would bring himself or herself up to sit, shield their eyes for a moment against the sunshine, and lift the baby from his spot in the shade. And then Joe or Nora would pad barefoot back up the hill and into the farmhouse, leaping over the rocks just outside the back door. Inside, Pip would get a little cleaning and a chance to rest from the heat, and the parent would unlatch the food basket and remove a flask of water or a piece of fruit. And then the family would be together again, would sit side by side on the edge of the pond and watch the strange way the cold transparent water would distort their feet, make their toes waver and appear clean and pale.

Nora would lean over and pull a large hat onto Joe's head, so that his fair skin would not burn. Joe held the baby and the baby paddled and played in the water. Philadelphia leaped into the water and swam in circles until she exhausted herself, then lay down to sleep with her head on Nora's lap.

Occasionally, the hum of a dragonfly would interrupt the quiet of their sunning and swimming. They would rise, prop themselves up on one elbow, and watch the insect make its way frantically across the pond, wings wildly beating and the sound of the flutter frantic in the wake of its flight. Then, because they had both been forced up and awake, Joe and Nora would wade into the water and swim out, racing each other to the other side and returning again. Nora ducked her head and swam underwater, caught the heel of her husband's foot in her hand, and pulled him down and under the water, too, so that neither ever won the race. What larks! They would flip over, suspended in the dark lake, wrestling and their arms slipping off each other's' bodies, until they remembered guiltily their son napping in the shade of the trees and pulled themselves up onto the grass again. The sun pressed its palms against their bellies and foreheads.

In the evening Nora hung their wet things on the clothesline. Phila followed her and sat, watching as each damp piece was clipped to the line. Inside the house, Nora untucked herself and fed the baby. Joe unpacked their dinner. He sliced the cheese and fruit with the same knife, so that the blade was crumbed in both, and then he licked it clean. Nora opened the windows, and the breeze came in soft and warm. The sun began to set and stretched long swathes of light over the floor of the kitchen.

When it was ready, they carried their supper down to the pond. Their hair, damp still from swimming, dried in wind that became more and more unpredictable, gusty, cold. Nora's hair, growing, growing, quickly now since she had given birth, curled and flew into her face, into her mouth. The wind came up from the south, roused tiny waves in the pond, and then from the west, and the waves on the water became confused and crashed madcap into one another. Nora and Joe ate their biscuits and fruit and cheese with their fingers. She leaned into him and rested her head on his chest. The wind kept coming, more insistently, and Nora stood and ran to take down the quilts and clothes before the wind loosed them and they danced away across the pond.

Inside, Joe sang to the baby softly. The dog stretched out and slept. Nora folded the quilt and closed the windows. She wiped the dishes they had used, and repacked the food they had not eaten. Joe came behind Nora and held her by the waist, leaned into her, and rested his chin on the top of her head. They had done so little, and felt so tired. They smelled like sunburn though neither had burned, like grass and water and their own sweat. Joe kissed the top of Nora's head. He knew she did not want to leave the house but stay there, instead, and sleep one more night in the home of her family, who she had loved. She did not explain but he understood, in the way it is between two people who have nothing left to explain, because this is how it is and has always been.

Joe took the sleeping baby and the baskets. He and Nora cajoled Phila into being tied to a length of rope. Joe and all these things returned to the village, to their home. Philadelphia cried because she did not like to leave Nora but Joe spoke soothingly to her.

Nora stayed behind, wrapped her body in the quilt, and walked her way again to the edge of the pond. Alone on the shore, the wind was very strong. She crouched down and pulled the quilt more securely around herself and lay down on the grass. She clenched her hands on the edges of the quilt. The wind would have blown her blanket away had she, accidentally, loosened her grip for even a moment. Nora lay flat on her back, warm enough and huddled inside the blanket. Cocooned, she fell asleep watching thin tendrils of her hair escape and dance upward into the wind. The wind above her face, the grass underneath her back and legs, and underneath that, the sound of the lapping and movement of the water.

When she woke, it was because the wind had pushed its way into her dreams, where she had seen people and things from her past aloft and whipping fast by in the wind. Her mother was there, sneering and feeling her way in the dark. Fernie held her hand by the sea; maggots writhed and she plunged her father's pitchfork into the dark heap of compost. Joe pressed a damp rag to her broken face. She dissected and took apart a pumping heart, the branching nerves inside a hand. Her baby brother was born again and Roger took his toy duck for a walk in the sunshine. Salderman tucked his hair behind his ear, looked away, turned away. Jules was laughing and Paul was singing. When she woke from her dreams, she kept her eyes clenched shut to petrify the images there. She felt her body tense and tight; every muscle was pushing against the wind and down into the ground. The back of her skull pressed itself mercilessly into the grass. The wind was higher and stronger than she could remember it having ever been. The wind pushed and pushed at her. She turned onto her side and curled her body into a fist. It was the dark and twisting lost center of the night. Nora tried to be still and to listen for the sound of the water. But she could not hear the water, only the great screaming gasps of wind. Nora opened her eyes, one lid peeled up against the wind and then the other.

Such a starry, starry night! And how still the stars were, how unmoving and constant. Sometimes only, coolly, blinking one bright
eye without hurry or energy. The wind could not jostle or unnerve
them. The night sky, the cool, even night sky.

It did not lessen, let up, or soften; the pond roiled and smashed,
loud, the spray soaked her quilt and face. Nora sat up and pulled the
sides of her blanket tight across her shoulders and over her head. The
force of the wind sent her over onto her side, and she struggled to be
upright again.

Nora squinted her eyes against the wind and could make out,
through the darkness, the uneven white crests of the breaking water.
They appeared and rose and vanished before she could trace their
shape or size: only they were there, and then were not.

High and arcing above her head, the white stars unruffled by the
wind.

She was cold, and wet, her eyes stinging from the strain of watching the wind. Her bones ached from pushing them into the grass
and dirt, and her dreams when she had half-slept had been of the
wind. She stood and, nearly toppling, pushed her way back toward
the house, her shoulders hunched and head down against the winds
which came from all sides. The door resisted and would not open
against the wind. She had to push and pull and heave. When it
opened and she slipped quickly inside, it slammed behind her. She
stood in the empty house, everything now quiet and still.

Chapter LII.
A Letter, Found in the Slough Home and Read Aloud to Joe Gallo

my deare Jo,

Jn 7:34 Ye shall Seek me and shall Not finde me

I write to you by my frend Agnes Slough the Midwife, who will reade this note to you so I need not fret it be myscarried or Lost. Let me stay & comfort feares, I am well, not sick or dead. I am left Chilling & gone away, to returne againe to our Home in a yeare or a tyme not more than 2 yeares. My dog Ph. is come along that I may be Safe and have a Loving Companion on my journey.

For the baby, he may be fed by Abigail Osgood in the day. In the night make a mixture of cow milk & a little yolk & some meale very finely grounde by the pestle & if it is the season, a little mash of pease. When Pip growes his teeth, soft bread wet in milk or water. Truely I know no man Alive better to care for This Boy. If the task weigh too heavy upon you the womyn will I knowe seek to help and rayse him vntil my Returne.

Some men are blacksmiths & others forge other mettles. We too know that life is only many Partings, welded together as from your fire & Hammer. I go to find the mettle I am to forge. In my minde I remember the Best thing of my lyfe, Joe the blacksmith in his forge at the old anvil, in the old burnt apron, sticking to his worke & singing to our Pip as he goes. I but see this in my minde & brought to Gratitude for the sake of you.

I verily believe and trust the Lord to remaine with you in my journeys & to comfort you. You haue the stroake of Gods hand vppon your face & I shall see it before me in the dark nightes I am away. I do not wish you to feel sad or despair. I am gone for me & not for you or wee Pip, whom I love and will Returne to be with againe. But it is not with me as it is with other euen Godly folk; who finde joy in the home & family & whom journeying can vnsettle & afear, & I am going only for the Necesity of going, not for the finding or arriving at any New Home. You are & will be all ways All and Wedded & I will Returne to you & live until we are taken to the Lord. But before I am in the home Forever I must go & move away, Wis 11:1-3 They journeyed through an uninhabited Wilderness and pitched their tents in untrodden places.

Gen 31:49 The Lord watch twixt me and thee whilst we are apart

Your Dearest Yoakefellow
Eleanor

Chapter LIII.
Satus House

Lily loved the autumn. Every year it took her by surprise. She would sweat through the night, toss and turn and damn the humid summer, swat at a mosquito and finally fall asleep, miserable and exhausted, well past midnight . . . and then wake up, the next day, to the fresh smell of wet leaves and cold rain. She could wear her coat in the autumn. She loved her coat because it was soft and had large deep pockets and a cavernous woolen hood that kept the rain off and her ears warm. Now that the Gallos had gone and all the men, Lily herself made the long trip to Chilling and back. She bought what they needed, and ran errands for her mother and Odette. During the walk Lily would pass through every part of the country. She began to love each part, in its way. From the top of the hill, she could see the ocean and the waves. In the forest she heard the rush as the brook began to rise with the season. But her favorite was when Lily reached the village, and she could smell the sharp soft smoke of the wood stoves as Chilling kept itself warm and dry and fed.

The leaves were beautiful, of course. But to Lily, the colors and patterns of the changing leaves were never as beautiful as the smell of firewood, of food cooking, of drying wool. Lily had been cloistered for a long time. She had a lonely childhood inside a house made out of secrets. Death and decay—even in its most vivid and glorious explosions of purples and oranges and colors that had no name on earth—could not equal for her the pleasure of a single, sure, steady plume of smoke.

With the men gone, Odette came downstairs much more often. She wrote in the library. In the mornings, Lily scrubbed the kitchen bricks with a hard-bristled brush. In the afternoon her mother started the soup and Lily walked to Chilling and back or, if they needed nothing, she would walk to the ocean. Sometimes she dug out clams. In the evening they all ate together at the kitchen table, and by October were forced to light candles in order to see their spoons. When they had finished Odette helped to scrape the plates and shake out the napkins and wipe the table.

The ritual of the day, even the work she did not particularly enjoy, had become a joy to Lily, because one thing led to the next and to the next, with unerring regularity, and the culmination of the day was always the same, and yet it was always different, and it was always wonderful. It was the best part of her day: when Odette brought out the books and they began to read. It was, she sometimes thought, the best part of her life.

To begin, Odette read out loud what Lily and her mother had struggled through the night before. Though they had deciphered it themselves, it was never boring to hear Odette read the lines again: the sentences were different when she pronounced them. Odette could do more than read. She could tell a story. And somehow, hearing it for a second time, the story expanded, grew grander and more intricate with retelling. Then Odette would finish and slide the open book to Lily's mother, and the work of learning to read would begin again.

Maga sounded out each word very slowly, very careful not to make a mistake. Odette helped and corrected. Lily would listen and try to spell the words she recognized on her slate, but spelling was very difficult and she was often distracted by the story, and by the tremendous sight of watching her mother attempt something so difficult. It was very slow work, but Odette told them that the most valuable work was always done very slowly, and her patience guided theirs. And each night their skill increased and their understanding increased and they were able to read a little easier, a little faster, a little more fluidly. They began to read words, and not just sounds, and then not just words but phrases, and then sentences, and then ideas, and then, sometimes, stories.

When Lily's mother had read her part, Odette would say, "Good," and it would be Lily's turn to read.

"'No more, my friend;
Greece is no more! this day her glories end;
Even to the ships victorious Troy pursues,
Her force increasing as her toil renews.
Those chiefs, that used her utmost rage to meet,
Lie pierced with wounds, and bleeding in the fleet.
But, thou, Patroclus! act a friendly part,
Lead to my ships, and draw this deadly dart;
With lukewarm water wash the gore away;
With healing balms the raging smart allay,

313

Such as sage Chiron, sire of pharmacy,
Once taught Achilles, and Achilles thee.
Of two famed surgeons, Podalirius stands
This hour surrounded by the Trojan bands;
And great Machaon, wounded in his tent,
Now wants that succour which so oft he lent.'"

As Lily read, her mother reached out and held her daughter's hand. Lily's eyes remained on the page. Her mother watched and felt gratitude for her life, but she did so without speaking, without interrupting.

"To him the chief: 'What then remains to do?
The event of things the gods alone can view.
Charged by Achilles' great command I fly,
And bear with haste the Pylian king's reply:
But thy distress this instant claims relief.'
He said, and in his arms upheld the chief.
The slaves their master's slow approach survey'd,
And hides of oxen on the floor display'd:
There stretch'd at length the wounded hero lay;
Patroclus cut the forky steel away:
Then in his hands a bitter root he bruised;
The wound he wash'd, the styptic juice infused.
The closing flesh that instant ceased to glow,
The wound to torture, and the blood to flow."

"Why are you holding my hand, Mum?" Lily asked, when she had finished the section.

Maga cleared her throat. "Nothing, Lil. I'm happy, happy you can read." Her voice broke and she cleared her throat again. "I am proud of you. I am so proud my daughter reads. You read so beautifully."

"Good," said Odette. "Enough for tonight."

314

Chapter LIV.
The Narrative of the Graveyard

When she came back again, it was springtime. The weather was very fine. The cow brother was in the forge; he sang and clanged his hammers; the child was walking by then, toddling with a dirty face and happy. The Slough woman came every day and knelt at her baby's stone; she was big, again, and would be having another child in her arms by the summer. It was warm, and the sun was good to us.

When the woman came back she had with her, at her side, the dog. She returned with nothing in her hands, nothing on her back, nothing at all but the black and white dog, half-blind, that obeyed her every sound and little move, like a tiny soldier. She did not go, right away, to see her child and husband. She came to me, where they had buried her family: Philip Pirrip, her father, and also Georgiana, her mother, and also the five small brothers. She stood for some time, not speaking, and the dog lay down at her feet and rested its head on her foot and went to sleep. She stood above their markers and looked down on them with such a strange expression on that hard thin face of hers . . . shall I tell you? What it reminded me of?

I have observed, again and again, the image of a man twisted onto the branches of a cruciform tree. And so much with the expression of this man—deep sadness, yes, deep pain, but also certainty, ruthlessness, and some joy—was her face. She walked into Chilling as though into a prison built only and gloriously for her.

I have heard this story a thousand times. The story of something disappearing, in secret, during the dead of night. The story of keeping the secret, the story of uncovering the secret, the story of burying it again.

You lost something once, too, didn't you? Something you needed. Your mother? Your leg? Your brother? The love of your husband . . . the love of your wife. Did you lose, too soon, a child? Your health? Your vocation, your work, your free will? It was something absolutely essential. Something you've been looking for, all this time. You will move across earth and heaven and the sea in between, seeking it. You will move, like the restless body that contains you must move. And when you find it you will see that it is better where it has been buried. Trust me. I will cover it with softness and weight and hide it under dark layers of heavy soil. I will keep it safe for you. I will do my work, slowly and unrelentingly. And one day you will feel the walls of earth on your skin: you will become a mystery, a darkness, a story that exists only in the memories and mouths of the living, and you will return, you will come home.

Epilogue
The Chilling Churchyard
February, 1842

An Englishman has come to visit Chilling. He is a vigorous young man, just thirty years old. He speaks a great deal and walks all over the village, into the forest and toward the sea, and back again. He carries a notebook and licks his pencil and scribbles furiously. It is a gray and misty morning, cold and wet. In the churchyard, he examines the stones for a long time, peering at each one and occasionally turning to his companion and asking a question, or making an observation or joke.

He bends over the stone of Philip Pirrip and also Georgiana. He stares at the letters and steps back to see the five small tablets for each of the five sons.

"Are there any more Pirrips buried here?" he asks his companion. "There are generations of other families, but only this small cluster for the Pirrips."

"No, sir," says the guide.

"And none still living?"

"Just the boy, sir. Well, an old man now. The blacksmith. We him call Pip, because he was a scrawny little boy."

"No one else?"

"His only sister is dead. And his sister's husband was the blacksmith before him. Pip still uses Joe's forge."

"Not married?"

"Never. No children, no wife."

"Sad story. The blacksmith with all his family dead."

The guide laughs. "You might not say that, sir, if you'd known the sister! A mean, bitter woman. Tongue like a whip and a heart like ice."

"Cruel woman?"

"A heart like ice."

The man takes a notebook from his pocket and writes a few sentences. He stares again at the gravestones.

"Someone must have loved her," he remarks.

The guide thinks a moment.

"The dog," he says, finally. "The dog loved her."

317

Zana Previti was born and raised in New England. She earned her MFA in fiction from the University of California, Irvine, and her MFA in poetry from the University of Idaho. Her work has been published in the *New England Review, Hayden's Ferry Review, the American Poetry Review, Ninth Letter,* and elsewhere. She was the recipient of Poetry International's 2014 C.P. Cavafy Prize for Poetry and the Fall 2016 Emerging Writer-in-Residence at Penn State Altoona. She is the author of the chapbook *Providence* (Finishing Line Press, 2017). This is her first novel.